FROM OUR ASHES

BOOK TWO

FIRE BETWEEN US

ALEX CROSS

Line and copy edited by Jessica Myburgh

Cover art by Lina Ganef

Cover typography by Get Covers

❋ Formatted with Vellum

For the ones who were told
they were too much—
You're not.
Fuck them.
Go light the world on fire.

CONTENT WARNINGS

From Our Ashes contains themes and content that may be distressing to some readers. This book includes:

- Cheating/infidelity
- Explicit sexual content
- Grief and the death of a parent (in the past)
- Parental illness, hospitalization, and medical procedures
- References to sexual assault involving a minor (non-graphic, off-page)
- Panic attacks and anxiety
- Unprocessed trauma
- Substance use (alcohol)

Please note that this novel is the second part of a duet and should be read after *When We Ignite*, as the story continues directly from book one.

Reader discretion is advised.

This is a work of fiction. Names, characters, places, and

events are the product of the author's imagination. Any resemblance to actual persons, living or dead, or to actual events is purely coincidental.

THE PLAYLIST

Listen, in case you're not aware, I'm Colombian, so when I decided to set this book in Madrid, my brain took that as full permission to be completely unapologetic about all the Spanish songs I added here. So yes, this is once again a completely unhinged mix, and I hope you enjoy listening to it as much as I enjoyed making it.

Nunca Estoy - C. Tangana (Prologue)
La Soledad - Laura Pausini (Prologue)
Thousand Miles - Tove Lo (Prologue)
Amores Extraños - Laura Pausini (Prologue)

Me Maten - C. Tangana (Chapter One)
Ateo - C. Tangana, NATHY PELUSO (Chapter One)

THE PLAYLIST

us. - Gracie Abrams, Taylor Swift (Chapter Two)
Fire for You - Cannons (Chapter Two)
People You Know - Selena Gomez (Chapter Two)

DtMF - Bad Bunny (Chapter Three)
Otro Atardecer - Bad Bunny, The Marías (Chapter Three)
superstar - Artemas (Chapter Three)

Good Luck, Babe! - Chappell Roan (Chapter Four)
No Fair - Ari Abdul, Ella Boh (Chapter Four)
good 4 u - Olivia Rodrigo (Chapter Four)

Nobody Gets Me - SZA (Chapter Five)
CLASSY 101 - Feid, Young Miko (Chapter Five)

everything i wanted - Billie Eilish (Chapter Six)
Potions - SLANDER, Said The Sky (Chapter Six)
Back to You - Selena Gomez (Chapter Six)

Control - Halsey (Chapter Seven)
Sinners - Ari Abdul, Thomas LaRosa (Chapter Seven)
HEARTBEAT - Isabel LaRosa (Chapter Seven)

True Disaster - Tove Lo (Chapter Eight)
Figure You Out - VOILÀ (Chapter Eight)
offline - Young Miko (Chapter Eight)

lovely - Billie Eilish, Khalid (Chapter Nine)
MIDDLE OF THE NIGHT - Elley Duhé (Chapter Nine)

Qué Pasaría… - Rauw Alejandro, Bad Bunny (Chapter Ten)
Envolver - Anitta (Chapter Ten)
BESO - ROSALÍA, Rauw Alejandro (Chapter Ten)

Do I Wanna Know? - Arctic Monkeys (Chapter Eleven)

THE PLAYLIST

The Night We Met - Lord Huron (Chapter Eleven)

struggle - Tove Lo (Chapter Twelve)
UN DÍA (ONE DAY) - J Balvin, Dua Lipa, Bad Bunny (Chapter Twelve)
you should see me in a crown - Billie Eilish (Chapter Twelve)

pay for you - Psylosia (Chapter Thirteen)
Cravin' - Stileto, Kendyle Paige (Chapter Thirteen)
Caroline - Artemas (Chapter Thirteen)
The Hills - The Weeknd (Chapter Thirteen)

ALL I WANTED WAS YOU - Ex Habit, Omido (Chapter Fourteen)
Just Want to Feel Something - Artemas (Chapter Fourteen)
El Mismo Aire - Camilo, Pablo Alborán (Chapter Fourteen)

Back to U - SLANDER, William Black (Chapter Fifteen)
Superhuman - SLANDER, Eric Leva (Chapter Fifteen)

TURiSTA - Bad Bunny (Chapter Sixteen)
Youth - Daughter (Chapter Sixteen)
You Are the Reason - Calum Scott (Chapter Sixteen)

Die For You - The Weeknd (Chapter Eighteen)
Ojitos Lindos - Bad Bunny, Bomba Estéreo (Chapter Eighteen)

Antes de Morirme - C. Tangana, ROSALÍA (Chapter Nineteen)
Stay - Ari Abdul (Chapter Nineteen)

southbound - Artemas (Chapter Twenty)
PLEASE - Omido, Ex Habit (Chapter Twenty)
Scream My Name - Thomas LaRosa (Chapter Twenty)

THE PLAYLIST

LA NOCHE DE ANOCHE - Bad Bunny, ROSALÍA (Chapter
Twenty-One)
Keep U Warm - SLANDER, William Black, Jordan Shaw
(Chapter Twenty-One)

Baby Girl (feat. Lalo Ebratt) - Mario Bautista (Chapter Twenty-
Two)
Mistaken - Tove Lo (Chapter Twenty-Two)
Come Undone - Tove Lo (Chapter Twenty-Two)

Always Been You - Jessie Murph (Chapter Twenty-Three)
Heaven Feels Like - SLANDER, Fairlane (Chapter Twenty-Three)

Favorito - Camilo (Chapter Twenty-Four)
Souvenir - Selena Gomez (Chapter Twenty-Four)

Worship - Ari Abdul (Chapter Twenty-Five)
You - Ari Abdul (Chapter Twenty-Five)

Paradise - Tove Lo (Chapter Twenty-Six)

Lucky - Zedd, Remi Wolf (Epilogue)
Fire on Fire - Sam Smith (Epilogue)

FOREWORD

Before you begin, a quick note on the timeline:

Sebastian left for Madrid in September.
The prologue takes place the following February.
The story itself begins in August, four years after he walked
away.

The epilogue of *When We Ignite* is set in the spring, when Ethan
receives his acceptance letters, leading directly into this book as
the summer begins.

Trust me, it will all make sense.
Eventually.

PROLOGUE

ETHAN

Just for a little while…

The words pulled me slowly back into consciousness, echoing in my head before slipping away from memory. Like a dream you can't quite hold on to—right at your fingertips, but… not.

My hands brushed the headboard as I stretched my arms above my head, the dull ache in my back and neck tightening before it eased. I rolled onto my side and spotted my phone beside me on the mattress. Not plugged in, just lying there—accusing.

Another night spent falling asleep clinging to images that were already starting to blur.

I tried to resist. A minute, maybe two. Probably closer to five seconds before I reached for it. The screen unlocked with my face, and sure enough, there he was—his picture waiting for me.

Sebastian.

He was so handsome.

It was the last photo he'd sent. I'd asked what he was doing, and he'd replied with a selfie. The background was dark, his face lit only by the bluish glow of his computer. The shadows carved deeper lines into his features, sharpening the cut of his jaw. One brow was arched, his lips mostly serious—just a hint of a smile curving at the corners. He was wearing a white button-down, collar undone, a few buttons left open. The faint outline of a necklace peeked out from beneath the fabric, barely visible, but I'd obsessed over it anyway.

My hand lifted on instinct, fingers curling around my matching medallion.

He's still wearing it.

That thought had kept me going these past weeks. Because that was how long ago he'd sent the picture—three *fucking* weeks ago.

Three weeks of one-word answers. Three weeks of silence where there used to be good-morning texts and late-night calls. Three weeks of the ache in my chest burrowing a little deeper every day.

Exhaling sharply, I flipped the phone face down, forcing myself out of bed and into the shower. It didn't help. Not even finishing with a blast of cold water could clear my head. My hands still itched to reach for it, to check—pointlessly—if he'd texted.

Once I'd changed and gathered my things, I slipped out of the apartment, making sure to leave before Maya woke up. She'd been mother-henning me a little too much lately, and I was getting sick of it.

Ten minutes later, as I walked to my first class with the frigid winter air biting at my skin, I caved.

ME
hey

I shoved the phone back into my pocket and waited for the vibration. It didn't come.

By my second class, I'd bitten my nails raw, anxiety coiling heavy inside me.

I should just delete the fucking text. He probably hasn't even opened it. But he must've seen the notification. Why the hell won't he answer? What's he doing? Who's he with?

And why does it feel like I'm the only one still reaching out?

My phone buzzed, and I checked it in a hurry, my chest deflating when I saw it wasn't from the Langley brother I wanted it to be.

HENNY LANGLEY

up for drinks? just landed

I tapped yes, then slipped the phone back into my pocket. As I did, I caught the eye of a girl staring straight at me. She turned quickly, whispering something to her friend before a wave of giggles broke out between them.

I pressed my back into the seat, trying to ignore it.

Fuck them.

I dragged my attention back to class, tuning out my phone, the laughter, and the doubt that had been building—steady and insistent—beneath my skin.

February.

Six months, and I still felt like this.

My grades were good—no, not just good. Since Sebastian left, they'd been fucking fantastic. Every bit of focus I had was going into them. Into myself. Into proving I could be more than what they all thought I was. More than the version of me he left behind.

Charlotte and Oliver had stepped in after both my parents stopped speaking to me—financially and otherwise. The trust set up on my mother's side would be released when I turned twenty-one, regardless of whether I had a relationship with them, and I did intend to use it. It was mine. But I didn't want to coast there.

Char was pregnant, and even though I knew the Langleys had more money than they could ever spend, it wasn't Oliver's responsibility to carry me until then. I needed to stand on my own two feet first—to prove to myself that I could.

And I could goddamn well do it. So as soon as I graduated— no, fuck that—*before* I did, I'd have a job, I'd have my trust, and I'd turn myself into a powerful man.

Just like him.

More than him.

Maybe then he'd actually answer my texts.

So I studied harder. Made sure I was at the top of all my classes and tuned out all the white noise around me.

When class ended, I walked up to the professor and asked about the last exam. He smiled and assured me I'd earned a top grade. Something like pride curled in my chest—right up until someone slammed into my shoulder.

It was one of the girls from before. She was smirking, her friends trailing behind.

"Looking for a hot date?" she whispered, her gaze flicking to the professor and then back to me before she walked away.

Heat crawled up my neck, and I pressed my lips into a hard line to keep from answering. Not for my sake—I didn't give a fuck what they thought about me. But I actually liked Professor Flintwood. He was almost seventy and married, and the last thing he needed was me handing them more gossip. After all, every time I opened my mouth, it turned into another rumor.

"Is everything alright, Mr. Bennett?" he asked.

I gave him a tight smile. "Everything's fine."

When I stepped out of the classroom, my phone vibrated again.

CREEP

hey

That was it. Almost four fucking hours, and all I got was a *hey*.

I stared at the screen until the letters blurred and my lungs felt too tight for air.

Doesn't matter. Don't care. You're doing fine. You have a whole life that isn't tied to him anymore. Remember?

But my thumb hovered over the keyboard like it had a mind of its own—itching to type, to poke, to pull a reaction out of him. Pathetic.

I took a deep breath and closed my eyes.

Another sharp laugh drew my attention to a group of girls, the same ones from the classroom. They weren't even looking my way, but my blood was already boiling. One more word from them and I knew I'd snap.

I quickened my pace, trying to avoid them, but they were directly in my path. Just as I was about to pass, one of them spoke. "Bet he can't pay what Sebastian Langley could."

I stopped. My jaw twitched.

Okay. No. Absolutely not.

So much for Bennett politeness.

Turning around, I walked straight back to them. One girl looked away, but I knew exactly which one had opened her mouth.

I smiled, slow and sweet. "Where do you want me to sign?"

She blinked. "What?"

"Well, you're clearly obsessed with me and who I'm fucking," I said with a shrug. "So I figured, autograph?"

Her friend's eyes went huge.

"I'm not—"

"I don't do it for free, though. But you already knew that,

right?" I stepped closer, lowering my voice. "Honestly, you don't look like you can afford me. But I'm feeling charitable."

An offended scoff left her. "Could you be any more arrogant?"

"It's not arrogance, sweetheart. It's confidence. The same confidence that got me Sebastian in the first place." I tilted my head. "Which is what's been killing you, right? Lying awake, wondering why he wanted me and not anyone else."

Their faces were priceless—insulted, curious, furious.

"Here's the secret," I said. "You're never going to know. Because it's not your fucking business. So maybe focus on your own technique and stop obsessing over mine." I turned on my heel before I said something truly unhinged, forcing my walk to stay calm and not a full-on stomp.

It wasn't even about them. Not really. But they'd lit the fuse, and I was done pretending I didn't want to burn something down.

Hey? Was he fucking kidding me?

I was the one getting all the backlash. Being called a rent boy four times a day. Being the laughingstock of this school. Being exiled from every family gathering—except ones the Langleys hosted. And I could handle it. I could. Because at least it was real. But lately, I was starting to fucking doubt it.

Three weeks of unsatisfying replies. Three weeks of ignored calls. Three weeks of excuses about why we couldn't make plans. And if I was being honest with myself, his affection had started fading even before that.

I knew it was over. We'd agreed to that at the end of September. But did that mean we couldn't even be friends? We'd been talking almost every day since he left. So what changed? What happened now? Had he found someone else already?

The thought hit low, burning like acid in the pit of my stomach. I hated how fast it spread, how quickly it twisted everything inside me.

By the time I got back that evening, I was drained. I

mumbled a greeting to Maya, closed my bedroom door behind me, and curled up on my side on the bed. My fingers found the medallion at my neck, and I squeezed my eyes shut.

This wasn't fair.

I missed him. So much. So fucking much. And it hurt, damn it.

Pulling out my phone, I stared at our chat. At that stupid, meaningless *hey*. Pain and longing swirled violently through me. I blinked furiously and started typing.

ME

I have spring break coming up

how about a getaway?

I stared at the screen.

He read it. Started typing. Then stopped.

My thumb hovered over the keyboard as I bit back the urge to remind him I'd grown my hair out—how *he'd* been the one to ask me to. A hollow laugh slipped past my lips. *Get a fucking grip.*

CREEP

I'm sorry darling

don't think I can

building a company remember?

It felt like a blade twisting deep. *Of course. Because work always came first, didn't it?*

Fuck him. Fuck this.

I stared at the blinking cursor, my heart pounding, fingers trembling over the screen. And then I typed.

ME

I can't keep doing this Ash

I'm done

A second later, a call came through. I shut my eyes tightly and scrubbed my face, willing away the wave of angry tears.

My phone kept vibrating, and I took a deep breath before answering.

"Pet—"

"Don't fucking talk." I cut him off before he could finish. I couldn't listen to him. His voice was my undoing. *He* was my undoing.

A hard exhale came from the other end of the line, but he said nothing.

"I'm blocking your number. I don't want this half-in, half-out bullshit, Ash. It fucking *hurts*. This hurts worse than you leaving."

Nothing.

"I want you gone from my life. For real. Don't call. Don't text. Don't come to the city. I need you to stop existing so I can fucking breathe again." My heart cracked a little more, but I knew this was what I needed. I needed to kill the hope that he was going to come back for me—that he still *wanted* to. "Please." The word left me as a whisper, stripped of strength.

The silence stretched again—heavier this time.

Oppressive.

Final.

"Okay." His rough voice tightened the vice already crushing my heart.

That was it.

No fight. No *I'm sorry.* No *I love you.* Just one word that ended everything instead.

I hung up before I could change my mind, doing exactly what I'd said. Erasing him from my life. This time, for good.

For a moment, I just sat there. My chest felt like it was folding in on itself. It didn't feel real—and maybe that was the cruelest part. That something this devastating could happen in less than a minute.

I curled onto the bed, my hand clamped around the medallion in a death grip. One tear slipped free. One.

But no more.

I wasn't going to keep crying over Sebastian Langley.

Unclasping the chain from around my neck, I pulled open the drawer of my bedside table and thrust it inside before slamming it shut.

Then I fell back against the mattress.

Turns out, waiting a few years was impossible. The things we'd said to each other months ago meant nothing now. The distance had broken us—and not the fucking ocean. The distance *he'd* always insisted on keeping between us. The emotional one.

I should've learned my lesson.

Don't be the one who cares more.

Don't be the one who waits.

If you don't let people in, they can't turn around and choose someone else.

I stared down at my open palm, the curve of the medallion's "C" imprinted deep in my skin. My only consolation was that it would fade.

One day, *this* would fade.

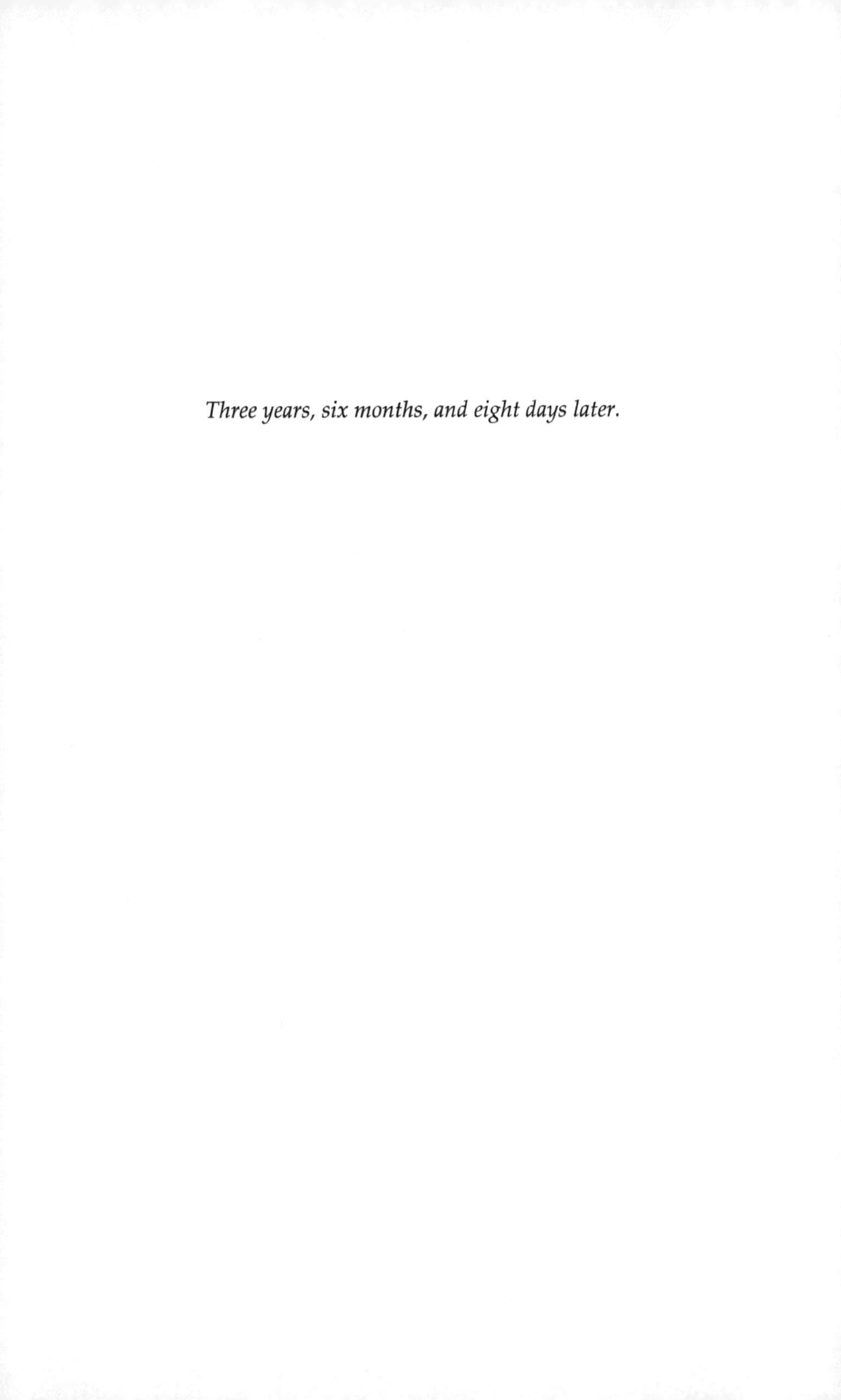

Three years, six months, and eight days later.

CHAPTER ONE

ASH

Summer clung to the city. September heat settled into the streets, stubbornly refusing to leave. Tourists still crowded the sidewalks bright with color and sweat as the city eased back into its everyday rhythm.

I navigated through the familiar chaos, sidestepping a stroller, ducking past a sunhat, until I spotted the entrance tucked between two high-end boutiques. The gate was already open.

I stepped through and followed a narrow hallway into a space I hadn't seen before. When I pushed through the side door, I stopped.

It was raw, but there was no mistaking the potential. Thick stone walls wrapped the room in quiet. Wooden beams stretched overhead, open to the cloudless sky—Madrid blue. Vines spilled from the top, untrimmed but not careless, like someone had told them exactly where to grow. The air inside was still, warm, and scented faintly with old dust and sun-soaked brick.

Of course Henry would find this place. My little brother had a knack for spotting beauty in places no one else would think to look.

"And the prodigal son returns at long last," Henry announced.

I turned to him with a smile.

He walked my way with arms wide and his signature grin intact.

"Are *you* the prodigal son in this scenario?" I wrapped him in a hug as soon as he came close enough. "We've been over this—Oli is the favorite."

"Yeah, well, he's not here, is he?" Henry's laugh echoed across the open space, and I let it settle over me like a warm blanket. It had been too long since we lived in the same country.

Four years.

Four fucking years.

Sure, we'd seen each other often—never more than a couple of months between visits—but the distance, the lack of a shared daily rhythm, had gone on far too long. I was used to Henry the way I was used to a limb. Life felt off without him.

"Finally, a little sanity enters the equation," came Raúl's voice as he crossed the room.

"Is he giving you a hard time?" I asked him.

Henry rolled his eyes. "He's been making budget cuts left and right. He's supposed to be a *luxury* consultant."

Raúl raised a brow. "I'm fairly certain that question was meant for me."

I laughed and reached out to shake his hand. Raúl was helping Henry with this latest opening, though I'd known him for years. As soon as Henry decided to open a club here, I knew bringing Raúl in was the right call—even if things had gotten off to a rocky start.

They were opposites, but in a way that worked. Raúl was a top-tier luxury consultant with years of experience behind him and a sharp, almost surgical eye for detail. He took his work seriously—like cathedral-seriously—and had a reputation for being meticulous, precise, and a little intimidating.

Henry, on the other hand, was chaos dressed in charm. I

knew firsthand how hard it could be to take him seriously. He was the most sociable of us brothers, all jokes and playfulness, which often masked just how clever he really was. And how deeply he felt.

Henry was a force of nature. In four years, he'd taken two clubs and turned them into eleven—eleven *highly* successful ones. He'd built an empire from scratch, far from the shadow of our father and our family name. And he'd done it by staying hands-on, never stepping back. The travel alone would have wrecked someone else, but not him.

I'd join him when I could—just never in one particular city. New York was still off-limits.

A thrill zipped through me at the thought of *him*—his pale blue eyes, that quiet smile. I shook my head, pulling myself back to the present.

Raúl crossed his arms. "We are not having marble statues, Henry."

"Just for the bathrooms." Henry grinned, tossing him a wink.

Raúl stared at him, exasperation etched across his face. "You're fucking with me, aren't you?"

Henry clapped him on the shoulder, laughing.

Raúl sighed and turned to me. "I thought you said he was serious."

"Nah. Just nepotism at its finest." Henry started walking backward, arms spread wide as if presenting a stage. "What do you think, Ash?"

"There's potential," I said, letting my gaze sweep over the stone walls.

"Potential?" Henry scoffed. "It's going to make Soho House look like amateur hour. Come on—let me give you the tour."

He waved me forward and walked me through the space, outlining everything in exhausting detail. By the end, I could tell Raúl was a little impressed—even if he wouldn't admit it out loud.

"I was thinking the bar could go here." Henry gestured

toward the far wall. "Make it a feature. Maybe commission an artist."

"We could ask my cousin," Raúl offered.

My smirk widened. "Oh, you *definitely* want his cousin." I chuckled when Raúl shot me a glare.

"What?" Henry's gaze moved between us. "Why?"

"He's a brilliant sculptor. Large-scale work—"

"He's also hot as fuck," I cut in.

Raúl let out a long-suffering sigh.

"Not my type," I added, "but definitely a nice view."

Henry's eyes narrowed with curiosity. "How hot?"

"I don't think that's relevant—"

"Thor-hot," I interrupted again. "Think Viking meets construction worker. The kind of guy you'd expect to see on a crumpled nineties pin-up, ripped jeans hanging open, leaning back on a Harley."

Raúl rubbed both hands over his face, pushing his glasses up into his hair.

Henry gave a low whistle. "Sounds qualified to me. Tell him we expect him to start on Monday."

"He's not in the country," Raúl said, "but I'll set up a meeting so you can actually review his qualifications."

"Don't be a spoilsport. Bring your hot cousin." My phone buzzed in my pocket, and I pulled it out, glancing at the screen before typing out a quick message. "Are we getting lunch?"

"Yeah, but we have to stop by my apartment first. It's on the way." Henry had that glint in his eye—the one that meant he was hiding something and found it incredibly entertaining.

"I'll politely decline this time," Raúl said.

"Really?" Henry tilted his head. "Such a shame. We could've used your sunny disposition."

Raúl clicked his tongue, and Henry snickered.

———

We moved through the streets of Salamanca, Madrid's polished little bubble where everything gleamed a bit more than it needed to. The buildings were all sharp lines and elegant stone. Real plants hung from the balconies, watered regularly instead of left to sunburn like everywhere else in the city. Cafés bled onto the sidewalks with silver trays and glass tumblers sweating into white napkins.

Beside me, Henry kept a brisk pace. "Come on," he said. "This way."

"Are you taking the place?"

"Yup," he said. "Signed the papers this morning. I'm thinking it'll probably be around six to eight months until we're up and running."

"That much?"

"There's a hiccup with the property. It's historical, so construction permits are rough. Bringing it up to code will be a pain."

"Yeah, that's pretty standard here. My apartment was a mess too. But it's going to be great, Henny—I can tell."

He tried not to grin outright, but the pleasure showed anyway.

"I'm proud of you."

Henry stopped abruptly, his eyebrows shooting up. "I beg your fucking pardon?"

I laughed. "Don't be like that. You know I am."

He shook his head, still amused. "You've gone soft in your old age."

"Oh, fuck off," I muttered.

Henry's grin widened. "What's it going to be—forty?"

"I'm turning thirty-nine, fuck you very much."

He sucked in a sharp breath through his teeth, and I rolled my eyes.

"Europe's definitely softened you up," he said, pressing his lips together to hold back a smile. "But I appreciate the sentiment."

A comfortable silence settled between us as we kept walking, still in sync.

Henry glanced over as we turned onto another street. "You know who's gone soft too?"

I let out a long exhale. "Are you about to give me the same speech Oli did? *Dad's changed; he wants to do better,*" I said, mimicking Oliver's calm drawl.

"I'm not saying the old man's perfect, Ash. But he's trying to be there now."

"For *you.*"

Henry shrugged. "And Oli. Char. The kids. When was the last time you talked to him?"

I looked away, trying—and failing—to remember. Didn't matter. I didn't owe him anything. He'd made it clear he wanted nothing to do with me.

"Look, I know it was bad, Ash. The last one was *really* bad. But you can tell he regrets it."

"How, Henny? How can you tell? Has he actually said the words? Has he told you, *Henry, I'm sorry I called your brother a fucking disgrace to the family name?*"

Henry grimaced. "Not in so many words..."

"Then no. I'm not folding first. If he wants me in his life, he can apologize like a grown man," I said for what felt like the hundredth time. I was done trying to keep the peace. It had been a relief to finally step away from his impossible expectations.

And right now? Was Henry kidding me? I already had enough on my plate, and he should've known that—it wasn't exactly a secret. When my name was on the line, the press wasted no time circling. By now our father had probably added this to his running list of *I told you so's.*

And then it hit me.

Three years ago. That was the last time we spoke.

It had been civil. Hollow. No apologies, no acknowledgment. Just a quiet, final kind of silence.

Now wasn't the time to break it. Not until this whole mess was fixed.

"Don't get mad, Ash," Henry said. "It was just an idea."

"A terrible idea."

"Fine." He sighed. "It's through here." He led us around the corner to a narrow entrance next to a bakery. The building was four stories, all clean stone and iron balconies.

My phone buzzed again, and I stopped to check it. "I'll wait for you down here."

"No, you won't. You're coming upstairs. I have a surprise for you."

I exhaled but caught the look in his eyes—the one that said I had no shot of getting out of this. Resigned, I smiled and nodded for him to lead the way.

"Promise it'll be worth it," he said in a singsong voice.

We stepped into the building's cool, marble-lined lobby—quiet and shaded. The walls were pale stone with gold-edged mirrors, and the scent of wood polish and something floral hung in the air.

Henry hit the call button, and the elevator arrived with a soft chime and a creak of effort. One of those old ones—gated, with a wrought-iron door you had to slide across by hand. The interior was wood-paneled, small enough that we had to stand close, shoulder to shoulder. The ride up was slow, the elevator groaning faintly as we passed each floor.

"You really know how to keep a guy in suspense," I said.

Henry smirked, eyes fixed ahead. "You'll thank me."

The elevator jolted to a stop, and the door opened with a metallic rattle. He stepped out, keys already in hand, and led me into his apartment.

The place was chaos—boxes stacked high, with barely any walking room in between.

"You know, there are people who can help you unpack."

"They're not mine," he said with a shrug. "This was an unforeseen problem."

I spotted his things underneath the boxes, mostly unpacked. Curious.

"Babe, I'm home!" he called out.

My eyebrow arched. "You're dating someone already?"

He turned with a grin threatening to split his face. "Why would that be a surprise for you?"

I was about to answer when a door at the back of what had to be the living room swung open.

And he walked out.

My heart stopped dead in my chest.

"Fucking finally, Henny." The voice was rough, low, and familiar. "I needed to see the landlord—like ten minutes ago. Can't do lunch. I'll meet you for a drink later, yeah?"

He didn't look up. Just sat on the sofa, pulling on his shoes, tying the laces like this wasn't the most important fucking moment of my life. Like I wasn't standing there, breathless, because after four years, Ethan Bennett was in the same room as me.

Four fucking years.

And time had only worked in his favor.

My eyes dragged over him—his tanned arms, the lean muscle lining them, his elegant hands, and that sharp jaw. His hair—god, *his hair*—was damp and curled messily across his forehead, longer than I'd ever seen it.

The only thing I hadn't seen was his eyes.

I let out a breath I felt like I'd been holding for hours, though it had only been seconds. "Well... aren't you a sight for sore eyes?"

His head snapped up instantly.

Ah.

There they were.

Those perfect baby blues landed on mine—and widened. His lips parted as he pushed off the couch, staring at me like he'd just seen a ghost.

All the air vanished.

From the room. From the planet.

And just like that, it was only *us*.

Ethan Bennett was standing right in front of me, and my chest could've exploded from the sheer amount of happiness it was trying to contain.

I smiled, holding his gaze. "Hello, darling."

CHAPTER TWO
ETHAN

Hello, darling.

Those soft words slid under my skin like a spell. Every lie I'd told myself about seeing Sebastian Langley again unraveled in seconds. The resentment. The hurt. The years of pretending I didn't care—gone. Fucking *poof.*

He was right there in front of me, and I knew instantly I'd been wrong about everything. About time dulling him. About distance making him smaller. About how quickly my body remembered him.

The truth was cruel in its simplicity: Sebastian Langley looked even better than I remembered.

He was older, sure, but it only made him more magnetic. His wavy hair was styled the same way, though streaked with a little more silver at the temples. The stubble I remembered had grown into a beard—longer now, but still impossibly neat. And, of course, he was impeccably dressed. Clean lines. Tailored fit. Everything about him radiated control.

He should've been intimidating. He would've been—if I hadn't known him. If that infuriatingly familiar smile weren't tugging at his lips, overflowing with fondness.

"I'll make myself scarce." Henry's voice snapped me back to reality.

I turned just in time to catch his smug grin and just knew he'd planned this. Even though he knew I'd wanted to do it on my own terms. *Rip off the bandage*, he'd said. And what a fucking rip it was.

As Henry left, a treacherous flush crawled up my neck. Sebastian took a step closer, shaking his head like he couldn't believe I was real. That made two of us.

"Hi…" It sounded awkward, even to me.

His grin deepened, and his gaze moved over me slowly, like he was memorizing me all over again. "You look so different." His voice filled every inch of the space, commanding attention the way it always had.

"Yeah, well… I'm far past my teens now."

Sebastian's eyes crinkled as his laughter rang through the room. It was such a rich sound—so achingly familiar it clawed at something buried inside me. Before I knew it, I was smiling back.

"Can I…" He stepped closer. "Can I hug you?"

The hesitation in his voice undid me, and I nodded without thinking. He closed the distance between us, his hands sliding around my waist as I rose onto my toes and looped my arms around his neck.

I shut my eyes and breathed him in.

He still smelled like himself, just not quite the same—a note missing I couldn't place. I let it crash over me; the indescribable, overwhelming feeling of being back in his arms. They tightened around me, the firm expanse of his chest pressed to mine, warming me in ways I'd thought were no longer possible.

I had missed him. So fucking much.

When Sebastian had left, it'd felt like he'd taken my heart with him, like something inside me had hardened just to survive his absence. I'd let him become the center of my universe, and when he was gone, I'd been left drifting through the emptiness he created.

We'd stayed in touch for a while, neither of us ready to let go, clinging to calls and messages that had only highlighted what we no longer had. I'd told myself it was enough, that hearing his voice was better than silence, but then the whispers in my head had turned into screams. Every look from strangers had begun to feel like pity or judgment, and the distance between us had become more than miles; it had been a wall, impossible to cross. I'd felt him slipping away, and the slow inevitability of it had destroyed me.

So I'd asked him to let me go. To let me erase him.

And, being Sebastian, he'd taken me at my word.

Then he was really gone.

But his influence had lingered in everything.

Sebastian had given me my drive—my ambition, my hunger for power. I admired how certain he'd been, how easily people followed him, and how commanding he was without even trying. I'd wanted that for myself. I'd gone from drifting to chasing, from aimless to determined.

He'd given me my confidence too. My humor. My edge. Sebastian had bulldozed through every wall I'd built and forced me to stop hiding behind what he called my Bennett politeness. I stopped worrying about keeping others comfortable, because he'd taught me how to take up space.

He had given me my preference for rough sex and older partners. I'd stopped fearing my sexuality, stopped overanalyzing every shift in my attraction, and just let it flow. I learned to embrace what I liked—what I craved—even when I knew I was searching for him in every touch. Trying, and failing, to recreate the spark he'd ignited in me with someone else.

Choosing to come to Madrid had been hard. I didn't want anyone to think I'd done it to chase him—especially not him. I'd done it for myself. For my future. But standing there, wrapped in his arms, I knew he'd influenced this too. Just like everything else.

His lips brushed my temple. "Your hair is longer." The words were soft, almost a caress against the raw edges of my soul.

A small laugh slipped past my lips. "I've had about a million haircuts since I last saw you."

His hands—warm and sure—moved to my neck, tilting my face back so he could really look at me. "I can't believe you're here."

I let my eyes trace his features too. "I can't believe you're almost forty. You look exactly the same."

He grinned, a quiet laugh rumbling low in his chest. "You don't." His smile softened as his thumbs brushed along my jaw, his eyes following the motion. "I didn't think it was possible for you to be even more beautiful than I remembered."

The words landed hard—tight in my chest, then lower. His eyes met mine again, and time just… stopped. Everything I'd ever felt for him hit me like a wave, dragging it all back to the surface. None of it had dulled. None of it had faded.

"It's so fucking good to see you," Sebastian whispered.

The breath that filled my lungs felt shared, like we were breathing for each other.

I couldn't remember the last time I'd let myself feel like this. My heart was making choices my mind couldn't keep up with, willing to throw everything away if it meant having him again. It felt like I'd gone back in time—to when he was mine—and I was just as reckless. Just as lost in him.

My fingers trembled as I covered his wrists, holding him there. "I missed you too."

The corners of his mouth curved. He leaned in until his forehead rested against mine, eyes closing.

I was free-falling.

He was so close. Finally, so close again.

He nuzzled his nose against mine in the sweetest, most

disarming gesture, and I melted into putty in his grasp. This couldn't be one-sided—it didn't *feel* one-sided. He had to be just as caught up as I was in this impossible rush of being near each other again.

Because this could be it, couldn't it? We could finally give *us* a real shot. Far from our families. Far from the cameras. Far from everything that had torn us apart. This could be our chance.

My tongue darted over my lips, and his gaze dropped to my mouth. I tilted my chin up in invitation, and he reacted instantly, his grip on my jaw tightening as he leaned closer, his breath ghosting over my lips. My stomach swooped, tingles skimming down my spine.

But then nothing happened.

Sebastian froze, the warmth between us flickering out.

A flash of confusion hit me first, then doubt. Maybe he wanted me to ask for it?

"Ash…"

The sound of his name barely left my mouth before his hands fell. He stepped back, eyes wide, blinking like he'd just woken up from a dream. I stood there, hands still open, grasping at the empty air between us.

The spell started to break.

Sebastian cleared his throat. "I'm sorry, Ethan." A strained, self-deprecating laugh slipped from him. "I got carried away. Sorry about that."

Ethan.

My lips twisted into a frown. "What just happened?"

His gaze went to the floor as he shrugged. "Got carried away."

Okay, so what? Who the fuck cared if he got carried away? I was about to say as much when his whole demeanor shifted. His hands went to his hips, and he tried to smile. It looked anything but genuine.

"But it's great to see you," he said. "Are you visiting?"

I stared back. I didn't think I'd ever seen him nervous. Sebastian was always cool confidence or calculated indifference—never this. This wasn't him.

"No. They didn't tell you?"

He shook his head, eyes still a little too wide.

"I'm doing my MBA at IE. I'm moving here."

From the way he flinched, you'd think I'd tried to punch him.

"What?"

"I thought for sure Oli or Henny told you. You really didn't know?"

He shook his head again. "I had no idea. But that's great—congratulations." His gaze darted around the room, lingering on the scattered boxes. "Are you and Henry living together?"

"No. I got an apartment nearby. Just haven't finished the paperwork."

He nodded stiffly.

My lips parted to ask why the hell he was acting so strange when Henry stepped out of his room.

His eyes bounced between us, eyebrows arched in surprise. "What are you doing out here? I thought for sure you'd be locked in the guest bedroom by now."

Sometimes I fucking hated him.

"Not at all," Sebastian said, his voice flat.

Not at all.

Three words, and they sliced clean through me. So what the hell had that been—the hug? Calling me beautiful? Where had all of that gone?

"Color me surprised," Henry said, and I shrugged under his questioning look.

"We're friends. Just that. Right?" Sebastian's smile was still plastered on his face, looking like it took real effort to keep it there.

"Right…" I echoed.

"We should have lunch," Sebastian added, too brightly. "Celebrate you being here."

Henry frowned. "Sure, Ash."

"On the weekend. I'll bring Luca along," Sebastian said, his eyes still fixed on Henry.

A little stretch of silence—the tense kind.

"Who's Luca?" Henry asked.

Sebastian slipped his hands into his pockets and cleared his throat. "My boyfriend."

Oh.

Oh…

It felt like a bucket of ice water had been dumped over me. Of course he was seeing someone. My chest deflated so fast it almost hurt.

"Boyfriend?" Henry shot me a quick glance. "Like, seriously?"

"Yes," Sebastian said. "For a couple of months now."

A couple of months.

He had a boyfriend—and had had one for months. And I'd let myself get my hopes up over a fucking hug? How stupid could I be? Four years spent healing from the trauma that was Sebastian Langley, only to watch the wound reopen in under sixty seconds.

Fucking pathetic.

"Can't wait to meet him," I said, trying to keep the bitterness out of my voice. "If he managed to tie you down, he must be the closest thing to a god there is."

Judging by their expressions, that hadn't landed.

After a couple of tense seconds, I said, "That was a joke."

To his credit, Sebastian tried to smile.

Henry rubbed the back of his neck, his expression painfully awkward. "So, pretending this isn't the most uncomfortable conversation I've ever been part of—Ash and I are off to lunch." He gave me a look that practically begged me to behave. "See you at eight?"

"See you at eight," I said politely. "It was great seeing you, Ash."

Sebastian smiled again, lips pressed into a tight line, and nodded once. "Same, Ethan."

They walked out, and I grabbed my phone, canceling my visit with the landlord.

Well, that was anticlimactic as fuck.

I'd be lying if I said I hadn't pictured it going differently. I'd spent weeks running through scenarios in my head—me cool, collected, and detached. Him flustered and desperate, the one chasing this time. In every version, I had the upper hand. And no matter which one—even the ones with stiff hellos, icy silence, or pretending nothing had ever happened—they all ended the same way: him in my bed, the two of us tearing each other apart.

Not with him in a relationship.

Not with him walking away.

———

Later that day, I paced my room, phone pressed to my ear. My landlord had insisted on talking to me; apparently, the *urgent* matter he needed to discuss was that the down payment hadn't gone through—which made no sense. He'd already told me another applicant was waiting on the property, and I'd been on hold with the bank for nearly an hour trying to figure out what had happened.

"Mr. Bennett?" a voice came through.

"Yes, I'm here."

"Thank you for your patience. We've reviewed the account, and it appears the transaction failed due to insufficient funds."

I frowned. "That can't be right. Are you sure you're checking the correct account?"

There was a short pause, the faint click of keys. Then he read back the account number—the one tied to my trust.

"That's the one," I said, a cold weight settling in my chest.

"We've also reviewed the recent activity," the representative continued carefully. "There have been regular withdrawals over the past four months. Substantial ones. It also notes here that there's a joint account holder?"

My stomach dropped. "Yes." Fuck. "There is."

"Were you aware of these transactions? If not, we can open an internal investigation, but since the co-holder is authorized—"

Fuck. Fuck. Fuck.

"No, that's okay," I cut in quickly. "I'll handle it privately. Could you send me the current balance?"

"Of course. Would you like me to stay on the line or email the statement?"

"Email's fine," I mumbled, swallowing hard against the knot in my throat.

He wouldn't. He couldn't have.

"We'll send it shortly," the man said before going through the polite routine of ending the call.

As soon as it disconnected, I searched for his number and hit dial. Straight to voicemail. *Coincidence. He's just busy.*

I stared at the screen—this had to be a mistake.

Rubbing my knuckles under my nose, my thumb hovered over the call button again, hesitating. But then a text came through.

CREEP

you know

That name hadn't popped up on my phone in years. I'd gone back and forth between blocking and unblocking his number so many times I'd lost count. Before coming here, I'd unblocked it once more—just in case. And here he was.

I stared at the notification until it faded off my screen, my thumb twitching. The screen lit up again. Another message from him.

Curiosity won before common sense could stop me.

CREEP

I really hate Henry for his ambush

I smiled to myself. At least that made two of us.

ME

he has a flair for the dramatic

can't say I'm a fan of it either

CREEP

I'm sorry for the freak-out

can we go back to the part where I'm ecstatic you're here?

My cheeks hurt with how much that last line made me want to grin. *Get a fucking grip on yourself.* Still, I scrolled up once more, reread his message, and tried to ignore the way my pulse quickened at just seeing his name.

ME

you're forgiven Sebastian

CREEP

did you start classes already?

ME

next week

He didn't respond right away. The typing bubble appeared, vanished, appeared again. I couldn't stop myself from egging him on. He'd texted first, so what was the harm, right?

ME

can I ask you a question?

CREEP

sure thing

I grinned, tapping my screen lightly.

ME

how do you have me saved on your phone?

A second later, he sent a screenshot. My stomach twisted at the sight of it—*Pet.*

The same name, just missing one small word. *My.*

He probably had to be careful now. Careful with *him.*

CREEP

some things never change

I arched a brow and typed before I could second-guess myself.

ME

some really fucking do

have you told your boyfriend about me yet?

CREEP

yes I did

That fast? They had to be close. I rubbed the heel of my hand against my chest, trying to ease the pressure.

ME

and how did you phrase it?

my friend moved to Madrid?

or my brother-in-law?

He took forever to reply again. The screen dimmed while I waited, my reflection faint in the glass.

CREEP

I told him my ex moved to Madrid who also happens to be my brother-in-law and my friend

Ex.

I never would've thought Sebastian Langley would use that word for me.

ME

is he looking forward to meeting me?

I can't fucking wait to meet him

CREEP

that sounded just the right amount of that
emotion you used to hate when I pointed it out

I scoffed, biting the inside of my cheek.

ME

I'm not jealous of your boyfriend

CREEP

of course not

nobody ever gets competitive around the
new guy

I chuckled under my breath, shaking my head at the screen.

ME

I meant I don't have a reason for it Ash

I seriously doubt you could top me

you couldn't have possibly found somebody
more front-page newsworthy

unless he's in high school

CREEP

he's not in high school

He didn't deny anything else, though. I couldn't tell if he was turned off or turned on by the verbal sparring—and that bugged the hell out of me. I was tempted to call him, just to hear his voice.

I wasn't sure what to type back, but he beat me to it.

CREEP

so

what do you have me saved as in your phone?

I laughed and sent a screenshot. He took his time replying, and I hoped it was because he was laughing too. I hoped his boyfriend was sitting right next to him while he did.

CREEP

I really fucking missed you

My smile faltered.

ME

Yeah?

What I really wanted to ask was *then why*? Why hadn't he broken up with him? Why had he stopped texting before? Why had he stayed away? But I didn't. I waited.

CREEP

I never stopped it's just more obvious now

My treacherous heart skipped.

CREEP

we should probably figure out how to be friends

you and I

That made me grin as I sank back against the pillows, my chest warm and my thoughts dangerously close to places they shouldn't go.

ME

sure thing ash

why don't we practice sometime?

I'll have my apartment next week

Fine. Maybe the teasing was uncalled for. Childish, even. I knew better than to goad any man in a relationship. But this wasn't *any* man. This was Sebastian.

Just a little jest between *friends*, right?

And where did he get off being in a fucking relationship, anyway?

CREEP

I knew you were going to be like this.

ME

like what Ash?

A new notification popped up on my screen—an email from the bank.

I sat up and opened it, my eyes skimming the words, trying to make sense of them. Until they landed on a line that was impossible to misinterpret.

Total balance: $0.00

Empty. It was fucking empty.

For a second, everything went quiet. No sound, no breath—just the rush of blood in my ears. My pulse thudded so hard it hurt.

The phone buzzed again, cutting through the silence.

CREEP

like fucking fire

My heart soared and sank all at once.

Because this image I'd been building for years—the version of myself I wanted to show him—was a fucking lie. He wouldn't think that about me if he knew just how much of a pushover I really was.

After all, who could be stupid enough to let themselves get scammed by their own father?

CHAPTER THREE

ASH

"I get why Henny did it—he's a fucking menace. But why the hell didn't *you* tell me?"

A thud came from somewhere off-screen, followed by a sharp wail.

Oliver glanced over his shoulder, half rising from his chair. "Need a hand?"

I narrowed my eyes. "No, you're not giving a hand. You're explaining yourself."

He sighed, turning back toward the camera. "Henny asked me not to."

We stared at each other for a beat.

"I'm sorry," I said, tilting my head. "I was waiting for you to discard that blatant lie and come up with a real answer."

Charlotte swept through the background, juggling a crying Liam and what looked like a half-empty jar of marinara. Amelia clung to her pant leg, while Julia—their nanny—trailed close behind, carrying paper towels and looking defeated.

"I'm good, we're good! There's just sauce everywhere," Charlotte said breathlessly, flashing me a frazzled smile. "Hi, Ash!"

"Hi, Charlie," I said, raising a brow at Liam's tomato-covered face. "I'm guessing Amelia's the artist?"

Charlotte laughed, a little too high-pitched. "Talk to your brother!" She disappeared out of frame with both kids in tow.

I leaned closer to the camera. "You heard the boss. Spill."

He sighed, slumping back in his chair without quite meeting my eyes. "Maybe I thought the surprise would be… nice."

I crossed my arms over my chest. "A nice shock to my system, you mean."

He tried for innocence and failed miserably. "Aren't you happy to see him? It's Ethan, Ash. I thought you'd be over the moon."

"Of course I'm happy." My voice was softer than I meant it to be. "But he's living here now, and how the hell am I supposed to keep my distance for two more years while he's in the same city?"

Oliver blinked. "Why would you?"

"You know why."

He dragged a hand over his face, thumb pressing into his temple. "You're being ridiculous."

I barked a dry laugh. "Weren't you the one who applauded my restraint four years ago? Told me how admirable my selflessness was?"

His mouth twitched, the faintest grimace. "Yes, okay. But plans change, Ash. Sometimes you've just got to ride the wave of chaos." He waved behind himself, where chaos was clearly thriving—laundry draped over chairs, toys littering the floor, and a toddler meltdown brewing somewhere in the background.

That wasn't like him. "Is everything alright?"

He exhaled slowly, eyes flicking to the hallway. "We're fine. Amelia's just… going through something. She's—" His lips pressed into a thin line. "Willful."

"I'll say," I muttered, smirking.

"She's three. It's a hard age. I'm sure she'll grow out of it." He ran a hand through his hair. "Liam's sick, so he's crying nonstop. And Charlotte's Wonder Woman-ing her way through it. We haven't slept in days." He looked exhausted; his voice had that hollow edge that came from running on fumes. "Or years."

"What you two need is a vacation."

Oliver snorted. Also not like him. "Vacation? I need four hours of uninterrupted sleep so I can get through the Core meeting tomorrow." His eyes were shadowed, and the stubble he usually kept neat had grown into the beginnings of a beard.

"Jonathan's still playing hard to get?"

He nodded, propping his chin on one hand. "Refusing to give us a fair price on the property. I'm this close"—he held up two fingers—"to telling him where he can shove it."

A laugh slipped out before I could stop it.

Oliver's brow arched.

"Sorry," I said, grinning. "Not laughing at your misery. It's just refreshing to see you so… over it."

"Yeah, well. Kid number two broke my spirit. I don't have the energy to care."

"Why not get a night nurse?"

He waved that off, sitting up straighter. "Char and I don't want our kids raised by an army of nannies. You know that. It's just rough right now because they're both so little. But it'll get better."

I offered him a small, unsure smile.

"Besides," he said, shoulders relaxing as his face softened, "even if they're feral hyenas ninety percent of the time, when they wake up at five in the morning and smile at you… there's nothing like it."

That was disgustingly heartwarming. And like so many times before, I felt that same dull ache: guilt, affection, and a longing to be closer. Not that I was exactly nanny material, but I could at least attempt to help.

"How about you, Ash? How are you holding up?" His tone was careful now, his posture almost bracing as he pushed the question out.

I couldn't blame him. The rock in my stomach dropped hard and fast, my mouth going dry.

"As well as can be expected." I shrugged, attempting a smile. "We're deep in the legal trenches right now, trying to find a solution."

Oliver drummed his fingers on the table, hesitating again, eyes sharp. "How much of your revenue was tied to state contracts? What's the loss?"

Through the screen, a burst of distant noise carried over. Amelia's laugh rang out somewhere in the background, followed by something clattering and Charlotte calling after her.

"Twenty-five percent."

Oliver's eyes closed as he swore under his breath. "Let me see if I can think of something," he said, looking back at me through the screen. "But, fuck, Ash…"

"Don't worry too much about it." I focused on the table instead of his face, letting out a brittle huff. "It is what it is. We're working through it." I felt like I'd said those words a million times over the past few weeks, and they were starting to lose their meaning. Their hope.

Charlotte reappeared and dropped into Oliver's lap, dissolving the tightness that had settled between us.

Her chestnut hair was a half-up, half-down disaster, and a red smear stained the side of her untucked white button-down. "What'd I miss?"

Oliver's arm slid around her waist automatically, and they melted together seamlessly. He glanced at me, a quick knowing look, before turning back to her. "Our children are feral." Oliver lifted his fingers one by one as he recited the list. "We haven't slept in four years, and he's mad we didn't give him a heads-up about E."

Charlotte nodded like that summed it up perfectly.

"Are the kids okay?" I asked.

"Oh yeah. Julia's got Liam in the bath, and Amelia's trying to help," she said. "I've got five minutes before I have to get back to the battlefield, so make it count."

They both looked at me, expectant.

I rolled my lips before shrugging. "I'm in a relationship."

"No!" they gasped in unison.

I nodded once.

"Did you tell E?" Charlotte asked.

Another nod.

"Oh my god." She turned to Oliver, eyes wide. "I have to call him."

"Ethan's fine," I said. "A little pissed, but fine. We'll get past it."

They exchanged identical skeptical looks. The synchronized-couple thing was really starting to grate.

"Is it serious?" Oliver asked.

I gestured vaguely. "Semi."

He blinked. "What the hell does that mean?"

"We've only been together a couple of months."

"And this is the first I'm hearing of…?"

"Luca," I clarified.

"Luca, because…"

"Because…" I hesitated, their matching stares pinning me in place. "Because I don't have to tell you everything. It would've come up eventually."

Oliver's eyes narrowed. "Right."

Charlotte crossed one leg over the other. "So you're going to keep dating him even though my brother just moved to the same city?" Her tone was edging toward accusation.

I smiled. "Is there something you want to say to me, Miss Bennett?"

She mirrored the smile, all sugar and knives. "Not that I want to meddle…"

"Of course not."

"But are you kidding me?"

"I'm with Char on this," Oliver said.

I shot him a look, but he just shrugged.

"We haven't seen each other in four years," I said. "We weren't supposed to keep our lives on pause forever. I'm sure Ethan's had partners too."

They exchanged a glance instead of answering.

"Right?" I pressed.

"Right," Charlotte said too brightly, that peppy tone back in full force. "I need to go check on the kids, but it was nice talking to you, Ash."

"You too."

She kissed Oliver's cheek, then disappeared partly from the frame. He caught her hand half off-screen, murmured something soft, and they shared a quick kiss before she slipped away.

He looked back at me, tired and expectant. "So?"

"We're having lunch on Saturday."

"Who's 'we'?"

"Henny, Luca…" I exhaled. "Ethan and me."

Oliver's eyes went wide before he burst out laughing. It started as a chuckle and snowballed into full-on hysterics.

"I'm glad you find this amusing."

"I'm sorry, Ash." He wiped a tear from the corner of his eye but made no effort to stop laughing.

"It'll be fine."

"Fine," he repeated, still grinning. "Oh god, you can totally tell you're not used to Ethan anymore if you think that's going to be anything but a disaster."

"I thought you were a fan of chaos now."

"I am—which is why this is so hilarious." Amelia's cry echoed somewhere behind him. Oliver winced, shoulders tensing. "I should probably go help."

"Wait."

Oliver leaned back in his chair, though the movement was tight, like his body was already halfway out the door. His attention was a fickle thing these days—understandable—but I needed one more moment of focus.

"What did you mean by that? That I'm not used to Ethan anymore?"

He pressed his lips together, gaze shifting to the side. The moment stretched, filled only by a muffled wail. When he finally spoke, his voice was thoughtful. "He doesn't really shy away from speaking his mind. At all."

A slow smile grew on my lips. *Attaboy.*

I had a feeling Ethan had come into his own. The version of him that only I used to know was now out in the world. Back when we were together, he'd stopped censoring himself around me, and I'd loved every second of it. It was bittersweet not having seen that grow into its full potential, but knowing it had was enough.

"That's a good thing," I said.

Oliver drummed his fingers on the table again, restless. "Yeah. It is. You know… under the right circumstances." The crying grew louder, and his eyes darted away once more.

"Go take care of that. We'll talk later."

He nodded, relief flickering across his face. "Thanks, Ash. And… sorry about the secret."

"I'll get my payback somehow."

His grin returned. "Please let me know how lunch goes. Can't wait to hear all about it."

I rolled my eyes but didn't bother hiding the smile.

"And I'll get back to you if I come up with anything," he added, giving me one more encouraging look before hanging up.

The screen went dark.

Silence settled over my home office, broken only by the distant hum of traffic drifting up from the street below. Madrid never really slept, but at this hour the noise softened into something muted. Files lay spread across my desk, legal notes and highlighted clauses blurring together under the lamplight.

I let out a slow breath and slumped into my chair, dragging a hand down my face. My shoulders ached from hours hunched over contracts and damage control. I should have gone back to work. There was more than enough waiting for me.

Instead, my thoughts drifted straight to Ethan. To our brief conversation. To his texts.

He still felt like the same person. He'd grown—that was the point of all this—but it wasn't like he'd become someone else.

I opened our chat, my eyes lingering on his words. My fingers hovered over the keyboard, itching to type something—anything—just to pick up the thread again.

But I set the phone down face-first on the desk and scrubbed a hand over my jaw.

I needed to get a grip. If I didn't, how the hell was I supposed to keep my distance?

Leaning back, I stared at the ceiling, but it wasn't legal documents or headlines or the impossible mess waiting for me in the morning that filled my head.

It was his smile.

Gorgeous. Familiar. Unchanged.

A quiet breath left me before I could stop it, and despite everything pressing in around me, I found myself smiling back.

He's here.

———

Saturday came too soon.

So soon, in fact, that I barely had time to prepare—myself or Luca—for what we were walking into. Between calls and meetings, there had been no space to think, let alone figure out how to tell him.

Now I was wandering through his apartment, waiting for him to get ready, bracing for something I couldn't quite name. Not that it had to be anything. I was probably making more of it than I should—at least where Luca was concerned.

"I still haven't been able to get that appointment," Luca called from his bedroom.

My eyes lifted from my phone. "Hm?"

"Casa Aurelio. I tried to get one to see the new collection, and they said they are too busy to schedule anything for the next couple of weeks. Have you heard anything?"

I stared at the half-open door, the words taking a second to land.

Luca walked out a moment later, a small, smug smile already in place. "You have no idea what I am talking about."

It wasn't a question. My best answer was my most charming smile.

Luca rolled his eyes good-naturedly. "I told you on Monday that I was looking for an appointment, and you said…" He waved a hand in the air, waiting for me to pick up the thread.

"That I knew someone and would make it work," I finished, my memory finally catching up. I'd completely forgotten. "I'm sorry. I've been distracted."

The thump of keys hitting the bottom of his bag echoed through the room as he started gathering his things. "It's okay, Ash. Just don't forget." He stepped closer, looking like he'd walked straight out of an ad, and stopped in front of me, giving me a once-over. "I like that shirt."

His palm slid up the fabric, and I placed my hand over his, holding it there.

"I wish you would change your mind about being photographed," Luca said. "We have a great concept for linen suits. You would look incredible."

I stiffened. "I'm sure you'll find someone who fits that role perfectly," I said, keeping my tone even.

Luca tilted his head, studying me. "That is another no?"

I smiled tightly and gave a small nod. After a beat, I added, "About this lunch…"

"Yes?" His hazel eyes stayed on my shirt, his other hand coming up, thumb brushing over the buttons. "Do you want to come back here after?" His tongue dragged slowly across his lower lip, the shift in his expression making his intentions unmistakable.

I let out a quiet, strained breath.

Luca closed his eyes, his head tipping back, already knowing what I was about to say, but still pressing close enough for his chest to brush against mine.

"You have work," he said, tiredly.

"I do. You know I do. And it's just for this—"

He lifted a hand, cutting me off. "I get it. I just thought I could cancel on Carla and we could have fun." His gaze flicked over me again, deliberate this time. "It's been a while."

I pressed my lips together. "I know."

He leaned in, brushing a quick kiss against my mouth before stepping away, already moving toward the counter. "I'll stop by your office next week. We'll figure out if there are any gaps in your schedule."

"Sounds like a plan." I slipped my hands into my pockets. "Luc, about this lunch…"

He nodded, pulling out his phone, thumb already moving across the screen.

"There are more people coming."

No reaction. The faint hum of the city drifted in through the windows, cars passing somewhere below.

"Raúl, who's an old friend. He's working with Henry, and…" *Just say it.* I cleared my throat. "And Ethan."

Two perfectly groomed dark brown eyebrows lifted. "Oh."

"You know he's my brother-in-law too. He and Henry are very close. And we're…"

Luca's attention shifted back to me, the ease gone from his posture.

"We're friends. He and I." The words sat there, thinner than I wanted them to.

Luca held my gaze for a second longer, then gave a small nod, like he was filing it away rather than accepting it. "Of course."

I forced a lighter tone. "It's nothing. Just lunch."

"Mm." His eyes dropped back to his screen, but his thumb had gone still.

"We should get going." I nodded toward the door. "Or we'll be late."

"Yeah." He slipped it into his pocket and grabbed his bag, heading for the door.

I followed him out into the hallway as he locked up behind us, the click echoing in the quiet space before we made our way to the elevator.

It could have gone worse, all things considered.

Maybe Oliver was wrong about this.

———

The restaurant was packed, and we sat out on the terrace. A parasol shaded us from the sun, but the heat still pressed in. Ten minutes in, and it was already going worse than I'd expected. The noise helped, at least, as a decent distraction from the tension simmering at our table.

Luca's eyes stayed on his phone, his expression set, thumb dragging across the screen without pause. He hadn't said much since we left the apartment, and whatever ease had been there earlier hadn't come back.

I shifted in my seat, the edge of the table pressing into my wrist, trying to ignore the way the silence kept stretching between us.

Two weeks ago, everything had felt… settled. Predictable. I'd been running a successful, growing business. My life moved in clean lines and controlled outcomes. Could it have used more color? Less quiet? Probably. But it worked. It was enough.

Now, sitting here, it felt like trying to force mismatched pieces together, something that might hold for a moment but would never really fit.

And the only thing that had changed was Ethan.

Work was work. Crises came and went. Being stretched thin was nothing new.

This was.

"Do you want anything else to drink?" I asked.

His glass of sparkling water sat untouched, the ice long melted. He shook his head without lifting his gaze. It wasn't unusual for him to disappear into his screen like this. Luca and his friends were always posting, snapping pictures, and talking nonstop. Victims of social media.

Still, something between us felt off—heavier than it should have.

"Luc—" I started, trying to salvage whatever this was before it slipped any further.

"Ash!"

Henry's voice cut through the noise, pulling my attention. Trailing behind him were Ethan and Raúl.

Now more than ever, I knew I'd been deluding myself into thinking this was going to be easy. Ethan looked like a ray of fucking sunshine breaking through darkness. Impeccably dressed—understated but elegant—and his hair, longer now, was dry this time. The light caught every shade of gold in those strands. He wore sunglasses—a very impressive pair, might I add—so I couldn't quite catch his eyes, but I felt him looking straight at us. At Luca, to be precise.

I cleared my throat and stood to greet them.

"You couldn't get a table inside?" Henry said, giving me a side hug. "It's hotter than hell today."

"Force of habit."

"Luca, I assume." Henry extended a hand. "I'm the little brother."

Luca's smile flickered back into place. "It is lovely to finally meet you."

"This is Raúl—he follows me around—and Ethan, our..." Henry paused mid-introduction, eyes narrowing slightly as he weighed his next word. "Brother-in-law."

"Nice to meet you both," Luca said, his smile tightening a fraction as he extended his hand to Ethan.

A tense second ticked by before Ethan took it.

"Same," he said, voice low, that familiar rasp curling around the word.

Then he turned to me, and his grin appeared—the full force of it hitting me square in the chest.

"Hey, Ash." He tugged lightly on my shirt, drawing me down, and kissed my cheek.

It read like a power play, and my stomach tightened once more. So maybe this wouldn't be smooth sailing after all.

Ethan dropped into the chair beside mine, and I caught Henry's barely contained amusement, shooting him a scowl.

The server appeared, tablet in hand, ready to take our orders.

"What's everybody having?" Henry asked.

"Macallan, neat," Ethan and I said in unison.

I bit the inside of my cheek to keep from laughing. Ethan chuckled under his breath, one shoulder lifting in that lazy, effortless way that always managed to pull focus.

Henry glanced at Luca, scanning the table like a host trying to keep the peace. "Luca, you want anything?"

"A glass of rosé, please." Luca straightened, posture polite, voice smooth. "Thank you."

Ethan made a soft sound beside me that could've been a scoff.

Henry started chatting with Raúl and Luca, clearly trying to smooth over the tension, but I couldn't follow a single word of it. My attention drifted to Ethan—watching him from the corner of my eye as discreetly as possible.

He was wearing white linen shorts that were just a touch too short and fit him perfectly. They matched his shirt—short sleeves that showed off his arms. A bracelet glinted on his wrist—not the one I'd given him, thankfully—and a couple of rings caught the light as he shifted. And the sunglasses—are you kidding me? Since when did a guy his age get his hands on a pair of Jacques Marie Mage and look that good wearing them?

Just then, one of his hands drifted close to the hem of his shorts, and he hooked a ringed finger under it, lazily pulling it back just a smidge. I couldn't help but take in the shape of his thighs, the dusting of golden hair over them. A sudden flashback of those same thighs wrapped tightly around my waist hit me hard, and my throat went dry.

A light tug on my sleeve pulled me back. "Ash?"

I turned to Luca. "Mh?"

"I was telling Henry that we met at a gala. Do you remember which one it was?"

I could barely remember my name right this second. "Fundraiser?"

"That is right. One of my friends organizes charity events at the opera house. That one was a fashion show," Luca said, his fingers tracing from my sleeve down to my forearm.

I let it dangle between us, trying to keep it out of Ethan's view. There was really no need to bruise his pride. Not that I assumed it would—but he *was* a little competitive.

I ignored the brief spark of satisfaction that thought brought.

Luca's gaze flicked to my cuff, then up to me. "At least you wore the right shoes that time."

A surprised laugh slipped out of me. "I maintain that no one noticed."

Henry looked between us. "What?"

"He showed up to a charity gala in mismatched shoes," Luca said, perfectly composed.

"Sebastian," Henry gasped, clutching his chest. "Not the shoes."

"They were both black," I muttered.

"They were not the same black."

Henry leaned back in his chair, delighted. "Please tell me there are photos."

"Unfortunately not," Luca said.

The corner of my mouth betrayed me anyway. "You're never letting that go."

"Never," he murmured.

The smile lingered, but something tight coiled low in my stomach. This had always been easy—slipping into shared glances and private jokes after too many rooms full of people performing importance. Two weeks ago, it would have felt perfectly natural.

Now…

"So, you work in fashion?" Raúl asked.

"Yes, in marketing, but with my family's fashion house," Luca told them, his accent charming enough to draw their attention without trying.

Ethan snapped his fingers, and we all turned toward him.

His head tilted slightly, a small smile playing on his lips, his full attention fixed on me. "I just figured out what's different about you."

"What?"

He lowered his sunglasses, giving me a calculated once-over. "You're not smoking. I can't smell it on you either. That sort of threw me off the last time I saw you too."

I couldn't help smiling. "I quit a year ago." I watched, riveted, as his smile deepened.

"And it stuck?"

"Yes, well, as the years go by, health starts being a more pressing matter."

"So you don't smoke at all?"

I pressed my lips together, looking away as I reached for my pocket. Pulling out a vape, I held it out to him.

He snatched it with a laugh. "You've got to be fucking kidding me. You vape? Sebastian Langley vapes?"

A chuckle made its way past my lips. "I try not to, but occasionally, yes." I couldn't exactly admit the only reason I'd brought it today was because this little meeting was setting my nerves on edge.

"Oh, please tell me it's flavored. I'll never stop giving you shit about it," he said, bringing it to his lips and taking a drag. I'd forgotten how gorgeous he looked doing that.

"Sorry to break it to you, but no." I took it from him and slipped it back into my pocket, resisting the urge to press it to my own lips. "No flavor."

"That would've been hilarious," Henry said, that same awkward look returning to his face.

Luca rested a hand on my thigh to catch my attention, though his gaze stayed on Ethan. "You do sometimes. Those watermelon-flavored ones."

An ache pulled tight in my chest. I turned to Ethan, watching his cocky grin falter. Then something softer—almost vulnerable—came through, and it speared me straight through the heart because we both knew exactly what that meant.

"Just when I'm feeling nostalgic," I said, offering a small smile. No use lying about something he could so easily see through.

A crease appeared between his brows, his lips pulling down into a frown.

Henry shifted in his seat. "So—"

"Missed the taste of me, did you?" Ethan cut in, his voice teasing. "Guess old habits die hard."

The air caught halfway to my lungs, and a startled laugh escaped before I could stop it.

"For fuck's sake," Henry muttered under his breath.

Raúl made a sound—something that might've been a cough or maybe a laugh he didn't want to commit to either.

Then Ethan leaned back in his chair, sunglasses low on his nose, the faintest smirk hinting at the corner of his mouth. "Relax," he drawled, voice softening into that lazy, self-assured tone that could disarm anyone. "Luca doesn't mind, do you?" His gaze flicked to my right. "He knows Ash was mine first."

From across the table, Henry gave Ethan a look that was half amusement, half *please, for the love of God, stop talking*. But something sparked through me—heat, thrill, denial tangled into one —and right behind it, a sharp surge of guilt.

As Luca froze beside me, his hand slipped slightly off my thigh, fingers curling against the fabric of my pants before retreating altogether. He smiled, but his jaw was working—the muscle there twitched in barely contained irritation.

Fuck. I was going to have to fix that later.

I leaned back, trying to mask my reaction with a slow exhale, but I could feel my pulse in my throat. Next to me, Ethan looked infuriatingly pleased with himself. Like he hadn't just gutted the table with one careless line.

The server showed up at that moment with our drinks— thank fuck—helping to dissipate some of the tension blanketing us.

"Should we make a toast?" Henry asked, seizing the lifeline.

"Why?" I asked, more surprised than anything. I had no idea what he thought was worth commemorating in this awkward excuse for a lunch. We hadn't even ordered food yet.

"Because..." He stalled, glancing at Ethan before shrugging. "Just because. Clink your fucking glass, Ash."

We did just that.

Out of the corner of my eye, I caught Ethan watching. His gaze dipped briefly to where Luca's hand had been resting on my thigh, but instead of the flare of anger I half expected, his mouth twitched—betraying his amusement.

Our eyes met over the rim of his glass, that slow grin spread wider as he took a sip and fucking *winked*.

Definitely not smooth sailing.

And fuck if that wasn't the most attractive thing I'd ever witnessed.

CHAPTER FOUR
ETHAN

Luca.

What kind of name was that?

I'll tell you what kind: one to match the ridiculously elegant, posh-looking man sitting next to Sebastian. His fucking *boyfriend*—his fashion-house-family, Italian *boyfriend*. Could the universe give me a fucking break?

I'd resisted the urge to look him up before coming here. To go digging through social media, to study photos, to measure myself against a stranger I didn't even know. I hadn't trusted what I might find—or what it might do to me.

Now I didn't need the internet.

They looked great together. It worked. Luca, with his hazel eyes, sharp jawline, tanned skin, and that annoyingly effortless wave in his brown hair. And Sebastian just being... well, Sebastian. Luca had to be way older than me, which kind of threw me, but still—they made sense. They looked like a couple.

Had we ever looked like that?

I shook off the unease that one single thought sent crawling through my body and tried to focus on the conversation in front of me.

We'd eased out of the awkwardness from my outburst.

Which was only fair. Luca kept touching Sebastian and staring at me like he wanted to make sure I noticed every second of it. Trust me, I was well fucking aware of how he was basically pissing all over him. So at the very least, now he knew I didn't give a fuck.

Which I didn't.

Sebastian could have a boyfriend. What the fuck did I care?

Plus, it didn't change the fact that he still couldn't stop looking at me. Just like his boyfriend, he kept stealing little glances. And after my last comment, he couldn't even hide the smile pulling at his mouth. Of course he liked the attention.

And I was not into it.

I wasn't.

Just like I wasn't into how much cologne he'd drenched himself in, or how it clung to me even though I'd barely touched him. Or how good his skin looked with that fresh summer tan. Or how badly I wanted to slide my hand up his nape and grab the longer curls brushing the collar of his shirt—

Christ.

What the hell was it about Sebastian Langley?

But, in light of everything, was it really that awful to want a little attention back? He was my ex—apparently—and if I was going to sit here pretending I wasn't flustered just being next to him, the least he could do was suffer a little too.

He owed me that much.

I rolled my shoulders back and tried to focus on Henry and whatever he and Raúl were going on about. Over the past week, I'd gotten used to Raúl's presence. He and Henry had been working around the clock, so I either saw them together at the apartment or ran into him when Henry dragged me out to the site.

"We're having the party at *Lumbre* for the birthday bash," Henry said, giving Sebastian a teasing smirk. His brother just rolled his eyes.

"Not this again…" Sebastian took a sip of his drink.

Not super keen on turning thirty-nine, are we? I smiled to myself.

"We should move it to *Senda*," Raúl said.

Henry shot him a curious look. "How come?"

"Adrian just got fired," he said flippantly. "The whole place is going to shit."

Henry's eyes widened. "You've been holding out on me." He slid closer, that tiny smile giving away how thrilled he was about this particular piece of gossip. "Dish right the fuck now."

"Who's that?" Sebastian asked.

I propped my elbow on the table and stole a glance at Luca. Just as confused as I was. *Good.*

"Adrian was the exec in charge of the Fama group," Henry said.

"That's the biggest club group in the city," Raúl added, meeting my eyes.

"So… big gossip?" I said, resting my chin on my palm.

"Very big."

Raúl usually had that faint glint of approval in his eyes when he looked at me—like he might've been into me—but he was careful not to let it linger. Part of me hoped Sebastian had asked him not to, though jealousy had never been his thing.

"So, what happened?" Henry urged.

Raúl's eyes slid to him; he shrugged, took a slow sip of his drink, then finally said, "Got caught fucking one of the hostesses in a supply closet."

"No!" Henry half gasped, half laughed. "That fucking asshole."

"That's it?" I asked.

"Adrian's wife is one of the founding members of the group," Raúl said to me. "I'm guessing that didn't go over well."

Yup. That'll do it.

"Can't believe he'd do that. How old is he now?" Sebastian asked.

I narrowed my eyes at him. Kind of hypocritical, but okay.

"Going on forty, maybe," Raúl said.

"Can you imagine being so horny you'd bang one of your employees at work? In a fucking *closet*?"

A laugh caught behind my teeth as I bit the inside of my cheek.

Sebastian cleared his throat and shifted in his seat. It was just a second, but it was enough for me to catch his eyes flicking to mine—and that tiny curve of his lips.

"He's a businessman with a reputation to protect," Raúl said. "He should know better." He shrugged. "Maybe if he was younger, but to get that primitive?"

"Kinda hot when you think about it. Not the cheating—just the I-have-to-have-you-now energy," Henry said, sipping his drink.

Sebastian's eyes met mine again, and we both looked away quickly. He coughed into his hand, and I pressed my lips together to keep from grinning.

"Is she younger than him?" I asked, keeping my tone innocent.

Sebastian shifted again as I kept my eyes locked on Raúl.

"In her twenties," Raúl said.

"Maybe he just wanted to prove he could keep up with her," I offered.

Sebastian tapped my foot under the table, like he was telling me to behave. I took a big gulp of my drink to hide my laugh.

"Forty isn't old," Sebastian said defensively. "There are plenty of people who have better stamina when they're older."

Henry and Raúl looked at him like he'd grown two heads.

"Have you seen Adrian?" Henry asked. "The guy walks around with an inhaler."

"Maybe a midlife crisis then," I teased.

Another tap on my foot, harder this time.

"That sounds more likely," Raúl said.

"Maybe trying to prove something? Fucking someone against a wall isn't that easy," I said with a sigh. "Reeks a little of overinflated ego."

Sebastian let out an offended scoff. But that curve at the corner of his mouth? Worse now. And aimed right at me.

"Actually, it doesn't sound like him," he said. "So it was probably the twenty-something waitress—"

"Hostess," Henry corrected.

"Who clearly has no impulse control. An affliction of the young."

"No impulse control?" I asked with a laugh.

Sebastian smirked.

Raúl tilted his head. "Do you know him?"

Henry's eyebrows shot up when he finally caught on. *The pantry.* He looked torn between bursting out laughing and scolding both of us.

Meanwhile, Luca and Raúl looked confused as fuck.

"No," Sebastian said smoothly. "But I can imagine."

A laugh slipped out of me, and both Langley brothers looked away, trying—and failing—to hide matching smiles.

"I'm going to the bathroom. Be right back," Luca said. He stopped by Sebastian's side, gave him a quick kiss on the cheek —one that left a bitter taste in my mouth—and walked off.

As soon as he was gone, Henry sighed. "You two are fucking unbelievable."

I put on my very best innocent face—betrayed instantly by the laugh bubbling up my throat. "Me?"

"It's all him." Sebastian tipped his chin in my direction.

I shoved his shoulder. "What?"

Sebastian bit his lip and leaned in, turning fully to me. "You're acting like a total brat."

I chuckled. "Haven't you heard? It's an affliction of my age."

That finally cracked him. His laugh rang out across the table, loud and bright, as he reached over to ruffle my hair. I swatted his hand away.

Raúl leaned back in his chair, looking between us. "I'm so confused."

"They're acting like children," Henry explained flatly, "because they got caught fucking in a closet once, and that was their clever little way of making fun of each other."

"A pantry," Sebastian and I said at the same time—then looked at each other and burst into laughter.

"Fucking children," Henry muttered, but his mouth was definitely curving.

If Raúl's eyebrows went any higher, they'd climb into his hairline. "Right. The scandalous ex. It all makes sense now."

That sobered Sebastian a bit. His laugh faded into a chuckle as he gave Raúl a shrug.

"So does he hate me?" I teased, keeping the mood light.

"What do you think?" Sebastian asked, smirking.

"I think I've been nothing if not cordial."

Henry barked a laugh. "Cordial? Babe, come on. Be so for real."

I shrugged. "It's your fault for giving me the opening."

"Are you going to behave now?" Sebastian leaned in, eyes locked on mine.

I mirrored him, lifting a brow in quiet challenge. "You don't get to tell me what to do anymore." I kept my gaze on his and mouthed, *Daddy*, barely containing my grin.

He laughed, shaking his head. "As if I was ever able to."

I grinned wider, still not breaking eye contact. It felt like a dare. Like pulling on a live wire between us. The temperature seemed to spike—or maybe the heat was just under my skin.

Henry cleared his throat loudly. "Reel it in."

We sat back at the same time, still lingering in each other's orbit until we physically had to look away. Until Luca came back to the table, and I had to pretend that little moment hadn't been fucking… electric.

Did he hate it?

It didn't look like he did.

Sebastian's smile didn't leave him the rest of lunch. He kept leaning closer, asking me things, pulling me into conversation, keeping us tethered in ways we definitely weren't supposed to be, especially with his boyfriend right next to him. We'd fall into our own little world for two seconds before remembering we had an audience. Exhilarating. And also incredibly fucking dumb.

Because Luca's hand kept slipping onto Sebastian's thigh.

And Sebastian kept letting it stay.

Like it belonged there.

After we were done eating and everyone was more than ready to leave the awkwardness behind, we gathered near the entrance to say goodbye. That's when a guy stepped out of the restaurant and gave me the most obvious once-over known to man. Spanish men were the boldest fucking flirts on earth.

I snorted a laugh—just at the audacity—which he apparently took as interest. He nodded like he wanted me to follow. I shook my head, and that should've been the end of it. But when I looked up, Sebastian was staring straight at me.

Of course he'd seen it.

And of course he wasn't jealous—just amused.

I leaned closer and whispered, "What?"

"Nothing," he said too quickly.

We were far enough from the others to talk without being overheard.

"Don't give me that," I pressed.

Sebastian stepped closer. "I like seeing you comfortable with yourself," he said softly. "It's a good look on you, darling."

And fuck—my heart kicked into a sprint.

Heat crawled up my neck as he stepped back again.

Fucking Sebastian.

They walked away, Luca beside him—not holding hands, but their shoulders brushed now and then. They didn't look all that close. Comfortable, maybe. But not the way we'd been. Behind closed doors, anyway.

"That wasn't so bad, was it?" Henry asked at my side.

"No." My eyes were still on them. "Not so bad."

Because the truth was, I still knew Sebastian. I knew what interest looked like on his face. I knew what his heated looks meant—what they felt like. And I'd seen them today too.

Not a single one had been aimed at his boyfriend.

A smile tugged at my lips as we made our way back to Henry's apartment.

Game on.

———

A soft rap sounded at my door, and Henry poked his head through the opening. "Babe, you busy?"

I rolled onto my stomach on the bed, shut my laptop, and slid it aside. "Nah, what's up?"

He stepped in, bypassing my still mostly unpacked luggage, and sat at the foot of the bed, eyeing the suitcase for a second before shrugging. "You know these open, don't you?"

My stomach tightened. "I'm moving out soon. I just need to find a new place."

I still hadn't told Henry what was going on with my finances —or my dad. I kept hoping I'd fix it before he ever had to know, but I still hadn't been able to reach my father. And things were getting bleaker by the day. My landlord had already sold my apartment to someone else, and I'd lied to Henry and said it was a plumbing issue.

I fucking hated it. Henny was the last person on earth who deserved to be lied to.

"You want my realtor to look at it?" he offered.

"I have a couple of places I'm looking at this week." More affordable ones, because God knows I wasn't going to be affording Langley prices anytime soon.

Henry nodded, then scratched the back of his head. "Or you could just stay..."

"Stay?"

"The place is big enough, E. You don't have to move out. Plus, the company is nice…" He gave me a giddy, hopeful grin. "We can be roomies."

I chuckled. "You don't have to do that. You need your own place to frolic in. I'll just get in the way."

"You won't—I'll frolic quietly. Promise."

"You don't do anything quietly."

"Fair. Then I'll ask you to join." He winked.

I shoved his shoulder, earning a laugh.

"I'm kidding—about the threesome, not about the moving in. At least think about it. Keep it on your list of possibilities when you look at places."

My stomach rolled again. "Maybe." Another lie. I definitely couldn't afford this place either.

"You know I'd be the best roommate ever. Keep you fed, drunk, comfortable. I'll fluff your pajamas and warm your bed for you."

I snorted. "Have you ever had a roommate before?"

"I grew up with my brothers—"

"Not the same. But just out of curiosity… did you fluff Oli's pajamas for him?"

"Obviously." Henry bumped my shoulder with his, grinning. "Speaking of which, how are you feeling? After yesterday's introductions?"

I sighed. "I'm fine, Henny."

"Really?"

I met his gaze and turned onto my side to face him. "I thought we had a rule."

"Yeah, I know." He rolled his eyes and mirrored my pose. "But we're all coexisting now, and I know this can't be easy for you. I'm just checking in."

"We are, which is why it's more important than ever that we pretend Ash isn't my ex and your brother. You can't get in the middle."

"I'm not, I swear. And I want that too. I'm fucking Switzerland right now, baby. You two can deal with whatever on your own—just don't ask me to pick a side."

"I'd never do that to you."

"Let's just avoid the scenario."

"Fine."

We held each other's gaze for a beat.

"But you *can* still tell me if you feel sad…" he added.

I rolled onto my back with a huff. "I'm not sad over your brother being in a relationship. I'm pissed I didn't see it coming, and I'm pissed that I'm pissed about that. But I'm over it. End of story."

"You didn't sound very over it yesterday…"

"Well," I said, pushing upright, "fuck off."

Henry laughed as I stood. He folded his arms behind his head, giving me that unimpressed, I-know-your-bullshit look. "If I were getting in the middle—which I am not—I'd say he didn't look very over it either."

"But you're not."

"You're right, I'm not," he said breezily. "So what I'm actually saying is that you can tell me if you're sad over the sky being blue or whatever—so we don't have to say the thing we both know we're actually talking about."

I blinked.

"That Ash is the sky, and blue is that he has a boyfriend—"

"Henny," I warned, lifting a finger.

"Yes, babe?"

I dragged my palm down my face and let out a slow breath.

Silence settled between us as I stared at the ceiling. He didn't push. Didn't fill the space. Just gave me the opening and trusted me to step through it.

I lasted all of three seconds.

"So he moved on," I said. "Good for him. Seriously. Good for him."

Henry didn't react—just watched me with quiet patience, like he'd known this was exactly where we'd end up.

"That's what people do, right? They move on. They date emotionally available adults with stable lives and matching shoes and shit."

The tension crept in, and the words slipped out before I could stop them. "I just don't fucking get him."

Henry's brows lifted slightly, his lips twitching as he fought a smile. "Get who?"

"Luca," I said. "Did you see him? The fundraiser, the gala, the opera house charity circuit… he looks like he belongs in a perfume ad, not next to your brother."

He pressed his lips together, clearly enjoying this.

"He's not even Ash's type."

"Oh?" Henry said carefully. "And what is Ash's type?"

I opened my mouth.

Closed it.

"You know…" I said.

Henry waited.

Heat crawled up my neck as I waved a hand through the air, very much not pointing at myself. "Short."

Henry stared at me for half a second, eyes going wide before he lost it—full-body laughter, doubled over, wheezing, absolutely no loyalty whatsoever.

"Fuck you," I snapped again, grabbing a pillow and throwing it at him. "You know I'm right."

He caught it, still laughing. "I can't believe you went there."

"Whatever," I muttered. "He can have his fashion-house boyfriend. I don't care."

Henry bit the inside of his cheek, trying and failing to look neutral. His eyes were soft, though. Gentle. He knew exactly what I was doing and was kind enough not to say it out loud.

"Okay." He pushed up from the bed and clapped his hands once. "New plan, roomie. You're coming with me."

"To where?"

"Site. Raúl's meeting us. His cousin too." He wiggled his fingers in the air. "Distraction therapy."

I grabbed my phone. "Fine." Because sitting here thinking about the things I wasn't supposed to be thinking about was starting to feel like a losing game. "He better be hot."

"That's the word around town."

I rolled my shoulders, surprised to find some of the pressure gone. Nothing had changed, but saying it out loud had made it feel… less like it was swallowing me whole.

We walked the five minutes it took to get there, this time without Henry badgering me about Sebastian—just him rambling about his plans. I tried my best to steer him away from talking about traveling together for the weekend to check out other clubs.

I had enough saved to last me through the year, but that was assuming I was paying rent and, you know, surviving. Not going on trips with Henry and his Olympic-level drinking habit. Even if he got half his drinks comped, he also loved buying rounds for the whole damn place—and I couldn't let him pay for everything. That wasn't how friendships worked. That wasn't how anything worked.

I was supposed to be able to handle my life on my own. And I'd been so fucking close, too. I checked my phone again—calls, emails, all of it—and still nothing. And every hour that passed without hearing from him made this whole situation feel a little more fucked.

The place still looked rough, but most of the heavy structural stuff was cleared out so they could start on the basics: floors, plumbing, the bones of it all.

I wandered around, trailing behind Henny, when Raúl walked in with his cousin—and yeah… they hadn't been lying. The guy was built. Rough around the edges in a hot way. Not exactly the kind of guy I went for, but sure, fuckable.

"Holy fuck, can you believe the men in this country?" Henry

asked, tugging at his shirt like he needed fresh air. "I swear everybody is fucking *hawt*."

I sucked in a laugh as they approached, and we all went through introductions. Mateo—that was the cousin—pulled a stack of papers from a bag, spread them across the floor, and immediately launched into a structural breakdown with Henry.

I stepped aside to give them space.

Raúl followed. "Did you start classes already?"

"Tomorrow officially."

"That's a great time—starting fresh," he said fondly. "I remember how ambitious we were back then."

"We?"

"Ash and me."

Right. Wharton friends. It felt weird meeting someone who'd actually known Sebastian in that world. I'd gotten so used to thinking of him as a loner, in spite of how charming he could be, that I couldn't even properly imagine him being my age and social.

"He still is," I said.

Raúl huffed a laugh and shrugged. "Sure. Not like before, but yes—he's still very much about carving out his future in a spectacular manner."

"Why not like before?"

"He's softer around the edges now," he said, glancing at Henry and Mateo still deep in discussion. "He's changed a lot these last couple of years. I couldn't believe it when he moved here. That he left his empire for a lesser title."

"Lesser?"

He looked back at me. "Because he was CEO before."

I frowned. "And now?"

"He's the CFO of VistaReal."

Seriously? That was somehow even more shocking than the boyfriend part. Sebastian actually stepped back? While starting his own company? That didn't fit. At all.

Raúl studied me for a moment, something like hesitation

flickering across his face. "I assumed you knew... with everything that's been going on, there are more eyes on him. Articles."

My pulse stumbled at that word—articles. "Knew what?"

He tilted his head slightly, as if reconsidering. "It's been... a demanding month," he said instead. "Nothing he won't outmaneuver."

Curiosity clawed up my throat, and I was about to push for more when Henry's laugh cut between us—loud and bright.

Raúl and I both looked over.

Huh...

Henry was standing, brushing invisible soot off his clothes like he'd just survived a mild explosion, very pointedly *not* looking at Mateo—who was smiling at him. Not a big grin, just... interested.

Raúl clicked his tongue and muttered a quiet string of Spanish curses before stalking toward them. Henry shook Mateo's hand way too fast, mumbled something, and immediately beelined for me before Raúl could open his mouth. He grabbed my arm and steered me off without so much as a backward glance.

"What just happened?" I asked, looking over my shoulder.

Mateo shrugged at whatever Raúl was saying—Raúl looked half-pissed, Mateo looked unbothered—and then Mateo's eyes drifted right to Henry's retreating back. Lingering.

"Nothing," Henry said. "Meeting's over."

"What did he say?" I grinned. "You're all flushed."

Henry pressed his lips together, still walking. "That I had a great smile."

My eyebrows shot up. "You *do* have a dreamy smile."

"The dreamiest," he said, nodding solemnly. "One of my most attractive features."

"And you love when people point that out."

"Yes."

"But not right now."

"No."

"Why not?"

"He might be my employee," he said. "That's unprofessional."

I scoffed. "Oh, come on. I've seen you flirt with every single one of your employees for years—"

"Excuse me? I am not a sexual harassment lawsuit waiting to happen. I'm not Adrian."

"You know you're a flirt, Henny. A respectful one, but a flirt." I nudged him. "So what was that?"

He shook his head. And for the briefest second, the humor drained from his face. Something tight flashed there, something I almost didn't catch before his usual easy smile slipped back into place. "He's just really not my type."

I stared at him, baffled, but he tugged on my arm again, ending the conversation. I glanced back at the de la Vega cousins —just in time to catch Mateo's gaze still fixed firmly on Henry's back, soft and intent.

———

Later that night, curiosity won.

I looked Luca up first. It felt safer somehow, like I was skirting the edge instead of stepping straight into the fire. The images loaded quickly. Event photos. Magazine shots. A few runway-adjacent appearances that made it painfully obvious he moved in circles far removed from mine.

Then I saw it—a photo of him and Sebastian at some gala, standing too close to be accidental. They were turned toward each other, Luca smiling, Sebastian's familiar half-smirk in place. It made bile rise in my throat. That single image felt more intimate than anything I had witnessed the day before.

I shoved those feelings into a small box and kept going, searching Sebastian's name.

The results multiplied instantly—interviews, features, market analyses, business journals—all of them recent, and none of them had anything to do with his private life.

My eyes fixed on one title, and my throat went instantly dry.

Langley Executive Faces Mounting Pressure Amid State Investigation

I read it again, like the words might rearrange themselves into something less dire.

They didn't.

CHAPTER FIVE

ASH

"When are you leaving?" Luca asked.

I lifted my head from my laptop, dragging my attention back to him. "I'm not. I'm here for the rest of the month."

"I leave next Monday." His thumbs were already flying over his phone. "Back on the twenty-third. Would you like to do XO on Friday?"

My lips parted to answer, but an email notification appeared in the corner of my screen. I glanced at it automatically, jaw tightening, before forcing my focus back to him. "Yes," I said. "Friday works."

Someone knocked at the door.

"Yes?"

It flew open, and Henry stepped in with a stack of takeout boxes. "Brotherly delivery. No excuses; we're doing a sushi lunch break—" He spotted Luca and stopped. "Oh. Sorry. Didn't know you were already busy."

"Like that's ever stopped you before," I said, pushing the laptop aside but not closing it. "We're just finishing up. Let's see what you've got."

Henry crossed the room and dropped the boxes on my desk before shaking Luca's hand. "Sorry for crashing your date."

"Don't worry—not a date. It is nice to see you again." Luca's gaze drifted to the spread. "And this is very sweet."

"Yeah, Ash is shit at feeding himself," Henry said. "As you must know by now. So I'm just putting in the work."

Luca turned back to me, a faint crease forming between his brows. "Are you missing lunch right now?"

"It's fine," I said, waving him off, eyes flicking briefly to the screen as it dimmed beside me. I tapped the trackpad to wake it. "I would've just asked Vanessa to get me something down the street in a little while."

Henry hesitated, then dropped into the chair and pretended to scroll through his phone, though his gaze lifted every few seconds.

"Oh. Okay, then. So... XO?" Luca asked.

I tipped my chin toward Henry, already reaching to silence another notification. "This'll just be a minute."

"That's fine." Henry blinked, face scrunching in confusion. "There's plenty in there for all of us."

Luca smiled politely. "I have to leave—I had plans already. Maybe next time."

"Sure..."

"I can do dinner on Friday." The words came out distracted, my attention snagging on the subject line that had just appeared in my inbox. "We'll figure out the rest after you get back."

Luca nodded, still tapping away on his phone.

Henry narrowed his eyes.

"Stop by Casa Aurelio before you leave," I said. "I got you the appointment. I'll text you the number—you're all set."

Luca's face brightened. "Thank you, Ash." He reached out to shake Henry's hand. "Bye, Henry."

Henry nodded back, still looking puzzled.

Luca stepped toward me, pressing a soft kiss to my mouth before heading for the door. Right before leaving, he paused and turned. "We're going out for drinks tonight with Carla. If you would like to come… both of you?"

My jaw tightened for a second. "Can't make it, Luc. I have a meeting with Elena tonight. Sorry, it's just this whole mess…"

"Right," he said. "No problem. Next time."

"Next time," I echoed, already reaching for my mouse.

Luca gave a small nod and slipped out of the office. The sound of his footsteps faded down the hall as we sat in silence. My inbox counter ticked upward on the screen.

"So…" Henry said. "Was this the first time you two met, or…?"

I blew out a breath, knowing this was coming. "What?"

"This just felt a little like walking into a business meeting, not my brother and his boyfriend."

I drummed my fingers on the desk. "Your point being?"

Henry leaned his elbows on the table, tilting his head. "Do you *like* him?"

"We're dating, Henny. What do you think?"

"That that was the most clinical exchange I've ever seen between two people who are, quote, unquote, dating."

"Just because we weren't all over each other?"

He wobble-nodded. "Not everyone has to be. But *you* can be. When you and Ethan—" He cut himself off abruptly. "Never mind. Not getting in the middle."

I grabbed one of the boxes and opened it. "Good choice."

"But I mean," Henry continued, "I've seen you be warmer than that with fuckbuddies. It's weird, that's all."

My phone buzzed on the desk, and I flipped it over. A text from Ethan. I'd messaged him this morning, and we'd been talking on and off throughout the day.

PET

just left quant methods

professor said numbers never lie but the
numbers in my spreadsheet have absolutely
lied to me

twice

I huffed a small laugh. The tension in my shoulders loosened a fraction.

ME

that's not the spreadsheet lying

it's begging for help

want me to take a look at it?

PET

are you implying my spreadsheet is dramatic???

and no thank you

I can tame them myself

ME

uh-huh

I'll be here when those "tamed" numbers start plotting a coup

I set my phone down as Henry finished unpacking all the makis. My stomach rumbled. Not that I wanted to admit he was right, but I had skipped breakfast for an early meeting—and the inevitable string that followed.

"So have you met his friends?" Henry asked.

I raised an eyebrow.

"Been to his place? Know his last name?"

I sighed. "Henny, we've been going out for two months."

"Right, right," he said, popping a roll into his mouth and chewing thoughtfully. "How long did your fling with E last? Summer, right? Couple of months?"

We stared at each other.

"You're being very annoying today," I said.

Henry let out his bark of a laugh. "You make it so easy."

My phone buzzed again, and I grabbed it while taking a bite of a salmon yuzu roll.

PET

please

I'd like to see them try

I've handled worse than a rogue spreadsheet

ME

forgot who I was talking to for a minute there

they don't stand a fucking chance

I'll still be around if you need saving though

PET

don't need the heroics

got plenty of red bull and have been vibing to this one song on repeat

kept me sane more than the class did tbh

ME

a song huh

what's got you vibing these days

PET

Lucky by Zedd and Remi Wolf

I'd ask if you've heard it but since you're a thousand years old and make the word vibing sound incredibly awkward I'm gonna go with no

"Little shit," I muttered under my breath, a laugh slipping out as I pulled up the lyrics on my laptop.

"Still working?" Henry asked.

My eyes skimmed the words, my grin widening as I picked up my phone and typed quickly.

ME

of course I have

and really?

so who are you clutching your pillow to these days? me?

I'm flattered but I guess it's nice to know you don't regret it

I lifted my eyes back to my brother. "Sorry?"

Henry was squinting again.

My phone buzzed in my hand.

PET

ooooh we're playing the cocky asshole game today?

my bad

let me think up an appropriate comeback

. . .

I laughed out loud before I could help myself, then pressed my lips together as I took in Henry's expression.

A slow grin spread across his face. "Oh, hello, teenage Sebastian!" he said with mock surprise. "It's been a while since I've seen you. Let me take a wild guess." He looked pointedly at my phone, not even trying to hide his amusement. "Are you maybe texting our brother-in-law right now?"

"No," I said too quickly.

My phone buzzed again, and our eyes dropped to it at the same time. We both reached for it, but thankfully I got there first, clutching it to my chest.

"You're so full of shit," Henry said, pointing. "You're totally texting him right now."

"So what if I was? I can't text him?"

"That's not the point."

"Then what is?"

"Five minutes ago you were acting like a fucking robot with your *boyfriend*"—he jerked his thumb toward the door Luca had walked out of—"and now you're here giggling and kicking your fucking feet while texting your *ex*? Shit, Ash, I'm about to blast Madonna and pull out the neon pink nail polish."

"That's not what's happening." I rolled my eyes and pocketed my phone to keep it out of his reach. "Ethan is just fun. You know this. He's your fucking best friend now—apparently," I said, trying my damnedest not to sound bitter. "And we know each other. It's different with him."

"Exactly, Ash." Henry's eyes widened as he nodded slowly. "It *is* different with him. Do you know why?" His tone was placating, like he was talking to a small child.

"You're dangerously close to getting right down smack in the middle of it, Henry."

That shut him up.

His chest visibly deflated, and he sank back in his chair,

poking at the sushi with his chopsticks. "I finally know what people who timetravel in movies feel like."

I snorted. "What?"

"You know… how they're supposed to not interfere and just let nature take its course. It's annoying as fuck."

I took another bite, this one harder to swallow. "I'm always going to have his best interests at heart, Henny. You know that."

He nodded, the humor slipping from his face. "I know I'm not supposed to call you out, and I know I was the one who asked for us to keep everything separate, so I'm just going to say one thing. Okay?"

I waited.

Henry met my eyes, his bottom lip twisting. "Don't fucking hurt him again."

And that hit me right in the chest.

Somehow everything with Ethan was always a mess. First my teenage affair when our siblings were getting married, and now he's my little brother's best friend. When I wasn't hurting Oliver, I was hurting Henry—and always dragging Ethan into the mix.

Fucking perfect.

"I won't," I said, hoping I could actually keep my promise this time.

Ethan's unexpected reappearance in my life was not ideal for so many reasons. But it was incredibly welcome. When my head was in chaos, just thinking about him could set everything right again. The ease. How he cut through the noise. That effect he had on me was so difficult to give up when all I wanted right now was some source of comfort. But my comfort shouldn't ever come at his expense.

Or Luca's, for that matter.

Things between us had turned a little tense since that lunch with Ethan—understandably—but it left a bitter taste at the back of my throat, an ache in my chest that felt too much like being caught doing something wrong.

Just thinking about them in the same space at the same time made something inside me twist. They didn't fit together. They couldn't. But that separation—the restraint it forced—made being around Ethan bearable. It gave me a way to hold the line.

Another pang of guilt followed close behind. Because that wasn't fair to either of them.

After we finished eating and Henry left, I finally pulled my phone from my pocket.

Ethan's messages were waiting.

PET

got it

you were the one smoking nostalgic watermelon vapes after claiming to fucking hate them so who's the pillow-clutcher in this scenario?

and that my friends is what I call a fucking buuuurn

I chuckled softly, but then my eyes flicked to the next line he'd sent a few minutes later.

Shorter.

Quieter.

PET

you busy or something?

Suddenly, *I* was the one going back in time—back to the nights when I'd forced myself to ignore my phone. To ignore him. And here I was, doing it again. Hurting him. Roughly half an hour after I'd promised I wouldn't.

Four fucking years, and I still couldn't control myself around Ethan.

ME

no

not busy

just got caught up with lunch

I might need some salve for that burn though

you win

I could at least give him that.

Since I was so keen on denying him everything else.

———

Madrid was already warm, that early kind of heat that clung to your shoulders no matter how fast you moved. I'd gone out before sunrise, hoping a run would settle my head.

It didn't.

My mind kept circling the same things—emails piling up, calls from legal I still hadn't returned, a board briefing I needed to survive without sparking panic, and the quiet but relentless question of who had signed off on the documents that started this whole mess. Every minute brought a new problem, and if I couldn't think of something fast, the next step would be layoffs.

Then there was Henry insisting on throwing me some big birthday bash, and, as the cherry on top, navigating my relationship with Luca when my head kept wandering into places it shouldn't. Work was an easy excuse right now, but whatever was happening between Luca and me felt increasingly misaligned. Forced. But I didn't have the bandwidth to touch that right now.

I was halfway through rehearsing what I needed to get done today—mostly to keep from thinking about everything I couldn't control—when something moved at the edge of my vision.

I looked up too late. Too late to avoid it.

Ethan was already jogging to me, lifting a hand in this easy, familiar wave, like running into me on an empty street at dawn made perfect sense.

Of course it was him.

And of course he fucking looked like that. It was worse than the tennis getup. Ridiculously short running shorts, a cut-out sleeveless T-shirt dipping low at the sides, and a cap barely containing the mess of golden curls. And the socks. Two-striped, criminally tight, drawing my attention straight to his calves.

Fuck. Me.

"Hey," he said, chest heaving as he pulled out his headphones.

"Hey."

His pale eyes did a slow once-over, and I swallowed thickly at the clear appraisal in them.

"You jog? What the fuck?" His laugh was delightfully raspy.

"Yeah, a few times a week when I have the time," I said. He tilted his head, waiting. "Health and whatnot."

His expression sobered a little. "But like… is it because there's something to worry about? First smoking…"

"Oh no, not at all, darling," I said, huffing an unwilling laugh at his worry. "It's an age thing."

His shoulders eased. Then his eyes did another scan, and he pressed his lips together in that shy fucking smile that undid me.

I couldn't tell if the flush on his cheeks was from the jog or the look. "What?"

"What the fuck are you wearing?" he finally asked.

"What's wrong with what I'm wearing? These are running clothes."

"Ash, it's like… skin-tight." His cheekbones were popping from how hard he was trying not to laugh.

"It's hot as balls right now, and these breathe."

"No, I can definitely tell they breathe. With the mesh"—he waved a hand vaguely at me, clearing his throat—"and you being basically naked and all."

I laughed out loud, all my worries melting away in an instant. "Nothing you haven't seen before, darling. So what's the harm?" I crossed my arms over my chest, biting the inside of my cheek when his eyes got stuck on it.

He gave in and laughed too. "You're too fucking full of yourself. I shouldn't even be surprised."

I couldn't stop myself from asking, "Are you done? Running?"

He nodded.

"Want to get coffee?"

He rolled his lips, looked away, clearly trying not to grin— then nodded again.

We walked to a coffee shop around the block, close to the entrance of my building, and settled at a small table outside by the door. It was still mostly empty, just a couple of regulars stopping by for their early morning jolt. Ethan's leg was bouncing under the table, his arms crossed on top of it while we waited for our order.

I could have tried to strike up a conversation, but in that moment I was completely entranced by him. It hit me all over again how much he'd changed—in the best possible way. His biceps were bulging where he had them tucked in, and Ethan might've still been fun-sized compared to me, but he'd filled out perfectly for his frame. And the angles in his jaw? Mouthwatering. Then he went ahead and flipped his cap backward, and I had to bite my tongue not to groan at the sight.

"So, you're a jogger now?" He arched a brow, smirk twitching.

"I've always done it, actually."

He frowned, clearly trying to place that. "Really?"

"I stopped for a while when I took over Langley Enterprises. Didn't have the time for it, but I've always been a junkie for early morning running endorphins."

The server stopped by and dropped off our identical double espressos.

He took a sip. "Guess that makes sense."

"How about you?"

He set the cup back down carefully. "I picked it up after I dropped tennis."

Well, that sucked. I loved that outfit. "You stopped playing?"

"Yeah," he said. "After I stopped talking to my dad."

Right. Because his dad hated my fucking guts. One more thing I'd fucked up for him. "You don't talk anymore?"

Ethan's face flickered through a string of emotions—hurt, anger, shame—before he brushed his knuckles under his nose, the rings on his fingers catching the light as he did. His little nervous gesture. My brows knit at the sight.

"No, we do—kinda…" His lips twisted into a small grimace. "It's complicated."

"I get that. Mine's pretty complicated too."

"But you stopped speaking with yours altogether." He didn't phrase it as a question. When I cocked my head, he continued, "I interned with LE last semester—shadowing your dad. He mentioned it."

I blinked.

What?

"My father mentioned—to you—that we weren't speaking?"

"Yeah. He asked me about you once. Like… kind of assuming we were still in contact. And when I told him we weren't, he said *same*."

"My father said *same*?"

Ethan smiled and rolled his eyes. "Like… that same intention but in your dad's very formal tone."

I chuckled. "Of course." My eyes drifted down to my cup as a frown tugged at my lips. He'd actually asked about me? And to Ethan of all people.

"Daddy issues, am I right?"

That surprised another laugh out of me. "Right." I took a bigger sip. "Those usually work in my favor."

Ethan let out a little huff. "Still? Luca doesn't look that young. How old is he?"

"Thirty-two."

His eyebrows arched, but he said nothing.

I opted for the safe subject change. "How did that internship work out for you?"

He sighed and leaned back. "Good. I worked with Oli too—when he could. It was fun. Hard but fun."

I finished my coffee, setting the cup down slowly. The soft murmur of early conversations drifted out from the café behind us, but between us the air felt tight. A little odd, considering everything had gone almost smoothly up until now. But I guess we couldn't ignore the bad things forever.

Ethan must've been thinking the same thing, because he got that resolute look on his face—jaw ticking before his eyes locked on mine. "Hey Ash, I need to ask you something."

My stomach rolled. "Sure, darling. Anything."

His leg picked up its bouncing again. "I just know it's going to bug the hell out of me, because here we are acting like nothing happened, and that's okay. It's nice to know things are still comfortable between us, but…"

"Yeah?"

He licked his lips. "Like I told your dad… you and I haven't talked in years. And we didn't exactly leave things on the best note, so. Maybe we should clear that up."

I nodded once. "What did you want to ask?"

He bit down on his lip, looked at his lap, then back at me. "Why did you stop texting?"

Fuck.

It wasn't even 7 a.m.

"Things had ended," I said. "But they didn't. I think it was doing more harm than good."

His mouth tightened. He was clearly trying to restrain his anger—not to spare me, but to keep me from seeing how much it affected him. Which was worse. I'd rather live in the fantasy world where he didn't hate me.

"Right. You could've told me that…"

"I'm sorry."

He shook his head, leg stopping for a beat before bouncing again. Then he looked at me, like he wasn't done. "That's not it, though. It felt like something happened, because one day you were there, and then you just weren't." Porcelain clinked softly as he tapped his ring against the rim of his cup. "Did something happen? Like… did you start seeing someone or something?"

I sighed and stared down at the table. How the hell was I supposed to handle this?

"Did you ever talk to Henny about this?" I asked as carefully as I could.

Ethan frowned. "Probably. But what does Henny have to do—"

Our gazes held.

His eyes darted over my face. "Why?"

I cleared my throat. "You should ask him about it," I said. "This feels a little tricky to navigate, and I think the right call is redirecting it."

"What the fuck is *that* supposed to mean?"

"It means I respect that you and my brother are friends. That you're close—closer than you and I are right now. So I think this is a conversation you and he should have. And if you still want to ask me afterward, then I'll be here."

"I guess that's fair." His eyes didn't move from mine. "So that wasn't it?"

"What?"

He shrugged quickly, eyes flicking down at his lap. "You weren't seeing anyone else?"

My lips curved into a smile before I could help it. I knew I'd put that idea in his head, and I knew it had hurt him, but I couldn't ignore the rush his jealousy gave me. That was new. I hadn't exactly been fond of it before.

"It took me a while to start dating again," I said. "After you. It wasn't exactly easy."

His gaze burned into mine. His lips finally twitched out of the firm line they'd been pressed into. "Same."

Some of the tension between us eased.

Then he hesitated, thumb brushing the rim of his cup. "Can I ask you something else?"

My shoulders tightened automatically. "Sure."

"Is everything okay at work?"

I stilled.

"I saw a headline," he added quickly. "Just… kind of stumbled on it. They're everywhere."

Yeah, fucking assholes loved throwing salt on a wound. Especially when the wound carried my last name.

A slow breath left me. "It's being handled."

Ethan stayed quiet for a moment, watching me over the rim of his cup. "That sounds like a no."

I huffed a light laugh, keeping my tone even. "It sounds like I'm not ruining a perfectly good espresso with corporate catastrophe at seven in the morning."

The corner of his mouth lifted, but the worry stayed etched into his expression. "Fair." He didn't push.

And I was grateful he didn't.

More than my own father, the idea of letting *him* down felt like acid burning in my stomach. I knew I shouldn't want him to idealize me. I loved that Ethan knew me—the real me. But this was never supposed to happen. I should have had better control over it.

Building this company had been one of the reasons I left him. The last thing I wanted was for him to witness it going up in flames. To watch me fail.

"Do you hate me a little less?" My voice came out almost like a whisper.

He caught it anyway. Ethan smiled, looking away and shaking his head. "Unfortunately, I don't think I'm capable of hating you."

Those words soothed an ache in my chest that had been lodged there for years. "Friends?"

He nodded. "Always."

I wanted to lunge across the table and kiss the hesitation off his lips.

No, Sebastian. We're not going there.

"I have to get to class," he said, raising his hand to get the check.

I pulled out my wallet and dropped the cash, plus the tip, before he could reach for his phone.

His eyebrows shot up.

"My treat. You can get the next one."

That shy smile he gave me, caught between genuine pleasure and mischief, felt powerful enough to tilt the world on its axis.

We stood and started walking in the direction of my apartment.

"So," Ethan said, "you're gonna keep running in those clothes?"

I bit down on my smile. "While the weather is this hot? Yes. I'm going to keep running in these clothes."

"I might take this route again then." Ethan smirked and added, "For the scenery."

I laughed, loud and stupidly pleased, and without giving it much thought, I draped my arm over his shoulders and pulled him closer. His body seemed to move on instinct—he chuckled and wrapped his arm around my waist as we kept our pace.

More than the flirting, it sounded… nice. Like this could be a new part of our routine. That wouldn't be too bad, would it? We weren't trapped in a confined space with all the tension simmering between us—it was easier to run and forget what he was wearing next to me. This way, I could keep him at my side from time to time.

Not too bad.

Also, nobody was awake at this hour to witness it.

As soon as that thought crossed my mind, we turned the corner, and my building came into view. Standing by the entrance was my brother, holding two to-go coffees. His eyes landed on us—on Ethan pressed against my side—and his easy grin dropped clean off his face.

Fuck.

Ethan stiffened beside me. I watched the ease drain out of him in real time, replaced by that stony, cold look he got when he was angry and trying to hide it.

Seems like no matter how much any of us wanted to avoid it, Henry was undeniably wedged between Ethan and me. And from where I was standing, it didn't look like a particularly comfortable spot to be in right now.

CHAPTER SIX

ETHAN

We stepped into the apartment.

Henry dropped his keys on the counter with a careless clatter, then turned just in time to catch the look on my face. "I feel like I'm the one who has the high ground right now, since you were the one caught in your secret rendezvous with my brother this morning. So why are you the one with the frowny face?"

The irritation simmering in my chest kicked up again. "Did you tell Sebastian to stop talking to me?"

Henry blinked, thrown. "No. Why the hell would I tell him that?"

"Not now, Henry," I said. "After he left."

I watched the realization drop into place as his shoulders sagged.

"You've got to be fucking kidding me," I muttered, shaking my head and pacing toward the couch.

Henry followed me. "Would you give me a little more context about what's happening right now? Because I feel like I have a perfectly good explanation, and this is being blown way out of proportion."

I spun around to face him. "Was that you not interfering? You telling him to fucking ghost me? You know how fucked up I was over that, Henry. What were you thinking?"

"I never told him to ignore you. Never." His hands lifted, palms out. "Look, E, you were fucking miserable, alright? You *both* were, and that toxic bullshit of having broken up but talking every single day wasn't helping either of you move on. So I told him you needed a clean break, but I didn't tell him to do it like an asshole."

Somewhere in the back of my mind there was a little voice speaking up, acknowledging that maybe what he was saying made sense, but unfortunately it was being drowned out by the other voice yelling—

"That was none of your goddamn business!"

"Hey!" His dark eyes went wide. "Calm the fuck down."

"No. You knew, Henry." I stepped closer, pointing a finger at him before dropping my hand. "You knew. You knew I've been villainizing him for years, thinking he really didn't give a fuck about me, and you knew that wasn't it."

"No, E, I didn't fucking know that was where your head was at. We"—he gestured sharply between us—"don't talk about him, remember? You never talk about anything going on with you."

"Oh, and you do?"

"This isn't even the fucking point!"

"You don't want to get between us, so stay the fuck out of it."

"I am! It was one fucking conversation." He raked his hands through his hair, frustrated. "How the hell was I supposed to know he was actually going to listen to me? He never fucking does—just turns around and does whatever the fuck he wants anyway."

"That's exactly what you did, Henry." My voice softened for half a second, then sharpened again. "And here I thought you hated when Ash did what he thought was best for you without asking."

Henry's expression faltered—a flash of hurt he smothered

almost immediately. "I can't believe you just went there," he said quietly. "You know that was *very* fucking different. Don't throw that in my face."

Guilt pricked at the back of my throat—ugly and immediate —but I shoved it down. "Just stay out of it."

Henry glared. "Fine."

"Fine!"

"Actually." He took a breath. "I'll say one more thing, and then I'll stay out of it."

I rolled my eyes and turned into the hallway. "Not listening."

"Yes, you are." He stayed planted where he was, like he knew I'd hear it whether I liked it or not. "First, it's sad that you don't realize how fucking manipulative it was for Ash to blame what he did on me."

I stopped walking.

"It's obvious as fuck, and you should know better by now, but the second he smiles at you, it's like you're under a fucking spell. Which brings me to the second thing—"

"You said it was one—"

"Well, it's two!"

I turned halfway back.

"This doesn't change the fact that he's with someone else."

My stomach dipped.

"And this little game you're playing is fucked up."

"I'm not playing any game."

"Yes, you are. You both are. And that is also really fucking obvious. I hope you think about your dad before you go diving headfirst into something you can't take back."

That one landed hard, and I went still as it hit me all over again—my mom asking me to keep her affair quiet, my dad's face when it all came out.

"Low fucking blow."

Henry lifted his hands in a soft shrug. "Had to be said. And you crossed a line first."

I breathed out hard through my nose, stepped into the guest room, shutting the door firmly behind me.

Fuck.

I pressed my palms to my face.

That had gone too far. Dragging up the worst thing that had ever happened to Henry like it was ammunition? Jesus.

I needed to take that back. But the stubborn, prideful part of me—the part that refused to give ground when I'd stood up for myself—kept my hands in place.

Because he had lied. Maybe not outright, but enough.

And underneath all of it, something else twisted in my gut.

Sebastian.

What Henry had pointed out—Sebastian blaming things on him—was manipulative, sure. But that wasn't exactly new. And the rest? It shouldn't have meant anything—it shouldn't have *changed* anything—but something didn't sit the same anymore.

The way Sebastian had looked at me this morning… I hadn't imagined that. It wasn't nostalgia. It wasn't loneliness. It felt different. Like maybe I hadn't been the only one gutted by the break. Like I wasn't the only one who'd never really gotten over it.

My head tipped back against the door.

Everything was a fucking mess. This shit with my dad and being basically homeless was fucking with my head. No matter how much I wanted to make it go away, the truth was that the funds in my account were running lower every day. And the resentment felt uncontrollable. I'd outgrown all of this, but lately my patience felt paper-thin.

Every part of my life was pulling in different directions, and I was running out of ways to hold it all together. Henry'd been the one constant these past years—the one person who'd been there for me through everything—and I'd fucking lashed out at him mercilessly. No way in hell was I going to keep living here after that. And now what? What the fuck was I supposed to do now?

I dragged in a rough breath, pushing my hair back, trying to center myself, but before I could get even a little bit there, there was a soft knock behind me.

"E?" Henry's voice came through—gentler, smaller. "I'm sorry."

I closed my eyes tightly.

There was some shuffling behind the door. "Can we try that again?"

The floor creaked softly outside before I opened it.

He was standing on the other side, looking sheepish. "I should have told you about it," he said quietly. "You were in a bad place, and I just thought… I thought it was better to distract you. Help you move on. Not keep dwelling on it. But I was also kinda terrified you'd hate me."

My shoulders sagged. "I don't hate you. And I'm sorry—I shouldn't have blown up at you like that. It wasn't fair."

His lips curved into a small smile. "Look at us. Being all mature and shit."

I chuckled, the anger bleeding away as his grin widened.

"I'm sorry for bringing up your dad and the cheating," he said, his face shifting into something more serious. "That was a shit move."

"Don't even. I said something worse."

"You were right. Kinda." He let out a small, humorless laugh. "Turns out I love making comparisons but don't notice them if they're about me. It was hypocritical. And I want you to know I really haven't tried to interfere again. You know, besides making you two meet the other day, but apart from that, I haven't. It's really fucking hard, in case you're wondering."

I huffed. "I get it—it would be hard on me too. I wish you would've told me, but I didn't need to yell. Sorry."

He leaned on my doorframe, arms crossed. "What's up with you?" His tone was softer. "You've been all over the place since we got here. Snappy. Is it just this whole thing with Ash?"

My throat went dry.

And now is when you're supposed to tell him.

Tell him.

I swallowed hard. "Yeah. Just the stuff with him. My head's kind of a mess right now. It's not an excuse."

He smiled and jerked his head toward the living room. "Let's get a drink and make up, okay?"

"If the drink is a smoothie, sure. It's not even eight."

He snorted. "Right." Henry rolled his eyes playfully. "Forgot you can be a prude."

"Let me hop in the shower, and I'll be right out," I said, and he nodded, body already shifting sideways. "And Henny?"

He turned back.

"I'm really sorry. You know I love you, right?"

He smiled. "Yeah, I do. Love you right back, babe." He gave the back of my neck a quick squeeze before walking into the living room.

Pulling in a long, steady breath, I tried to find the nerve to face this.

I was going to tell him, but I needed to make sure this was really happening. I needed to get my dad on the phone. It had only been a little over a week. Maybe I *was* blowing everything out of proportion.

Whatever this was—stress, fear, old shit I hadn't dealt with—it was starting to get the better of me. And if I didn't figure it out soon, I was going to make things worse.

I needed to get my head on straight.

Fast.

———

Classes started out okay, in spite of everything.

That first week, I was really apprehensive that things would be just like last time, but nobody was interested in me—not the way they used to be, with all the gossip. Here, it felt like slipping into anonymity, which was a welcome relief. And when I actually talked to people, they seemed more interested in *me*, not my last name or my past.

I was still looking at places near campus, even if Henry kept insisting I could stay. The tension from our fight seemed to have faded for him completely in a matter of hours, but I still felt like an asshole for not telling him what was going on. And if I couldn't solve this, I couldn't just keep living off him.

Charlotte had definitely picked up on something. Naturally, she thought it was about Sebastian and his boyfriend and not the family shit—because even though I'd been in touch with our dad for a while, I hadn't exactly told her about that either.

She'd cut off all contact with him a few months after the wedding, after everything went down. We hadn't talked about it, but I had a feeling something else had set it off. But, staying on brand, neither of us brought it up. Like we had an unspoken agreement—never talk about him, and it's like it never happened. And apparently, I was a fan of replicating that strategy with everything else in my life.

Still, she'd been calling more often to check in—like now, as I walked into the apartment after a full day of classes, wrapping up my first week and already feeling wrung out, with two unanswered emails and five straight-to-voicemail calls to my father. I was already trying my best to keep it together.

"Have you talked to him again?" she asked.

I hummed, dropping my keys and my bag on the counter. "Texted a bit." I was keeping the Sebastian talk vague.

"Are you really not going to give me more than that? I'm home with two kids all day—I need grown-up gossip."

"I've already told you about the last time I saw him, and that was three days ago." I pulled out my laptop and logged in. "I have no more updates for you."

"Oli and I are thinking about popping over for a visit. Without Liam and Amelia." Her tone wobbled, just a bit.

"Are you ready for that?"

"I need a little time to myself, E. And with Oli. I love them to death, but that whole losing-your-identity thing is no joke. Just a little breathing room, you know?"

"You don't have to explain yourself to me. I think it's a great idea. For both of you." I refreshed my email. Still nothing. "When were you thinking?"

"We wanted to go for Ash's birthday, but it doesn't look like we're going to make it. Maybe a couple of weeks after that… maybe."

"Well, I think you should, but I'm completely biased and being extremely self-serving about it."

She laughed. "You sure you don't want to talk about it? Him?"

My phone buzzed. I pulled it from my ear to check the screen —my dad.

"Shit—I have to take a call, Char," I said quickly. "Talk to you later."

"Sure. Everything alright?"

"Yeah, perfect—just need to take this."

"Okay, then…"

I apologized before switching over.

"Ethan," Dad's voice boomed through the line.

I let out a rush of air. "Dad—finally. Where the hell have you been? I've been trying to reach you since last Monday."

He was silent for a second—long enough for the unease to claw its way back.

"Been busy. Thought we should have a chat before I leave for Boston."

I frowned. "Boston?"

"Yes, I'm handling a new investment there."

I tapped my fingers on the counter. "What?" It came out as a whisper.

"The one I told you about."

"Yeah, but we said we were going to talk about that before—"

"I had to take the opportunity before it was too late. You can understand that, right?"

More tapping. Harder. "Dad, that was my—"

"You'll earn it back. It's not like you need it anyway," he said, tone dismissive. Like he hadn't just stolen my fucking life out from under me.

"What do you mean I don't need it? Dad, that was the whole thing. I'm doing my master's right now—I'm not working. I couldn't even get a place to live."

"You don't need it, Ethan. You've been smart about the choices you've made. I'm proud of you for that."

Those words should've felt good. Should've meant something. Instead, they jammed somewhere in my head, and every alarm in my body went off at once. "I don't get it."

"With the Langleys," he said. "Your sister will support you no matter what. You have Henry there with you. And I know you went to Madrid after Sebastian. He definitely has more than enough to keep you comfortable for the rest of your life." He laughed—like any of this was actually fucking funny. "Several lifetimes, in fact."

My heart fell straight through the floor. "You can't be serious…"

"I'll let you know when the investment starts paying off. Thanks for being there for your old man, son."

"Dad—"

Silence. Wrong, heavy silence.

"Dad?"

I held the phone away to look at the screen. He fucking hung up. I tried calling again, and an ominous automated voice informed me the number I'd dialed was no longer in service.

He didn't… He didn't actually just block me?

Fuck.

Don't panic—

My breath started coming in short, clipped bursts.

Don't panic. Don't panic. Don't panic. Don't panic.

I dragged a hand through my hair and pulled. "Fuck!"

This didn't just happen. It couldn't have. He stole it? All the fucking money? He could just run off into the sunset with it? What was I supposed to do? Call the police? Tell Charlotte?

Charlotte—*fuck*. How the hell was I going to admit any of this to her?

I was such a fucking idiot; believing he wanted to reconnect with me. Why the fuck did I trust him?

My eyes burned as I paced the kitchen, thoughts slamming around in my head with no rhyme or reason, just: *You fucked up! You fucked up!* Over and over again, like a notification ping—cruel and mocking.

What the fuck had I done?

He wasn't going to give it back—it was as good as gone, and I couldn't tell anybody. I couldn't let anyone know how stupid I'd been.

I pressed my back to the wall, knees giving out as I sank to the floor, holding my head in my hands, fingers twisting, pulling. "Idiot."

My chest tightened painfully. I wasn't getting enough air.

A soft patter hit the floor beneath me.

Great. Now you're crying. What a fucking—

"Idiot. Idiot. Idiot." Each word came with a harder tug. My teeth clenched so tightly it felt like they might crack.

The door creaked open.

"Idiot. Idiot. Idiot."

Footsteps.

"Henry?" Sebastian's voice called out.

No.

Are you fucking kidding me?

My head snapped up, and our eyes met. Sebastian was standing by the doorway, body angled to the living room but gaze locked on me—curled on the floor by the fridge, crying like a fucking kid.

Why did it have to be him?

His expression shifted instantly—from surprise to worry—

and he hurried to my side, dropping to his knees. "Darling, what's wrong?"

Idiot.

"Nothing," I muttered, rubbing my hands over my face.

"Ethan." His fingers brushed my wrists.

I flinched. "Nothing. Can you go away? Please go away."

"Hey." His voice softened, as he slid in closer, heat radiating off him. His bent knees boxed in my sides, and his hands settled gently on my shoulders. "I'm not leaving you alone like this. You don't have to tell me if you don't want to, but I'm not leaving." His rough, deep voice vibrated in the small space between us.

I shook my head.

Sebastian's hands slid to my shoulder blades, applying the faintest pressure—just enough to ask a question without saying it. My body answered before my mind caught up, and I leaned into him. The backs of my hands, still covering my face, pressed against his chest.

His arms came around me, and he lowered his chin to the top of my head. "It'll be okay, my darling," he whispered.

My eyes squeezed shut. "It won't."

But breathing was getting a little easier.

"It will. I promise. Anything that's been broken, we can fix. I'll help you in any way I can."

I let my hands drop and shook my head against his shirt. "I don't want *you* to fix it."

Because then he wins. Then he's right.

"It can't be you."

We stayed silent for a while, a small stretch of time where he kept gliding his hands over my back. Comforting.

The longer it went on, the more I melted into him, until my ear was pressed over his heart and its steady thumping drowned out the noise in my head. Everything smelled like him.

His palm brushed over my arm.

Up and down.

Up and down.

How could I have been so stupid?

"I'm always going to be on your side. Always, okay?" His voice was even deeper now, rumbling straight from his chest. "Even if you feel like you can't tell me, I promise I'm never going to think less of you."

Was that true? How could he not? I was supposed to be a grown man. I was supposed to be proving a point right now. Instead, the only thing I was proving to him—of all the fucking people in the world—was that I was still too naïve and immature to function in society.

"I fucked up," I said.

"Tell me about it. If you don't want my help, that's fine, but I can still listen. I can still be here for you while you figure it out."

Fuck.

And he was even better than before. Of course he was. It felt like the universe was mocking me. Why wouldn't Sebastian Langley suddenly become mature and empathetic?

I took a deep breath. "I really fucked up, Ash. I don't think there's any way to fix this."

His arms tightened around me. "Big problems feel like that sometimes."

I bit my cheek and closed my eyes. "Do you promise you won't tell anybody?"

"Not a soul."

I sat up—not exactly pulling away, but enough to see his face. "I mean it. Nobody."

Sebastian's eyes ran over mine, his lips twisting a little before his thumb brushed a tear off my cheek. He nodded, concern still written all over him.

"I lost my trust," I said, the words almost too quiet to hear.

But he did. His shoulders tensed just a little as he waited for me to continue.

"I've been talking to my dad again. I don't know if you knew about that, but Char stopped talking to him too after..." My eyes dropped to my lap. I shrugged. "After."

Sebastian's hand returned to my arm, his knuckles moving back and forth in slow strokes. "Oli said something about that a while ago."

"He showed up again last year. He apologized—for how he acted after the wedding—and said he wanted us to have a relationship again." I bit my lip, a fresh wave of guilt washing over me. "He said we should keep it between us."

Sebastian's fingers stilled for a fraction of a second.

"And I did. I didn't tell anybody we were talking again." My eyes stayed on the hem of my shorts. "It felt… normal. We went out for lunch, chatted. Neutral topics only. Then he started mentioning he was having a hard time."

Sebastian shifted closer, his posture going just a touch rigid.

"He got a big settlement with the divorce, but my mom's family funds everything. He told me he'd had a couple of bad investments and that he knew a good one that would definitely work this time…"

"Does your dad not work?"

"Kinda. He used to. Then he started consulting. If I'm being totally honest, I never really asked after he moved out. I figured he was still doing that."

"So you loaned him the money?"

I nodded. "At first. It wasn't much. And as soon as I did, he'd drop it, and we'd go back to normal. But every time he asked, it was more. And it was… insistent. Like the conversation couldn't move forward until I said yes. I just wanted it to stop because every time he asked, it felt like everything between us was about to break again." I swallowed hard. "Around March, he asked about a big one—I said no. But he said he was having a hard time covering expenses, so I thought, why not help with that? I could give him access to the funds, and then he'd use what he needed and stop asking."

The rock in my stomach slammed down hard. I had been so stupid. He hadn't even asked for it. I was the one who offered it.

Fucking idiot.

"And when I did, everything went back to normal. Everything was easy again. That was months ago, Ash. Months."

"What happened?"

"The payment for my place here got declined, so I called the bank. They told me the account had been cleared out. It's all gone."

Sebastian's breathing was the only sound between us.

"They said since the person was co-authorized, they can't open an investigation. And I tried calling him after that—" The words rushed out of me like I couldn't get them out fast enough. "He didn't answer his phone for almost two weeks—fucking weeks—then he finally did today, and he admitted it. Told me I didn't need it anyway, that I'd be fine. That he'd send me the return on the investment, and I'm really fucking sure that's a lie. It's fucking gone, and—" my voice cracked, "—and he had the gall to say he was proud of me."

"Why?" Sebastian asked quietly.

"Because I had been smart enough to associate myself with all of you. Oli. Henny. And… you. Because that meant I didn't need my trust anymore."

Sebastian's breath left him in one long exhale. "That's not your fault, darling. None of it is."

"How can it not be? I was the idiot who offered him the access. He was just using me this whole time, and I didn't even realize it."

"Not your fault." Sebastian's hand slid down to my shoulder. "Do you think anybody has an easy time saying no to someone they love? Especially when they're in need?"

"Charlotte said no."

"You haven't talked to your sister about this. You don't know how things were for her."

"I know she didn't lose everything." I swallowed the knot in my throat as best I could. "What am I supposed to do now?"

Sebastian tilted his head, the faintest smile adorning his mouth. His palm cupped the side of my neck. "You're going to fight your way out of it, like you always do." His fingers tightened on my nape. "You're tough as nails, remember?"

I shook my head, eyes squeezing shut, but he followed the movement with his hand, keeping that steady pressure.

"Yes. You are."

"It's not fair."

"No." His forehead dipped toward mine, not touching, just close enough that I felt his breath. "It isn't. But you can't drown yourself in that thought." His thumb stroked the line of my jaw again. "Can I try to help? I know you don't want me to make the problem just go away—that's not what this is. I promise."

I stared into his dark eyes, his face inches from mine. "Okay."

"Stay here with Henny. Talk to him about this—tell him everything—and stay."

"Ash, I can't just—"

He tightened his grip on my nape again, gentle but impossible to ignore. His other hand rose to cradle the side of my face, thumb brushing the salt from my cheek. "Henry loves you," he said softly. "And he'll do anything for the people he loves. He'll want to be there for you because you're in a tight spot. If he were in the same one, would you ask him to move out?"

My eyes lifted to meet his again, and I shook my head.

"Exactly. So talk to him. Take one weight off your shoulders."

I took a deep breath, still fighting it. I couldn't just live off Henry. It wasn't fair.

Sebastian's fingers skimmed the back of my neck. "Now," he said, "for the next part. Can you work a job around your schedule?"

"Maybe. Depends on the work."

He hesitated. It was brief—anyone else might have missed it —but I saw the shift in him. The calculation behind his eyes.

Then he said, "You can come work at VistaReal."

I froze. Working with him meant stepping into the middle of a fire he was already trying to contain. I couldn't do that to him.

Sebastian watched me carefully, like he already knew where

my mind had gone. "I know," he said. "The timing isn't ideal. But it would give you income. Structure. Breather space while you figure things out."

I shook my head slightly. "Ash—"

"You wouldn't be working for me directly," he added. "And if it ever felt uncomfortable, you'd walk away. No questions asked. No hard feelings."

"You have enough on your plate," I said. "I'm not adding myself to the list."

His whole face softened. "Darling, you're not a problem to solve."

My eyes burned again, and I blinked hard.

"You'd just be letting me help." He rolled his lips as he thought something through and added quickly, "And let me get someone to figure out where the money went."

"No—Ash, I don't want this to turn into a thing."

"Quietly," he said, voice dropping. "Let me look into it quietly. I can't promise you'll get any of it back. Actually, there's a very big chance you won't. But let me look, okay? No legal pursuit. No police. Just my guy."

A dry laugh escaped me. "You sound like a mobster."

His lips curved into a small smile. "Whatever works for you."

I sat with it for a moment, forcing myself to look at the offer for what it was—not a rescue, not a favor, but a way to keep my feet under me.

"Okay." I swallowed. "Let me think about the job. But the rest of it..." My shoulders sagged. "...okay."

"You've got this." His fingers carded through my hair. "This isn't bigger than you. You're a force, darling. This is just a little roadblock you'll look back on in a couple of years and smile at how you conquered it."

My eyes welled again. "I'm so fucking pissed."

"I'm sorry he did that to you. Nobody deserves to be

betrayed like that. Especially not by your father. But he's the one losing here."

"Say that to my bank account—"

"He doesn't have *you*," he said, and the argument died in my throat. "There's no bigger loss in this life than not having you in it. Trust me, I'd be the leading authority on the subject."

That… completely disarmed me.

We stared at each other. I got lost in the depths of his eyes, in the warmth radiating off him, and a quiet understanding settled into place.

He wasn't trying to control this.

He wasn't trying to own the problem or make it disappear.

He wasn't telling me who to be or what to feel.

He was standing beside me—seeing me—and believing I could survive it.

Something in my chest cracked open—something I'd buried years ago because it hurt too much to carry.

He was still looking at me like that. That hadn't changed. The intensity. The way he focused on me like I was the only thing in the room. For the first time since everything fell apart between us, I didn't feel like something temporary in his life.

I felt *his*.

My pulse stumbled.

I want him back. I want him to be mine again.

I wanted to feel his skin and the shape of his lips and his weight over me.

I wanted all of it.

My insides went weak for him all over again. There was no more lying to myself about this—about how much he still meant to me. Having him here again sent something blazing through me, consuming every rational thought. He was so close, our eyes still locked, and I swore I could feel his hands on the bare skin of my back, feel his breath ghosting against my mouth—the heat of him searing through the space between us, turning my world into an inferno of need.

I'd never felt this way about anybody. Not since him, and there was no after him. Not for me.

His hands were still on my face, his soft lips parted just slightly, and his thumb swept across my cheek. My hands acted without permission, sliding up the warm line of his neck, finding the gap in his shirt. That small stretch of skin that had been teasing me for weeks felt even better than I remembered.

Sebastian didn't flinch. He leaned into it—into me. Our faces were only a breath apart.

"Thank you, Ash," I said into the space between us. "For believing in me so much."

"Always, my darling."

My tongue darted over my lip, and his gaze flicked down, fireworks bursting behind my ribs.

Kiss me. Please, just fucking kiss me.

He softened into it, his forehead coming to rest on mine, his nose brushing gently over my own. My fingers dug into his skin, and he hummed, pleased. It felt like we'd gone back in time, like the rest of the world had vanished. Just us, nothing stopping us from falling back into the comfort of it.

His lips hovered a breath away from mine, my body already arching into him—

And the sound of the door opening shattered the spell.

"Hey! Heads up," Henry called from the doorway.

Sebastian and I jerked apart, our hands dropping, but our eyes stayed locked. His were a little wide.

"Ash is—" Henry stopped short when he saw us, still on the kitchen floor. "Here." His gaze bounced between us before settling on my face. "Are you okay?"

I was probably still flushed and tear-streaked. I dragged my hands down my face and straightened. *Pull it together.* "No, actually," I said. "Do you think we could talk?"

Henry's attention sharpened, the surprise draining from his expression.

Sebastian shifted beside me and rose first, offering a hand. I took it, letting him pull me up.

"What's this about?" Henry asked.

My eyes drifted to Sebastian. He gave me a tiny smile as his hand landed on the small of my back, giving me a bit of courage.

"My housing situation," I said, drawing in a breath. "And my dad."

"Okay." Henry nodded once, already turning toward the living room. "Let's talk."

Sebastian and I lingered a second behind him, both of us still reeling from whatever the hell had almost happened.

"Thanks," I said again.

"Don't mention it." His expression softened into something closer to the Sebastian I knew. "I'll leave you two to it."

"Ash," I said before he turned. "Could you stay a little longer?"

He paused.

"I mean, it's fine if you're busy," I added quickly. "But you can stay—for the talk… and after? Maybe figure out the job. It's not every day you get a CFO volunteering to help sort out your entire life."

A quiet huff left him, almost a laugh. He hesitated—long enough to make my chest tighten.

"Sure," he said at last. "I'll just make a call."

Relief slipped into my smile. "Thanks."

Sebastian felt like magic in that moment. After one of the most overwhelmingly horrible calls of my life, he had somehow breathed calm into me.

That didn't just happen.

What we had wasn't chance. It wasn't something that could exist with just anybody.

We were bigger than everything else.

I knew we were.

The rest of the fucking world was just going to have to deal with the fact that we were meant to be.

Sebastian was meant to be mine.

CHAPTER SEVEN

ASH

"So, is this the *best* idea you've ever had?" Elena asked from her spot, arms crossed, leaning on her desk, and looking out the glass screen.

Afternoon light spilled through the floor-to-ceiling windows behind her, painting the skyline in warm gold. Her office—sleek marble, dark wood, not a single thing out of place—looked like it had been built to intimidate lesser men.

"No." I didn't need to follow her gaze to guess exactly what she was looking at. "Definitely one of the worst."

"A self-aware man. I love that. *Don't* love the HR nightmare you just sent my way." Her tone stayed light as she pushed off the desk. Her heels clicked softly on the polished floors, her tailored black suit cutting a razor-sharp silhouette.

"It doesn't have to be forever, and he's in a different department. It's only part-time—I'm not even his boss, and I barely deal with marketing—"

"Ash, you're one of the heads of this company," she cut in. "You're the boss of everyone."

I rolled my lips and shrugged, giving her my best doe-eyed expression.

Elena huffed a laugh before rubbing her temples, rings

glinting under the light. "God. Please just keep this professional, Sebastian. The last thing we need is an internal relationship becoming ammunition right now."

"There's nothing going on between us," I said firmly. "There's nothing to report."

She gave me an unimpressed look, which made me drop my gaze to my lap.

There was something about Elena that screamed woman in power. Impossibly put together. Always three steps ahead. The kind of executive who could make a whole boardroom fold with a single inhale. She saw right through my bullshit every time, which was both annoying and extremely useful. After losing Aria to Henry a couple of years ago, I'd apparently needed a replacement emotional nanny—Elena had filled the role.

"He needed a job," I continued. "And with what he wants from his career, VistaReal was the logical option for him. I already spoke to Marcela in Marketing—she's thrilled to have him on the team. But," I said, emphasizing that last word as she rolled her eyes, "if you are really against it and he turns out to be a liability—which I'm a hundred percent certain he's not—then I'll figure out where else he can go."

Her brown eyes narrowed.

"And I'll report to HR that we used to be an item," I added, more subdued.

"Thank you." She turned back toward the glass, posture effortlessly regal. "He's very cute, I'll give you that. Inappropriate—but cute."

"That could be our motto," I joked.

"The disclosure form is on my desk." She pointed a perfectly manicured finger at the folder waiting for me. "Before the end of the day."

I reached for it, skimming the lines, each one more humiliating than the last.

"You're still seeing that Italian model?"

"He works in fashion—not a model. And yes, I am."

"And you're sure this isn't inviting drama into the company at the exact moment we cannot afford drama?"

I arched a brow. "You invited drama the day we signed the founding documents."

"Fair." She slipped into her chair behind the massive walnut desk. "Are you ready for the board meeting?"

"Almost. I still need to review the revised forecasts. The last set was…" I exhaled. "…tight."

She considered me for a moment. "Tight as in manageable, or tight as in we start making decisions we don't want to make?"

"Let's hope it doesn't get that far."

Because if the freeze held much longer, we'd be looking at halted projects, shrinking liquidity, and conversations I refused to have.

"Keep me posted," she said.

I nodded.

"And about our new research assistant too."

"There'll be nothing to report there," I said. "Don't worry."

Her eyes narrowed again. "Why are you so sure?"

"Because I'm nothing if not a strategist with a plan. And that's not part of the plan."

"Plans can go to shit," she said, deadpan. "Just take a look around."

A soft chuckle slipped out of me. "Touché. I promise I'll let you know if mine do too."

Stepping out of her office as our impromptu meeting ended, I was greeted by the sight of Ethan walking down the hall with a couple of people from marketing—junior analysts, by the look of them. His pale eyes found mine instantly, and he lifted a hand in a wave, an easy, bright smile on his lips. I nodded back, not managing to stop myself from returning it with one of my own.

Of course he looked incredible in office attire. Another reminder of the hole I was digging myself into. But who could blame me? How was I supposed to walk into that apartment and watch him fall apart and not rush in to do anything—*everything*

—to make him feel better? I was only human. And if that resulted in him being in my office most days of the week…

Yes, this was definitely a bad idea.

I'd also had to cancel my dinner plans with Luca so I could stay and help Ethan after he talked to Henry. Worth it, though. He looked lighter today. More relaxed. His smile was more genuine than I'd seen since he'd gotten here. Only—unfortunately—far too often directed at me.

And then there was that slip. The almost kiss. I had gotten so caught up in how he was opening up, how he was letting me in again, that I didn't even notice how close I'd gotten to him and how unable I'd been to keep my hands to myself. And he hadn't pulled away. Not even a little. We had come so close. So close that now the image was burned into my mind, replaying every time I blinked.

Now here I was, welcoming him into my safe space—my workspace—like an idiot. Letting him parade around all day in those perfectly tailored pants and aim those soft, ridiculous smiles at me from across the floor while regulators combed through our files.

Fucking perfect, Sebastian.

Well fucking done.

———

The office was dark except for the glow of my monitors. Legal emails. Compliance updates. Cash projections. Three different timelines showing how long we could keep things moving if the freeze dragged on.

None of them were acceptable.

"I'm not interested in waiting," I said into the phone, pacing behind my desk. "Waiting is how we bleed out."

Oscar exhaled quietly. "We can't move forward on the state projects until the auditors clear the authorization chain."

"I'm aware," I said, jaw tight.

Three hundred units stalled mid-construction.

Two infrastructure bids suspended.

Millions in progress payments frozen.

Payroll, however, was *not* frozen. Neither were vendor contracts. Nor insurance. Nor the lights currently burning money above my head.

"We're prioritizing private work," he continued, cautious. "But if this review runs longer than expected—"

"It won't."

Silence met me on the other end of the line. I knew I couldn't will this problem away. Oscar knew it too. Which was why the tension stretched between us—it was him waiting to see if I'd finally lost it.

Get it together, Sebastian.

"I need updated projections tonight," I said. "Best case. Worst case. Model thirty days."

"That's… aggressive."

"That's realistic."

Another pause. Papers shifting.

"We're still trying to identify what triggered the audit—"

"It didn't trigger itself," I snapped. "Somewhere in that authorization chain something doesn't match, and until we find it, we're fucked. So dig."

"We are—"

"Dig faster." The words came out sharper than intended, but I didn't take them back. "I want every document tied to those approvals reverified. Every signature. Every submission. If something is missing, I want to know before the auditors do. Send it to me. Everything."

"Yes, sir."

I ended the call and pressed my fingers hard against my eyes.

The building hummed around me—elevators, distant voices, the steady rhythm of a company still functioning while a critical artery remained clamped shut. The circulation hadn't stopped yet. It was just running on what had made it through before the whole fucking mess imploded.

Somewhere in that chain, one missing authorization, one irregular document, one overlooked detail had stalled every-thing. Until we found it, we were stuck in place. Burning time. Burning money. Burning credibility.

A soft knock sounded at my door.

"One second," I called, not looking up.

The silence lingered.

Then—

"Bad time?"

My head lifted.

Ethan stood in the doorway, backpack slung over one shoul-der, tailored trousers sharp, that hesitant smile tugging at his mouth like he wasn't sure he should interrupt.

In the middle of this chaos—and decisions that could cost people their jobs—he looked like relief.

I straightened, forcing the tension out of my shoulders, tucking the crisis back into its box for five minutes. "No," I said. "Come in."

"Sorry to interrupt," he said, taking a couple of steps inside. "Just thought I'd pop in and say hi. First week and all."

"How did it go?"

His eyes roamed over my desk, taking in the mess of paper and folders. "You look busy."

I pushed up from the chair, flipped on the light, then crossed to the bar cart. "I am, but a quick break won't sink the company. Want one?" I glanced at him as I poured.

"Sure," he said, setting his bag on a chair before dropping to the one beside it.

"So…" I handed him the glass and went back to sit behind my desk. "How was it?"

"Good. Everyone's nice." His mouth curved into a smirk. "Had to have a chat with HR, sign a form."

"Me too." I rolled my eyes and took a long swallow. "Just a formality. Don't worry about it."

"It was kinda weird," he said, swirling the drink, "but everybody's being oddly neutral about it."

I raised a brow. "What do you mean?"

"You know, no one's said anything about this…" He gestured between us. "Nothing mean anyway. I was kind of expecting it."

"How come?"

He took a sip, then looked away, his gaze dragging over the bookshelves like he was trying too hard to be casual. "Got used to it."

I frowned, about to ask him what he meant by that, when he cut off my train of thought.

"I'm officially all moved in—or unpacked, I guess. Henry's ridiculously happy about it."

"I bet he is." I smiled around my drink. "He loves having people around. He got so upset when Oli and I left for college without him. Kept showing up with lunch while he was supposed to be at school."

Ethan chuckled. "I can totally see that."

"I'm glad you two finally talked. Are you feeling better?"

"Yeah. Better." His lips pressed into a line, though a small smile began to form. "It still sucks, but I don't feel so hopeless now."

His pride was probably taking another hit just talking about this. I couldn't imagine what he must be feeling right now. I wanted to kill his fucking father.

"And Charlotte?"

He shook his head. "One step at a time, Ash."

I opened my mouth to insist he talk to his sister before he cut in again.

"No boyfriend today?"

The leather of the chair creaked as I leaned back. "No. We don't see each other every day." I tried to keep it vague. For his sake.

"Sebastian, the relationship guy," he said, widening his eyes. "Who would've thought?"

Another laugh escaped me. "*The relationship guy* seems a little extreme. I've had a couple."

He pinned me with those icy eyes. "You don't do the casual thing anymore?"

I shook my head.

"Why?"

"Something you said stuck with me."

The ice in his glass clinked softly as it stopped halfway to his lips. "Me?"

"Yes, you," I said, grinning at his shock. "Why does that surprise you?"

"It just does." He shrugged. "What life-altering comment did I make to change your wild ways?"

"You told me I should get to know the person before I decide if it's worth fucking with their head."

A raspy chuckle drifted through the room, and he downed the rest of his drink. "That does sound like me."

"You don't remember? We were fighting on the boat ride before we even really started fooling around."

He nodded, cheeks faintly flushed.

"Anyway, I moved here, and after many months of self-imposed celibacy, I decided I'd actually get to know people first." I lowered my glass, studying the amber liquid for a moment. "That turned into dating. Then relationships. I've had a few boyfriends. Luca isn't the first."

"Really? How many have you had?"

"Over these four years?" I rubbed my hand over my beard, thinking. "Two semi-serious ones."

He leaned forward in his seat. "Is he one of the serious ones?"

"I don't know, darling." I finished my drink and set the glass down. "We've been together less than three months. It's new, and you know my workload has been... excessive lately.

Three months with me is like three weeks of an actual relationship."

Those perfect lips curved into a smirk I was becoming too familiar with. "Are you downplaying it for my benefit?"

I laughed. "Maybe a little. Why do you want to know that?"

He bit his lip, a shoulder lifting in a coy shrug. "I want to know if he's the love of your life. If that's what I'm dealing with."

A breath punched out of me before I could stop it. I couldn't pretend I didn't find this blunt side of him exhilarating.

Still, I narrowed my eyes. "Why do you ask questions you don't want the answer to?"

He grinned. "You're being cagey. Fine. I'll allow the subject change." He looked entirely too pleased for some reason.

"What about you?"

"What about me?"

"Now who's being cagey?"

Ethan tried to hide his smile by rolling his lips. "Haven't dated."

I blinked. "At all?"

"I tried it your way." He adjusted in his seat. "That stuck."

My stomach sank as the meaning landed. "You mean you've just had hookups?"

He nodded, rubbing his knuckles under his nose. "Yeah."

"That's… not good," I finished lamely.

Ethan's brows knit. "Why? You can do it, but I can't?" His tone edged sharper, the kind I knew could turn into an argument in seconds.

"Because it isn't like you. *You* told me that."

His eyes held mine. "It's been years, Ash. You don't know me anymore."

A knife to the chest would've been kinder. "Do you really believe that?" The words came out soft, almost hushed.

His jaw ticked. A couple of tense seconds stretched between

us before his lips twisted—down first, then into a small smile. "Maybe." His eyes flicked to my empty glass. "Another one?"

"Sure." God knew I could use it after the blow he'd just delivered.

He grabbed both glasses and moved to the bar, pouring refills. He didn't sit, though—he came around my desk, handed me mine, and leaned back against the edge with his ankles crossed, casual and tempting as sin.

"So, Boss—"

"Marcela is your boss," I corrected.

He smiled like he enjoyed that. "Why don't we set some boundaries? So we don't get called into HR again and you don't get into trouble. You and I were always shit at being friends. We might as well try, right?"

Something about the look in his eyes—the heat simmering right behind it—started raising the temperature in the room. That and him sitting there like he owned my desk. It did things to me it really shouldn't have.

Okay, I'll bite.

I took a sip of my drink. "Like what?"

"First one—look, don't touch."

My lips twitched into a smirk. "Wait… what exactly counts as touching?"

He rolled his eyes, but the smile decorating his mouth gave him away. "Just platonic stuff. Nothing with intent."

I couldn't help myself. "Intent to what?"

"Fuck off, Sebastian." His face was flushed in the prettiest way while one of his rings tapped against the glass in his hand. "Your turn."

I rocked my chair back. "We only see each other in public. No hanging out at each other's apartments."

"Fair," he said, then added, "No calls or texts after midnight."

I ran my tongue along my canine, trying to figure out his angle. "What about flirting?"

He grinned. "That's a tricky one."

That's what I thought. "How about nothing we couldn't say in front of Henny?"

He laughed. "Sure." Then he lifted a hand to run his fingers through his hair, the light catching every golden strand. It was fucking mesmerizing.

I leaned forward, elbow on the desk. "How platonic is hair touching?"

Ethan scrunched his face like he was genuinely considering it. "No pulling, no grabbing. Definitely no stroking."

"And brushing it back?" *Heel, boy.*

"That's not so bad," he conceded.

I stood and stepped closer. From this angle, I towered over him—his chin tipped up, neck exposed, that teasing smile curling at his mouth. *Sinful.*

My hand lifted, brushing a lock of hair behind his ear, lingering longer than I should've. "Not so bad…" I was hypnotized instantly—by the closeness, his scent, his entire presence tilting the ground beneath my feet.

Before I knew it, my finger hooked gently under his chin, lifting his face up to mine. "What about compliments? Endearments?"

He went still. Perfectly still. Obedient in a way that made the air combust.

"You wouldn't be you without them," he murmured. "But I think that counts as flirting."

I hummed, considering, then let my hand fall. "We'll stick to 'darling,' then. And I'm sorry—your hair looks fucking fantastic like this. It's hard to restrain myself."

His gaze dipped from mine, dragging slowly down my chest before lifting again.

"You're still hot as fuck," he rasped. "So I get it."

Oh *god…*

RIP, shy Ethan. Make way for the phoenix taking his throne.

He had me—completely. And it was effortless for him. He didn't even realize the damage he was doing.

I stepped closer. "That came out laced with intent."

A low chuckle slipped from him. One shoulder rolled in a lazy shrug. "Oops."

He was a fucking menace.

I exhaled sharply, a dry laugh slipping out as I forced myself to take a step back—trying to break whatever spell he'd cast over the room. "Boy, are we going to be great friends or what?"

Ethan just grinned, bright and wicked, and it was fucking everything.

My computer chimed, breaking the moment. I forced my attention back to the screen.

"What are you working on?" he asked, lifting his glass again.

"The freeze," I said, sliding my chair forward. "Compliance flagged an authorization inconsistency in one of our state submissions. Until it's cleared, everything tied to it is stalled."

His brows lifted. "Everything?"

"Projects. Payments. Bids. Cash flow." I exhaled. "It's a nightmare. A quarter of our business is tied to state work." I glanced at him. "You've probably noticed the mood around the office."

His mouth tilted slightly. "Hard to miss." He set his glass down slowly. "Can I look? I've been buried in documentation all week. Might help me understand what you're dealing with."

I angled the screen toward him. "Be my guest."

He stepped closer, leaning over my shoulder. His arm rested along the back of my chair, his heat bleeding through my shirt. I tried my best to ignore it.

"This is the authorization package?" he asked.

"Yes. The one that triggered the review."

He scanned the page in silence.

After a minute, his brows drew together. "Is this approval reference number supposed to be the same across projects?"

My stomach tightened. "No."

He pointed to another tab. "Because this one has the exact same authorization chain ID… and it's for a different site."

I leaned forward, pulse kicking up.

He opened a third file.

Same number. Different project.

Cold slid down my spine.

"That's the state authorization stamp," I said slowly. "Each project should generate its own chain."

Ethan clicked into the file properties. "These were created from the same template."

"Holy shit," I breathed. "It's not just one submission."

He leaned back slightly. "Is it bad?"

I dragged a hand over my jaw. "It means the auditors won't stop at the original file. They'll start checking every submission tied to this template." I sank back in my chair, staring at the screen. "I need to find out how far this spread."

If it ran wider than the initial package, the review wouldn't stay contained. It would expand, delaying everything. Maybe expose us to penalties we couldn't afford right now.

"I'm sorry," he said. "I didn't mean to make it worse."

"You didn't." My voice came out rough. "You just confirmed this isn't a one-off mistake." Panic pressed at the base of my throat—but I couldn't keep the admiration out of my voice. *He fucking did it.* "We've been trying to figure this out for weeks."

Ethan gave me that soft, dangerous smile. "Then you're welcome," he said quietly. *"Friend."*

Jesus Christ.

A strained laugh escaped me. I caught myself before I did something reckless, like pulling him into my lap. "Careful," I muttered. "You keep being useful, and I'm stealing you from marketing."

He grinned. "Corporate poaching already?"

"Hostile takeover."

Our faces were only an inch apart, and even though my world was threatening to collapse beneath my feet, I couldn't deny the rush that came from watching his mind work. And from having him this close.

The moment held for half a breath too long, then reality slammed back in.

I pushed back from the desk and reached for my phone. "I need to call Compliance," I said, already scrolling through my contacts. "And Legal. And Elena."

Ethan straightened, the warmth between us settling into something steadier. "Do you want me to flag the files that match the template?"

My eyes lifted to his.

Fucking perfect.

"Yes," I said. "Please."

He nodded once, all focus now, settling into my chair as he turned back to the screen.

Just like that, he was beside me in it—not watching from the sidelines, not expecting me to fix everything—but stepping into the fire with me.

"First week, and you might actually have earned a raise."

"Don't need it." He didn't look up, eyes fixed on the screen, nimble fingers moving over the keys. "I'll just pull your camera footage and start building my case for sexually inappropriate behavior. The settlement alone will keep me comfy for life."

A laugh broke out of me—real, unexpected—even through the fear.

And I found myself wondering how the hell he made it feel easier to breathe just by being here.

CHAPTER EIGHT

ETHAN

Midday at VistaReal meant the heat was building—the AC was nonexistent on my side of the room—and people were getting restless, already eyeing the exits for lunch. I wasn't planning on joining them. Not with me as the new guy—splitting my time between morning classes and this place—buried in authorization packages, compliance logs, and a stack of files I barely understood and was now expected to flag for inconsistencies.

But today was an exception. I'd only had one class this morning, and I'd made it in early, so for once, I wasn't rushing to fit everything into the day. Henry had insisted on taking me out because of it, but I wasn't completely sold on the idea. That thing with Sebastian last week—spotting the duplicated authorization chains—had apparently put me on people's radar. Not in a dramatic way. Just enough that a few more heads lifted when I walked past, a couple more emails landed in my inbox, and Marcela had started forwarding documents with a quiet *Can you double-check this?*

Oddly, it drew more attention than the fact that I'd once dated the CFO, which was… refreshing, I guess.

But I could feel the pressure creeping in because, one, I didn't want to screw this up, and two, I still had school to keep up with. And I'd barely gotten my footing there before being dropped into a company-wide compliance freeze.

"Ethan!"

Plus there were other nuisances.

"Hey, Bruno. What's up?" I tried my best not to sound as annoyed as I felt.

He perched on the side of my desk, all smiles and charm. "We're going out. You want to come with us?" Bruno had a slight accent, which would've been endearing if he didn't keep interrupting me every five seconds. He didn't even work in my area—we just had the tiniest overlap since he was a junior analyst, and after one meeting on my first day, he decided I was either his new best friend or the new option on the menu, judging by how much he kept eyeing me.

My gaze dropped back to my screen, fingers tapping fast to get the idea down before it fled my brain. "Can't. I'm waiting for someone."

"How about drinks after work on Friday? You didn't make it last week, and it's our newbie tradition." Another charming smile.

"Maybe," I said, trying not to get on his bad side too soon. "I've got so much schoolwork to catch up on. I'm not sure I'll have any spare time until I figure out how to juggle everything."

"What? Our genius research assistant?" he teased. "You'll conquer the world in no time."

I huffed a laugh. "Not likely, but I appreciate the confidence."

He scooted a little closer on the desk. "Anytime."

Jesus, this guy.

"I actually have to get this done before I can leave," I said, nodding at the screen. "It's for Marcela."

"Right, right." He nodded, dark eyes lingering on mine. "So, is it a lunch date?"

Don't roll your eyes. Don't roll your eyes.

I forced out a polite smile. "Something like that."

"Babe, are you done? Got the reservation for one!" Henry called out—too far away and far too loud, but in this case, I was incredibly grateful for his lack of subtlety.

"Just about. Give me five, okay?"

"Cool. Gonna pop in and say hi to Ash, and I'll be right back," he said, pulling his sunglasses down to peer at my desk companion over the rims. "Hiya, there."

"Hi," Bruno said, suddenly looking uncomfortable.

Henry walked off to Sebastian's office.

"Your boyfriend?" Bruno asked.

I shook my head, lips curving slightly as I kept scanning the numbers on my screen. "Brother-in-law."

It took him a minute to piece it together. Henry was always walking around here like he owned the place, but I guess not so much around marketing for everyone to know who he was.

"Ash, as in Sebastian? Is that the other Langley brother?"

"Yup. In the flesh." I clicked a tab and started typing the conclusion to the report, copying in the images and original file. "I really do have to finish this."

"And he's your lunch date?"

Could this guy not take a hint?

"Not a date," I said, still typing. "Just my friend and room-mate. And I'm going to be late if I don't send this out now. Can't chat."

Bruno looked more and more puzzled by the second. "You live with one of the Langleys?"

"Bruno, *come on.*" The annoyance slipped through before I could hide it.

He straightened, sliding off my desk. "No, cool. Got you. See you around," he said quickly—his smile way too big for someone who'd supposedly "gotten the hint." Yeah. I could expect more interruptions in my future.

I nodded and went back to my file, doing a final read-through before sending it off.

"The fanboy left?" Henry asked, stepping up beside me a few minutes later.

This time, I did roll my eyes. "Don't even get me started."

"Do you want me to let him know you're violently allergic to flirting with anybody under thirty?"

I shot him a look, and Henry laughed as he reached over and plucked a sticky note from the edge of my monitor.

"I can fend for myself, thank you." I snatched it back and slapped it into place.

Henry leaned down with a mischievous smirk. "Yeah? And how's that working out for you with the big boss?" Thankfully, he kept his voice low.

"Don't even fucking bring that up while we're still in here." I swatted him away and hit send on the file. "There. Let's go. And reservations? We agreed to keep things in *my* budget, Henny."

He slipped his sunglasses back on and checked his phone. "No, I said I'd *consider* it. Have *you* considered how selfish it is to not let me eat what I want from time to time?"

I scoffed. "You could just eat by yourself."

He gasped dramatically, hand to chest. "Like Sebastian? No, thank you. I rather enjoy life."

"Henny…"

"I'm kidding. But I really do want to try this place. You can just pay whatever your pride requires you to, and I'll handle the rest. Okay?"

I wanted to be mad at him, but a part of me loved that he was still himself around me—no pity, no walking on eggshells. Just Henry.

Hitting the elevator button, I smiled. "Fine. But next time, I choose, and I'm picking the cheapest, most questionable food truck we can find."

Henry grinned, sliding his sunglasses down just enough to raise a brow at me. "Baby, you had me at *questionable*."

Before the elevator doors closed, I caught a glimpse of Sebastian in Elena's office. He'd practically been stationed there all week, pulled into meeting after meeting as the crisis tightened its grip. Now he stood off to the side, arms crossed over his chest, listening with an intensity that made the entire room seem smaller around him.

He looked commanding. Authoritative. And hot as fuck in his tailored suit.

I sighed as the doors slid shut, thinking about how good that beard would feel against my jaw. Or the inside of my thighs.

Henry led us to a restaurant a few blocks away, and as soon as we sat down, they set his drink in front of him.

He raised his brows when I gave him a look. "What? It's not my fault people like me." He took a sip, ice clinking softly. "Do you want something, or are you using the I-have-to-go-back-to-work-in-an-hour excuse?"

My eyes skimmed the menu, the faint hum of conversation around us spilling over from nearby tables. "Not an excuse."

"Don't bother with that. I already ordered."

I set the menu down with a sigh. "Do you have an ulterior motive for bringing me here? My Spider-Sense is tingling."

He tried to look innocent for all of two seconds. "Okay, so Mateo has this gallery event with four other artists, and he invited me. I get to see his work, but it's also a sneaky move on his part to get me out on a social call."

Right. Mateo. We'd been going in circles over this since they met. Henry kept avoiding him and, at the same time, couldn't stop bringing him up. And even though I respected his reason for wanting to stay away, he was still very clearly into him, and Mateo was a total sweetheart.

"You want me to go?"

"I *need* you to." His expression was practically pleading.

"Why wouldn't I?"

He grimaced. "They also invited Ash." We stared at each other. "And plus-one."

I groaned, dropping my head back for a second.

"I know it sucks, but Aria is going to be there—and a bunch

of hot local artists. And free drinks, and you love me and can't say no."

"Fine."

The server dropped off our appetizers and a Diet Coke for me.

"So when is this?" I asked.

"Next Thursday."

I grabbed a potato, dragging it through the orange sauce beneath it. "And you talked to your brother about it?"

Henry's eyes lifted to mine mid-chew.

"He said he was bringing Luca?"

Another chew.

"Like… still?"

Henry swallowed. "Yeah, as far as I know. Why?"

I popped the food into my mouth. Spicy. "Have you hung out around them a lot? Are they, like, coupley?"

Henry pressed his lips together. A soft hum slipped out of him, growing louder until he practically yelled, "Ding! Ding! Ding! Alarm bells are going off, ladies and gents. Ethan Bennett has crossed the fucking line!"

I fixed him with a flat look. "It was just a question."

"Do I need to remind you that you screamed at me that this was none of my business not too long ago?"

"I'm not asking you to pass notes. I just wanted to know your read on the vibes."

He let out a humorless laugh, stabbing a piece of food a little too aggressively. "No. You want me to validate your claim on him."

"It's not—"

"Ya-huh, it is. You want me to say Luca is terrible for Sebastian, that they have nothing in common, and that he needs to get out of that relationship fast so you can be like, *Well, okay, guess I'm going to keep flirting with him then.*"

I scowled.

"God, I swear." Henry shook his head and went back to his

food. "You two are so fucking toxic."

We ate in silence for a beat, the clatter of cutlery and low chatter around us filling the space.

My eyes slid up to him. "So…"

Henry sighed and set his fork down. "He acts like a fucking robot around him. It's weird."

The corners of my mouth curved. "Really? Who does? Ash?"

"Both of them. It's like they met two days ago. Everything is polite as hell, and you know Ash—he doesn't even cuss around him."

"Did you ask him about it?"

"Yeah, and he told me to mind my own business too, which is what I should be doing right now."

I bit down on my lip. Interesting. And frustrating as hell. Why was he still with him?

"Thanks for being honest with me."

"It was a terrible idea. I can see the little cogs turning from here." He twirled a finger toward my head, and I leaned out of reach. "Please don't do anything rash. Maybe just sit Sebastian down and have a conversation like two adults?"

I shrugged, grabbing another bite just to busy my mouth.

"Right, where's the fun in that? Let's cause more trouble for Henry," he muttered.

"What trouble?"

"Having to deal with you and Ash in crisis mode at the same time, and the club, and Mateo's incessant, unwelcome flirting, and I have to go back to the States next weekend because Vivian is terrible at handling anything with our dad."

"Wait." I held up my fork. "What about your dad?"

Henry's shoulders sagged, his expression going from sullen to vulnerable. "He's got some tests he needs to get done, and it's kind of a mess. He doesn't want anyone to know because reputation or whatever. It's fucked. He hasn't even told Oli. And he keeps asking about Ash."

My stomach sank, fingers tightening around my fork. "Like he's sick?"

Henry made a noncommittal gesture, then fixed his gaze on me. "Actually, now that I think about it, you could help me."

"Anything. I just don't know how much help I'd be…" I had zero medical expertise, but, fuck, if something was wrong, I wanted to do something.

"Could you talk Ash into calling him?"

My jaw dropped. "Seriously?"

"Yeah, he listens to you. And look, I know right now you're in the dads-suck club and all, but you worked with him. You know he's different. He's trying. He's just old and shit at showing it. But he's our dad, you know. I don't want both of them to live with regret forever."

It made my heart ache. And he was right—they did deserve that chance.

Even if it was just for closure.

Maybe?

All my dad had ever done was fuck my life up.

Teddy *had* changed, though.

Henry must've seen the uncertainty on my face because he shook his head. "I'm sorry. I'm putting you in a tough spot right now. After what you've been through…"

"No, it's okay. If it's important to you, of course I'll try. I just don't know how much Ash will be willing to talk to me about that."

Henry gave me a wry smile, leaning his elbows on the table. "Are you kidding me? You're literally the only person in the world Sebastian has ever opened up to." His voice softened. "He doesn't let people in when things are falling apart. If he's letting you in now… that's not small."

The butterflies kicked up a frenzy in my stomach. I was stupidly pleased by it. "I'll try."

Henry smiled again. "Just don't use that as an excuse to keep hitting on him."

"That's not what I'm doing." I stared down at my plate, lips pulling into a tiny smirk. "If I were, he wouldn't know what hit him," I muttered.

"Heard that."

———

Casa Umbral, in the Carabanchel district, used to be an old warehouse before it was repurposed into a contemporary art gallery. I hadn't explored much of the west side of the city, but the industrial landscape was just as striking as anywhere else I'd been.

Inside, the place was crowded with modern and abstract pieces, everything arranged in those clean, impossible-to-replicate lines that made you stand a little straighter. The room buzzed with the artsy crowd of the city. Servers drifted by with trays of champagne, though plenty of people clutched small beer glasses instead. It didn't feel overly pretentious—more like a niche corner of Madrid that somehow managed to feel exclusive without crossing into annoying.

I was—however—annoyed.

First, because the reason I was here at all was to be the emotional support friend of Henry Langley, who had decided at the last minute that bringing a date was better than bringing *me*. Something had definitely happened between him and Mateo this week, but he wasn't sharing, which meant I was free to keep being irritated about being abandoned tonight.

The second reason was currently holding a glass of champagne in one hand while his other arm was looped through Sebastian Langley's, posed like a polished little ornament. They'd walked in looking like the perfect couple, and even though Sebastian refused to take any official pictures, the people orbiting them—presumably Luca's friends—were all about the selfies.

And I was wandering around aimlessly—alone—while the Langley brothers annoyed the hell out of me. Again.

It didn't help that Sebastian looked fucking impeccable as always. I took some small comfort in the fact that the second he spotted me, his eyes dragged over me appreciatively before landing on mine. He threw me a wink, and my stomach did that traitorous dip I absolutely did not authorize.

"Ethan!"

My head snapped in the direction of the voice, and I immediately lit up, arms open as one of my favorite people in the world barreled toward me.

"Ari," I laughed as she wrapped her arms around my neck.

"I've missed your face," she said, squeezing me a little too hard.

"Very much the same. Please tell me you're staying for more than a day this time."

She stepped back, whiskey in hand. "I wish. Henry's here, so I've got to take care of the rest. I'm off to Greece tomorrow night —still a few weeks left before offseason."

"Work, work, work." I lifted my glass with a smirk.

She mirrored me. "Learned from the best. Or maybe the worst?"

"Definitely the worst."

"Speaking of which..." She craned her neck, eyes sweeping the gallery like a hawk tracking prey. "There's the devil and... the devil's new boyfriend?" Her gaze flew back to me.

"Yup. That would be him."

"And do we like him? What are we doing? What's the plan?"

"We are attempting maturity, but..." I made a face. "We might be failing a little."

"Sounds about right." She bumped her shoulder against mine lightly. "How's school?"

"Great. Actually a little overwhelming, since I started at VistaReal a couple of weeks ago."

She froze mid-sip. "Excuse me? Started as in... working?"

Her eyes widened. "Are you Sebastian's employee? Did you two somehow manage to make your relationship even more complicated?"

"There's no relationship to complicate this time," I said. "We're just friends. And I'm just part-time, so don't look at me like that."

She rolled her eyes so hard it was a miracle she didn't sprain something. "Most unrealistic thing I've heard this year." Then, more seriously, "So you know about the whole thing? How's he holding up? Those fucking articles—I swear—people just love making him miserable."

My eyes flicked to Sebastian. To anyone else, he looked the same as always—composed, untouchable, perfectly put together. But I could see it. The faint shadows under his eyes. His hair was getting longer, like he hadn't had time to maintain it. The tightness in his shoulders even when he stood still. Stress clung to him. It was unsettling seeing him like this—scrambling, carrying too much, looking one bad turn away from drowning in it.

"They'll figure it out," I said. "Ash, Elena… everyone at the company is pulling their weight. And if they can't resolve the freeze, they'll find another way to absorb the hit." I said it with complete certainty. Because I believed in them. I believed in *him*.

"I'm sure they will." Her eyes lingered on me. "Did he get Oli on board?"

I opened my mouth to admit I had no idea when she edged closer, leaning in.

"Incoming," she murmured.

"We all know each other. Don't be weird."

Sebastian was already walking toward us, smirk firmly in place and aimed at Aria. "Well, well, well—if it isn't my favorite oathbreaker?"

Aria laughed. "Gosh, you're still such a geek."

"You got the reference, though," he said, wearing that ridiculously attractive, warm smile as he hugged her. "Please tell me you're turning your back on my brother and coming back to me."

"Not a fucking chance," Henry said, appearing out of thin air. He handed an empty glass to a waiter and grabbed a new one in a single smooth motion. His date—a beautiful Spanish woman whose name I wasn't a hundred percent sure of—stood beside him.

Aria stepped back. "Plus, you can't afford me anymore," she said, eyes on her former boss.

"*I* can barely afford her," Henry muttered, half hidden behind his glass.

Aria shoved his shoulder before extending her hand to Luca. It was curious how nobody seemed to know he existed until recently.

A second later, Raúl and Mateo joined us, and once the introductions wrapped up, I took a quiet sip of my drink just as Luca tightened his hold on Sebastian's arm.

Interesting.

Luca always seemed to get a little more territorial when I was around. I caught one of the glares he shot my way and had to fight the urge to smile. I was guessing he'd found out I was working under his boyfriend. That probably hadn't gone over well.

I hid my amusement behind another sip of my drink.

Mateo ended up beside me, looking smart in a linen suit with his shoulder-length, dirty-blond Viking hair down. He also looked a little sad, gaze drifting to Henry, who downed his entire drink in one go. Something was definitely off there.

"It is an incredible piece, Mateo," Luca said.

"Thank you. Do you like sculptures?" Mateo angled his body toward him.

Luca nodded. "All art."

I scoffed under my breath. Truth be told, it sparked every one of my insecurities. Luca, I'd learned during my light stalking, was an art major—just like Charlotte. So not only was he older and attractive, but he was cultured and smart too, and that really rubbed me the wrong way.

I tried to tell myself most of what he said sounded generic.

"I like art that forces you to take up space with it," Luca added, turning toward the massive sculpture. "Pieces that don't just sit in a room—they change the way the room behaves. Yours reminds me a little of Serra, the way it reorients you without you noticing."

Mateo's brows lifted, a small smile tugging at his mouth. "That is very high praise. Thank you, Luca."

Fine. That might have been a little impressive.

Sebastian hummed, eyes still on the sculpture. "It does take up the room. There's no denying that."

"Ash is not big on modern art," Luca said, his palm casually pressed against Sebastian's stomach.

"That's not true. I'm very appreciative of the work of Iris van Herpen and Issey Miyake," Sebastian said, deadpan—like he hadn't just named two fashion designers at an art exhibit.

I was about to jump in when—

"Of course. Next you will tell me Balenciaga is your favorite painter." Luca nodded solemnly, then turned to Mateo. "Sometimes I forget he was raised in a boardroom."

And then Sebastian laughed. His drink was halfway to his lips, his mouth twitching into a grin before he let out a warm huff of laughter. Not the full goofy one, but still real.

"That was a little harsh, don't you think?" Sebastian leaned closer to him, eyes softening in that playful way that always made my chest tighten. When it was aimed at *me*.

"Somebody has to knock you down a peg," Luca replied easily.

"And thank God for that," Henry chimed in.

Everyone laughed—light, easy, natural. Even Mateo.

Meanwhile, I just stood there with a bitter taste in my mouth and a very strong urge to get the fuck out. I gulped down my drink instead and took a small step back.

"Oli's the art enthusiast of the family. Ash and I are kind of hopeless," Henry said, his Spanish bombshell giggling as she moved closer to him.

Mateo's eyes moved between them.

Luca looked up at Sebastian. "There had to be a catch."

"Why do I suddenly feel like I'm being graded on my ability to appreciate beautiful things? I think I'm fantastic at it, actually."

Aria laughed. "It's good to keep you grounded, Ash. That way not everybody's dying to be a Langley."

Another ripple of laughter moved through the group. Sebastian rolled his eyes; Luca smiled up at him—perfect, effortless.

Mateo drifted a little closer to me, and when our eyes met, something unspoken clicked into place. The quiet sting of being on the outside. The Langley rejects.

Fitting.

"Can I get you another drink?" Mateo asked, his gaze dropping to my empty glass.

Relief loosened something in me. I nodded, finally turning my back to the happy little circle. "I don't think I've ever wanted anything more."

We made it all the way to the outdoor bar. Mateo ordered two whiskeys while I leaned back against the counter, letting the night air cool my face. The glass doors were wide open, giving us a clear view of the gallery inside—unfortunately.

"I'm sorry, but this event is terrible."

Mateo chuckled as he handed me the glass. "I agree with you on that one."

"I'm always going to be on Henry's side of… everything, really. But this kind of sucked, and I'm sorry you're getting your feelings hurt."

"I'm sorry you're getting your feelings hurt too."

My first instinct was to scoff and pretend none of this bothered me, but whatever—we were in the same boat. "They're just looking a little too perfect tonight." I shrugged. "I hate that. We never looked like that."

Mateo frowned, eyes flicking toward the Langleys before coming back to me. "Maybe. But I don't think so. I've only met Sebastian a couple of times, and I've never seen the two of you together like that, but with Luca?" He made a small, unimpressed face. "There's no warmth."

I stared at him. "What?"

"When people connect—when they're meant to be together—there's this thread you can see," Mateo said. "Even from the outside. I can't see it. Can you?"

Hope swelled in my heart.

"Henry didn't tell you?" I muttered. "My judgment is not to be trusted here."

"Why?"

"Because he's not supposed to be with anybody else." The truth slipped out before I could stop it. "He's mine."

Mateo didn't flinch. Didn't judge. He just lifted his glass. "Then slow and steady wins the race, right?"

A smile curled onto my lips. "If this is you trying to buy my affection as his best friend… well done." I clinked my glass against his.

His rough laugh vibrated between us.

"And with Henny…" My gaze drifted back to them—Henry pulling away from his date, drinking like he was racing the clock. "He's got his own shit to deal with, but he's not trying to hurt you. His heart is huge. He just doesn't know what to do with that sometimes."

Mateo's expression softened. He nodded once. "Thank you."

We chatted for a little while after that, until he was called away, and then I was left to stew in my own misery again. I didn't feel like drinking anymore, and I definitely didn't want to circle back to that group just to say goodbye. I wished I could just disappear for the night.

Even if what Mateo said had made me feel a little better,

Sebastian was still back there with him—laughing, teasing, probably going back to his place after and—

Nope. Did not need that visual in my head.

I sighed and pulled out my phone as it buzzed. Four new texts from… seriously? When did he even get my number?

"For fuck's sake," I muttered as I typed back.

"Who do you need me to get rid of?" Sebastian's voice came from my right. I looked up as he slid onto the stool beside me and lifted a hand for a drink.

My eyes flicked over his shoulder, expecting his boyfriend, but it was just him. "One of your junior analysts can't take a hint."

Sebastian chuckled. "Unwanted attention?"

I nodded, tucking my phone away. "Very much so. It's crossed from persistent into full-on stalking."

He took a sip of his drink, completely unbothered. "Unfortunate," he said lightly. "But not surprising. Have you seen yourself lately?"

My heart did a somersault—then dipped.

Fuck him.

Why was he always playing with my heart like this?

I smirked instead of calling him out. Instead of turning around and walking away. "Where have your eyes been roaming to? Your boyfriend's still by the sculpture." It wasn't supposed to sound bitter, but some things were inevitable.

Sebastian's lips twitched. "Just pointing out the obvious."

I shook my head. That line—the one I knew I should be holding—was already stretching, bending, becoming way too flexible. "What's so obvious?"

He grinned, devilish as ever. "You're gorgeous, darling."

His voice dipped to that perfect, low rumble, and I melted. Like an idiot. I leaned in on my elbows, closing the space between us. Our eyes stayed locked.

"Who could blame anyone for falling head over heels with one look?"

My smile pulled to one side. "Now, would you really say that in front of your brother?"

Sebastian laughed quietly and shrugged. "Why not?"

Was this still just a game to him?

Well, fine. It could be a game for me too.

I scooted closer, lowering my own voice. "I don't know, *friend*... Why don't you tell me what's so gorgeous about me, and I'll let you know?"

He didn't miss a beat. "So many things."

What was he doing?

"Like what?" I whispered.

The crinkle at the corner of his mouth deepened. "You. Everything. We're big on art appreciation tonight, in case you haven't heard, and we've established it's not any one thing—it's the sum of all the parts." His brows lifted knowingly.

I bit my lip. "Is it my dazzling personality?"

"That too."

"My eyes? My hair?"

"All of it." He almost purred the words.

I couldn't make sense of it.

"Are you just telling me what I want to hear?"

His smile stretched slowly—too slowly—like he was deciding how much truth he could get away with. Then he leaned back, putting space between us. "You looked upset. Nothing's a lie, but you looked like you needed to hear it."

My smile slipped. I was one second away from telling him to go fuck himself or pulling him in by the shirt and kissing him senseless.

I swallowed thickly. "I don't—"

"Ethan!"

We both turned. Mateo was running toward us, urgency written all over him. The moment our eyes met, he waved me over and spun around, already heading the other way. I didn't hesitate, following with Sebastian close behind.

"What is it?" I asked, keeping pace.

"Henry—I'm not sure. He keeps saying your name," Mateo said, breath uneven.

"What?"

He pushed through the crowd and slipped through a doorway into a back room—bare walls, scattered supplies, ladders leaning in the shadows. I opened my mouth to ask again when I saw him.

Henry.

He was on the floor against the far wall, knees pulled in, hands tangled in his hair. An overturned glass lay empty by his feet. He rocked slowly, like he couldn't quite keep himself steady.

"Henny?" Sebastian's voice came from just behind me.

Henry's head snapped up, and his eyes landed on me. Red-rimmed. Streaming.

Oh shit—

CHAPTER NINE

ASH

"Ash..."

The water was running hot in the shower, steam filling the entire room until everything blurred.

"Henny, what—" My heart stopped dead in my chest.

He was lying on his side in the shower, curled against the tile, clothes still on, completely drenched.

His dark eyes—so similar to mine—lifted to me, slow and unfocused. Red-rimmed. "A-Ash?" His voice shook, his whole body trembling, his teeth clenched around my name.

I dropped to my knees, jeans instantly soaking through, and I brushed his hair back, trying to get a good look at him. "What happened?"

My little brother's gaze broke from mine, filling again with tears that vanished into the wetness on his face. "He—I..."

I waited.

Seconds.

Minutes.

Hours.

Nothing came.

"Henny?" I kept my voice soft, even though panic was crashing through me.

The water still roared in the background, and I reached up and turned it off. The sudden silence was almost deafening—broken only by the pitter-patter of water dripping off surfaces.

"Henny?"

He blinked—dazed—like he was waking up from a dream, and in an impossibly small voice, he whispered two words.

"I'm... hurt."

The dull clatter of glass rolling across the stone floor snapped me back to the present.

"Babe?" Ethan was kneeling in front of Henry, cupping his face in his hands.

A sharp, unpleasant twitch hit deep in my gut, twisting my expression into a scowl. I shook it off. That—and the panic. The panic of finding him like this again. Hurt. I was never supposed to let him get hurt.

And it was always the same people doing the hurting.

I spun on my heel and got in Mateo's face. "What the fuck did you do to him?"

Mateo lifted his hands, eyes widening. "Nothing. We were just talking, and he—" His gaze drifted back to Henry. "I don't know what happened."

Ethan was saying something to Henry, but the words blurred under the hard thrum in my ears.

I shoved Mateo's shoulder.

The contact startled us both.

"And you expect me to believe that?" My voice sounded rough, unrecognizable. "He was fine outside." I pushed him again—not hard, but enough to force a step back. "What did you do to him?"

Mateo steadied himself, confusion flashing across his face. "I didn't touch him."

Another shove, both hands on his chest now. "What did you do to him?"

"Nothing!" He stepped back, a flash of anger breaking through his usual calm.

"Like fuck—"

"Sebastian!" Ethan's voice cut across the room, loud and stern.

I turned.

"You're not fucking helping." He was glaring at me. "Cut it out."

Behind him, Henry was struggling to pull air into his lungs, chest heaving, still trying to fold in on himself.

"If you want to be useful," Ethan said, flicking his eyes toward the table beside us, "hand me the ice in that glass and shut the fuck up."

I blinked.

Mateo moved first, grabbing the ice and placing it into Ethan's outstretched palm, then stepping back quickly. Ethan lowered his forehead to Henry's, speaking softly as he pressed the ice to his wrists, rubbing slow circles.

What…

"Panic attack," Mateo said beside me. His voice was low, like he was trying to make sense of it too. "That's clever—the ice…"

That familiar pang of uselessness hit me—hard. Tight. Suffocating. Like the room had shrunk without warning.

As Ethan kept talking, Henry slowly started to calm—bit by bit—while I stood there, doing nothing.

The air felt too thin. My pulse too loud. My grip on the moment slipping through my fingers no matter how hard I tried to lock it down.

You didn't keep him safe.

"Ethan," I said, a tremor in my voice I hadn't expected slipping through.

He tilted his head toward me, anger gone—replaced by worry. "Can you get us a car?" Then to Mateo, "Is there a back exit or something?"

"Yes," Mateo said immediately.

"I can't leave. I have a date," Henry tried, voice shaking.

That tone—fuck, that tone—made my hands unsteady.

"She's a big girl, Henny," Ethan murmured. "She'll get back safe. Let's go home, okay?"

Mateo stepped closer. "I'll make sure she does."

Henry still wouldn't look at him. He just stared at Ethan's chest and gave a stiff nod.

Like hell Mateo didn't do anything—then why the fuck was Henry acting like this around him?

"Ash," Ethan said. His eyes were bright and pleading. "Call the car."

I nodded once and pulled out my phone, making sure the driver would be waiting right outside.

The seconds stretched longer than they should have.

Ethan helped Henry to his feet. He swayed a little, but he looked better already.

"They're outside," I told them.

Mateo walked us to the back door. Ethan and Henry huddled together behind me, and he held the door open for them.

"Henry," Mateo said quietly.

Henry still wouldn't look at him. "I'm sorry. Not right now."

Ethan leaned into the Spaniard, lowering his voice. "I'll let you know how he is in a little bit. Don't worry too much—he's okay."

I frowned at that exchange.

Henry got into the back seat. Ethan was about to climb in after him but stopped when I reached for the passenger door.

"Ash, don't," Ethan said. "I've got it."

"I'm not leaving him alone right now."

"He's not alone. I'm with him—"

"Ethan." My voice dropped. "I'm not leaving my brother alone. Get in the car."

He looked like he wanted to argue but thought better of it, and he slid inside.

I shut the door after him.

Taking a breath, I turned to Mateo, still standing by the curb. "If I find out you did anything to hurt him," I said, voice low and cold, "I'm coming back for blood. I'm not fucking kidding."

His hazel eyes went wide.

I shut the door with a sharp snap, and the car sped away.

When I looked back, Henry was staring out the window, face still ashen—his hand clasped tightly in Ethan's, their fingers intertwined.

I faced forward again and watched the city blur past, trying to swallow down the doubt creeping up my throat.

———

Back at the apartment, Henry looked much better and kept repeating that Mateo hadn't done anything. He didn't say much else, though—not to me. He went straight into his room, and Ethan followed, closing the door behind them.

I probably should've left. Instead, I sat there for over an hour, whiskey in hand, scowling at the goddamn door.

If Mateo didn't do anything, then what the hell did they have to talk about? What was taking them so long? What were they doing in there?

Questions and resentment circled my brain like vultures.

If I'd never left them alone, would they even be this close? What did I miss? What was happening between them?

The thoughts sat wrong in my chest. And at the same time, Henry needed this. He deserved someone he trusted. Someone he could open up to. I should be relieved he'd found that. I should be proud of Ethan for breaking through walls none of us ever could. Instead, bitterness settled in, stubborn and unwelcome.

The creak of the door jolted me out of my spiral.

Ethan stepped out, eyes tired, giving me a small smile as he shut it carefully.

"I thought you'd left." He walked to the bar, his back to me. The soft pour of liquid into a glass followed.

"Without saying goodbye?"

Ethan's brows lifted as he turned and came to sit beside me. He sank into the couch, legs spreading lazily, still somehow managing to look inviting even in exhaustion. "Why are you mad?" His voice was rough, worn thin around the edges.

"I'm not mad, darling. I'm worried."

He pressed the rim of his glass to his mouth and took a slow sip. "Mateo didn't do anything to him, Ash. Henny had a panic attack."

"Why?"

His lips pulled down. "He got triggered."

"Why?" I pushed.

"Why do you think?"

"Don't be fucking coy with me, Ethan. If Henry wants to protect that guy—"

"Do you honestly think I'd let someone hurt him and walk away?"

I scoffed. "You're the one who pointed out I don't know you anymore, remember?"

He cocked his head. "Are you sure you're not mad?"

"I'm not." I placed the glass on the coffee table and leaned forward.

The couch creaked as Ethan moved in closer. My gaze stayed on the table until I felt the tip of his finger at the corner of my mouth. Then I caught the amusement in his eyes, lingering on my lips.

"You get a little line here," he said. "It dips when you're mad." He finally pulled his hand away, along with that quiet curiosity.

"Why can't you tell me what happened?" The question came out in a whisper.

"Because he'll tell you when he's calmed down. Reach out tomorrow," he said. "You were the one who taught me people have to voice their own stories, *remember*?"

His soft tone loosened something in my shoulders.

"I have to say, watching you get all macho is kind of hot," Ethan teased, though there was seriousness beneath it. "But misguided. And unnecessary." His eyes drifted over my face, then to my hair. "Are you doing okay?"

"I'm not the one who got hurt today—"

"Henry didn't get hurt, Ash," Ethan cut in gently. "He's okay. Are you?"

No.

Yes.

No.

Everything was going to be fine. I just needed to get everything back in order.

I blew a breath out through my nose. "Why do you call each other that?"

Ethan stretched out, arm over the back of the couch, head resting on his palm, a lazy smile tugging at his lips. "Babe?"

I leaned back into the leather, relieved he wasn't pushing anymore. "Yes."

His grin widened. "That was your fault."

I arched a brow. "How could that have possibly been my fault?"

"Do you remember that guy you used to fuck? Chris?"

My lips curved at the bitterness lacing his tone. "Yes."

"One night, we ran into him at a club opening. Henry and I had done way too many shots. Chris kept calling everyone babe —you know how he is."

"I do," I said with a huff. "It's so fucking annoying."

"It is. But drunk us thought it was hilarious, so we started saying it to each other. And then it stuck." He shrugged. "See? Your fault."

We held each other's stares, trying not to smile.

"And that's it?"

"That's it."

A knot loosened in my chest. The tension from tonight

drained out of me bit by bit, and I let myself be soothed by his presence once more. Sinking into it.

"Is he okay?" I asked.

"He will be," Ethan said. "You Langleys don't like facing the things that hurt you. You just bottle it up."

"Is that where you learned it?"

Ethan chuckled, closing his eyes and arching his neck over the back of the couch. How could someone be so effortlessly sexy?

He licked his lips, pale blue eyes drawing me right back in. "I'm really fucking tired, Ash. I'm going to bed." His lips twitched. "There's plenty of room if you need to crash."

He was baiting me. And still, my whole body hummed. "In your bed?"

He nodded through another stretch. The urge to scoop him up and have him writhing like that on top of me burned low in my gut.

"Your call," he said, slipping off the couch and finishing his drink.

"Technically, I shouldn't even be here. Do those boundaries not apply to your bed?"

He strutted toward his room, unbuttoning his shirt as he walked. One shoulder slipped free, exposing just enough skin to spike the heat in my body instantly. And I knew what it was— even as I tilted my head to watch him. Payback. For earlier. For flirting when I shouldn't have.

I just hated making him look sad. It was always easier when he was angry at me.

"I would *never* make my boss sleep on the couch," he said, leaning against the doorframe with a wicked smirk. His shirt hung open, and even in the dim light I could see the lines of muscle over his stomach, the rise and fall of each breath.

"Goodnight, darling."

"Goodnight, Sebastian." He disappeared behind the door, his smile lingering even as it shut between us.

I closed my eyes and rubbed my palms over my face. A quiet "fuck" slipped out.

Slowly, I walked to his room. My fingertips grazed the wood of the door, sliding down until they hovered by the handle.

Just one turn. That's all it would take.

I shook my head and stepped back.

Stick to the plan, Sebastian. You cannot afford more chaos. Not right now.

A dull ache spread through my chest as I walked away, each step heavier than the last.

———

Elena's office felt unusually still.

Morning light washed the skyline in pale gold beyond the glass, traffic threading through the city below as if nothing in the world had changed. Inside these walls, however, everything felt suspended in time.

I hadn't slept. Not properly.

Henry's departure this morning kept looping in my head—the quick hug, the careful smile, the way he'd accepted my apology for basically attacking Mateo without offering much back.

I should have pushed. And now he was somewhere over the Atlantic while I sat here, waiting for another verdict I couldn't control.

The door opened behind me. Elena stepped in, tablet tucked against her side, her expression composed in the way that meant the news wasn't good. "They've reviewed the corrected submissions."

"And?"

"They're expanding the audit scope."

The words landed with quiet finality. Of course they were. Which meant more files, more scrutiny, more time. More money burning while we waited.

I leaned forward, elbows on my knees, forcing my voice to remain even. "How long?"

"They won't give a timeline," she said, dropping to her chair.

"That's not acceptable."

"It's not negotiable."

Rising to my feet, I crossed to the windows, dragging a hand down my face as the city blurred beyond the glass. "We can't just sit on our hands. There has to be a way to accelerate this."

"There isn't," Elena replied calmly. "Not from our side."

I turned back to her. "We corrected the error. What else do they want?"

"Time," she said. "And proof that the problem isn't systemic."

The word lodged under my ribs. *Systemic.* As if the company we had built could be reduced to a compliance failure.

"As long as this review is active," she continued, "they will assume risk. And risk slows everything down."

I let out a breath that felt scraped raw. "We can't afford slow."

"No," she agreed. "Which is why we stop trying to control the review and focus on what we *can* control."

I stared at her.

She held my gaze, unflinching. "Private development," she continued. "Bridge financing. Reallocating crews. Preserving liquidity. We ride it out."

Ride it out. The words didn't sit right. "That sounds like waiting."

"It sounds like surviving," she corrected.

The low hum beyond the glass pressed in, steady and indifferent.

Somewhere in the back of my mind, Henry's voice surfaced again—the careful distance, the refusal to open a door I didn't know how to knock on. Control slipping in one place was one thing, but control slipping everywhere felt like failure.

"We built this to withstand pressure," I said. "If we just sit here—"

"We are not sitting," Elena cut in, more forceful now. "We are *adapting*." Her tone softened, but her eyes did not. "This is not just on you, Sebastian—it's on all of us."

It felt like it was.

Like if I had caught it sooner, tightened the process, burned that template the second it was approved, demanded better oversight, demanded sharper eyes, and demanded perfection the way I always did, then maybe this wouldn't be happening. Maybe the review wouldn't be expanding. Maybe the crews wouldn't be idle, and the money wouldn't be bleeding out by the hour, and the company wouldn't be standing here waiting to be judged.

You didn't keep them safe.

This wasn't the plan.

This wasn't the fucking plan.

CHAPTER TEN

ETHAN

The week after the art exhibit felt too calm.

Henry had flown back to the States to see his dad. He seemed to be doing okay, and I thought he might finally be close to agreeing to talk to someone. A professional. Someone who could actually help him deal. He'd talked to Mateo too, and that seemed… fine. Even though the last time I'd seen Mateo leave our apartment, he'd looked like a kicked puppy again.

And then there was Sebastian and me. A whole different disaster.

I had no idea where we stood. I hadn't spotted him on the running trail again, and most of our office interactions were distant—well, our version of distant. Not nods, because we didn't do nods, but the winks and lip bites we threw at each other from across the room weren't actual intimacy.

And they shouldn't have been.

Because he still hadn't broken up with his fucking boyfriend.

The only reason I knew this was that Vanessa—Sebastian's assistant—and I were friends now. Lunch-break friends. And she let slip a couple of times that Luca had come by or had been calling him.

Sebastian himself had barely been visible. When he was, he moved through the floor like a storm front rolling in—phone to his ear, jacket slung over his shoulder, tie loosened, beard darker against the hollowing shadows under his eyes. More than once I'd caught sight of him late in the evening when I was leaving, still in his office with the lights low, the glow of his monitors reflecting off his face. He was working insane hours. Even by his standards.

And every time our eyes met, he still found the energy to smirk at me like nothing in his world was on fire.

I should've been focusing on my schoolwork—and I was. The Sebastian obsession was just a side project. The classes were interesting and challenging, and unlike some in uni, I felt like they actually prepared me for the real world, which I was also a part of.

Budgeting was its own challenge, but I'd worked out my credit card debt with the bank, turning it into smaller payments I could actually manage. I'd only received one paycheck so far, but for the first time in months, I felt like I had my life under control again.

When Henry returned on Saturday, he announced we'd all been invited to a club opening. Not a surprise—he got invited to these every day of the week—but he came back from his trip a little off. Exhilarated and light, but also more chaotic. Still, after working, studying, and overthinking full-time, I was craving a shift in pace, so I didn't complain.

Not when we showed up a little early for the VIP party.

Not when we both started drinking faster than usual.

Not when we got our picture taken, and Henry posted it on social media, and it blew up in minutes.

Nope. Tonight was going to be a fun night out.

An hour and a half later, Henry and I were well past tipsy, swallowed by the dance floor, surrounded by a pack of strangers who had instantly become our new best friends. Henry's arm hung over my shoulders; someone else kept shouting along to the music. The bass rattled my ribs. Sweat clung to my skin. The whole room smelled like cologne, alcohol, and bad decisions.

Henry yelled something in my direction, but the chorus drowned him out. Then—

"Oh! Hey!" He peeled his arm off me and waved wildly.

"What?"

He leaned in until his hair brushed my cheek and shouted in my ear, hot and loud, "Everyone's here!"

Flinching, I followed his line of sight… and of course. Mateo. Sebastian. Luca. And the little entourage glued to him like decorative barnacles.

I groaned. "Why did you invite them?"

"Because I like my brother, and they're my friends?"

"I can't be drunk around him." I frowned and took a half-step back. "Now I have to stop drinking."

"You do whatever you think is necessary," Henry said, patting my chest. "Just keep Slutty Ethan under control and you'll be aces! Let's go say hi." He latched onto my hand and dragged me through the crowd.

They were gathered around a tall table in the VIP area, the lights softer here, cooler, the music more muffled under the balcony. Luca and his friends were a little farther off, snapping pictures of everything—again.

Henry said hi first, stopping beside Mateo, slipping his hand onto Mateo's shoulder as he leaned in to talk animatedly into his ear. Mateo nodded at me in greeting, trying to follow whatever Henry was babbling about.

I faced Sebastian Langley. Our eyes met, and just like every other day this week, we both tried not to be too obvious about our stupid, hidden smiles. But something in his felt… strained. Like it arrived a fraction too late.

Then again, he'd shown up tonight. Things couldn't be that bad.

Sebastian leaned a little closer, a glint behind his eyes. "Are you two having fun?"

There he is.

I grinned. "So much fun. Doesn't it look like we are?"

"So much," he echoed, mouth tilting in a low chuckle. Then his gaze dropped—and so did his grin.

I frowned at the sudden change, followed his stare… and saw it. My hand still wrapped around Henry's. When I looked back up, his expression was composed again, perfected into that polished, controlled calm he wore like a second skin. But that tiny crack? That brief flicker of something real?

Cute. And *telling*.

Was he actually bothered by that?

I'd been wondering since the art exhibit—the change in his mood, the tension, the way he'd loosened the moment I explained the whole *babe* thing.

Sebastian couldn't still be jealous of his own brother, could he?

That was insane.

And it absolutely needed to be confirmed this very second.

"Mateo," I called.

He leaned over the table, Henry tipping a little into him and dropping my hand to steady himself.

I grinned. "Do you dance?"

Mateo chuckled. "Some. Not much."

"You should ask Henny to dance. He's an *unbelievably* sexy dancer."

Henry blinked at me, slightly horrified by the grenade I'd just handed him, and I bit my lip to keep from laughing.

Mateo only smiled, cocking his head in Henry's direction. "Is that right?"

Henry visibly swallowed. "I'm… capable. Better than Ash, in any case," he said, trying to deflect.

I looked back at Sebastian. His face had gone still, eyes narrowed just enough to give him away.

Bingo.

I shifted a little closer, my shoulder brushing his arm. His eyes dipped straight to mine.

"He's not so bad," I said.

The little smile he gave me was mouthwatering. *Okay, pack it in.* I needed to get some water in me. Soon.

A glass was set in between Sebastian and me, making me take a step back. I was startled when I realized it was Luca, moving in next to his boyfriend.

"Hi, Ethan," he said, tone and stare cold as ice.

Well, hello. What's this? A little honesty from Mr. Perfect?

"Hey."

"Ash, you know what?" Henry said, moving in closer. "One of the owners said he knew you. Come say hi with me?"

Sebastian stiffened, his gaze flicking from Luca to me. "Sure."

They left, and I expected Luca to go back to his friends, but he stayed right where he was, staring at me.

"I think it is time for you to stop," he said.

My brows knit. "Stop what?"

He smiled, but it was tight, forced. "Your need to be so close to him all the time."

And there it was—Sebastian's boyfriend finally calling it out.

A sharp discomfort twisted low in my stomach. Just enough to make me pause. Just enough for the smallest voice in my head to whisper that maybe he had a point. Maybe I *should* step back, acknowledge the boundary, and stop hovering around someone who was technically still in a relationship.

I should have.

Too bad my restraint was nonexistent.

I leaned in, meeting his stare without flinching. "We're just close like that. You know—old friends."

"Working for him? Really?"

"What can I say?" I shrugged. "We share a lot of interests."

He didn't move. "People notice. They talk. It reflects on him."

Ah.

So that's what this was about. His perfect image.

"I'm good at what I do," I said evenly. "The only thing I reflect on him is success."

No polite smiles this time. "You are making everybody uncomfortable."

"Everybody? You sure about that?" I took a step closer, refusing to shrink under his stare. "Look, I'm always going to be in his life. You should be getting used to it, not feeling threatened—"

"I don't feel threatened by you," he cut in quickly.

I smirked. "Could've fooled me."

Luca used his height to his advantage, moving in. I clenched my teeth and held my ground.

"You act too desperate to be threatening," he said. "Just keep your distance tonight."

He grabbed his glass and walked away, while I stood there, jaw slack.

A hand landed on my shoulder. "Ethan," Mateo said, a warning under his breath.

"Did you *hear* that motherfucker?" I snapped, outrage punching straight through me. "He called me desperate."

"He's jealous too, Ethan. Think about—"

"No. No thinking." I blew a sharp breath out through my nose. "Desperate? I'll fucking show him desperate."

I spun toward the Langley brothers but paused—one tiny alarm bell going off—then tapped Mateo's arm. "Hey, you know Henny and I have *zero* feelings for each other, right? Like none whatsoever."

Mateo gave me a confused little smile, then nodded.

"I need his help right now, so whatever you see, keep that in mind."

Mateo just chuckled and waved his hand, like saying, *Go forth.*

Say no fucking more.

I resumed my storming, and when I reached them, I slid under Henry's arm and wrapped mine around his waist. Henry barely registered it, but his brother—standing right beside him—definitely did. Sebastian was talking to another guy and stopped mid-sentence for a beat before continuing.

Gotcha.

"Hey, babe, come dance with me?" I asked Henry, lowering my voice just enough to make sure it carried.

"And shots?" Henry asked, already smiling at me.

"And shots."

He started steering us away, and I let my hand drift over his back until my thumb slipped into his belt loop. I resisted the urge to look back.

———

There was a certain magic to slow reggaeton tracks. Sultry as fuck, all bass and heat, Spanish lyrics rolling low and heavy through the speakers. In a room thick with strobing lights and sweat, they hit even harder. They made everything feel more vivid—every brush of skin, every sway of hips—an invitation to get away with touches you wouldn't dare anywhere else. Perfect for right now. Perfect for the way Henry had his hands on me, guiding me into something almost obscene, both of us milking the rhythm for everything it could give.

For him, it was performance. Showing off for the person watching him across the room—the one he actually wanted but couldn't walk up to.

For me, it was the same game, except I didn't want Sebastian to just watch. I wanted him to *crave*. I wanted him to *burn* at the sight of me in someone else's arms. I wanted that careful control he kept around me to finally fracture. I wanted to be the spark that made him snap.

Henry slid his hands from my hips to push his hair back, sweat plastering it to his forehead. I reached up and did it for him, dragging my fingers through the strands, slow enough to sell the moment.

He arched a brow, hands returning to my hips as he leaned into my ear. "Are you up to something?"

My smile didn't budge. "What?"

"You're being excessively affectionate, and it's starting to make me uncomfy—and you know it takes a lot to do that."

"Luca called me desperate."

Henry hissed. "And he's still alive?"

I shrugged. "I figured I'd show him what a desperate man really looks like."

Henry narrowed his eyes. "Oh, *bad* Ethan. You're using me to make Ash jealous? Why am I getting dragged into this? I'm having a happy day."

"He'll get over it."

Henry grabbed my hand and pulled me toward the edge of the dance floor—still in Sebastian's line of sight, but out of the crush of bodies and sweat.

He scanned the room, then looked back at me. "He looks like he wants to murder me."

I snorted at the flat look he gave me. "Sorry. That's enough for tonight."

Henry sighed. "You owe me one."

I tugged on his shirt to bring his attention back. "What do you mean, a happy day?"

His lips curved—not tense. Just soft. "I talked to my dad about everything. It was... a good talk."

Warmth rushed through my chest. "Yeah?"

"Mhm." A small shrug. "I think I'm gonna try the therapy thing again. See if it sticks."

"That's a great idea, Henny."

His eyes drifted to our table—to Mateo, obviously—before dropping to his feet. "I don't want to keep missing out on every-thing anymore."

When he looked back up, his eyes were a little red, and it hit me right in the gut. I threw my arms around his neck and yanked him into a hug.

Henry chuckled. "Come on, now. I don't want to die right after I've had this epiphany."

"I'm so fucking proud of you," I said, tightening my hold until his arms finally squeezed back. "You deserve everything in this world, okay? All the best things. They should all be yours."

Henry sniffled, a wet little laugh escaping him. "God, you're a sappy drunk."

I loosened my hold and cupped his face. "I'm not drunk. I just love you and your stupid face."

Henry's eyes glistened. "I love you and your stupid face too."

I pushed up and pressed a quick peck to his lips before hugging him again. "Want to go back?"

"Yeah, sure."

"I need the bathroom first."

Henry raised a hand as we parted. I pushed my way to the bathroom, stood in line for what felt like forever—fucking clubs —and then headed back to the table.

I was halfway there when I spotted Sebastian walking away, shoulders tight, posture stiff. The magnetic pull between us dragged me after him, bypassing the VIP section entirely.

He was leaning against the end of a corridor, probably leading to the offices—Sebastian's favorite kind of hiding spots. He looked serious, brows drawn and lips pressed into a thin line.

"What are you doing, stranger? Lurking in the back like a creep," I teased.

His eyes flicked up to mine, then away. No humor. Just a low hum in response.

I smiled to myself. *Look at him, all jealous.* A sharp flicker of thrill shot down my spine—that dangerous, addictive lure that had always lived in the space between us.

Stepping into the corridor, I leaned back against the opposite wall, facing him. My tongue dragged over my lower lip, unable to help the grin tugging at them. "You mad at me?"

His jaw twitched.

It was hot back here, and I probably looked like a mess from dancing—hair pushed back, shirt open more than it should be. He, of course, looked great. Weatherproof, as always. Even the faint sheen on his neck somehow worked for him.

I tapped his shoe with mine. "Say something."

Sebastian shook his head tightly, gaze still fixed anywhere but on me. "Aren't we supposed to be friends?"

"We're friends."

A dry, humorless laugh scraped out of him. "That didn't feel very friendly."

I pushed off the wall and took a step closer. "You know we're just—"

But he'd reached his limit. "You know I try my best not to show any kind of affection," he cut in, dark eyes finally locking on mine. "Not in front of you. I told you I would never do that to you."

Something in his voice made my grin falter. "What are you talking about?"

"With Luca."

My stomach dropped.

But he wasn't done.

"I don't do it because I don't want to hurt your feelings. Because I fucking care about you." He straightened, shoulders squaring, taking up more space—and I hated how much taller he looked. How small I felt.

And suddenly the heat between us felt different. Like a different brand of danger.

"Don't give yourself so much credit," I said, the words coming out clipped. "You didn't hurt my—"

"Well, you hurt mine!" Sebastian snapped.

I froze, lips parting.

Shit.

I hadn't meant—

"Whatever happened to you not doing that to me?" His brows were low, voice shaking with anger—or something close to it. "To not doing it with my own fucking brother?"

"I'm not doing anything to you," I said, softer now, attempting to slow down his spiral. "Henry and I are just friends, you know that."

His expression hardened instead of easing. "Because you act like that with all your friends, do you?"

I gave him a small smile. "Ash, we were just dancing."

It didn't work.

"You dance with your friends like that? Touch like that?"

"Yeah—"

"Kiss like that?"

I blinked. "Kiss like…" My eyes widened as it hit. "That was a fucking *peck*."

His chest rose unevenly. "You still kissed him."

"This is ridiculous." I shook my head, trying to rein it back in. "It was innocent. You know that. And you have a whole fucking boyfriend, and you're giving me shit for kissing my friend—"

"My brother," he corrected instantly.

"My friend," I said, quieter but firm. "And we were having a moment. You've never done something like that?"

"No."

"Oh, come on."

He crowded into my space. "You knew that was going to hurt me."

"No, I didn't." I stared up at him, refusing to step back. "That's like thinking patting someone on the back is going to hurt your feelings."

"You *kissed* him," he insisted, but the words sounded less like anger and more like something breaking loose.

I exhaled slowly. "You're acting like a kid having a tantrum."

"Because you're lying. You don't kiss all your friends—"

"Oh, for fuck's sake." I fisted the collar of his shirt and yanked him down, pressing a quick kiss to his lips. "There, see? It's just a—"

I didn't finish.

Couldn't.

Because his mouth met mine again, cutting off the argument entirely.

It was a short kiss. Soft.

But the shift in energy was *seismic*.

Neither of us moved. His gaze held mine, dark and impossibly intense, before dropping again. His breathing had changed—shuddering, shallow pulls, controlled like he was forcing it to stay that way.

And I could *feel* it—the need burning behind his eyes was a tangible thing.

I was free-falling off a fucking skyscraper. No air. No sense. Just him and my heartbeat thundering in my chest. His eyes lifted back to mine, and beneath the heat there was something fragile, almost unsteady. A question.

Can I?

Before I could think—before the consequences could even take shape in my head—I nodded. And then, in a movement more instinctive than breathing, our lips met again.

And again.

And again.

Each time we pulled back, we hovered—breath brushing breath—before falling in once more. Gentle, impossibly soft passes of *his* mouth over mine. *His* breath warming my lips. The faint scratch of *his* beard.

Because it was *him*.

Oh.

My.

Fucking.

God.

I was kissing Sebastian Langley.

My brain finally lurched back online, sluggish and scrambling, fighting against the sensory overload to catch up to what my body already knew. This was real. *Happening.*

And then something snapped.

He must've registered that same reality at the same exact moment, because suddenly my back hit the wall, and he closed the space everywhere, his mouth stealing helpless pants from mine with every slow press, as if he couldn't get enough air, enough contact, enough of *me.*

His tongue brushed the seam of my lips—tentative—and I all but surrendered, parting for him, letting him in, finally tasting him again.

Fucking whiskey.

Sweet and smoky, colliding with my own breath on my tongue. And the sound he made—low, wrecked—vibrated straight through my soul.

My body arched into his, hands sliding up to cup his face just to *feel* the solid rasp of his beard under my palms. I opened up for him once more, letting the kiss deepen, and his hands roamed—hot on my arms, my waist—pulling, urging. One of my legs lifted instinctively, rubbing against the side of his thigh, and I rose onto my toes, chasing the contact.

When I opened my eyes, his were already on me—searching, unguarded, stripped of every layer he wore in the daylight. My gaze went to his lips, parted and glistening, the same lips that had been on mine a second ago. Our eyes locked again, and something like lightning shot down my spine, flooding every inch of me with violent, dizzying want.

Sebastian let out a breath that sounded almost like surrender, his gaze dragging over my face like he was mapping every detail again. Then his hands moved—up my neck, over my jaw, into my hair—fingers tangling, gentle at first and then tightening with a little more grip. His eyes followed the movement hungrily before lifting back to mine.

The look we shared was everything—one beat of recognition, of *shit, we're really doing this*—before we dove back in. No slow, no subtle. Just the raw hunger of two men absolutely starved for each other.

I groaned into his mouth as his fist tightened in my hair,

dragging me into the angle he wanted while he devoured me. I bit down on his lower lip, and he answered with a sharp nip of his own, like he'd been waiting for an excuse to lose every ounce of control.

Then he stepped in—really stepped in—pressing me into the wall, chest-to-chest, thigh sliding between mine, and every coherent thought I had evaporated. I'd been hard from the second his mouth touched mine, but when his leg pushed up between my thighs and my hips jerked forward without permission, there was no pretending. We both felt it. Both reacted.

Suddenly nothing in the world mattered except getting closer —impossible as it was.

I grabbed at him—his jaw, his shoulders, his shirt—anything to drag him closer. He was solid under my palms, heat rolling off him like a furnace, the back of his shirt damp with sweat. Every brush of his stubble scraped fire across my mouth. Every drag of his hands lit my nerves up like they'd been waiting their whole lives for this exact touch.

He crowded lower, into every inch of my space, and I rose onto my toes again to meet him, desperate to align our bodies properly. It was messy and frantic—my knee bumping his hip, his hand skidding down my side before gripping tight, hauling me flush against him like distance was no longer survivable— but fucking perfect. His thigh pressed up again, and I gasped into his mouth, my hands fisting in his shirt like I could fuse us together by force alone.

The wall was cold at my back, but I barely felt it. Everything was heat and noise and *him*.

His mouth.

His hands.

His breath mixing with mine.

The way he groaned when I dragged my fingers through his hair, pulling him back down for more. He felt incredible. Felt *right*.

I could just melt right here and now. Melt straight into him.

The bass from the dance floor pulsed through the wall—deep, slow vibrations rolling up my spine—but it felt miles away. Like the whole club had sunk underwater, muffled and blurred, leaving only the two of us breathing in the same tiny pocket of air.

"Seriously?" The loud voice registered somewhere in the back of my brain—but not enough to pull me out of him.

"Sebastian!"

That one did. Him. Not me. The second he tore his mouth from mine, I was already leaning in again, chasing him like a fucking maniac.

"For fuck's sake, help me unglue them," Henry grumbled, presumably to someone else.

"Not yet," I said, grabbing the back of Sebastian's neck and pulling him down to my mouth again. He actually responded for a second before a hand planted itself on my chest—firm, unrelenting—and pushed me back against the wall.

But it wasn't his.

I blinked slowly, finally focusing on Henry's very unimpressed face.

"Will you calm the fuck down?" he said, then flicked his gaze to his brother. "And are you two aware you're making out in a literal open corridor? While everyone—including your boyfriend—is out there and could walk past whenever?"

That word—*boyfriend*—hit like someone had tossed cold water over both of us.

Our eyes met again, and guilt shot across his expression.

Sebastian exhaled hard, face scrunching like reality had just caught up. "Fuck," he breathed, rubbing a hand over his face before taking a step back.

But this is mine. He was mine first.

Immature? Yeah. Probably. But he was supposed to be *with me*, not him. It wasn't fucking fair. He clearly wanted me too.

"Now," Henry said, snapping the moment in half, "do I need to ice you, or are you good to walk out of here?"

Sebastian nodded once and took a couple more steps back.

That's when I noticed Mateo standing nearby, watching all of this unfold. He gave me an apologetic little smile and a look that carried just a hint of pity. A quiet *You know this is a mess*, even though he didn't say it.

I swallowed hard, the heat of Sebastian's mouth still buzzing under my skin.

Henry sighed. "Let's go."

Sebastian didn't look at me again—I caught the moment he almost did, then forced himself not to.

But I couldn't look away.

And that was how we walked out of the corridor—him pretending nothing had happened, and me still trying to remember how to breathe.

CHAPTER ELEVEN

ASH

uck.

Fuck. Fuck. Fuck. Fucking fuck fuck.

FUCK.

What the hell was that, Sebastian?

Where did control go, huh?

How did you just... lose it like that?

Eyes locked on the path ahead, I trailed Henry through the crowd, trying not to choke on my own heartbeat. Trying not to puke from the sudden, gut-deep wave of guilt clawing up my throat.

Shouldn't have done that.

Fucking hell.

Couldn't believe I'd just done that.

The table—and of course, Luca—came into view, and I fought every instinct screaming at me to turn around and disappear. Couldn't do that. I was supposed to be a fucking adult.

It had been a very long time since I'd craved a cigarette like this.

Just one.

Or five.

Before we reached them, before anyone spotted me, I

grabbed Henry's arm and held him back. Out of the corner of my eye, I saw Ethan stop too, only for Mateo to lay a hand on the small of his back and guide him forward.

Henry glanced at me, wide-eyed, curious—and very much like he wanted to mock me. That alone made my teeth grind. Because he was part of the fucking problem too.

"What do you need?" he asked.

Deep breath. *Calm. You are going to calm down.*

"Why did you make me come to this thing?" The accusation in my voice was embarrassingly obvious. *So much for calm.*

His eyebrows shot up. "Excuse me?" A dry laugh. "Is this somehow *my* fault?"

"Yes."

Another laugh. "You're fucking delusional."

I stepped in closer. "Why the fuck do you have to keep touching him all the time? You know it messes with my head. Why do you keep doing it?"

Henry's expression snapped through shock, confusion, and straight into outrage so fast it made me dizzy.

He grabbed my arm and pulled me a little farther out of view, leaning in. "First of all, how fucking dare you? Are you seriously accusing me of making a move on your guy right now? Because you know damn well I would never do that to you. Ever."

Guilt hit hard once more—shoving some of the anger out of its way.

"Second, if you're pissed about the touching, take that up with Ethan, not me. *He's* the one who wanted to rile you up to get back at Luca."

What?

"I've told both of you to stop putting me in the fucking middle," he went on. "Because I am *not* choosing a side when this blows up in your faces."

I stared at him, lips parted.

"And third—what the fuck, Sebastian?" He threw me a look

full of disbelief. "You're being a dick. Just make up your mind already."

"I don't need to—"

"Oh, no? You don't?" He was mad—Henry was genuinely mad at me—and something inside my chest tightened another notch. "You think you can just keep going on like this and not make a choice?"

"That's not—"

"You need to either break up with your robot boyfriend— who is very fucking aware that you still have feelings for Ethan —or you need to ask Ethan to back the fuck up. But you cannot keep playing the nice guy, flirting with everybody like there won't be consequences. Because in case you haven't noticed, you've completely lost the plot."

I blinked, stunned.

"I get you're under a lot of stress. I get that. But you don't do shit like this," Henry said, jabbing a finger at me. "Almost getting into a fistfight with Mateo? Oli told me you haven't been answering his calls *for weeks*. Picking a fight with me? And now cheating?"

My body locked, absorbing each word like impact after impact.

"And yeah, why don't we talk about that too? Because it seems to me like you're doing what you always did with your 'relationships,' just slapping a boyfriend label on it this time to make it look more presentable. And I know you don't give a fuck what people think about that, so the only logical reason you could keep up this charade is to force distance between you and Ethan—which means you're just fucking using that guy. Do you realize that? How fucked up that is?"

The words were caught in my throat. Nothing came out.

"I don't know what the hell is going on with you, Ash. You're a goddamn robot yourself. What the fuck happened to your programming?"

The panic surged again—fast, rising from somewhere I

couldn't reach or control. The floor felt unstable beneath my feet, like everything I had carefully kept aligned was coming apart all at once. He wasn't wrong—and the fact that he wasn't, made something inside me cave in. Every plan I'd set out for myself—for us—was crumbling, and somehow, I was still the one it all led back to. Even if I had no idea how the fucking wrecking ball had picked up this much speed, I'd been the one to set it off.

I swallowed hard. "I don't know." My voice came out small. Unrecognizable.

Henry didn't answer right away. He just stared at me, chest still heaving with leftover anger, like he didn't know what to do with the version of me standing in front of him.

The silence stretched.

Some of the fight left his shoulders. "Fuck," he muttered, scrubbing a hand over his mouth. "That was harsh. I'm sorry—"

"No." My hands settled on my hips, needing something solid to hold me upright. "No. That was called for."

He studied me for another second, the anger fading into something heavier. "I know you're not a robot," he said more gently. "You just pretend to be. But lately… you're not doing such a great job of it."

A humorless laugh left me.

"It's messy," he went on. "Everything is messy."

"I know."

"I thought you didn't like messy."

I didn't.

Everything needed to get back in order.

"I'm sorry. It's not your fault," I said, dragging my hands through my hair. "Clearly."

Henry just watched me like he was trying to decide whether to push again or back off. "What are you going to do?"

What I should've done the second I saw Ethan in Madrid.

"Leave."

He nodded and gave my back a quick pat as we moved toward the table again. The second I saw the back of Ethan's head, heat flared through my chest—my body reacting on instinct, remembering his mouth, his breath, those barely there sounds he made against my lips. Denying what I felt for him had always been a losing battle. I'd known it since the night we kissed in the Hamptons. I'd been gone for him ever since.

The closer we got, the more I noticed the tension in him: shoulders creeping up, arms crossed tight, and weight shifting from foot to foot. He was annoyed. Or pissed. Something was winding him up again.

Then I saw who he was talking to. Not Mateo. Not Luca. That guy from the office. The one who wouldn't stop hovering around him. Bruno. Ethan always looked like he'd rather be anywhere else when that man was near—and tonight was no exception.

The impulse to step in burned through me, but I tamped it down. First things first.

I sidestepped them and stopped in front of Luca, touching his elbow lightly. "Luca."

He turned with a smile. "Yes?"

"I'm going to take off. Come with me?"

He nodded, but as his eyes drifted over my face, the smile slipped. What did he see? Was it written all over me that I was still reeling from that kiss?

"Let me say goodbye," he said.

Behind him, Ethan stepped back again, Bruno following with a grin that made my jaw tick. Normally I could've brushed something like that off. Right now it hit me like a flare to the chest.

Ethan took another step back.

The guy leaned in closer.

My body twitched—an involuntary urge to move toward them.

"Okay, I'm ready," Luca said, rejoining me.

We rounded the table, closing in slowly, the crowd's heat

brushing against my shoulders, strobe lights flashing across Ethan's pale hair.

"I'm not really in the mood to dance right now." His voice carried through the music.

"You are going to tell Henry, yes?" Luca asked, leaning closer.

"He knows." I didn't take my eyes off Ethan.

Then Bruno stepped in again, hand sliding onto Ethan's waist as he said something into his ear. Ethan looked like he was seconds from rolling his eyes, and I knew he could handle himself. I knew he could.

But apparently my programming really was broken.

I stepped up behind Ethan and laid a hand on the guy's shoulder. He looked confused for half a second once he noticed me—probably thinking it had been Ethan who had touched him —definitely not his boss.

His eyes went wide.

"How many different ways does he have to say no for you to get it?" I said.

He parted his lips but didn't speak.

Ethan didn't move—not even a twitch—and his scent hit me again, warm and damp from dancing. All I could think of was his mouth on mine.

"What?" the guy finally asked, eyes flicking to Ethan.

"Go find someone else." I leaned in close enough that Ethan's hair brushed my neck. "Touch him again and you won't just be out of a job at my company—you'll be out of one in this city."

He swallowed hard, then gave a jerky nod.

"You should've taken the hint." Ethan stepped back slightly —pressing his back against my chest. "In case it wasn't obvious, you're not my type—and you're staring at it right now."

Those words—

Fuck.

They sent something wild and possessive through me, a

violent urge to wrap myself around him, to claim him so completely the entire room would understand. The entire world.

I locked my muscles in place.

The guy finally walked off, and when Ethan turned his head, my attention followed the line of his gaze.

Straight to Luca.

He was standing right there. The lights flickered over his face, sharpening the tension around his mouth—nothing like his usual careful composure.

Ethan fitted himself closer to me without hesitation. "Doesn't he look pretty when he's jealous?"

The words weren't for me. They were *about* me.

As Luca all but sneered at him, the moment settled into place with brutal clarity.

Ethan wasn't the problem here.

I was.

I was the one who had let this blur into something reckless. The one who hadn't ended things when I should have. The one who kept standing too close, touching too long, and wanting too much.

Enough.

"Ethan," I said, my tone firm as I stepped back, putting space between us.

His pale eyes snapped to mine, pupils blown wide—want written openly across his face. His lips curved into a slow, flirtatious smile. "Did you need something, Ash?"

I shook my head. "Ethan." This time it came out as a warning. A boundary. A plea.

The smile faded—just slightly—as something in my voice landed. He sighed and looked at Luca. "I'm sorry." Flat. Not sincere in the slightest.

"We're leaving," I said.

A flicker of something—surprise, maybe fear—crossed Ethan's face. "What?"

I ignored it with effort. A staggering amount of it. Because walking away from him felt like tearing muscle from bone.

It always had.

"Bye, Ethan." I pressed my hand to Luca's back and guided him away, the music swallowing us as we moved.

The heat of Ethan's body still clung to my chest.

I forced myself not to look back.

———

Things weren't looking up in the morning.

I'd hoped sleep would settle everything from yesterday, but sleep never truly came, and when it did, it was flooded with *him*. The feel of his body against mine. That impossible intensity in his baby-blue eyes. The rough warmth of his voice when he said my name.

And then Luca's face. Angry. Hurt. Humiliated.

The tightness in my chest refused to ease—and why would it? The kiss hadn't been the worst part. It was everything that came before it. The constant pull toward Ethan. The messages. The flirting. The way my thoughts circled back to him no matter how hard I tried to redirect them. The way, even now, my body remembered exactly what it felt like to have him in my bed.

The boundaries we set had come too late and held too loosely. That was on both of us.

But this—this was mine.

Henry was right. I'd lost the plot.

And it wasn't just about Luca. It was the company I couldn't save. The people depending on me. The look of disappointment on my brother's face. My father's voice in my head, reminding me that my ambition would cost us everything.

And Ethan—god—Ethan was air.

Everything I needed.

But he didn't fucking deserve this mess. He was supposed to get the best version of me, not the one scrambling through the wreckage of what I'd burned down. I knew not choosing was its own kind of cruelty, but choosing Ethan in the middle of this would be worse.

Last night had made that brutally clear.

We'd almost made it to his apartment in silence. The tense kind. The city slid past outside the window, streetlights flickering over the dashboard.

"We need to talk," I said.

"Yeah." Luca's jaw tightened. "We do." The coldness in his voice didn't surprise me, but it made me aware of how stiff his posture had gotten.

"Are you coming up?" he asked, still looking away.

Traffic hummed past us as I bit the inside of my cheek and forced myself to push forward. "No."

Luca let out a hollow laugh. "You are unbelievable."

"Luca—"

"This was never about your rules," he snapped, turning toward me. "It was never about work. This is about your obsession with that guy."

I froze for a second, then adjusted in my seat. How could I deny it? "I'm sorry, Luca."

He shook his head, muttering a long string of Italian that I was sure were insults meant for me. "You've barely kissed me since—" He bit the side of his thumb, staring at his lap. "It is him. This is so fucking humiliating."

His hair fell over his eyes. Passing headlights flashed across his face, lighting up the frown tugging at his mouth.

I reached for him, but he pulled his arm away.

"Don't."

"I'm sorry," I said again.

I couldn't keep doing this. Faking it. Dragging him through the mess I'd created. Even if our relationship wasn't ever going to deepen, we'd been friends before everything got fucked up. I respected him, and I'd stopped acting like it.

The car slowed to a stop in front of his building. Neither of us moved.

I leaned a little closer—careful not to touch him. "Can I explain?"
A notification ping snapped me back to the present.
My phone lit up with a text.
Ethan.

PET

what you doing stranger?

My thumbs hovered over the keys. Always fucking hesitating with him.

ME

coffee?

PET

are you drinking it or do you want to get one?

ME

remember the café near my place?

PET

yeah

I needed to get this over with. The sooner, the better.

ME

can you meet me there?

He typed. Stopped. Typed again.

PET

be there in ten

ME

okay

This is it. Stop being a coward.

Changing quickly, I made my way downstairs and stepped out into the warm October afternoon. I walked the short distance to the café and chose a table outside, one of the small round ones tucked against the brick wall.

The street was alive with weekend noise—scooters whining past, low conversations drifting from nearby tables, and the clatter of cups and saucers from inside. The air was dry, threaded with the smell of coffee and cigarette smoke. It hit the back of my throat with a familiar bite, and for a brief, treacherous second, my body remembered the ritual—the slow inhale, the burn in my lungs, the illusion of control.

I flexed my fingers against the tabletop instead.

After signaling the server, two espressos arrived in quick succession, their bitter steam curling into the air. I set them in front of me and focused on the dark surface, willing my mind not to rewind to last night.

I spotted Ethan the moment he rounded the corner. Sunglasses, and one of those coordinated sets where the loose shirt matched the pants—effortlessly clean, understated, elegant. Very him.

Forcing my smile away, I schooled my expression into something neutral despite the heat gathering at the back of my neck.

"Hey," he said, voice low as he slid into the seat across from me. A small mercy that he didn't lean in to kiss my cheek this time.

"Hey." I nodded toward the cup in front of him. "Hope that's okay."

He pushed his glasses up and took a sip. "Perfect. Thanks."

Cars rolled by, sending warm bursts of air across the table. Inside, the espresso machine hissed, small sounds filling the space between us.

Ethan's eyes stayed on mine, a faint curve at one corner of his mouth that almost looked playful. But the tension in his body told another story. His leg bounced beneath the table, tapping a restless rhythm against the metal frame.

"So why the coffee place?" He rubbed his knuckles under his nose. "We could've gone up to yours, no?"

I looked toward the street, toward anything that wasn't him. "We have a rule about that."

His leg stopped, then started again, faster, a ringed finger drumming against the cup. "Yeah, but…" Something flickered behind his eyes. Not quite a question. A nudge.

"We need to be stricter about the rules," I said. "Otherwise—"

"Otherwise what?" His voice sharpened.

"Well… we're just friends, right?"

His mouth tightened, gaze dropping to his lap. "Right." After a beat, he pushed his chair back, the scrape loud against the stone floor as he stood.

"Ethan—"

His hands slid into his pockets. "Did you break up with him, Sebastian?"

The noise of the café pressed in around us, filling the space I didn't.

He let out a short breath through his nose, almost a laugh. "Okay."

"Ethan—"

"Fuck you." He started to walk away, then stopped and

turned back, facing me with something flat and furious in his eyes. "For the record," he said, "this is not how you keep the door open for someone." His jaw tightened. "You fucking lied."

Then he left.

And somehow, the calm on his face was worse than his anger.

I'd hoped for shouting—anything but that quiet certainty, like he'd already made peace with expecting nothing better from me. The guilt hit immediately, heavy and inescapable, settling inside me as I watched him disappear around the corner.

I didn't even manage an *I'm sorry.*

He's going to reach his limit with me. I'm screwing this up. Permanently.

I stayed there long after Ethan had gone, staring at the half-finished espresso growing cold in front of me. The street noise blurred into nothing until, finally, Luca's voice pushed through my head.

"No, I do not need your explanations. I can see very clearly what is going on between the two of you."

"I'm sorry. I didn't mean—"

"No more excuses, Sebastian," he said. *"You are practically foaming at the mouth every time he comes around. I actually thought you were better than that."*

That hit a nerve. "Better than that?"

"You are obsessed with a guy half your age—who acts like it—just because he is attractive and desperate to fuck you."

That's not what this is. That's not what we are.

All I managed was, "You don't know what you're talking about."

"I thought you were serious," he continued. *"That you wanted something real in spite of your stupid rules. But you have no idea how to be in a relationship, do you? You don't know how to stay for some-one. With you, it is always work. Always appearances."*

"That's not true."

Was it?

He let out a bitter laugh. "It isn't? I have never met anyone more addicted to the chase than you. You want trophies, Sebastian. Not people. This is not how you treat people." He shook his head slowly. *"I almost feel sorry for him. The disappointment he'll feel when his god, Sebastian Langley, finally comes crashing down."*

I held his gaze, saying nothing.

"You will keep him at arm's length. You keep everyone there."

The low hum of the engine filled the space between us.

"It is incredibly sad watching a man your age mistake obsession for love," he said, his voice turning cold. *"But it is not my fucking problem anymore."*

I remembered him opening the car door, the cool night air hitting my face.

"Have a nice life." The door slammed behind him.

My heart had been pounding—part anger, part something far worse.

Doubt.

Images flooded behind my eyes: Ethan's easy laughter, the way he refused to be pushed away, the way he stepped straight through every boundary I tried to build and stood there anyway, unapologetic and bright and impossible to ignore. The way he filled a room simply by existing in it. The way he looked at me like I was something worth reaching for. Like I was someone he believed in.

He wasn't the problem. He never had been.

Ethan was fire—open, reckless, alive. And I was the one standing too close to it, pretending I wouldn't burn.

Luca was wrong about many things, but not about this. I had no business reaching for something real when I could barely keep the rest of my life from splintering apart. Look what I'd already done. To Luca. To Ethan.

I couldn't do it. Not like this.

It was too soon. Too unfair to him.

So I did the only thing I knew how to do when the ground shifted beneath my feet.

I pulled everything back under control.

CHAPTER TWELVE
ETHAN

I walked into the apartment, straight to my room, and dropped face-first onto the bed. I squeezed my eyes shut against the burn gathering there and pulled in a deep breath to calm myself down.

It didn't work.

Fucking Sebastian Langley. Why did he have to be so goddamn stubborn?

"Hey," Henry's voice came through the door, followed by a knock and the soft creak as it opened. "How'd it go?"

I pushed myself upright and faced him.

His shoulders sagged the second he took in the expression on my face. "Oh, fuck. What did he say?"

My gaze dropped to my lap, a dry laugh slipping out. "That we're *friends*. I don't think I've ever hated that word more."

"Aw, babe, I fucking hate *this*."

"Don't." I slumped back on the bed, rubbing my hands hard over my face, hoping it might wipe the sting of tears away. "I knew this was going to happen." My lip wobbled anyway, and I bit down on it, trying to keep it together.

The mattress dipped as Henry sat beside me. "Maybe a little time…"

"He doesn't need *time*," I muttered into my hands. "What he needs is a glass of ice water to the face. Something to shock him out of whatever delusional restraint he's clinging to."

Henry huffed. "That would be fun to watch."

My stomach twisted painfully. All I could think about was last night—the way his body had given in to mine, the urgency in his mouth, the way he held me like he'd been starving for it. Compared to that, the stiffness from earlier felt like a punch straight to the gut.

"Why doesn't he ever choose me?" My voice came out small.

The mattress dipped beside me, Henry's fingers settling gently on my head. "E, Ash always chooses you."

My face tightened into a frown.

"I don't know what's going through his head right now," he said. "But don't ever think it's because he doesn't care."

I turned onto my side, finally looking at him. Henry was propped on his elbow, brows drawn, expression soft.

"I want to hurt him," I said quietly.

His eyebrows shot up.

"Not like that." My eyes drifted to the ceiling. "I want him to realize he's making a mistake. I don't want to be the one—" I shook my head. "I want *him* to beg. Not me."

Henry shrugged, face scrunching thoughtfully. "I mean, I guess I get that. Sounds fair."

"I'm so mad at him. Why the fuck didn't he break up with him?"

Henry blinked. "He didn't?"

"I don't think he did. I asked, and he just sat there staring at me with his stupid, broody eyes."

"Hey, we have the same stupid, broody eyes. Watch it."

I shoved his shoulder. "Don't be cute—I'm fucking pissed."

Henry chuckled. "I'm trying to lighten your mood."

I rolled onto my back, anger and ache clashing inside me, neither willing to give.

"Hey..." he said carefully. "I feel like I need to ask you something."

"What?"

"Have you actually tried talking to Ash about this? Like, have you two had an adult conversation about still having feelings for each other?"

"We talked about boundaries and being friends."

"While flirting and crossing every single one of them..."

"Well, yeah. That too."

"That's not what I asked." Henry pushed himself up slightly, his attention locking onto me. "Have you told him you want him back?"

We just stared at each other.

"You haven't, have you?" He let out a slow breath. "E... wanting him to admit it is fine. But pretending you don't care unless he says something first?" His brows lifted like he couldn't believe I was even arguing it. "That's bullshit, and you know it."

I swallowed, something in me bristling at how close that landed. "I'm not pretending."

"You are," he said. "You're acting like it's just about sex because that's safer. Because if he chooses you first, you don't have to risk anything."

My jaw clenched.

Henry watched me for a moment before speaking again, quieter this time. "And you know him better than anyone. You know he digs his heels in until someone forces him to move." He dragged a hand over his mouth, as if he was choosing his next words carefully. "I'm not saying that's on you," he added. "But this... game you're both playing? It's not getting either of you anywhere. I know it's scary—"

"I'm not scared," I cut in.

He tilted his head, clearly not buying it. "Sure, babe. You're behaving like a completely mature and well-balanced adult."

"You're the one who taught me I could get him to do what I wanted if I took my clothes off."

Henry barked a laugh. "That was fucking ages ago. I'm all grown up now—soon to be therapized and shit. My new advice is: you can't seduce him into being in love with you."

The sheets rustled softly as I moved.

"You can get him into bed," he added, "but that's not what you want, is it?"

I tilted my chin. "What if it is?"

Henry gave me a wan smile, one that said he knew better, then shrugged. "Then you're the one not playing fair, because that's not what he wants."

That made me pause, my walls dropping just a fraction. "He's still with his fucking boyfriend. What do you mean that's not what he wants?"

"Come on, E," he said. "You know him better than that." He sat up on the bed, offering me his hand. "Don't sell yourself short. Ask for what you really want."

I stared at his hand.

What I really wanted…

My mind tangled instantly—Sebastian and his games, my father and his, years of feeling unseen and unheard, wanting things I was never supposed to ask for. What was the point of wanting anything when no one ever wanted to give it to me? Life never handed me shit. If I wanted something, I had to take it.

"I know what I want," I said, rising from the bed without his aid.

Henry let his arm drop. "You do?"

I shrugged, a smile forming at the corner of my mouth. That wasn't how this was going to end.

This time, Sebastian didn't get the last word.

———

Work that week was somehow both fun and horrible.

VistaReal had turned out to be a great fit for me. The job was demanding, but it leaned straight into the things I was good at—reading a room, connecting dots no one else bothered to look at, catching what people muttered under their breath, and turning it into something useful.

Marcela noticed. That's how I ended up sitting in meetings people at my level usually heard about through office gossip instead of firsthand—because I could walk in, read the dynamics in thirty seconds, and hand her exactly what she needed. Did I understand every spreadsheet on sight? Absolutely not. But I always knew which questions to ask and which ones to save for a late-night Google deep dive. And every time I cracked something open or held my own in a room I technically had no business being in, it made me more confident—more certain I could get whatever the hell I set my sights on.

The company itself, though, felt… tight.

Phones rang more often and got answered faster. Conversations dropped to murmurs when certain names came up. Finance people walked the halls with clipped steps and tight jaws. Words like *audit scope, liquidity,* and *reallocation* floated through conference rooms as if everyone had suddenly learned a new language overnight.

And to top it off, the CFO of the company was now actively avoiding me.

Which was incredibly annoying, since *I* was the one avoiding *him.* How the hell was I supposed to punish him for his terrible decision-making if I didn't actually see him?

The truth was, he barely existed in the building anymore. When he did appear, it was between meetings, phone pressed to his ear, expression carved from stone. The few times I caught sight of him through glass walls or at the far end of a corridor, he looked like a man holding an entire structure upright by sheer force of will.

And even those tiny sightings made my stupid heart race. Every time I heard the click of expensive shoes in the hall or caught a trace of his cologne—Halfeti, of course—my whole body went on alert like I was being hunted.

I didn't know how to handle this new distance between us. Even through my anger, I didn't want to be away from him.

Confusing. Everything with Sebastian was always so fucking confusing.

Fortunately, Charlotte and Oliver were coming in a couple of weeks. That alone was enough to boost my mood. Spending time with my sister was the exact touching-grass moment I needed right now—a reminder that there was a whole life outside the Langley universe. I mean, technically she was in it too, but she was still *my* sister.

Also, that was probably going to force interactions between us. He could avoid me at work, but he sure as hell couldn't avoid me in social gatherings.

If there was one unexpected bright spot in the middle of all this, it was Vanessa. Sebastian's assistant had somehow become my lunch-break companion—and, possibly, my best chance at understanding what the hell was going on inside his fortress. She had proven to be an invaluable source of insider intel.

Not that I was gathering information.

I was just… staying informed.

She found me out in the courtyard on Thursday, the midday sun warming my shoulders while the wind tunneled between the buildings and chilled my ankles. Madrid couldn't commit to a temperature.

Much like someone else I knew.

"Why are you out here?" Vanessa asked, dropping onto the bench beside me.

"It was getting stifling in there."

That—and Mr. Boss Man had asked Marcela, in an unsurprising turn of events, to keep their meeting to department heads only, effectively running me out of it. He didn't even look at me when he said it. Just a polite smile. No eye contact. Like I was a fucking intern he'd barely met.

Out here, at least, I could breathe without feeling the weight of his dismissal pressing down on my lungs.

"There's AC in there," she pointed out.

"Allegedly." I took a bite of my sandwich. "Also, the vibe screams *impending financial apocalypse.*"

She snorted. "Fair."

A gust of wind lifted the edge of my napkin.

"Are you going to Sebastian's party tomorrow?" she asked.

The bite became significantly harder to swallow. "I'm not sure yet…"

"Henry's called me three times today alone to check on Sebastian's guest list."

I frowned. "How come?"

"Says he needs RSVPs for masks or something." She poked at her lunch with a plastic fork.

"That's weird."

"You know what's super weird?" Vanessa looked at me through her fringe with a sly smile.

"What?"

She went back to eating with the most fake-disinterested expression I'd ever seen.

"Why are you edging me?"

She laughed, then turned toward me again. "Luca hasn't RSVPed."

"Seriously?" My eyebrows shot up and my pulse jumped— way too obvious—and I took another bite to hide it.

She nodded, scooting a little closer. "I asked Sebastian about it today, and he said Luca was out of town—but that seems weird, right? Like… it's his birthday. And he hasn't been over in a while."

God, I loved her.

"Maybe they're fighting."

"Maybe." Another bite. Then, "So… are you going?"

I leaned back, staring across the courtyard where employees

hurried between buildings like nothing in the world was shifting under their feet.

He could avoid me in the halls, in meetings, behind glass walls, and with polite smiles, but he couldn't avoid me at his own party.

"It's Saints and Sinners, right?"

She nodded.

"What's he wearing?"

"A hot-as-sin suit from Prada. I picked it up for him two days ago."

I chewed as an idea began forming—slow at first, then picking up speed, turning into something wicked.

He wanted control? Wanted distance?

Perfect.

Let him try to keep it.

"Do you know any good costume shops?"

She leaned back on the bench. "Are we talking prim and proper or provocative?"

"Provocative." I grinned. "Definitely provocative."

CHAPTER THIRTEEN

ASH

stared at myself in the mirror.

The suit worked perfectly—dark burgundy with smooth silk lapels, tailored to fit like it had been sculpted onto my body. One of a kind. Striking. The kind of thing that should have sparked something—vanity, satisfaction, or a flicker of pride.

Nothing.

Just a flat, hollow quiet.

I lifted my glass of whiskey—my third in less than an hour—and let it burn on the way down before setting it on the table beside me.

Thirty-nine.

Thirty-*fucking*-nine.

And what did I have to show for it?

I had walked away from my title in my father's empire—a father I was no longer speaking to—to build something of my own, and now I was getting to watch it implode in slow motion.

My relationships with both of my brothers felt strained, and the fault sat squarely with me. One I couldn't face after my professional disaster. The other I'd hurt by doing the exact opposite of what he'd asked of me—which had been so simple. Don't hurt his best friend.

And my love life—god. It had always been a mess, but right now it was collapsing in spectacular fashion, entirely of my own making.

Nothing was the way it was supposed to be.

And adding another year to my age only made the humiliation harder to ignore.

My reflection looked the same, but I felt older. Brittle around the edges. Exhausted in a way sleep never fixed—the kind that came from endless hours staring at spreadsheets and contracts, from late-night calls and emergency meetings, from trying and failing to find a way to stop everything from falling apart.

I picked up the glass again and drained it.

A tap sounded on the doorframe. "Jesus, Ash. Pace yourself." Henry leaned against it, dressed in sleek black from head to toe, the crisp white collar of a very stylish priest costume giving him a holier-than-thou edge he absolutely did not deserve. "It's your party, not your funeral."

I kept my eyes on the mirror. "Feels like both."

"You're being dramatic. Forty is not that bad."

"You know I'm turning thirty-nine," I snapped.

"And apparently that comes with a loss of humor." He sighed. "And here I was, ready to come in and give you a hard time. But you seem to be managing that well enough on your own."

I let out a slow breath and poured myself another drink—one for Henry too. "Are you going to give me shit about Ethan again?"

Henry pushed off the doorway and came to lean against the mirror's edge, hand outstretched for his glass. "That *was* the plan." His eyes flicked over my face, and for once he wasn't wearing a smirk. "You look sad, Ash. Are you okay?"

"You know I'm not a fan of birthdays. It gets worse with each one."

Another drink gone. I adjusted my tie, fingers a little too

precise. "Is Ethan coming?" My voice dropped before I could stop it.

Henry shrugged and took a sip, eyebrows lifting in appreciation. I'd pulled out the good stuff. Getting older and all that.

"He didn't say. I haven't seen him all day." He stepped beside me, checking his reflection. "How about Luca?"

I turned from the mirror and crossed to the vanity, grabbing my cologne and giving myself a couple of sprays. The familiar scent settled in the air as I rolled my lips, debating how much to disclose. I didn't want to lie to my brother—but I had a feeling he wouldn't keep the information to himself. Just like my lovely assistant, who had recently decided that Ethan was the best thing to happen to the office. And she *really* had trouble keeping things to herself.

I settled on a very vague "Who knows."

"Are you still fighting over the party?"

My lips pulled into a frown.

Henry cocked his head. "Does he know you kissed E?"

"Are you trying to make this day even more miserable?"

His eyebrows lifted. "No. You seem to be doing fine on your own."

Another fucking pang of guilt.

"Let's just get this over with," I mumbled.

"Gee, thanks, little brother, for putting together this amazing party in my name. Oh no, Ash, it's my pleasure. Anything for my big brother. It wasn't a problem at all." He walked in front of me, miming the whole conversation.

"Thank you, Henny."

He turned back to me, sheepish. "It's not fun if you're actually in a bad mood."

I shook my head. "I'll get over it."

We rode to the venue, not too far away, while Henry kept chatting beside me. He had a habit of doing that—filling the silence when he was uncomfortable or when he knew someone else was having a hard time. Normally, I'd let him distract me.

Tonight, I didn't have it in me to play along. I just needed to get through the evening so I could spend tomorrow at home wallowing in dignified self-pity.

The venue was… a lot.

Red drapery hung from the ceiling in long, dramatic swaths, pooling into the shadows like spilled silk. Chandeliers glittered overhead—massive, obsidian-dark structures dripping gold and throwing warm light across the room, so everything glowed in shades of crimson and candlelight. Every surface gleamed. Every corner flickered. It was decadent in that curated, slightly sinful way Henry adored: a room built to blur the line between indulgence and excess.

Roses—deep red, almost black—sat in narrow vases, looking more like props than flowers, their shadows long and theatrical against the walls. Servers moved as if they'd rehearsed it, slipping through the room with trays of champagne and lowball glasses. Somewhere above, an aerialist swung lazily on a ring, her body carving slow arcs of shadow across the draped ceiling.

It smelled like wine, roses, expensive perfume, and melted wax. Saints and Sinners, Henry had said. More like a cathedral built for sin.

"This is amazing, Henny," I said, readily accepting the glass a server offered. I took a sip. Perfect.

Henry paced in front of me with his arms spread wide, the picture of smug delight. "A night to remember, right?" Then he held something out—an ornate mask.

I lifted a brow. "Really?"

"Fit for the devil," he said, grinning as he slipped a rosary over his neck like it was an accessory instead of sacrilege.

I turned the mask over in my hand. Red leather, deep ridges carved into the brow, sweeping upward into stylized horns. Silk ties, of course. Henry wouldn't allow elastic anywhere near his aesthetic. I sighed, resigned, placing my drink on a nearby table, and donned the mask.

"Well," Henry said, stepping back to admire his work. "Terrifying. Exactly what we were going for."

He drifted toward someone across the room, already pulled into conversation, leaving me alone just as Elena appeared at my side, immaculate as ever, a glass of champagne poised between her fingers.

"Happy birthday, Ash." She brushed a kiss against my cheek.

"Thank you."

Her gaze moved once around the room before settling back on me. "I was under the impression we agreed to stop pursuing the state follow-up."

My stomach tightened. I took a measured sip of my drink. "We did."

"Oscar seems to think otherwise." Her tone remained even. "He mentioned revisions. Calls."

Heat climbed the back of my neck.

"We are under review," she continued. "This is not the moment to test boundaries."

I held her gaze, jaw set.

She held it longer. "We agreed to pivot," she said. "Not to push."

The music swelled behind us. Laughter broke out somewhere near the bar.

"I want you in Seville on Monday," she added. "Private consortium. Infrastructure and energy. Be useful there."

Be useful. Not fix this. Not lead. Not solve. Had I lost her trust already?

I nodded once. "Send me the details."

"Try to enjoy your party, Ash." Her expression softened just enough to remain human. "Life is so much more than this. Don't lose sight of that."

The words landed somewhere deep and unwelcome. For a split second, I saw what she meant—a life not measured in balance sheets and crisis calls, in victories wrestled from collapse. A life where tonight could simply be a birthday, not a ledger of failures.

I shut the thought down before it could take root.

This was the job. This was the cost.

Seville would mean distance, not surrender. If I couldn't push here, I would push there. Quietly. Away from the microscope.

I nodded once.

She gave me one uncertain smile before she moved back into the crowd.

I finished my drink in one swallow.

"Hey, look at that—ran out already," Henry said, eyeing my empty glass before guiding me deeper into the room, his hand warm at my back as he steered me through the press of bodies.

We slid up to the bar. Henry leaned over the counter with practiced ease, and I followed, setting my glass down.

The bartender—masked, shirt half-open, fully on theme—inclined his head toward it. "Another?"

I lifted a brow in answer, and he reached for the bottle.

Beside me, Henry said, "You know, if you keep drinking like that, you'll hit forty before midnight."

"Perfect," I said into the fresh glass. "Maybe then the rest of my life will catch up."

Henry's smile pulled a little tight as he looked me over. "You're really going through it, huh?"

I lifted a shoulder—nothing else to give him.

He tapped the toe of his shoe against the bar. "You know who's getting older too?"

I shot him a look, waiting for the pitch.

"Dad," he said, hopeful in that annoyingly Henry way.

My eyes went up before I could stop them, rolling back. "Henny, come on. Right now? Really?"

"I mean..." He shrugged. "As long as life is feeling all vulnerable and shit. Just a call, Ash. You know you're the bigger person. And what if you regret this?"

I dragged a hand down my face, turning my back to the bar. Absolutely not. "Not tonight."

"But, Ash—"

That was as far as he got, because in that exact instant the world stopped.

It wasn't gradual. Not subtle. It was a full, visceral *halt*—like my brain short-circuited and my body forgot its basic functions.

Near the back of the room was a staircase—elegant, spotlighted, and unfortunately positioned directly in my line of sight. And standing at the top of it, descending slowly—deliberately so —eyes locked on mine…

Was Ethan.

But not *just* Ethan.

Ethan dressed in the most exquisitely sinful way I had ever seen him in my life.

His summer-warm skin gleamed—actually gleamed— candlelight dragging gold across it with every step. And there was so much of it on display. An alarming, illegal amount. Because the only thing he was wearing was the smallest, most perfectly arranged Greek robe.

Golden straps wrapped up his calves in tight, crisscrossing lines, drawing my gaze up the firm cut of his legs. The miniature skirt hit high on his thighs—far too high—and a single white sash crossed over his otherwise bare chest, leaving every line of muscle exposed. His curls were a chaotic, beautiful mess around his face as he moved, each step unhurried, like he knew exactly what he was doing to me.

And then—because apparently my sanity wasn't fragile enough—he had wings. A small, fluffy white pair of angel wings perched on his back, soft and ridiculous and devastating, because the rest of him looked like sin carved into flesh.

This wasn't a costume. It was a provocation.

And I was speechless.

"Hey, are you alive?" Henry's voice came from somewhere to my right.

Still no words. No breath. Just Ethan continuing his slow descent. Heads turned as he passed—double takes, outright stares—and that small, tantalizing smirk on his mouth.

A hand waved in front of my face. "Ash?"

"Oh my fucking god," I whispered. My body reacted before my brain caught up, heat unfurling low, the kind that made thinking nearly impossible.

"What—" Henry shifted beside me, following my line of sight. "Oh boy."

Ethan reached the first floor and started toward us—toward me—while the crowd seemed to part for him like he was some goddamn deity stepping down from Olympus.

"Ash." Henry's hand landed on my shoulder, firm. "Ash, pull it together."

"What?" It didn't even sound like my voice.

"He's getting closer. Pull it together," Henry hissed, shaking me like he could physically shove sense back into me. "Pull it together. Pull it together."

Whatever he was trying to aim for, it wasn't working.

"Okay—fine. Then at least close your mouth?"

My jaw clicked shut on command just as Ethan stopped in front of us, chin tipped up to hold my gaze.

"Hi, birthday boy," he said, voice even raspier than usual.

A sound came out of me—something caught between a hum and a groan and absolutely *not* a dignified greeting. I cleared my throat like that might erase it.

Ethan's perfectly plush lips curved. "Save me a dance?"

My throat refused to function, so I lifted my glass and gave what I hoped passed for a nod.

He grinned—slow and intentional—and that's when I noticed the golden leaves woven into his curls.

Jesus *fucking* Christ.

"Gotta make the rounds," he murmured, then winked. Naturally. He turned, walking away with the kind of confidence that guaranteed I'd be watching. His entire back was bare, the tiny skirt downright obscene, pulling my gaze down the line of his spine to the flex of the back of his thighs.

Another sound slipped out of me—this one undeniably a groan.

"Christ," Henry muttered, pressing his fingers to his temple. "I've never felt secondhand embarrassment this bad. Absolute cringefest."

I rounded on him, setting my glass on the table before grabbing his shoulders.

His eyes went wide. "What?"

"You cannot leave me alone with Ethan tonight, Henry."

His lips parted, tongue pushing into his cheek as his gaze flicked away for a beat. "Yeah, that's fair. You're already drinking like a maniac, sad because you're turning—"

I shot him a warning look.

"*Thirty-nine,*" he said carefully. "And he's dressed as what I'm guessing is your biggest fantasy. You've gotta hand it to him, though—the kid's smart."

I gave him a shake. "Henny."

His eyes snapped back to mine.

"It's imperative."

He slipped out of my grip, smoothing his shirt like I'd wrinkled his soul. "Okay, yeah. I get it. Keep you two apart. Super easy, by the way." The sarcasm was back in full force.

I reached for my drink again, but Henry stopped me halfway, palm to my wrist. "Are you really going to make my job harder?"

Now I wanted the drink purely out of spite. Unfortunately, he wasn't wrong.

"Now what?" I asked, defeated.

"Now we mingle." Henry adjusted his collar, grinned, and pulled me straight into the crowd.

What followed was a blur. Hour after hour of greeting people

—colleagues, clients, business associates, all drinking behind masks while the room tilted a little more with each passing minute. Henry dragged me through photos and endless toasts, and I did my best to pretend my smile wasn't so fake it could've cracked off my face, aware of eyes lingering a second too long, of the quiet appraisal that came with rooms full of investors and partners.

And every time I caught a flash of golden curls or warm, shimmering skin somewhere in the crowd, I turned away immediately, focusing on anything else. Anyone else.

My brother deserved a fucking award for shepherding me through the night.

Until he spotted Mateo.

One smile—that was all it took. Henry veered off like a heat-seeking missile, leaving me stranded with a pack of investment bankers and absolutely no emotional support. Apparently, the Langley brothers shared a crippling lack of responsibility in the face of sexual attraction.

The second I could excuse myself, I drifted away and through the crowd, nodding at passersby, lifting my glass in greeting, trying to look like a functioning adult instead of a man circling a breakdown.

Eventually I found an exit—a stone balcony draped in roses, with a few scattered tables and chairs. Blessedly empty.

I sagged into the nearest chair, slumping back with a groan. Tugging the mask off my face, I let the cool evening air hit my skin, and for the first time all night, I actually breathed in. Unfortunately, the way the balcony tilted when I closed my eyes probably wasn't a great sign.

"What a surprise," a husky voice said. "You're hiding again."

My eyes lifted—baby blue hit me straight in the chest. Ethan stood in the doorway, arms crossed, curls a mess around his face.

Fuck. Me.

"Needed fresh air." At least I could get words out now. Improvement, technically.

He smiled, then walked over and sank into a seat. The tables were tiny, the chairs shoved close together, so his thigh brushed mine immediately and stayed there. Bare. Warm. Glimmering.

Don't look. Don't look. Sebastian, don't—

"Nice party."

My gaze drifted over him before I managed to drag it back to his face. Not much safer. I fucking loved his face. "Henry's good at that." I finished what was left of my drink and set the glass down, maybe a little harder than I meant to.

Ethan's eyes flicked to it. His lips twitched, and then his hand moved—fingers walking over until they found my wrist. Heat shot up my arm as his thumb traced lazy circles on my skin.

"Are you having fun?" he asked, voice low, hypnotic. It always did things to me, but tonight—Christ, it was worse. Or better. Both.

Alarms should've been blaring, but apparently, I was ignoring all of them. I leaned in automatically, careful not to disturb his hand. "I am now."

Ethan grinned. "Do you like the outfit?" His leg slid between mine, his thigh tensing against me. The gold shimmer on his skin caught the moonlight.

"I love it," I said before I could stop myself.

He looked entirely too pleased with that.

"How did you know?"

We were closer—his hand had somehow reached the bend of my elbow now. I'd ditched the jacket and rolled up my sleeves earlier, so the slow drag of his thumb there felt... really fucking good.

"You said something once," he murmured, swallowing. "That I looked like a Greek statue come to life. You told Charlotte. Remember?"

I nodded dumbly. "So... was this for my benefit?"

"Happy birthday," was all he said.

I licked my too-dry lips, and his eyes followed the movement like he wanted to taste it. "What did I do to deserve such pleasure? I thought we were fighting."

Ethan hummed, moving into me. Of course I followed. His hand slid up from my arm, fingertips brushing over my beard in a slow caress.

"You're supposed to get gifts on your birthday."

A low chuckle slipped out of me. "And are you mine?"

Something flickered in his eyes—too quick for my drunken brain to catch. Then he leaned in closer, guiding my face with a soft press of his fingers until his cheek hovered right beside mine.

"You know what I'd do if I were?" he whispered, warm breath spilling into my ear and sending a full-body shiver down my spine. "Yours."

"What?"

His hand glided from my neck down to my chest, curling into my shirt and tugging me closer. "I'd take you somewhere dark," he breathed, "but still in plain view. Crowd you against a wall, hold your hips in place."

My pulse hammered, my restraint snapping thread by thread.

"Then I'd get on my knees."

My cock—which had been hard from the moment he appeared on that staircase—throbbed in my pants.

His fingers released my shirt, then traced slowly downward, stopping at my belt. "I'd pop this button, drag the zipper down, and reach inside..." His voice dropped into something lower, filthier. My eyes fluttered shut. "...pull that big cock out, and give it a few slow strokes. Just enough to make sure it's nice and hard for me."

Fuck.

Fuck. Fuck. Fuck.

"And then," he whispered, "I'd run my tongue all over it—"

The warm drag of his tongue against the shell of my ear made a sound tear out of me, raw and helpless.

"—before taking it into my mouth and making you cum down my throat."

Hard. I was so hard it was painful.

My body was coiled tight, mind emptied of every rational thought. Everything except *him*. Taking him. Having him. Pulling him into my lap, kissing him until he melted, getting him naked and open, and letting him ride me however the fuck he wanted—

I reached for him without thinking, my hand sliding to the thigh pressed between mine, my palm molding to the heat of his skin, and a broken sound almost slipped out of me at the relief of finally touching him.

Ethan was panting softly into my ear when his fingers closed around my wrist. But instead of guiding me where I wanted, he lifted my hand away. "Too bad you don't get to touch."

What?

My mind lagged behind, still trying to process what he'd said, while my body had already surged ahead, already choosing him without hesitation.

He leaned back just enough for me to see his face—close, but out of reach. All that molten warmth gone, replaced with something cold.

"Too bad you made the wrong choice," he said, head tilting slightly. "So instead of doing all of that…"

He let the silence drag, punishing.

"…the only thing you get to do is go back to your apartment —alone—and jerk off thinking about me."

The words landed like a slap.

Realization filtered through the haze, piece by brutal piece, until I understood exactly what this was. "We're still fighting." It wasn't a question. It landed in my chest like a weight.

Ethan nodded once, dropping my hand. "Happy birthday, *friend*." Venom coated the word.

I sank back into the chair, humiliation burning up my throat. I had no right to feel betrayed—not after everything—but the denial, the distance, the reminder of what I had forfeited twisted something raw inside me. I closed my eyes and tried to breathe through it.

You chose this. You let this happen. You failed him. You failed everyone.

Pressure built behind my ribs, tight and relentless, Elena's voice folding into Henry's disappointment, into my father's warnings, into the audit and the freeze and the slow collapse of everything I had built, until the weight of it pressed down so hard it felt impossible to draw a full breath.

And Ethan—right here, within reach and yet utterly out of bounds—was the one thing that had always quieted the noise; the one place I could set the burden down, and now even that was closed to me.

I couldn't control anything.

Not the company. Not the damage. Not myself.

The guilt raked through me, sharp enough to tear, and without the thin layer of restraint I had been clinging to all night, the words slipped out. "Why are you here?" The accusation sounded foreign to my own ears, jagged and raw.

Because if he wasn't here, I could think.

Because if he wasn't here, I wouldn't feel myself splitting open.

"Why did you have to follow me here?" My voice cracked. "I can't think with you *everywhere*."

Silence answered me.

Too much of it.

I forced my eyes open—

And the look on his face knocked the breath from my lungs.

Wide eyes. Wounded. Unprotected.

Because I had put that there.

My stomach dropped.

No. No, no, no.

"That's not what I meant," I said quietly, uselessly, but it was already too late.

Ethan pushed to his feet, jaw tight, eyes bright in the low light, and without a word, without looking back, he turned and walked out, leaving me sitting there like the world's biggest fucking idiot.

What the hell had I just done?

My phone pinged, the sound slicing through the noise in my head.

I stared at it for a moment before reaching into my pocket, my hand unsteady as I pulled it free. My breath turned shallow, pulse hammering as I looked down.

ARIA

I hate being the bearer of bad news

but I thought I'd give you a heads-up

I had this one taken down but you know they have a habit of popping up anyway

Happy birthday Ash

A link waited beneath the message. Somewhere in the middle of it, I'd stood. I hadn't even felt it happen.

My thumb hovered before tapping down. The page loaded slowly, and when it did, two photographs filled the screen. The first showed Luca and me arriving at Mateo's gallery opening, his hand at my back, cameras catching us mid-step as if we were something curated for display. The second was from the café— *that* afternoon, the day I had set out to break Ethan's heart. They had captured the exact instant he'd looked up at me, smiling warmly, something open and unguarded in his face, something that had never belonged to anyone but me.

Below the images, a headline stretched across the page—not kind in the slightest—accusing me of exactly what had happened and dragging both of them into public scrutiny once again.

"Fuck!" The word ripped out of me, loud against the terrace air, taking the last thin thread of sanity I had left with it.

Happy fucking birthday to me.

CHAPTER FOURTEEN

ETHAN

The apartment door slammed shut behind me, the echo carrying through the space as anger surged under my skin. But beneath it—under the heat and the sting—something far worse pulsed. Something empty.

He doesn't want me.

Why the fuck did I even come here? Why the hell was I in this city, dressed like this, chasing after what? A man who couldn't even look at me without flinching?

Tearing at the costume—the sash, the skirt, the stupid wings—I yanked everything off in one frantic motion. Storming into the bathroom, I twisted the shower to hot until steam swallowed the mirror, then grabbed a fistful of makeup wipes, dragging them over my skin with shaking hands, scrubbing at the shimmer, the bronzer, the glitter clinging like a reminder of how stupid I'd been.

Desperate. I looked desperate.

Because that's what I was, right?

Desperate to have him.

Desperate to matter.

Desperate to be someone worth choosing.

So fucking desperate that when my dad took everything from

me, I just… let him. Didn't fight. Didn't defend myself. Didn't even ask why.

And this job? This city? I had to run straight to *him*. Of course I did. I insisted on staying close because I always fucking do that. I always choose the people who won't choose me back. I gave him my heart once, and he shoved it straight back at me. Because who would want it in the first place?

I scrubbed harder until my skin went red under my fingers and the wipes piled up in the sink. The shower roared behind me, fogging the mirror until I couldn't see myself at all.

His words replayed over and over, hitting deeper each time.

Why are you here?

I can't think with you everywhere.

My breath stuttered out of me.

I stepped into the heat, but the shower didn't help, because underneath the humiliation, the shame, the glitter smeared across my hands… was the truth I hated most:

I'd wanted him to look at me the way I've always looked at him.

And he couldn't even stand to be around me.

Nothing was helping. Nothing slowed my thoughts or steadied my breathing or eased the raw burn in my chest.

Why did you follow me here?

The tone of his voice—his beautiful, smooth voice—turned cold and resentful. Turned on me.

He didn't want me.

I pulled on sweats with clumsy hands, shut off the lights, and crawled into bed, yanking the covers over my head as if that could silence everything. Like darkness could drown the noise.

My heart wouldn't settle on a single emotion. It ricocheted between heartbreak and rage so fast it made my head spin. My eyes stung, and I blinked hard, refusing to let that happen. I was not crying over him. Not again.

Why did I have to provoke him?

Did I just fuck this up? For good?

No.

No, I wasn't letting this take me apart. If he didn't want me like this—

He did.

I knew he did. I saw it in the way he looked at me tonight, like he was starving. But I didn't know how to reach out for the thing I actually wanted from him. Not sex. Not the power play. Not the games.

Henry's voice crept in: *Ask for what you want.*

What if what I want sends him running? What if he rejects me again?

An hour passed. Maybe more. An hour of lying there, trapped between longing and self-loathing, between wanting him and resenting him, between hating myself for caring and hating him for making me feel like this. An hour of wanting sleep and knowing I wasn't going to get it.

And then the buzzing started.

I pushed the covers down and checked my phone.

A call from the doorman? At this hour?

"Hello?"

"Mr. Bennett, Sebastian Langley is here for you, asking if he can come up."

My stomach dropped. First relief—*he came, he fucking came—*then indignation rising fast.

"Let him up," I said, already pushing out of bed.

I walked to the front door, every step fueled by everything he'd said to me tonight, but paused with my hand braced against the frame, forcing a slow breath into my lungs.

This was close to what I wanted. But not close enough for me to give in.

By the time I stepped into the hallway, the softness had already sealed itself away. A moment later, the elevator opened, and Sebastian stepped out—rumpled, flushed, eyes going straight to mine. He didn't look angry anymore. He looked wrecked.

My chest ached, but I held the line. "You've got some real nerve showing up here right now."

He stopped in front of me, jaw tight. "Ethan—"

"No." I cut him off immediately. "I didn't let you up here for you to take the easy way out."

He faltered, guilt written all over him. "I came to apologize—"

"Yeah," I interrupted, "but you're not doing it drunk in the middle of the night because you're lonely on your birthday. You don't get the easy way out." My arm stayed braced across the doorway, keeping him where he was.

"Then what?"

Do it, Ethan. Fucking do it.

Ask for what you want.

"You're going to break up with your fucking boyfriend, *then* you'll apologize." I leaned in a little. "And you're going to admit you fucked up. With me. With all of it. But you're not doing it like this."

His gaze stayed locked on mine.

Ask. For. It.

"You're going to do it on your knees, Sebastian," I said, my voice unsteady despite the control I was forcing into it. "I want you to *crawl* to me. I want you to *beg*."

His eyes widened—probably more at the conviction behind the words than the demand itself—and for a split second, something in them broke through. Not arrogance. Not control. Something raw and unsteady. It hit me deep in the chest—the same place he always reached without trying, making my resolve waver. I could end this right now. Pull him inside. Let him hold me. Let everything fall back into the shape it always took when he touched me.

But if I folded now, nothing would change. I would still be the secret. The almost. The thing he reached for in private and denied in daylight.

I held his gaze and didn't move. "And you're going to be

stone-cold sober when you do it," I added. "I deserve that much."

He swallowed, then nodded once.

"Go home." And I closed the door before he could say anything else. I stayed there against it, breath unsteady. "Fuck."

He deserved that.

He really did.

But doubt pushed at me anyway, trying to wedge its way in. I dragged my hands down my face.

From the other side of the door came the soft scrape of his shoes, then a dull sound—maybe his forehead resting against it. "You're right," he said. "You don't deserve this."

Pressure built under my ribs as his steps retreated. The elevator chimed—metal slid shut, and he was gone.

Again.

I slid down the door until I was sitting on the floor, elbows on my knees, head in my hands. "Fuck," I whispered. "Fuck."

———

Charlotte was about to arrive. Henry had stepped out to get groceries and then stayed downstairs, waiting for them to get here. They'd landed a couple of hours ago, gotten settled at the hotel, and were coming straight over. After that, Charlotte would stay with me, and Oliver and Henry would go see Sebastian.

Because that's where we were right now. Like a divorced couple splitting up the kids.

This last week had been terrible. I'd felt solid in my resolve, waiting for Sebastian to come find me and finally say *I'm sorry*. But he hadn't.

Vanessa told me he'd left for Seville on a work trip, which—fine—at least meant he wasn't actively avoiding me again. But he'd been back since yesterday, and when Henry suddenly announced that tonight was brothers' night, I hadn't been invited.

I was fucking miserable and one short step away from crying or breaking something.

No.

Not breaking. The anger had quieted—backed down from rage and gone stale. It didn't feel better, though. It felt heavy. And I couldn't ignore the fact that he still hadn't chosen me. I didn't even know whether he'd broken up with Luca or not.

I thought I was holding it together, but that illusion shattered the moment I opened the door and saw Charlotte standing on the other side of it. My eyes welled instantly, and her easy smile turned into concern in under a second. She wrapped her arms around my neck, and I let the tears fall quietly against her shoulder, holding on, something in me giving in. Her perfume—warm jasmine—was familiar enough to crack me wide open.

"Hey, E. What's wrong?"

"I missed you."

Her arms tightened. "Is that all?"

I shook my head, and she didn't push. Just held me.

Oliver looked confused and a little worried when we finally stepped apart. I wiped my eyes, tried to keep the conversation light, and after the Langleys left, it was just Charlotte and me on the couch with glasses of red wine and takeout on the way.

"Okay. Done." She set her phone down, took a sip, and fixed me with that *Charlotte* look. "Let's talk about it."

I slumped deeper into the couch, practically sinking into the cushions. "Sebastian and I are fighting."

"I figured. About the boyfriend?"

"That and… a bunch of other stuff." My gaze flicked to hers, sheepish, fingers picking at a loose thread on the couch cushion. "We kissed."

Her eyes widened. "What? When?"

"A little while ago."

"And was it like…" She let the implication hang.

"Cheating, yeah."

Her expression didn't just shift—it hardened. The disappointment was clear, turning my stomach sour.

"Ethan…"

"It's Sebastian," I cut in quickly, the words coming out defensively before I could make them anything else. "This isn't like—they weren't all that serious."

"Come on, E. Don't make it smaller than it is."

"I'm not," I muttered.

"But you're acting like it's not a big deal." Her voice took on that familiar edge—too tight to be calm. "You don't get to do that just because it's Ash."

Something in me pushed back immediately, instinctive and stubborn. "He's not just—" I stopped, exhaling sharply, dragging a hand through my hair. "This is different."

"Is it?" Her brows lifted. "Because from where I'm sitting, it looks pretty similar. Someone on the outside, convincing themselves it means more. That it's justified. That it's—what—inevitable?"

Heat flared under my skin. "It *is* different. You don't get it."

"I do get it." Her voice didn't rise—it dropped, controlled in a way that made it worse. "And you do too." A beat. "You know what this does to the person on the other side. You've seen it happen."

The guilt hit hard, but I pushed against it once more, clinging to the only thing that made this make sense in my head. "He was mine first," I said, quieter now, but no less certain. "Before all of this. Before Luca."

"Ethan." Charlotte's gaze didn't waver. "That doesn't give you a free pass to hurt someone else."

My gaze dropped to my hands. "I'm not trying to hurt anyone."

"But you did." The words settled heavily between us. She ran a hand through her hair, exhaling, some of the tension slipping but not disappearing. "I'm not saying this is all on you. Sebastian should have known better," she said. "But I'm going to take a wild guess and say you were pushing all the right buttons?"

My stomach roiled. "Fine," I muttered. "Fine. Yes. I fucked up."

Charlotte's lips curved into a small smile—relieved. Her hand landed on my knee, giving it a light squeeze. "Admitting it is the first step. I get that things can get out of hand, E. I do." She hesitated, her tone softening. "I just… don't like seeing you be that person."

I scrubbed a hand over my face. "Me neither." I didn't know what to do with that. Did Luca even know? About the kiss. About any of it? Or was he still walking around thinking everything was fine?

If I was being really honest with myself… he wasn't the bad guy here. He hadn't done anything wrong—he'd just been there. I was the one who crossed the line.

And that made it a hell of a lot harder to sit with.

Charlotte propped her elbow on the back of the couch, fingers threading through her hair. "There are a couple of pieces floating around online. You, Sebastian, and Luca. I thought it was just gossip."

I rolled my eyes. "There's always gossip." It barely registered. People had been talking about me long enough for it to blur into background noise.

But the thought snagged a second later.

Sebastian hated that noise. Hated the scrutiny. He'd spent years keeping his life sealed off from it—no personal interviews, no social media, no trail that wasn't strictly professional—especially after the first time our names had been dragged through the headlines.

And now, with the company already being picked apart, with articles dissecting every move VistaReal made, this would only feed the narrative. Personal scandal layered neatly over professional instability.

I reached for my glass and took a longer sip, unease settling in heavier over the whole mess.

"Did he break up with him?"

I sank even further into the couch. "I don't know."

She blinked. "How do you not know?"

"Because he's annoying and can't say anything to my fucking face in a way that's actually clear." I rubbed my feet on the carpet. "The only thing I know is that Luca hasn't been around or calling because his assistant told me. And he didn't go to Sebastian's birthday."

She arched a brow. "His assistant?"

I reached for my glass too fast, sloshing the wine a little. "We're office friends."

"Right… because you're working with him." Her voice softened into suspicion. "Can you explain to me why? Because that's a question you've been avoiding too."

I didn't want to tell her the truth about everything. My eyes dropped to the wine, watching it swirl around the bowl of the glass, my thumb tracing the stem over and over just to give my hands something to do.

Guess I was just as good as Sebastian at sidestepping conversations—hiding what mattered until it spilled out somewhere public and messy.

Fuck that—

I told her everything instead.

Right from the beginning with Dad, all the way to that final call and me having to accept everything was gone. Charlotte went through her glass of wine. Then a second one. Her eyes kept getting wider through the whole story, and that little vein at her temple started to throb.

By the time I finished, she was pacing in front of the couch, shaking her head like she could barely contain herself.

"I'm going to fucking kill him," she declared.

Whoa. Charlotte swearing?

"There's a line for that," I muttered.

"That slimy weasel"—she jabbed a finger in the air—"And Mom did tell me he moved. She was furious because he left without telling her and apparently owed her money. This is just too much."

Yeah… I really was never going to see a cent of it again. Things genuinely couldn't get worse.

She sat down again, hand landing gently on my thigh, eyes huge and pleading. "Why didn't you tell me? I could've helped."

"I figured it out, Char." I swallowed. "Sebastian helped, but… I figured it out. And I don't want you to worry or feel like you need to support me. The last thing I want is for him to be right and for me to just live off the Langleys forever."

Her expression didn't budge. "If you didn't want the money, that's fine. But why didn't you let me help you *go through* all of that? Just talking. Listening. There are other ways to help, Ethan."

I stared at her.

"When the whole thing with Sebastian blew up, I told you to stop doing this," she went on, voice tight. "To stop carrying everything on your own. You and me? We're it for life, E. If something like that happened to me, would you want me to hide it and go through it alone?"

"Of course not."

"Then stop thinking letting people in makes you weak."

My brain stalled. Literally *stopped*.

Because she was right. And because—god—it hit somewhere deep enough that something inside me flinched. I could picture myself saying that exact same sentence to Sebastian. And that was the part that gutted me.

When had I started behaving like him? When had I turned into the thing I spent so long resenting?

"I just…" The words scraped on the way out. "I just don't want people to have a reason to leave me."

Charlotte's eyes welled the second I said it—like she'd been waiting for me to say something that honest. "That's not going to happen."

But it already had. Over and over.

I never realized how much Sebastian leaving was carved into me. How deeply my parents' bullshit had lodged under my ribs. And now… this. All of this fucking mess. I'd crossed the same line I'd spent years hating them for.

And instead of dealing with it, I felt myself shutting down all over again. Every disappointment made me colder. Every time it happened, I pulled further back. Suddenly I was looking at myself through her eyes and realizing—

Was that what it was like for him too? Carrying everything alone until the fractures began to show somewhere he couldn't control? Was he just… shut down? Not because he didn't care, but because he genuinely didn't know how to reach out?

The thought was so sad my eyes burned.

Charlotte's arms wrapped around me again, fast and tight, and I leaned into her without thinking.

"Fuck, this is sad," I said against her shoulder.

She let out a wet laugh. "A little."

"I'm sorry. You're finally away from the kids, and I have you here looking after me."

She pulled back just enough to pinch my arm.

I yelped, hand flying to the spot. "What the hell was that for?"

"Stop apologizing for being human, Ethan. We all are."

I rubbed the sting, a small smile tugging at my mouth as something in my chest unclenched. "I hope that's not how you correct your kids. This kind of thing is illegal now."

She smacked my arm—lighter—before grabbing her wine and downing it. "I would *never*. You just need extra help."

The tension in me eased after that.

We ate, we talked, she curled her feet under her on the couch the way she always did, and for the first time in days, the noise in my head felt manageable. I felt more grounded. More like myself and less like the spiraling mess I'd been since arriving in Madrid. Probably before that, honestly.

And when I finally lay in bed later, replaying everything—our fight, his voice in that doorway, his face when he looked at me—it didn't hurt the same way.

It gave me clarity.

Because even if I understood him better now—even if I could see the parallels between us—I didn't have to turn into him. I knew Sebastian wasn't intentionally cruel; he just didn't know how to offer more. But I deserved better, and I wasn't going to settle for scraps.

———

Three days later, there was no more avoiding it. Not for either of us.

The space between Sebastian and me hadn't eased—not even a little. We hadn't spoken since the night he showed up at my door. No text, no call, no attempt to fix what'd been broken.

By the time lunch rolled around, I'd rehearsed exactly how to handle being in the same room with him—calm, civil, braced for whatever version of him I'd get. Guarded enough that nothing slipped through the cracks I'd spent the week stitching shut.

November had arrived quietly, slipping into the city without ceremony. The light felt thinner now, the sun lower even at midday, and the chill that lingered in the shadows followed you indoors if you let it. The restaurant was meant to feel casual, but the private room felt stifling the moment I stepped inside.

Henry had invited Mateo and Raúl; Sebastian sat beside Elena and a couple of directors; Oliver, Charlotte, and a few friends filled the rest of the table. I slid into the seat beside my sister, quietly putting as much distance between us as I could.

We didn't say hello.

Our eyes met for a second—his unreadable, mine trying not to show anything—and then we both looked away.

It was strange how quickly things had changed. How we'd gone from wanting to be near each other, from the effortless pull that used to drag our gazes together and tug smiles out of us… to this quiet separation. To silence. To regret.

Maybe he didn't care as much as I thought.

Maybe I was waiting for a version of us that was never going to exist.

Halfway through lunch, while I was debating getting up and leaving, Sebastian's phone buzzed. He frowned, murmured an apology, and stepped away to take the call.

Something about it immediately put me on alert.

I watched his back as he listened.

In a single heartbeat, his posture changed—shoulders locking, head dipping forward. When he turned slightly, his eyes were wide, startled in a way I had never seen on him. His mouth moved fast, voice low and too far away to pick up.

Then he looked back at the table… and his gaze caught on mine.

Not pleading.

Not asking.

Just raw emotion leaking through the cracks he usually kept sealed shut.

I was on my feet before I realized I'd moved, my chair scraping softly against the floor.

Charlotte tugged on my sleeve. "E, what is it?"

"I don't know," I whispered—because I didn't, not exactly. But something in me recognized it was bad.

Sebastian turned toward us again, eyes bright with something dangerously close to fear. That was what got me moving, my feet already taking me to him.

"Calm down and—" Sebastian's voice shook as he spoke into the phone. His chest rose and fell too fast. "What happened?"

"Ash?" I said quietly.

His eyes snapped to mine. He didn't answer. He didn't seem

capable of it. His free hand twitched at his side—just once—like he was fighting the urge to reach for me.

So I made the choice for both of us. I took his hand, interlocking my fingers with his. His grip closed around mine instantly—too tight.

I steadied him with a small nod and turned to the table. Most of them were already standing, alarm rising like heat in the room.

"Henny. Oli," I called.

The panic on their faces twisted something sharp inside me.

Sebastian squeezed my hand again—harder. "Where is he now? Vivian—" His voice cracked on her name.

Oh, fuck no.

"Vivian, where are they taking him?" His breathing sped up, thin and uneven.

He listened, eyes darting from side to side as he tried to piece together words we couldn't hear. Oliver and Henry rushed to us, Charlotte right behind me.

Finally, Sebastian looked at his brothers, and his grip tightened around my hand until it hurt. He lowered the phone slightly, not speaking into it but still listening. "It's Dad," he said. "They're taking him to the hospital."

Shit.

CHAPTER FIFTEEN

ASH

A sharp ringing filled my ears, the loud thump of my heartbeat pounding through it.

Thump. Thump. Thump.

"He was confused and grunting... in pain. We called the ambulance, and the doctor said he could be having an—"

"Slow down." My voice didn't sound like mine—thick, underwater. "What did the doctor say?"

Thump. Thump. Thump.

"Henny, call the pilot." *Ethan.* That was Ethan. "We need to get over there right now."

I closed my fingers around the warm hand gripping mine, the ridges of his rings digging into my skin.

Thump. Thump. Thump.

The room tilted—just slightly. Or maybe it was me.

"He said he was having an episode. I don't... he just collapsed!" Vivian's voice shot sharp through the line. "On the floor! In the middle of breakfast!"

On the floor... The words didn't land right. They scattered.

Why is she lying on the floor?

I pulled the phone away. It didn't help. None of it made sense.

Thump. Thump. Thump.

Keep your brothers in here—

"Ash." A soft sound, followed by a tug on my hand.

I turned toward it and found pale blue eyes watching me, tight with worry.

Thump.

Thump.

Thump—

Vivian's voice vanished. Someone took the phone from me, and suddenly there were hands cupping my face, holding me still.

"I need that back," I said—at least, I thought I did.

Ethan shook his head. Voices circled us—Oliver, Henry, tense and too loud.

I needed them safe. I needed—

"Hey," Ethan murmured, stepping in and lowering his voice so it was only meant for me. "Breathe in for me. One deep breath."

His thumbs brushed my cheekbones.

I swallowed and inhaled.

You have to keep your brothers in here—

THUMP.

"And out," he said.

Again.

In—

Keep them—

And out...

"That's it. Come back to me." His hands stayed on my face, steadying my focus, guiding me back into my body.

The ringing in my ears ebbed. Sounds returned in fragments —chairs scraping, hurried footsteps, someone speaking into a phone. Ethan's face sharpened into something fully there—not just a pair of eyes, but the whole person in front of me.

My hands lifted to his wrists—not pulling him closer, just making sure he stayed.

"I'm here." Something loosened in him when he saw me breathe. "One more?"

I inhaled through my nose and let it out slowly. The rest of the room came back: Oliver holding one phone, Henry speaking into another, Charlotte typing fast.

"The car is outside," she said.

Henry pocketed his phone. "Plane will be ready by the time we get there. Let's go."

Ethan's hands slipped from my face, but when he stepped back, I didn't let go. Our fingers caught and laced in the same motion. He didn't question it—just held on and led me toward the door.

The restaurant blurred behind us, then the hallway, the rush of cool air outside, the car pulling up fast. Oliver took the passenger seat, and the rest of us slid into the back.

"I'm getting his doctor on the phone," Oliver said, already dialing. "I couldn't understand half of what Vivian said."

Thank God. Not just me.

My hand flexed around Ethan's. He stayed close, knee pressed lightly against mine, eyes flicking up to check on me before he looked away again.

Get it together, Sebastian. They need you.

A vague memory surfaced—Henry mentioning tests, something I hadn't paid much attention to at the time.

"What were the tests?" I asked, leaning forward.

The sound of my voice startled all of them.

"The ones from a few weeks ago?" Henry said. "Cardiac panel. EKG. They were checking for an arrhythmia."

"So it could be a heart attack?"

He exhaled. "Yeah… it could be."

Fuck.

"He's conscious," Oliver said. "That's good." He straightened as someone picked up on the other end. "Hello?" His tone changed instantly.

Another squeeze of my hand.

"You'll be there in no time," Ethan said quietly.

Something about that phrasing jolted me. *"We* will," I corrected. "You're coming, right?"

He blinked like he hadn't expected the question. "I have classes and work—"

"Ethan, I own the company. You're coming." The firmness didn't even sound like me—it was threaded through with panic I couldn't hide.

He couldn't stay behind. I needed—

God.

I *needed* him.

After a beat, Ethan nodded without arguing. "I'm there."

The knot in my chest eased just enough for me to breathe in again. He adjusted in his seat, the side of his body a steady pressure against mine. The contact helped, and I finally let the breath out. A shaky one.

My head felt stuffed with cotton, but Oliver managed to get someone on the line who could actually explain what was happening. The doctor said they were treating it as a possible cardiac event. He'd collapsed, was disoriented and in pain, and they couldn't say yet whether it was a heart attack or something else. They wouldn't call it anything definitive until the tests were done—an EKG and bloodwork to check cardiac markers.

He'd been conscious when the paramedics arrived, which they said was a good sign, but they rushed him to Mount Sinai for evaluation anyway. Until those results came back, there was nothing more they could tell us.

That was it. That was all we got.

By the time we reached the plane, he'd already been taken in —sedated and being prepped for the rest of the tests. And we still had nearly nine hours in the air ahead of us. Nine hours of not knowing. Nine hours of holding myself together while every part of me braced for the worst.

The car slowed, and before it had fully stopped, Henry, Charlotte, and Oliver were already moving, heading for the jet. We followed without a word, Ethan's hand still in mine, only loosening as we passed through the cabin corridor. The crew greeted us politely—voices lowered, movements careful, as if they were holding their breath too.

I dropped into the window seat in the larger lounge, the one arranged so we could all sit facing each other. Charlotte and Oliver took the seats opposite me. Henry settled onto the couch to our left. Ethan sat beside me without a word, close enough that I could feel the warmth of him through the armrest. After what felt like a lifetime, the engines roared to life, vibration settling into my bones as the plane began to move.

Henry leaned forward, already talking logistics with Oliver. "We can set up camp in my apartment," Henry said. "I'll ask them to get it ready for you. And the kids, if you want."

"Definitely." Oliver's eyes dropped back to his phone, a deep crease between his brows. "I'd rather stay close."

"I'll get my mom on the phone and have her bring them over tomorrow," Charlotte added. Her gaze flicked to me every so often, like she wanted to say something but didn't know how.

Ethan stayed beside me. Quiet.

I stared out the window as the ground began to blur, the city stretching into something distant and unreal.

My father almost died today.

The thought moved through me without resistance, too large to fight.

I'd spent weeks—years—obsessing over timing. Over consequences. Over doing things right. Holding the line. Managing outcomes. Containing fallout. As if control alone could keep everything from breaking apart. And none of it meant a damn thing if you ran out of time to do the things that actually mattered.

He almost *died*.

While I buried myself in problems I couldn't fix—contracts unraveling, Elena's measured disappointment, headlines dissecting my company and my name—I kept telling myself I could contain them. That if I pushed hard enough, worked fast enough, absorbed enough pressure, I could stop everything from collapsing.

Instead, I watched control slip through my hands piece by piece.

The company.

My authority.

My brothers' trust.

Luca, waiting for something I couldn't give.

Ethan, held at arm's length because I didn't know how to choose him without breaking everything else.

And still I dug my heels in. Refusing to call. Refusing to speak to my father until he apologized first. As if pride could buy time.

What if we didn't make it there in time? What if his last memory of me was a cold phone call and silence?

Why did I keep wasting time like this?

I knew better. I knew how fast things changed. How quickly you could lose people.

Keep your brothers in here—

I squeezed my eyes shut, trying to push back the pressure building behind them.

The seatbelt sign chimed.

Beside me, Ethan moved, his hand brushed mine—tentative, almost unsure if he was allowed anymore. I didn't even remember when I'd let go, but I fucking hated that I had. I hated the distance. I hated that I'd been the one to create it.

Fuck control. It was costing us everything.

I reached for his hand and closed mine around it, firm this time. "We broke up."

Ethan stiffened beside me.

I didn't look at him when I said it. The words came out flat and low, but the silence that followed spread through the cabin. When I finally turned, he was staring at me like he was checking to see if I was real.

"Get up," he said quietly.

I stared back at him, blank, the words still lodged somewhere in my throat.

"Come with me." His voice softened, but his hand was already urging me to my feet, pulling me gently toward the bedroom at the back of the plane.

For the first time in a long time, I didn't hesitate.

The door clicked shut behind us, sealing us into the quiet of the back cabin. Ethan moved deeper into the room, his back to me. He paced once, twice, then stopped.

I sat on the edge of the bed, waiting for him to turn, part of me braced for anger. But when he did, his expression was still soft.

"Ethan—"

He shook his head, lifting a hand to stop me. "It's not the time to have this conversation, Ash."

"I just need to say—"

"I know." His tongue flicked over his lip before he took a step closer, stopping between my knees, his hands settling on my shoulders. "And you can. Just not right now."

"It has to be now."

"Your head's not in the right place," he said. "You're in shock. It's like you're drunk, and you don't cross that line, remember?" One hand lifted, his knuckles brushing under my chin.

With me seated and him standing, the height of the bed put us almost face-to-face. For once, we were level. He only had to look down slightly.

"I'm so sorry," I said anyway. Because even if I couldn't say the rest, I needed him to hear that much.

His eyes dropped for a second. "Ash..."

Tentatively, my hands settled at his hips, expecting him to pull away.

He didn't.

"I didn't mean what I said," I went on. "Or how it came out. I want you here. I *need* you."

His blue eyes strayed, then locked on mine.

"Sometimes I need you more than air," I said softly. "Like right now."

His brows drew together, and his expression softened.

"I'm sorry for ever making you feel like I don't. That's the biggest lie I've ever told."

He searched my face, eyes moving slowly, like he was deciding whether to believe me. Then he nodded. "Okay."

The tension in my jaw eased. Some of the urgency drained out of me, leaving fear in its place.

Ethan must have seen it, because he stepped closer, his hands sliding into my hair. "I'm not leaving you, Ash. I can be angry at you. I can need time. But I will never turn my back on you when you need me. Never."

A weak smile broke through my expression, and whatever resolve I had left shattered. I pulled him in by the waist, wrapping my arms around him. A second later, his came around my shoulders, holding me just as tightly. The warm press of his body, the clean scent of him, the way he fit against me—everything about him—quieted some of the ache spiraling inside me.

How could one person hold this much power over another?

His fingers traced my shoulders, then slid into the hair at my nape. "When did it happen?"

I didn't need to ask what he meant. "After we kissed. That same night."

His body relaxed a fraction more. "You're an idiot for not telling me."

I nodded into his neck, eyes closing as I nuzzled closer. "I am. I'm sorry." My arms tightened around him.

Ethan exhaled softly against my temple. "What's going on in that head of yours?" His voice dropped. "Will you talk to me?"

My first instinct was to deflect—to joke, to flirt, to pull us out of the moment before it could cut too deep.

But I couldn't. Not now. Not with him.

"I'm scared." Saying it felt like stepping off solid footing.

The engines roared around us, sealing us into a private bubble. Just him and me.

"Of what?"

I buried my face in his neck for a moment longer, breathing him in, buying myself a second before lifting my chin. My gaze drifted past his shoulder to the endless white of clouds beyond the window. "Of things changing," I said quietly. "Of losing something again. Of having the ground pulled out from under us—Henny, Oli, and me."

The words settled between us. I felt them land—on him, as he tried to understand, and on me, as I realized how true they were.

His hands cradled the back of my neck, fingers moving slowly through my hair. "Are you thinking about your mom?"

The drop in my stomach was immediate. All the words I had vanished, caught in the tight knot in my throat. I nodded.

"That does sound scary," he said. "Life does that sometimes. But I'm here, okay? And your brothers are right there on the other side of the door."

My eyes burned, and I closed them again.

"They don't need you to carry this for them," he went on. "You can do it together. All of you. And I'm here too."

He didn't have to say the rest. I heard it anyway.

You're not alone this time.

Fear still pressed against my ribs, familiar and stubborn, slow to release its grip.

"Don't close up on us," he murmured. "It's not the same."

My eyes burned harder, and I tucked myself back into the curve of his neck—half hiding, half holding on.

"Thank you," I whispered.

"Anytime."

Night started to settle around us, the plane humming steadily beneath our feet, and we stayed there in that same embrace for a while—my heart slowly finding its rhythm again, Ethan holding me through it.

I used to wonder what it was about him. Why he had this effect on me. Why he made me feel seen and… safe. Of all the people in my life, why him?

I'd asked myself that question for years.

And right then, wrapped in his arms, with everything stripped down to what actually mattered, the answer came to me —soft and simple.

With him, I didn't have to hold myself together. I didn't have to be careful, or controlled, or strong. I didn't need to anticipate the next fracture or brace for impact.

I could just *be*.

And somehow, in the middle of everything falling apart, he made the chaos feel fucking beautiful.

———

The house was quiet.

It was the wrong kind of quiet. The kind where people held their breath in the same space, tense and afraid.

I dropped my bag by the door. People moved through the house— none of them familiar. Some glanced at me as they passed, then quickly looked away. No one said a word.

The living room wasn't empty. People stood scattered, like they didn't know where to put themselves. My eyes locked onto the one thing that didn't belong.

My mom.

I couldn't see all of her, just her feet, but I knew it was her.

Why is she on the floor?

I hadn't even finished forming the thought when hands closed around my shoulders and pushed me back. My father's face filled my vision.

"Sebastian, go upstairs," he said.

"Is Mom okay?"

Silence.

His face looked wrong too—flushed, eyes too bright.

"Go upstairs," he said again, firmer this time.

"Mom?" I twisted my head, trying to look past him, but his hands came up to my face, cupping my cheeks and holding me still.

"Your mother's gone."

Gone where? She's right there.

My body reacted before my mind caught up. My eyes burned. My breathing turned shallow, uneven.

"Gone where?"

He might have answered. I wasn't sure. All I could hear was the ringing in my ears, everything else muffled and far away. When I didn't move, he grabbed my arms and pulled me with him, steering me up the stairs and into their bedroom.

Oliver and Henry were sitting on the bed. Oliver's face was red, his eyes swollen. Henry started to wail the moment he saw me, even though his cheeks were already streaked with dried tears.

I turned back to my father, standing in the doorway.

"You have to keep your brothers in here," he said. "Don't let them come downstairs."

"Dad—"

"You have to keep them in here."

"Dad, what—"

The door shut behind him with a hard, final thud.

A hand landed on my shoulder, jolting me awake.

"Fuck," I breathed out, blinking through the darkness, slowly making out my brother's face.

"Sorry," Henry said, offering an apologetic smile. "We're landing soon." His eyes flicked to the space beside me. "You'll need to get back in your seat."

I followed his gaze. Ethan was stretched along my side, half curled into me. There was barely enough room on the chair for one of us, let alone two, which left us pressed together beneath the thin blanket.

"I'm up." My voice was rough with sleep, and I cleared my throat.

Henry gave us one last smile before heading back to his.

We'd stayed out in the lounge together. All of us. Waiting for updates. Sitting in the quiet after they told us he'd need surgery. It hadn't been a small heart attack. Multiple blockages, which meant a bypass. When I'd finally drifted off, they were already prepping him to go in.

Sleep never settled properly after that. I'd slipped in and out for hours, memories tangling with nightmares. After one particularly bad one, Ethan had unbuckled his seatbelt and, without a word, slid in beside me. I'd stretched the chair flat, pulled the blanket over us, and let the warmth of his breath and the press of his forehead against mine pull me under again.

For a moment, I studied his face while he slept, brushing his hair back from his ear. A sharp wave of panic hit me as I watched him—the aftershocks of the dreams still clinging to me.

I couldn't lose him. I wouldn't survive losing him.

Keeping the contact light, I pressed a kiss to his forehead, then his cheek. He stirred, beginning to surface. Watching his lashes flutter open felt like relief. Real relief—even though I'd known he was only asleep.

As he blinked and rubbed a hand over his face, I wondered how much rest he'd actually gotten. The last thing I remembered before sleep had claimed me was his hand tracing slow circles over my back, his eyes still wide open.

"We're landing," I whispered.

He nodded, rolling onto his front as much as the space allowed, stretching with a soft groan. "Fuck," he muttered. "My neck."

I hummed in agreement. "Did you get any sleep?"

He made a face. "Barely. I'm gonna go wash up." His voice was still low, meant only for the two of us, rough with exhaustion.

I couldn't stop staring at him.

With one last stretch, he leaned in and pressed a kiss high on my cheek. "Be right back."

I trailed my hand over his arm as he stood, watching him disappear down the narrow aisle. Rolling my neck, I straightened the chair and pulled the blanket off. When I looked up, I was met with three identical stares. Henry, Oliver, and Charlotte —all sitting upright now, rumpled and watchful.

"Any news?" I asked, shifting the focus away from myself.

Oliver leaned his elbow on the armrest. "Still in surgery."

I dragged my palm over my beard. "Christ."

"They might be done by the time we get there," Oliver added. "But he's going straight to the ICU. It'll still be a while before we get any real updates."

"We're all going straight to the hospital, right?" Henry asked.

A wave of quiet agreement moved through the cabin.

"Coffee, anyone?" he said, already pushing to his feet. "We're in for a long night. Or day. Or whatever time it is."

More nods.

"I'll help," Charlotte said, and they headed toward the front.

Oliver's gaze lingered on me, his lips pressed tight. After a brief hesitation, he moved into the chair beside me. "Ash."

For a second he looked both younger and older than me. His dark brown eyes were too bright, and a nauseating wave of shame rolled through me again. He hadn't deserved the silence I'd left him with, not after always being at my side. He was the one person I trusted with anything work-related—until it was me fucking up. Then I couldn't bear the thought of hearing disappointment in his voice.

I exhaled hard. "I'm sorry for not—"

He shook his head, his hand settling on my shoulder. "I know. I know you, okay? I know it's not about me."

I bit the inside of my cheek. "It's not that I don't trust you."

"I know, Ash. I know you do."

He was still looking at me, but I couldn't hold his gaze. I tried. I couldn't. So I did the next best thing.

The honest thing.

"I just wanted to fix it."

Oliver nodded, his grip tightening slightly. "I know," he said again. "Let's just put that aside, okay? We focus on this. I just don't want you to—"

"I won't." My hand covered his, keeping it there. "Not this time."

When I finally looked up again, Oliver was still watching me. A small smile tugged at his mouth. It wasn't even close to happy. But it was real.

I answered with one of my own—fragile, unsteady, but there. We stayed like that a second longer, hands still clasped, the silence between us no longer oppressive.

Footsteps approached from the galley. Henry's voice carried first, followed by Charlotte's softer reply. Ethan appeared behind us, one hand braced briefly on the back of the seat as the plane jolted. He glanced at me—just a check-in—and I nodded once.

He didn't come back to my side. Instead, he slid into the seat beside Henry, close enough that our feet could still touch if either of us moved. Charlotte settled across from us again, passing out coffee cups with quiet efficiency.

Oliver's shoulder remained warm against mine.

This week, when I'd finally had to face him in person, I'd kept things light, deflecting anything real. I hadn't been ready for him to see how much was already cracking beneath the surface. It had been easier to keep the distance. Easier—and far more isolating.

This felt so different. Like a wall lowering, brick by brick.

And knowing he was here—that all of them were—made the thought of stepping off this plane feel a fraction less suffocating. We still had to face the hospital. Our father. Whatever waited on the other side of those doors.

But we wouldn't be walking into it alone.

———

Hours later, we were ushered into a waiting area just outside the ICU.

Not the main one—this was smaller, quieter, tucked behind a set of double doors that never stopped opening. Nurses passed through without looking at us. Doctors spoke in low voices that blurred together. Machines beeped somewhere beyond the walls, steady and impersonal.

We sat. And we waited.

Time stretched into something unrecognizable. No one checked their phone anymore. No one spoke above a whisper. Charlotte sat rigid beside Vivian, arms crossed tight over her chest. Oliver leaned forward with his elbows on his knees, staring at the floor. Henry stood, paced once, then sat again— only to stand back up minutes later.

Ethan stayed beside me. Not touching constantly, not hovering—just there. Every so often, his hand would find my wrist, and I could breathe a little easier.

I kept staring at the doors.

My father was in there. Cut open—his chest split apart. His heart stopping and starting again under someone else's hands.

When the doors opened one more time, we all startled. A man in green scrubs stepped through, surgical cap still on, mask hanging loose around his neck. He looked tired.

His eyes scanned the room once. "Mr. Langley?"

All of us were on our feet instantly.

"That's us," Henry said, his voice tight.

The surgeon nodded, already turning toward a quieter corner of the hall. "Let's talk over here."

That walk—those few steps—felt longer than the flight.

He stopped, folded his arms, and took a breath. "The surgery is over."

My lungs burned with the sudden rush of air.

"Your father had a significant myocardial infarction," he continued. "There were multiple blockages in three major coronary arteries. We performed a triple bypass."

It felt like we were all clinging to that breath like a lifeline.

"The procedure itself was successful," the surgeon said. "He's stable right now, but he's still in critical condition. The next twenty-four hours are vital."

His eyes were on me, so I nodded once—an automatic gesture.

"He's sedated and on a ventilator," the surgeon went on. "That's expected after a surgery like this. We're keeping him asleep to reduce stress on his heart while his body adjusts."

Charlotte's hands went to her hips as she rocked slightly on her feet, her gaze flicking anxiously toward Oliver.

"Is he—" Oliver started, then stopped. Swallowed. "Is he going to be okay?"

"He's where we want him to be, given the circumstances," the surgeon said. "There were no major complications during the surgery. That's good. But recovery will take time. Days in the ICU. Weeks in the hospital. Months after that."

Ethan's fingers curled into mine.

"Can we see him?" Henry asked.

The surgeon nodded. "Briefly. One at a time. He won't wake up yet, but it can help."

Help whom?

"Ash, you go." Henry's hand landed on my back, giving me a gentle nudge.

"This way," the surgeon said.

My fingers slipped from Ethan's as I followed him past the doors. Inside, he handed me off to a nurse who guided me through the ICU—past rows of glass walls and softly glowing monitors. The antiseptic smell hit me square in the chest, my pulse spiking as she turned the corner and yet another room came into view.

She didn't let me inside. Just close enough to see him through the glass.

He lay in the bed, surrounded by wires and tubes. The ventilator whirred beside him as his chest rose and fell mechanically.

He looked smaller like that. Just a man—impossible to please, to read, to reach—lying there, broken open, kept alive by machines. My father.

My gaze dropped to the bandage across his chest. It rose and fell with his breathing as my hand lifted to the glass.

Up.

And down.

Up.

And down.

A wave of relief passed through me, loosening the death grip fear had wrapped around my heart.

He's alive.

The world tilted back into place.

"Hello, old man," I whispered, my breath fogging the glass.

He was alive.

I held onto that.

CHAPTER SIXTEEN

ETHAN

Something changed.

Hours had passed since the surgeon came out to speak with us. The brothers had been going in and out for a while. We'd eaten bad hospital food, survived on massive amounts of coffee, dozed off in uncomfortable chairs, and watched the same commercials loop endlessly on the waiting room TV.

When Sebastian had stepped through the doors again, he hadn't looked like a man on the verge of a breakdown anymore. That sharp edge in his eyes had been gone, the tight press of his mouth loosened. And the moment he'd taken the seat beside me, I'd felt it.

Something changed.

It reminded me of how soft he used to get after we'd had sex —how his walls would lower just enough for me to glimpse the real Sebastian underneath. The one without such a punishing grip on control. The one who could sink into the chair beside me, whose eyes turned molten when they found mine, who leaned in close and spoke in a voice meant only for me.

The version of him that, little by little, had made me fall in love with him the first time.

That Sebastian was back.

But beneath the familiarity, there was something different now—something quieter, stripped raw by fear and exhaustion and the long night we'd just survived. Sebastian had always been affectionate—at least with me. But this wasn't the same. The way he sought it now, the way he kept reaching for it, wasn't about claiming or commanding. It was softer. Like he was letting himself be held. Like he wanted to be taken care of.

And that—out of everything I'd been through with Sebastian—was the part that really fucked me up.

Because this was Sebastian Langley we were talking about.

Sebastian *I don't need anybody* Langley.

Sebastian *I can handle everything myself* Langley.

Sebastian *I keep my emotions locked down and function like a goddamn machine* Langley.

Right now, none of that armor seemed to fit.

He was letting me in.

And it didn't feel like a responsibility or a burden. Being there for him came more naturally than breathing. From the moment he got that call—when I watched him freeze in place—I knew exactly what I had to do. Where I had to be. If he needed me, I was there. I didn't stop to dissect what that meant about boundaries or pride. It didn't feel reckless.

It felt inevitable.

Just like the pain of being this close to him... and not having him. But for now, that would have to wait.

There was an unspoken agreement between all of us: we weren't leaving the hospital until the first twenty-four hours were over. The doctor had made it clear how critical that window was, so we stayed—through the fatigue, through bad coffee and worse chairs, through the slow, suspended hours that made time feel unreal.

No one said it out loud, but none of us were willing to be anywhere else.

It was just after five in the afternoon the next day when my mother arrived.

I'd been sitting beside Sebastian and Henry, listening to Henry ramble about contracts, when Sebastian's expression changed. The strain lifted, replaced by a smile so warm it caught me off guard. One that softened his entire face.

A second later, his arms opened wide as a high-pitched squeal cut through the room.

"Uncle Ash!" Amelia barreled into him, her tiny arms looping around his neck. Sebastian closed his eyes as he hugged her back, holding her like she was something precious.

"My favorite little troublemaker," he said.

And fuck if that wasn't the most heartwarming thing I'd ever witnessed. I felt myself soften completely just watching them—Amelia saying something I didn't catch, Sebastian laughing, his hand ruffling her hair near her ear like it was the most natural thing in the world.

"This one was asking for you," Charlotte said.

I looked up at her, at the dark circles under her eyes—probably mirroring my own—and the quiet, content smile she wore as she shifted her youngest on her hip. Liam stretched his arms toward me, letting out a soft, excited "eee."

I held my hands out, and she passed him over without hesitation. I pulled him in close, pressing a kiss to his cheek. "Hi, sweetie," I murmured. "Missed you."

He settled into my lap easily, like he'd done a hundred times before.

"This makes no sense," Henry declared with a huff. "I'm the fun uncle, you little traitors."

Sebastian laughed again, quieter this time, and something in my ribs ached in the best way.

Charlotte's hand settled on my shoulder. "Heads up," she said, tipping her chin toward the entrance.

I leaned forward and saw my mother standing beside Vivian

and Thomas. "Shit," I muttered. My chest tightened—for a completely different reason this time.

Thomas noticed me first, offering a polite smile and a nod before drawing my mother's attention in my direction. Our eyes met, and that familiar knot of guilt and irritation settled in my gut. It tightened further when her gaze flicked to Sebastian sitting beside me, her mouth flattening in unmistakable disapproval.

"Guess there's no avoiding this," I said, pushing up from my chair.

There was movement at my side, and I turned to find Sebastian already standing, close enough that his arm brushed mine. He was still murmuring something to Amelia, his hand resting lightly at her back as he carried her. It was like his body had shifted into autopilot, one simple directive running through him—stay close.

I adjusted Liam in my arms, his weight settling easily against me, then stepped forward, the rest of them following a beat behind.

"Hey," I said when we reached them.

My mother turned toward me, her expression already composed. "Ethan."

Thomas smiled easily beside her. "Hey. Rough few days."

"Yeah," I said. "You could say that." Liam's fingers toyed with the collar of my shirt, giving me something else to focus on.

"Ethan's been a godsend," Vivian said. "Found somewhere with decent coffee. The one in the hospital is terrible."

I gave her a grateful smile, which she returned. Vivian had always been kind to me—so had the rest of the Langleys. The contrast only made my mother's reaction even more noticeable, after years of barely seeing her.

"I can make another run if anyone wants." Henry stepped in beside me, clearly trying to redirect the attention.

Sebastian was still quietly talking to Amelia, a soft laugh passing between them, holding some of the tension at bay.

But my mother's gaze lingered on me a second longer than necessary.

"You've let your hair grow out," she said. Not unkindly. Not warmly either. Just… observant. "It doesn't suit you like this. You always looked more put together when it was shorter."

There it was.

Another reminder of how little she knew me. Of how much she disliked the person I'd become—the one I'd kept hidden for years just to keep her comfortable.

I opened my mouth, already exhausted by it, but Sebastian spoke first.

"I like it," he said, taking a small step closer, his eyes still on Amelia.

My heart thudded in my chest.

Surprise flickered across my mother's face before she smoothed it away. "Oh."

Sebastian adjusted Amelia on his hip, unbothered. "I think it suits him perfectly."

The silence that followed was immediate and thick. Henry rubbed the back of his neck. Charlotte's lips pressed together. Even Thomas seemed to suddenly find the floor fascinating.

My mother smiled, thin and polite, the kind that didn't quite reach her eyes. "That's… nice."

Henry cleared his throat, the sound a little too loud in the stillness. "Okay," he said, clapping his hands once. "Well. Since we're all here and nobody's actually combusted yet—"

Charlotte let out a tired huff that might have been a laugh.

Sebastian moved then, stepping closer to me without making a show of it. Just enough that his arm brushed mine again. I handed Liam back to Charlotte, and she adjusted him over her hip, palm absently patting his back.

"Plans," Henry went on. "Because at some point, all of us are going to need sleep. Or at least showers."

Right on cue, Oliver appeared from down the hall, phone still in his hand. "He's okay," he said. "Stable. Still sedated, but they're happy with where he is right now." He scrubbed a hand over his face, dragging out a breath with it. Some of the tightness in the room eased. Just a notch. "We should do shifts," Oliver added. "No reason for all of us to crash at once. I'll take the first one tonight."

Henry nodded immediately. "Yeah. That makes sense." Then to Oliver and Charlotte he said, "Why don't you guys head over to mine, get a nap in, shower?"

Oliver turned to my sister. "You go with the kids. I'll come over once we get the okay later."

Charlotte hesitated. "You need sleep too."

Oliver sighed, shaking his head.

"The nanny's already there," Henry said, "getting everything set up. We're all close, Oli. Ten minutes away."

Oliver looked at him like he wanted to argue.

"It's just a couple of hours," Sebastian said quietly beside me. "You'll still be right here."

"Exactly." Henry squeezed Oliver's shoulder. "They're fixing up the office for E. Another room for Ash. And I have a driver there; you can come over whenever…"

My gaze snapped to Sebastian. He was rocking Amelia gently in his arms, but his eyes were on me. I lifted my brows, just enough to ask the question.

Is that what you want?

His lips curved, and he gave me a small shake of his head.

"Hold that thought," I said, turning back to them.

Every pair of eyes landed on me.

"Ash and I are staying at his apartment."

Silence dropped hard around us.

"Kids take up more room," I added mildly. Almost casually.

I felt my mother's stare before I saw it. When I looked over, her eyes were wide—unguarded for the first time since she'd arrived. I didn't shrink under it, just smiled a little.

"Okay then," Henry said quickly. "Let's sidestep that too and get a car for Char and Oli."

Sebastian's arm brushed mine again. This time, he didn't move away. He stayed right where he was, and the awkwardness still hanging in the air loosened its grip on me.

Because I was so used to carrying this—the judgment about him and me—by myself.

This time, he was here.

And he had my back.

———

Teddy Langley was declared stable a few hours later.

He was still heavily sedated, still in the ICU, and likely would be for another couple of days—but it was enough to let us all breathe a little easier. Once Oliver returned from the apartment, we split up. Henry went with Charlotte and the kids. Sebastian and I headed to his place.

The moment the door slid open, it felt like time folded in on itself. Too many memories rushed in at once—of us, of what this place used to be—and I had to clear my throat to hide how much it affected me.

Sebastian had a guest bedroom. A small one I realized I'd never actually seen before.

He offered it, and I took it without hesitation. I showered, letting the heat strip away the hospital smell still clinging to me. I tried not to think about those dark eyes drifting toward his room, then back to me, lingering too close to a question we both knew he wasn't supposed to ask.

Sebastian had gotten clothes for me. I had no idea when, but they were waiting on the bed, neatly folded. Something about the quiet thoughtfulness of it settled warm and heavy in my gut.

When I finally stepped back out, I half expected him to be in his room, already asleep. Instead, he was sitting on the couch, the glow of his phone lighting his face. He looked fresh out of the shower too, his hair still damp, brushed back with a few loose strands refusing to stay put.

There was something about Sebastian out of his rigid work clothes that always affected me more than it should. In dark sweats and a T-shirt, he looked almost ordinary. Human. Just a man sitting on a couch. Not the untouchable figure the rest of the world seemed to see—the one he *let them* see.

I moved farther into the room, my nerves ticking up at the realization that it was just us now. "Any news?"

He glanced up, his eyes sweeping over me before dropping back to his phone. "Still stable. I was ordering us something to eat before heading to bed." A pause. "Are you hungry?"

I sank onto the couch—probably closer than I should have. "Starving."

The food arrived not long after. We ate right there, side by side on the couch, and the familiarity of it pulled at me in a way I couldn't ignore. His presence. His scent drifting over to me. The way my body kept wanting to lean closer without permission.

This version of him was dangerous.

Watching his forearms flex as he lifted his fork, the casual intimacy of bare feet against the floor—it all made my thoughts stray in directions I didn't want to follow.

And it didn't help that he kept offering without saying a word. A thigh brushing mine. His leg falling open just enough to press against me. A touch that lingered a beat too long before he pulled back.

Every part of me wanted to close the distance. To curl into his side. To remind myself how it felt to touch him like he was mine.

I forced myself not to.

This wasn't an all-clear. This didn't erase what he'd said or the way he'd hurt me. Being here for him didn't mean everything was suddenly okay. It didn't mean I didn't still deserve answers. Apologies.

This was just a pause.

So I sat there, back against the couch, both of us on the floor in front of it, and listened to him talk.

"Anyway," Sebastian went on. We'd been talking about a holiday trip when they were kids—a week of cabins, snow, and chaos. "Henry, at the tall age of six, saw Oli's scraped knee and declared he was going to have to cut it off."

I chuckled softly.

"Oli was horrified," Sebastian said, a faint smile on his lips. "But resigned. Luckily, I got there before he went for the kitchen knives."

"Jesus," I huffed.

Sebastian took one last bite and placed the container on the coffee table. "It's always been like that. Henry taking charge while being completely feral. Oliver worrying. And me..." He stopped, something in his eyes going a little sad.

I wiped my hands on a napkin. "You fixing."

He turned to look at me, then nodded once. "Yeah. Something like that."

The silence that settled between us wasn't heavy or oppressive. It felt necessary. I watched him gather his thoughts, the way his eyes drifted, the way his hand clenched briefly over his knee. He wanted to say more.

With a quiet exhale, he finally did. "It was always expected of me," he said. "It's easy to know what role to play when you're handed the part."

My elbow was propped on my knee, my chin resting in my palm, all of my attention on him. "What do you mean?" The question was a gentle push, an invitation to stay instead of retreat into himself.

His lips twisted, and he shrugged, suddenly looking younger than I'd ever seen him.

"I can't stop thinking about it," he whispered, his gaze drifting somewhere far away.

"About what?"

"The day she died."

I'd known it was coming, but hearing him say it still felt like a rock landing in my stomach. The pain in his expression softened something inside me in a way I couldn't fight. This time, I didn't stop myself. My free hand went to his arm, smoothing over the skin before my fingers slipped under the hem of his sleeve.

His hand closed around my wrist, holding me there. "We don't have to—"

"I want to listen," I said quickly. His eyes lifted to mine. "If you want to tell me about it… I want to listen."

He looked away again. A quiet moment stretched between us, filled only by his breathing and the distant hum of New York traffic beyond the windows.

"It was sudden," he said. "Completely out of nowhere. There hadn't been anything wrong with her. That morning, we'd had breakfast together. She was joking with us, Henry sitting on her lap like he always did. He was always glued to her."

My eyes burned at the image. They'd been so little.

"When I got home from school, the house was packed," he went on. "And I saw her—not all of her, but enough. On the floor. Before my father pushed me out." His jaw tightened. "He told me she was gone. Then I was upstairs with Oli and Henny, and he told me to keep them there. I think they were taking her out, and I just—" His grip on my wrist tightened. "I broke. I started crying. Everything hit me all at once, and I couldn't stop it."

My chest ached so much for them. For him. "Ash…"

He shook his head. "It scared them. Henny jumped off the bed and ran to the bathroom, banging on the door, calling for her, like she was supposed to be there. That made Oliver cry harder, and that's when it really hit me." His voice dropped. "Nobody was going to comfort them. Those cries were only going to meet silence. So it had to be me."

A tear slipped free before I could stop it, and I wiped it away quickly.

His eyes stayed on the floor, red-rimmed but dry. "It felt like I was being torn apart," he said. "But I couldn't let myself feel it.

When I picked Henry up, I kept looking at his hands. His tiny hands. And it hurt more—but it also made everything else go quiet." He swallowed. "I focused on that. Then on Oliver's hands once I had him tucked under my arm. And somehow… breathing got easier."

Because he made it about them.

Fuck—Sebastian.

"It's all I can think about now. Every time I let my guard down, every time I start to fall asleep, I'm back in that bedroom. That same feeling—being ripped apart and terrified I won't be able to keep them safe."

My hand slid free of his grip and went to the back of his neck. "I'm so sorry."

His eyes lifted to mine, lips curved just slightly—not enough to chase away the sadness—as he reached up to wipe my cheek. "It's okay, darling. A bit of unprocessed trauma is practically a staple at my age."

A joke. Of course.

"That was a long time ago, Ash," I said. "You don't have to keep holding everything together anymore."

He looked away again.

"Maybe that's why it keeps coming back," I added carefully. "You never stopped carrying it."

He didn't respond right away. Just sat there, still, maybe turning my words over, maybe sinking somewhere deeper than he was ready to share. I stayed quiet, unsure if anything else I could say would help.

After a moment, he said, "Thank you."

"I told you—"

"I know." He turned fully toward me, his shoulder leaning into the couch. "I still need to say it."

I mirrored him without thinking.

"Thank you for staying with me," he went on. "For being here." A beat. "I know you're still mad at me."

"Ash, let's get some sleep, okay?" I said. "I promise we can talk about this tomorrow. We're running on fumes."

And I wasn't sure I was ready for that conversation yet. Not after everything he'd just shared. I wasn't sure I'd be firm enough.

"Today can just be about this," I added. "About you. I'm not going anywhere."

His eyes searched my face, like he was looking for something to contradict him. When he didn't find it, he nodded.

He leaned his elbow on the couch and dragged a hand through his hair, the movement drawing my attention to his neck, to the collar of his shirt.

Something caught the light.

My heart kicked hard in my chest, and I reached out without thinking, fingers closing around the chain and lifting it.

Until a necklace rested in my hand.

Until the medallion lay warm in my palm. Gold. A simple *P* etched into the surface.

"Why are you wearing this?" I whispered.

He didn't answer right away. When I looked up, his expression was open again. Vulnerable.

"I always wear it."

I shook my head slowly. That couldn't be right. I would have noticed. *I would have known.*

"I don't when I run," he said. "But otherwise—it's on."

"Why?" I watched him closely, waiting for him to shut down, to deflect, to pull away.

He didn't. He tilted his head, a small smile touching his mouth. Soft. Familiar. "You know why."

So I can always keep you close to my heart.

That's what he'd said.

Four years ago, right before he left.

His gaze dropped to my neck, bare where the chain should have been, then lifted again. Something pained flickered there.

"Did you throw yours away?" There was a trace of humor in his tone, but it didn't hide the truth underneath it.

"Of course not, Ash," I said. "It's safe. I just don't—"

"I get it," he cut in quickly. "You didn't have to keep it. It's okay—I had that coming."

My heart slammed against my rib cage, like it wanted to break free and go to him. I let the necklace fall, the chain sliding back into place over his chest, settling above his heart.

"I don't… I don't know what to say."

Sebastian smiled—that stupid, fond smile—and before I could process anything else about this conversation, he leaned forward. Not in one smooth motion. He stopped. Hesitated. Gave me room. When I did nothing but stare, he closed the distance and pressed his lips to mine in a soft, fleeting kiss that sent fireworks through my entire body.

But it was just one.

Then he pulled back, giving me space again.

"Tomorrow?" he asked, hope threading through his voice.

I nodded. "Tomorrow."

He rested his forehead against mine. "Can I convince you to sleep in my bed with me?"

My stomach swooped. I shook my head.

His fingers lifted to my jaw, his thumb brushing gently over my skin. "How about the couch? We could just sleep out here."

"We've been sleeping in chairs for two days," I said. "Do you really want to keep that streak going when you have a perfectly good bed available?"

His lips twitched. "If it means I get to stay close to you, yeah. I'll take the couch."

Fuck. Me.

"Fine," I said. "I'll get the pillows."

Sebastian smiled again, brushing a kiss to my cheek before standing, looking almost giddy. "I'll grab the blankets."

We moved the couch cushions to make more room, gathered pillows, and settled in facing each other under a thick blanket.

We managed to keep our distance for maybe a second before our legs tangled together, the soft brush of feet against calves and thighs sending warmth through me. His hand rested at the back of my neck, his mouth only a breath away as I held him by the waist, keeping him close.

"Goodnight, my darling," he said, so soft.

I nudged my nose against his. "Goodnight."

As I closed my eyes, exhaustion finally claiming me, I felt his lips brush mine again—just a whisper of a kiss, one I answered before sleep pulled us under.

Then we fell fast, wrapped in each other.

———

I was lifted, the movement almost startling me awake, but I was too groggy to fight sleep. I curled into the body holding me, pressing my face into the warm skin of his neck.

Ash.

"What are you doing?" The words came out tangled together.

"Taking you to bed," he murmured. "Keep sleeping."

A moment later, I was lowered onto the bed, blankets pulled up around me as I sank into the mattress. I felt him tuck them in and press a kiss to my temple.

"I'm going to the hospital."

My hand reached for his shirt, fingers curling weakly.

"Everything's okay." He caught my wrist. "I'm just giving Oli a break. Sleep."

I nodded, eyes still closed, face buried in the pillow.

One last kiss, and he was gone.

Seconds later, I heard the rush of water from the shower. I cracked my eyes open just long enough to take in the room—the bedside table, the doors I knew led out to the terrace.

He'd left me in his bed.

I smiled to myself, nuzzling into the pillow again. "Sneaky fucker."

CHAPTER SEVENTEEN

ASH

The doctor met us just outside the ICU doors, a chart tucked under his arm and a paper coffee cup in his other hand. It was the kind you got from the hospital— the really bad kind. Maybe he was used to it by now.

"Your father had a good night," he said. "He's off the ventilator now—breathing on his own. His vitals have been stable since late last night."

The pressure in my chest loosened. Not relief exactly. More like a slow release from impending doom. I'd arrived hours ago, and we still hadn't been given a full report. Oliver had been going back and forth about leaving, restless and eager for this conversation so he could finally relax. I couldn't blame him. Even with Ethan close beside me, I'd woken up with my heart in my throat, needing to be here in case anything changed.

"He still needs to be in the ICU?" Oliver shifted in place, anxious.

"For now," the doctor replied. "That's expected after a bypass. But he's past the most critical window."

Henry let out a breath, rubbing at his jaw. His stubble had grown in, making him look rougher than usual. "So he's out of immediate danger."

"Yes," the doctor said without hesitation.

The word settled between us, and the fear lost its hold.

"Is he awake?" I asked.

"On and off. We're keeping him lightly sedated so he can rest, but he's been responsive. Oriented. A little irritable—which I'll take as a good sign."

Oliver huffed out a laugh.

"Can we see him?" Henry asked.

"In a bit." The doctor tucked the chart more securely under his arm. "It'll be a short visit. He may not remember much, but hearing familiar voices still helps."

"And recovery?" I asked because that part I understood. Structure and timelines.

The doctor didn't rush the answer. "He'll be here another day, then moved to step-down. Cardiac rehab will be important. It'll be weeks before he's steady. Months before he feels like himself again."

I nodded once.

"But," he added, meeting my eyes directly, "the surgery went well. His heart function looks good. We expect a full recovery."

Silence followed—not the suffocating kind this time. The kind that came after something fragile was finally said out loud and held.

"We'll let you know when you can go in."

When he walked away, Henry scrubbed a hand over his face and exhaled slowly. "So," he said. "He's going to be okay."

"Fuck," Oliver breathed, his face scrunching before easing as the tension finally broke.

I grabbed him by the back of his neck and pulled him into a hug, feeling the relief pass through both of us. "He's going to be okay."

"He's a stubborn fucker, that's for sure." Henry's voice wavered just enough to give him away.

Oliver pulled out of my arms and went straight to Henry,

hugging him tight. Henry tipped his head, but I caught a glimpse of his too-bright eyes, and my heart thudded.

Keep them safe—

The thought surfaced instinctively, old and automatic.

I let it pass. Ethan's words from last night steadied me—this wasn't mine to carry alone anymore. Not this time.

"Are you finally going to sleep?" Henry asked when they drew apart.

"You two keep forgetting that, out of the three of us, I'm the only one who's evolved to function without sleep."

"Yeah," Henry shot back, "but you don't *have* to."

Oliver's gaze drifted to the double doors. "I'm going to wait until I can go in. Then I'll leave." He looked back at us. "Deal?"

Henry and I agreed a little reluctantly.

We headed for our usual spot—the small table just outside the waiting room. Close enough that the nurses knew where to find us, far enough away that we could breathe for a minute. That was where life kept catching up with us. Work calls. Texts. Apologies wrapped around urgent requests that didn't care where we were.

By the time Ethan arrived—coffees balanced in one hand and paper bags in the other—Oliver and Henry had already been in to see our father, and I was answering my third call of the morning.

We were half-huddled around the table, shoulders brushing, paper bags spread between us like a makeshift camp.

"I'm so sorry to bother you right now," Oscar said the moment I picked up. "I know where you are. I wouldn't if this wasn't important."

"It's fine," I said, turning slightly away from the table. The movement made a dull pressure bloom behind my eyes, as if something tight were cinched across my temples. Lack of sleep. Too much coffee. Or both. "What's going on?"

Behind me, wrappers crinkled as Henry muttered something about hospital food being a human rights violation.

"We need confirmation on the revised figures before this goes upstairs," Oscar said. "There are discrepancies between the projections and reported revenue. If we send it as is, it's going to trigger questions."

A slow pulse started behind my right eye. I pressed my fingers briefly to my temple, trying to force my focus back into place. "Send the files," I said. "All of them."

"I'm really sorry to bother you right now—"

"It's okay. Send them." I ended the call and stared at my phone for a second longer than necessary, willing my brain to cooperate.

It didn't.

Across the table, Ethan swallowed around a bite, sliding a coffee toward me without interrupting whatever Oliver was saying.

I tried to listen. Caught half a sentence. Lost the rest in the low thrum building behind my eyes. Christ.

I didn't have it in me to look things over right now. But... Ethan was good at this kind of thing. He could help.

I bit the side of my thumb before clearing my throat. "Ethan."

Three heads lifted.

He stilled immediately. "Yeah?"

I hesitated—the instinct to say never mind rising fast and familiar—and then pushed through it. "Can you do me a favor?"

His posture shifted, attentive. "Anything."

"Oscar's sending over a report," I said. "Revenue discrepancies. I just need it flagged—anything that looks off, anything that doesn't track. Would you mind looking it over and letting me know?"

Henry's brows shot up. Oliver's coffee froze halfway to his mouth.

Ethan didn't react to any of that; he just nodded once. "Of course."

Relief moved through me so quickly it almost felt like

vertigo. "I don't have my laptop," I said, my hand drifting back to my temple as the pressure tightened again.

"I can help with that," Oliver said immediately. "Call my assistant. He can get one here."

"That's perfect, Oli. Thank you. Here—" I pulled up the contact and handed it to Ethan. "Use my phone. The files are there. You can take a look after you call."

Oliver's thumbs were flying over his screen. "I've texted him. He knows what it's about."

Ethan stood, already dialing. "I'll take care of it." He paused, studying my face. "Want me to get you something for that headache?"

I smiled and shook my head. He squeezed my shoulder as he passed—brief, comforting—then stepped toward the quieter end of the corridor, voice low as he handled the details. I watched him go a second longer than I meant to.

When I looked back, Henry was staring at me like he'd just witnessed a solar eclipse. Oliver's expression was quieter, but no less stunned.

I reached for my coffee. "What?"

"Nothing." Henry looked down, biting back a smile. "Not saying a word."

Oliver swallowed, a small curve to his lips. "He's good, right?"

I arched a brow.

"He's clever," Oliver went on. "When he worked at the company, he even had Dad impressed."

Something warm and fierce swelled in my chest. "He's amazing," I said. "Marcela—the head of marketing—loves him. People above his pay grade…" I let a grin slip. "Not so much."

Henry leaned his elbows on the table, still pretending to be focused on his bagel. "So, as long as we're talking about E…" He glanced over his shoulder, then back at me. "What, pray tell, does your boyfriend think of all this? Slumber parties and whatnot?"

Both of them waited.

"We broke up."

Oliver sank back in his chair. "Oh, thank fuck."

"Jesus Christ, Ash." Henry set his breakfast down, the paper crinkling softly. "Way to keep us all in suspense. You couldn't just say that?" He frowned. "When?"

"A little while ago," I said. "Ethan knows. I told him on the way over."

"So what now?" Oliver asked.

"Finally admitting to what everyone with functioning eyesight has known for years?" Henry chimed in.

Oliver snorted into his coffee as I shot Henry a look.

"Now we talk." My gaze flicked to Ethan, still pacing with the phone pressed to his ear. "It's long overdue."

Henry followed my line of sight, then looked back at me, something like relief flickering across his face. "Okay," he said, nodding once. "Good. That's… good."

"So you're getting back together?" Oliver asked.

I took a slow sip of coffee. "If he'll have me."

Henry rolled his eyes. "He moved to another continent for you, is fixing your mess from a hospital hallway, and hasn't taken his eyes off you since we got here. I'd say your odds are decent."

Oliver's mouth twitched.

"You more than anybody know how badly I've fucked this up. All the time I wasted…" I shook my head. "There's a lot of groveling to be done. A lot to mend."

I'd made so many mistakes with Ethan from the moment we met that they blurred into one long chain, each one another blow to his pride. To his heart. Even if he wanted to be here for me—even if he'd told me he did—believing we could grow past this was another thing entirely. Believing I could give him what he needed… and that he would trust me enough to accept it.

Oliver's hand landed on my shoulder, bringing my attention

back to him. "We all fuck up, Ash. That's just life." He shrugged. "It's how you show up after that counts."

His words touched on more than just this—on the mistakes I kept making with them. The ones I'd been making for years.

I bit the inside of my cheek, my leg bouncing as I held his gaze. "I'm sorry I didn't let you in. With the freeze." My eyes flicked to Henry. "Both of you."

The way they looked at me then made my chest tighten—like I was back in that bedroom years ago, both of them looking up at me, waiting.

But I got it now.

They weren't waiting for me to make things better.

They were waiting for me to stay.

I exhaled hard. "It's—" My lips pressed together. "I can't fix it. It fucking kills me that I can't."

Neither of them rushed to fill the silence.

Henry leaned forward first, forearms on the table. "What did Elena say?"

I dragged a hand down my face. "She wants to offset the loss through private sector contracts. Fast. Aggressive expansion." My mouth twisted. "I've barely looked at them. I've been... focused on making it go away."

Oliver nodded slowly, absorbing that. "Ash."

I already knew that tone. I braced for it anyway.

"Why are you trying to do this by yourself?"

My spine stiffened. "I'm the one who—"

"You're the one who *cares* the most," Oliver corrected gently. "That's not the same thing as being the only person responsible."

"There are entire departments whose job it is to handle fallout like this," Henry said. "You don't get to martyr yourself just because you hate losing."

"I'm not martyring—"

"You're exhausted," Oliver cut in, not unkindly. "You're running on caffeine and stubbornness. That's not strategy."

My jaw tightened. They weren't wrong. I hated that they weren't wrong—and that it had taken me this long to listen.

"We can look at it together," Oliver continued. "Loop in Elena. Finance. Marketing. Pivot the strategy—focus on private sector expansion for now. You don't have to solve it in one sleepless night."

My instinct was to refuse. To push back. To take it all back into my own hands where it belonged. But the pressure behind my eyes pulsed again, dull and relentless.

I couldn't keep this up.

"We'll figure it out," Henry added. "Together. That's what we do."

I looked between them—really looked—and felt something give, just a little.

Before I could respond, Henry's phone buzzed on the table.

He glanced down and pushed back his chair. "Vivian's here. I'm being summoned." He squeezed the back of my neck as he passed, a quick, grounding gesture. "Everything's going to be okay, Ash."

Then he was gone.

Oliver watched him disappear down the corridor before turning back to me, hand already reaching for his coffee.

My gaze drifted past him instead.

Ethan stood at the far end of the hall, leaning against the wall, one phone tucked between his ear and shoulder as he scrolled through files on another. Focused. Calm. Completely unbothered by the chaos around us.

Then, as if he felt my eyes on him, he looked up. Whatever was on my face must have given me away, because his expression softened immediately.

Oliver followed my line of sight, a small smile tugging at his mouth. "You're different with him."

"Am I?"

"It's sweet," he said, taking a sip. "I never really got to see you two together. I wasn't expecting it to be like that."

I tilted my head. "Like what?"

"You know." He waved a hand, widening his eyes like that was supposed to explain anything. "I expected you to be all... *Sebastian* about it. And it's not. Which is a good thing. I just didn't know."

If Oliver was fumbling for words, he'd definitely reached his limit.

"I don't think you function as well as you think you do without sleep."

He laughed, setting his coffee down. "You're leaning on him. I've never seen you do that. With anybody."

My lips parted.

"I figured you'd be all protective and authoritative," he went on, "and you're just..." He let the word hang.

"What?"

"Soft," Oliver said. "You're softer with him."

Couldn't argue with that. Ethan just brought it out of me. Yet another thing I couldn't control around him—one I didn't want to. Not anymore.

I hummed, and Oliver rolled his eyes, a hint of amusement there.

"It's good that you feel safe with him, Ash," he said. "It's a really good thing."

"If it works out," I muttered.

"It will." He smiled at me, the kind that didn't leave room for debate.

"Maybe."

Oliver stared into his coffee like it might hold answers, then let out a quiet chuckle that grew into a full laugh, the sound edged with exhaustion and disbelief.

I frowned. "You need to sleep."

He nodded, wiping at the corner of his eye. "I do. But god— you do realize we're going to have the same in-laws?"

"And that's funny to you?"

"They don't like you—at all."

"I've assumed as much," I said. "I'm not crazy about them either."

He made a dismissive wave with his cup. "Margaret's always been too preoccupied with what people think," Oliver went on. "And just because he's older, it doesn't make the age gap disappear, you know?"

My stomach twisted, the guilt I'd carried about Ethan—and the disparity in our ages—surfacing all over again. "I know."

"Do I think she's aiming her anger at the wrong thing? Absolutely." He shrugged. "But part of me gets why it bothers her so much. No one wants that for their kid. To watch them struggle like that."

My brows drew together. "Because of how different our lives will be?"

"No. Because of how hard it was on Ethan."

That caught me off guard. "When I left?"

"People were horrible to him. You know this," he said casually, taking a sip of his coffee like he hadn't just wrecked me with that single sentence.

"I—"

His eyes lifted to mine.

"I didn't know that," I said quietly.

Oliver's expression fell. "I mean, Ash... what did you expect? That the scandal would just leave with you?"

Yes. That had been exactly what I'd thought. It sounded stupid hearing it out loud.

"How was he struggling?"

Oliver glanced at Ethan, now talking to Henry, the two of them smiling easily, before turning back to me. "He didn't really have much of a life in college. As far as I know, he kept to himself. Mostly stayed at the house with us or went out with Henny—and even that was rarely in the city."

Something tight closed around my ribs. I watched Ethan laugh at something Henry said, like the past Oliver was describing belonged to someone else entirely.

"His own family wasn't talking to him," he said. "Going to Madrid was the right call, I think. Not just for you two. He needed a fresh start. He needed his life back."

Fuck.

And then he'd gotten there, and I'd been a complete asshole to him.

No wonder he'd been so angry.

I'd blown up his life and then hadn't even had the decency to really see it. To see him. Or what I'd done. Or tell him how much he'd meant to me all along.

I'd been a fucking idiot.

"Hey," Oliver said. "You're working on it now, right? Making it better? That's what matters."

I nodded, but the knot in my chest stayed tight. It would stay there until I actually did something about it.

Ethan needed this. He needed me to be honest. To show up—the way he kept showing up for me. And I was fucking done half-assing things with him.

"I'll make it better," I said, my voice firmer this time.

Oliver smiled. "Exactly." He shrugged, then looked away. "At least you don't have to deal with his father anymore."

Another sinking feeling settled low in my stomach. "Actually… we should probably talk about that."

Oliver's expression sobered instantly.

My eyes found Ethan one more time, lingering there a second longer before I leaned forward and laid it all out—the shit piling up in the background.

CHAPTER EIGHTEEN

ASH

Around seven that same night, I was pacing in the waiting room.

Oliver and Henry had stepped out to grab dinner for us, and Ethan had left a little while earlier to catch up on schoolwork. The hospital was quieter now, the usual sounds softened into a low hum—machines beeping somewhere down the hall, footsteps passing, the muted squeak of a cart being pushed by.

Right now, it was just Vivian and me.

The doors swung open, and she stepped out, her eyes finding mine immediately.

"How's he doing?" I asked.

She smiled, small but genuine. "Better, I think."

Vivian and I had never really had much of a relationship. Our father had remarried a while after our mother passed, but back then I hadn't been able to see her as anything other than a replacement. I knew my coldness wasn't necessary anymore. Still, some habits were hard to kill.

She took a couple of steps toward me. "He's awake right now. I think he's going to fall asleep soon, but… this might be the right time if you want to go in. Say hello."

I froze, staring at her. I hadn't been back in there since the first time. Back when he'd still been unconscious.

"I don't want to upset him," I said after a moment. "That can't be good for him right now—"

"It won't be a surprise," she said. "He knows you're here."

My throat went dry. "I—"

"He was asking about you," she added. "I told him. Hope that's okay."

I drew in a slow breath, curling my hands into fists to keep them from shaking. "I'm not sure that's the best idea."

She nodded, unoffended. "I think he'd really appreciate it if you went in. Not for long. Just hello."

Her eyes weren't unkind—just not the ones I knew. A dark shade of blue instead of the rich brown I'd grown up with—my mother's.

I clicked my tongue, exhaling through my nose.

"Just think about it," she said before she turned and walked away, leaving the waiting area behind her.

Then it was just me. Me and my pride.

Or maybe not pride at all.

Maybe it was just fear.

I ran a hand through my hair, noting absently how long it was getting. Before I could talk myself out of it again, I turned and pushed the doors open.

"For Mr. Langley?" a nurse asked as soon as she noticed me hovering.

I nodded once.

"This way."

I followed her down the same path as last time, though I barely remembered it, until we stopped at his room.

His eyes were closed. The ventilator was gone, and a blue sheet rested over his chest, rising and falling slowly with each breath.

I suppose this would be easier if he wasn't awake.

Stepping into the room quietly, I stopped at his bedside and looked down at him. He still seemed smaller—but less so without all the machines. Older, too. That realization hit me harder than I expected, settling heavily within me.

I was staring at his hand when I heard it.

"Sebastian." His voice was rough. Hoarse.

I turned, and our eyes met. They softened in a way I had never seen before. Not once. And then they glimmered.

My heart kicked painfully against my ribs.

Something tugged at my hand, and I startled when I realized he'd grabbed it, his grip weak but insistent.

"I'm here, Dad," I said, my voice steadier than I felt.

"Sebastian." His face twisted into something like relief and pain all at once. "I'm sorry."

For a second, I thought I'd misheard him. But then he said it again, clearer this time.

"I'm sorry, son. I'm so sorry."

My eyes filled as his did. I tightened my grip on his hand, reaching over with my other to rest it on his shoulder. "It's okay," I said softly. "We're good. It's okay. You're okay."

He nodded, holding on to me like he was afraid I'd disappear. His eyes closed, and a small, tired smile curved his lips.

I swallowed hard. "It's okay."

———

By the time I got back to the apartment, the adrenaline had burned itself out, leaving me feeling stripped raw and strangely weightless.

The place was dark and quiet when I stepped inside. No lights on. No movement. I toed off my shoes by the door and paused, listening, but the only sound was the low hum of the city filtering in through the glass. Ethan must've crashed—jet lag finally catching up with him.

I moved through the apartment slowly, my father's voice still echoing in my head.

I'm sorry.

The words felt heavier now that everything else had gone silent. He'd never said them before. Not to me. And I didn't know yet what I was supposed to do with an apology like that— offered so late, wrapped in tubes and weakness, and a hand clutching mine like a lifeline.

But it mattered.

It mattered that he'd said it. That he'd seen me. That, for once, he hadn't looked at me like something that needed to be shaped or corrected or hardened.

I stepped out onto the terrace, leaving the door slightly ajar, and the cold hit immediately—cutting through my shirt, stealing the warmth from my skin in seconds. The city opened around me in a wash of distant sirens, traffic, and scattered light, my breath fogging faintly in the air.

The outdoor space was just as I'd left it—low couch, small table. The place I used to come when I needed air and a vice I could justify. Where we used to come out together.

Reaching into my pocket, I pulled out the pack I'd bought earlier and sank into the couch, crossed my ankles on the table, lit the cigarette, and took the first drag slowly, letting the burn settle into my chest. The smoke curled upward, disappearing into the night, and for the first time all day, I let myself just sit there.

Breathing.

Feeling.

Letting it all land.

My father was alive, and he was going to be okay.

"Busted." His voice startled me.

Ethan was leaning against the doorway, arms crossed, a familiar smirk in place. The low terrace light caught the sharp lines of his face, softened by the wear of the day.

I let out a quiet chuckle. "You caught me. Thought you were asleep."

He shrugged, stepping out onto the terrace and moving to

the railing. "I had a paper to turn in. Got wrapped up in it and didn't bother turning on the lights." He leaned back against the rail, propping his elbows on it. "And I wanted to make sure you got back okay. You need to rest."

I took another drag, resisting the urge to close my eyes and sink too far into the familiar burn. "In a little while." Pulling another cigarette from the pack, I held it out to him. "You want one?"

Ethan's smile lost some of its edge, something like déjà vu flickering between us. "Yeah."

He crossed the space and stopped in front of me. I lifted a brow, uncrossed my legs, letting the invitation hang there without words. He pressed his lips together in that shy, almost-boyish smile before nodding and stepping in, lowering himself between my thighs and settling back against me, his spine fitting easily to my chest.

This was already better than the cigarette.

I leaned forward and lit his for him, watching the way he inhaled, then exhaled slowly, smoke curling into the night.

"Haven't done this in a while," he said, holding it out in front of him.

"Me neither."

His hair brushed my cheek as he tipped his head back onto my shoulder. "Why now?"

I took another drag, my free hand lifting instinctively to his hair, fingers sliding through it, nails scraping lightly against his scalp. "I saw my dad earlier."

"Yeah?" Ethan angled his head to look up at me.

I nodded. "He fell asleep a few minutes in. But he saw me." My voice dropped. "Said my name. That he was sorry."

Ethan pulled back slightly, just enough for me to see his eyes widen. "Wow."

I huffed out a quiet laugh. "Tell me about it."

A shiver ran through him, small but unmistakable, like the cold had finally slipped past his sweats. Without thinking, I tucked him into my side, my palm sliding up and down his arm to warm him.

He didn't protest. If anything, he leaned in. "Are you doing okay?"

I shrugged, the movement lifting him with me. "Better than the last couple of days. It's just been… a lot."

His lips pressed together at that, but before I could decide what it meant, he slipped the cigarette back between them. "It has been…"

"Did you find anything?" I asked.

Ethan nodded. "A few irregularities in the projections. I flagged the areas that don't track and sent everything back so they can reconcile the numbers." He watched me for a moment. "Do you want to look it over?"

The old reflex kicked in. Review it. Confirm it.

I paused, taking a long drag. Then I shook my head on the exhale. "Tomorrow." I scrubbed a hand over my face. "Thanks for helping. Don't know what we'd do without you."

His chest rose and fell as he smoked, flicking the ash away before bringing the cigarette back to his mouth, and I watched every small movement up close. Entranced.

I stubbed my cigarette out in the ashtray as his knuckles brushed over my skin. I looked down to find his finger hooked around my necklace, his eyes fixed on it.

"You'd get another research assistant," he said lightly, killing his smoke too.

A chuckle slipped out of me as I shook my head. "Impossible. There isn't another *you*."

"You're good with words, Mr. Langley. I'll give you that."

I smiled. "You think I'm smooth-talking you?"

"I know you are," he said. "That's your thing."

Amused, I let a low sound escape me. "Do you still think that? That I'm only saying what you want to hear?"

"Obviously."

His hair slid between my fingers as I reached for him again, twisting it gently and tugging, drawing him closer until we were nose to nose, his breath warm against my mouth.

"My thing," I said softly, "is meaning every ridiculously infatuated word I've ever said to you. I don't do flattery. Not with you. You should know that by now—I've been hopeless where you're concerned since the moment I saw you."

His lashes fluttered, and for a second he didn't say anything—just watched me, like he was deciding whether to believe me.

"See?" he murmured.

"What?"

His finger twirled around the chain. "That. That's the smooth-talking."

I smiled, unable to help it. "I'm not trying to convince you of anything," I said. "I'm just telling the truth."

He turned more onto his side, his body fitting even closer. "Mhm," he hummed, low and unconvinced.

My hand went to his neck, holding him there as his eyes traced my face—my nose, my jaw… my mouth. The interest in them made my stomach swoop.

"You don't know how you take my breath away," I whispered.

His blue eyes snapped back to mine, and something in me gave. Melted. Everything about him felt overwhelming in the best way. "You're so fucking beautiful."

Ethan's lips parted. His gaze dipped, lashes shadowing his cheeks, and then his hand fisted in my shirt, pulling me in with quiet, desperate strength. I barely had time to register the heat of him before I was there—against his mouth, soft and warm and already opening for me.

The kiss wasn't gentle. Not frantic either.

It was deep. Intentional. Like we were finally meeting in the middle.

Our lips moved together, slow at first, then hungrier—tongues sliding, pressing, relearning the shape of each other. I felt his breath hitch every time I kissed him harder, the quiet sounds he made sending a jolt straight through me. My hands came up without thinking, steadying him. *Us.*

Then we were kissing. Really kissing.

And I did it like I'd been holding back for months. For fucking years. Like my body finally remembered exactly where it belonged and refused to let go. Like if he didn't keep opening for me—keep letting me feel him like this—I might actually shatter in his hands.

When we finally broke apart, we were both breathing hard. I rested my forehead against his, our noses brushing, the space between us charged and fragile and *alive.* Our breaths mingled in the cold air, warm bursts against chilled skin. I leaned in again, ready to give him everything—

And stopped at the firm press of his hand against my chest, holding me back.

"You're like fucking human crack or something," he muttered. "Fuck."

"Darling—"

"No." His voice was firm—so was the rest of him—as he pushed me back and stood, turning away. "We can't be trusted with this, Sebastian. We're alone. Unsupervised. We can't."

"Why not?"

He scrubbed his hands over his face, shoulders tight. "Because it's complicated. You know that."

Right.

Because it was time.

And I was done pretending it wasn't.

"Darling," I said, "would you look at me?"

"No." His voice broke just enough to betray him. "Every time I look at you, everything gets fucked up."

The movement was slow as I slid down onto the floor. My knees hit the cold stone, the chill biting through my skin. I didn't reach for him. Didn't touch him. I stayed where I was—spine straight, hands open at my sides, palms up.

No control. No armor. No defense.

Just me.

"Please."

He turned. And froze.

His eyes dropped from the couch to the floor—to me—and went wide, like his mind couldn't quite catch up to what he was seeing. Like the image didn't make sense yet.

"You said you wanted me to beg," I said, steady despite the way my heart threatened to tear itself out of my chest.

His lips parted.

"So here I am. And I'm ready to do just about anything to earn your forgiveness. Even if you say no. Even if you have every reason to."

He didn't move. Didn't breathe.

"I'm sorry I left," I said. "I'm sorry I stopped trying. I'm sorry I filled my head with excuses and plans to keep us apart."

His throat worked.

"I'm sorry I didn't break up with him the moment I saw you. I'm sorry I let you believe—even for a second—that you were optional. That you were something I could walk away from."

Ethan's fingers curled at his side, knuckles whitening. He didn't look away.

"And I'm sorry it took me this long to say it out loud," I went on, my voice rough now. "Because I've known it for years."

He shook his head faintly. "You're upset—"

"No," I interrupted, stopping the thought before it could finish forming. "I'm not. I know exactly what I'm saying."

"This—this whole thing just fucked with your head," he tried. "You don't mean—"

"Ethan."

He stopped, whatever he'd been about to say falling away.

I drew in a breath and pulled everything to the surface— every truth I'd buried, every feeling I'd locked away—because he had always been able to read me. Because there had never been a version of this where I could lie to him and get away with it.

My lips curved, just barely. "Can we just pretend…"

His breath hitched. His eyes gleamed.

"Just for a second," I continued, "that I didn't fuck this up beyond repair. That you still trust me. That you know no one has ever had me—has ever held my heart in their hands—the way you do. Please?"

The word sat between us. Raw. Exposed.

I stayed where I was, on my knees, letting him see all of it. All of me.

The indecision was written all over his face—the want, the fear, the years of damage I'd caused.

And still—

He nodded. A small, careful thing.

I swallowed hard, pulse roaring in my ears.

And jumped off the ledge.

"I love you, Ethan."

His eyes went impossibly wide.

My heart slammed against my ribs so hard it hurt, but the words didn't scare me the way I'd expected. They felt inevitable. *Necessary*.

"I love you," I said again.

Because I finally could.

CHAPTER NINETEEN

ETHAN

My heart was beating in my ears. Loud and unrelenting.

Each thump echoed as I kept looking down at him—at Sebastian Langley, on his knees, for me.

I'd asked for it, but never in a million years had I imagined it would come with those words. With this piece of himself I'd never truly believed he would give me. Not like this. Not willingly.

I love you.

He wasn't terrified, and that was the thing. His shoulders had eased, just slightly. His eyes stayed locked on mine, like something heavy had finally been set down. Like he'd said it—and could finally breathe.

There he was, waiting. Waiting for me to react. To acknowledge what he'd just done.

And all I could do was stare through the pounding of my heart.

My lips were still tingling from his kiss. I could still taste him—smoke and heat and us, lingering on my tongue. Every instinct in my body told me to move. To close the distance.

Experience kept me exactly where I was.

"You love me?" The words slipped out, disbelieving.

"Yes," he said, without hesitation.

"I don't—" I stopped, not even sure where I'd been going with that.

Sebastian's palms rested on his thighs as he sat back on his heels. "Please forgive me." Moonlight caught the sharp lines of his face, softening him in a way that made my chest ache.

I love you.

"Please give me a chance to make this right. To prove to you how much I mean it. How much I need you with me."

He was actually begging.

I love you.

My heartbeat sped up, each thud crowding the next, chest rising and falling too fast. My fingers tingled with the urge to touch—to take—to *feel*.

"Please…" The word came out on a breath, quiet and wrecked.

He loves me.

My body moved before my head could catch up. I crossed the distance in two steps, hands fisting in his shirt, in his hair, hauling him up as I dropped on him and caught his mouth in a bruising kiss. It felt like impact—like collision—like every second I'd spent holding myself back finally snapped.

His breath left him in a broken sound against my lips.

I kissed him like I needed to feel it in my bones. Like it had to hurt a little, just to know it was real. Everything blurred into warmth and pressure and the persistent pounding of my heart in my ears. The world narrowed to the slide of his mouth against mine, to the way his hands tightened like he was afraid I'd vanish if he let go.

I didn't think.

I couldn't.

I just kissed him back—hard and deep and desperate—like saying yes without words. Choosing him all over again.

His hands found my waist, pulling me close, sliding lower

until they slipped under my thighs. I nodded frantically into the kiss, and he pushed up from the floor. My legs locked around his hips, holding myself there as he carried us into his bedroom without breaking stride. The terrace door clicked shut behind us, keeping the warmth in.

As soon as my back hit the bed, I fisted my hands in his shirt and hauled him down over me, not giving either of us a second to think. Nobody was going to slow this down. Not now.

He was mine. He was finally fucking mine.

A sound broke from me as I pulled at his clothes, fingers clumsy on the buttons of his shirt when I realized I couldn't just rip it off. He didn't have the same problem—one rough pull, and my sweater and shirt were gone, and he was back at my mouth, helping me finish undoing his shirt.

Then his bare skin was over mine, and I went dizzy with it— with how badly I wanted him, with how long this hunger had lived beneath the surface. His hips pressed down on mine, his body settling perfectly between my legs, and there was nothing left to hide about how badly we wanted each other.

I slid my hands between us, reaching for his waistband when he broke the kiss.

His forehead rested against mine, his mouth a breath away, hot and panting. "Are you sure?"

"Yes." I arched up into him, catching his mouth again.

Sebastian pushed my sweats down, taking my underwear with them. He barely got them past my ass before his hand came back, grabbing, squeezing—rough with want. The clink of his belt cut through the room, and I fumbled to undo it, groaning when I felt the hard line of his cock slide against mine.

"F-fuck—" I'd missed that. I'd missed him so much.

We both wanted the same thing—to move together, to close the distance completely—but our half-assed attempts at getting undressed kept getting in the way.

I pushed him back, breaking the kiss. "Take your fucking clothes off."

Sebastian huffed out a short, amused breath before stepping back off the bed and doing exactly what I asked. I finished kicking off my sweats as I watched him. As he bared himself, his eyes stayed locked on mine.

He was still a work of art—toned without being excessive, skin tanned and dusted with dark hair, familiar and devastating all at once. He looked broader than he used to. Stronger. The sight of him like this sent my pulse spiking. And his dick—fuck —it stood at attention, full of promises of what was about to happen. I wanted to run my tongue over it. Ride it until he screamed my name.

The clatter of the bedside drawer snapped my attention back to his face as he reached inside, pulling out what he needed and setting it on the mattress.

His jaw was tight when he looked at me. "Pillows."

I crawled back onto the bed, opening my legs in clear invitation, silently telling him to come back to me. He did, his mouth curving into a smirk as his eyes traced every inch of my exposed skin. And then he was back in my space, crashing into my mouth before either of us could even think about slowing down.

I ran my hands all over him—down the broad span of his back, my nails scraping as I went, over his ass as he rutted against me, sending waves of pleasure through my body. Into his hair, gripping and tugging. I couldn't make up my mind. I wanted all of him.

Sebastian's mouth finally broke away from mine, kissing along my jaw and down my throat, sucking hard enough to pull a moan from me. My body rocked beneath him with every movement, the agonizing pleasure of his cock dragging over mine, again and again, driving me wild. His hands were open and hot against my ribs, then under my thighs, bracing my legs around him, holding me exactly where he wanted me.

His lips slid up, close to my ear, and in that deep, gorgeous register, he rumbled, "I missed you, my pet."

I groaned loudly, the name landing harder than it ever had before. "Fuck—fuck me, Ash. Right now."

His forehead rested against mine again, his dark eyes locked on my lips. "Is that what you want?" His voice was unsteady, rough with want, his hips grinding against mine.

"Ah—" I gasped. "Fuck yes. Now."

He moved back to my neck, kissing and licking over my collarbone. I was about to protest when I heard the unmistakable click of the lube opening. A second later, slick fingers were at my taint, sliding back to rub over my hole.

My neck arched, head pressing into the pillows as my fingers twisted tight in his hair. "I want to suck your dick," I said, breathless.

Sebastian hummed, his mouth trailing down my chest until he reached my nipple, drawing it into his mouth. "Later." His fingertip kept circling, coaxing, almost teasing me into relaxing before pressing inside.

My legs fell open at my sides. "More. Don't go slow. I can't— fuck." His finger sank deeper. "I can't do slow right now."

His mouth stayed on my chest, licking and nibbling, the pleasure sharp enough to make me hiss before he moved to the other side.

"Then relax for me, my darling," he murmured. Another suck. "So I can get inside you." A bite. "And fuck you the way you want me to." He pulled his finger out and replaced it with two.

A loud groan left me, and he followed with one of his own.

"That's it, pet. Loud," he whispered against my lips, licking his way into my mouth. "Make it loud for me."

He kissed me deep, swallowing every sound his fingers drew out of me as they kept moving—sliding in, curving just right— until stars burst behind my eyes. When he worked a third in, my whole body coiled tight, ankles digging into the backs of his thighs to keep him close. My cock leaked against my stomach, desperate for attention.

As if reading my thoughts, he broke away from the kiss and traced his mouth down my body until he reached me, licking the head.

My hips lifted, my eyes rolling back. "Fuck!"

"Are you close?" he panted, his nose brushing along my cock before he buried it in the hair at the base, inhaling deeply, his hand cupping my balls before giving them a tug.

"Yes." I didn't bother lying. The edge in his voice told me he was close too.

He pulled his fingers free without warning—gentle but decisive—and moved off me. The sound of the condom wrapper tearing echoed in the room, my body vibrating with anticipation as I watched him settle on his knees between my legs, slicking himself with more lube before working a little more into me.

He crawled back over me, hands hooking under my knees and pressing my thighs toward my chest.

Sebastian kissed me again, softer this time, lingering, pulling me into it. "Ready?"

I nodded as the blunt head of his cock pressed against me. He didn't push in—just dragged it over me like he couldn't help himself. The look on his face, completely lost in this, knocked the breath out of me. It had been so long since I'd seen it.

"Come on," I groaned. "Push it in."

A grin curved his lips as he adjusted his weight, the pressure building.

My lips parted on a breath as he ran his tongue over them—

And the head of his cock slipped inside.

"Fuuuuuck..." My thighs trembled in his grip as he kept going, inch by inch, pulling back just enough before pressing deeper again. His breath panted into mine, our mouths meeting in brief, broken kisses neither of us could sustain, all our focus on him finally getting all the way in—driving himself home.

He dragged out once more, then slid fully inside, lifting my ass from the bed until I was nestled over his hips, and we both breathed out into the space between us.

Sebastian pressed a soft kiss to my lips. "You feel so good," he whispered hoarsely. "So much better than I remembered."

I rolled my hips, clenching around him, and smiled when his eyes fluttered shut and a quiet gasp slipped free.

"Fucking heaven," he groaned, shifting his hips slightly as he dipped to kiss my neck. The scratch of his beard against my skin raised goosebumps instantly.

My hands went to his hips, over his ass, nails digging in as I pulled, urging him to move. "Come on, Ash."

"How do you want it?"

I smiled to myself. "You know the answer to that." My blood burned beneath him, under my skin, waiting to combust the moment he started to thrust.

"Fast?" he breathed against me.

I nodded, biting down hard on my lip.

Sebastian pulled his hips back, the drag of his cock lighting me up from the inside.

"Rough?"

"Yes."

He eased back just enough for our eyes to lock again. "Hard?"

I dug my nails deeper into his skin, watching him bare his teeth, a soft hiss pulling from him.

"You know what I want, Sebastian," I said. "Give it to me."

He grinned, his gaze sweeping over my face, and practically purred, "My pleasure."

Then he snapped his hips forward, hard, rocking me into the bed and setting me on fire.

Pleasure sparked through my body, all the way to my toes, curling tight as he began to thrust in earnest. His forehead pressed to mine, breath hot against my mouth, soft grunts leaving him as skin slapped against skin.

"Fuck—yes. Like that."

My neck strained as I arched back, lifting my hips to meet his punishing thrusts. He hit exactly where I needed him, again and again, until my mind went blissfully blank from the feel of him. I didn't hold back a single sound, knowing how much he loved it—how much he *needed* it. And it wasn't a show. He was driving me insane with every thrust, racking pleasure through my entire body.

My hand slid into his hair, keeping him close as I watched him now, trying to hold on to every second of it. This was Sebastian—his body over mine, his cock buried inside me, his shoulders flexing and straining as he moved. He looked down at me, his expression etched with pleasure, yes—but also something softer. Almost reverent.

The realization that this was actually happening—*with him*—pushed me closer to the edge more than the frantic movement of our bodies ever could. My cock was trapped between us, untouched and slick with precum, straining for friction.

Sebastian's breathing grew more labored, his chest rising and falling faster, his control clearly fraying. I loved seeing him like this. Loved that I was the only one who could make him give in to his instincts.

I tightened my grip on his hair. "Make me come."

"Anything for you, my pet." He tilted his head, bracing himself on one hand as the other slid between us. "Anything." His lips crashed back onto mine as his hand wrapped around my cock, no patience left in the way he stroked me.

"Fuck—"

My thighs clung to him, heat coiling low in my gut, pressure winding tighter and tighter until it was almost unbearable. My balls pulled tight, my breath stuttered, everything in me straining toward it—right there—

"God…" he breathed, awed, like he was watching something sacred happen.

I cupped his face, beard rough beneath my palms, needing him close, needing him with me. "Come with me."

He nodded against my forehead, breath shaking, thrusts turning messy and frantic. "Fuck—yes—"

The pressure snapped.

I gasped.

He groaned my name like it hurt, hips jerking hard as he stayed buried deep, his cock throbbing inside me as he came. The sounds he made, the way his body shuddered, the heat flooding through me—it all tipped me over the edge, and I spilled into his hand, pulse after pulse breaking free.

Everything blurred. My head went light, the edges of my vision soft and hazy as I watched him breathe, watched the way he stayed over me, still connected, still holding himself inside like he couldn't let go yet.

I thought, distantly, how much I would've loved it if he'd actually filled me.

Next time.

"I love you," he whispered against my mouth, voice wrecked, body slowly easing as the aftershocks faded.

I let go of his face and wrapped my arms around his neck, pulling him down with me into the shared heat of the bed. Sebastian pressed a kiss to my throat and stayed there, breathing me in, his weight warm and familiar.

For a long moment, neither of us moved.

The haze began to lift, and little things came back into focus —the muted city noise drifting through the window, the rumpled sheets beneath us, the steady rise and fall of his chest against mine. This room. This bed.

Look at us back here.

I traced a slow line over his shoulder, reacquainting myself with the feel of him, letting the silence settle between us.

Sebastian pulled out, slow and careful, disposing of the condom before returning to my side. He pressed soft kisses along my cheek and down my neck, unhurried, like he had nowhere else to be.

I smiled, letting myself take it in.

He grabbed something—a shirt maybe—and gently wiped

my chest, then his. "Do you want water?" His voice stayed low, as if anything louder might break the moment.

I turned just enough to brush my nose against his cheek. "Don't leave."

His arms came around my waist, drawing me closer, fitting us together again. "I wouldn't dream of it."

His fingers mapped slow, lazy patterns along my back; up and down, while we watched each other in the quiet. There was something fragile about this—something new and tender. Neither of us rushed to break it.

I brushed a strand of hair from his forehead. "What are you thinking about?"

He moved closer, pressing a kiss to the tip of my nose. "That it's been a while since I've felt this happy."

"Yeah? Since when?"

His eyes softened, open in a way I wasn't used to seeing. "Since the wedding, probably."

Something tight pulled in my chest. Aching. I leaned in and kissed him, and he met me without hesitation, like he'd been waiting for it. Our mouths brushed, and I felt it—that dangerous swell of something I'd been trying to keep buried.

This was too much. Too good. Too close to the thing I'd lost once and wasn't sure I'd survive losing again.

I closed my eyes. "My head's a mess right now."

Sebastian slid an arm beneath me and pulled me in, holding me close, his hand smoothing through my hair. "I'm not going to hurt you again," he said quietly. "I promise."

I didn't answer.

I wasn't sure how.

I could lie and say I believed him—but did I?

"Do you want to sleep?" I asked instead.

He shook his head. "I don't think I can." Sebastian brushed his cheek against mine, kissed it, then dipped to my neck. "You're in my bed, darling—I can't." His kisses turned urgent, demanding—his tongue sweeping over my skin, his mouth hot and open. "I want you all night. Fuck until thinking isn't even an option."

My cock twitched at his words. "Fuck," I whispered.

"I'll be right back," he said, kissing my lips before moving off the bed and into the bathroom.

I buried my face in the pillow, scrunching it tight as emotion swelled in my chest.

Don't get ahead of yourself.

This can all disappear in a second.

It's just sex. Not a fucking marriage proposal.

I forced my breathing to steady, listening to the water run, then his footsteps returned. Warmth pressed to my back as his mouth found my neck and a damp cloth brushed over my chest. I sighed, soaking up the attention.

Sebastian moved the cloth slowly—over my stomach, my cock, then along my back, between my cheeks—kissing my neck, nuzzling into my hair the entire time.

As he moved lower, his kisses followed—trailing down my spine, along my ribs, over the small of my back.

My breath hitched when he set the cloth aside, spread me gently, and kissed his way down my crease.

"Fuck," I breathed, unsteady.

His tongue brushed over my hole, and I flinched.

"Does that hurt?" he murmured, not pulling away, his voice already thick again.

"No. Just feels weird—sensitive. Don't stop."

"I'll keep it soft." His tongue returned, slower, gentler this time. His nails scraped lightly over my ribs, his face buried between my cheeks, his beard rough in the best way. "Hold yourself open."

I did immediately, reaching back to give him more room, my face burning. Sebastian groaned, his free hand cupping my balls before sliding forward to stroke my cock as it began to swell again.

His tongue pressed, patient, waiting for my body to yield—

and when it did, when he finally slipped inside, I clutched the pillow hard, panting into it.

"Ash…" I breathed as I heard him opening the lube again.

He kissed his way back up my spine, keeping me on my side. "I'll go slow."

I knew it was a question, even if he didn't say it like one. I nodded, helpless.

He was careful with his fingers, even though my body was already loose, already open. And when the head of his cock pressed back against me—condom on—he stopped, chin resting over my shoulder. "Do you want this?"

"More than anything."

A tortured moan left me as he eased inside.

"Slow, my darling," he murmured against my shoulder. "Let's fuck so slow we burn this bed to the ground."

I reached back, tangled my hand in his hair, holding myself in place as he rocked his hips in a deep, unhurried grind, barely pulling out before pressing back in.

Sebastian brought his hand to his mouth, spat into his palm, then wrapped it around my cock, stroking in the same slow rhythm. The slick glide made me shudder.

"Good?"

"So fucking good," I groaned, pushing back into him.

"Perfect," he said softly. "You're perfect."

———

The shower was running behind me.

I stared at myself in the mirror—at the mess of tangled curls on my head. There were bags under my eyes, but my skin looked fucking radiant. Glowing.

My gaze traced over it all. To the hickey blooming just under my jaw, dark and unmistakable. To the bite mark peeking over my shoulder, the one he'd left when he came. To the raw redness across my chest, still tender from the scrape of his beard.

Steam began to curl through the room.

Sebastian stood by the glass door, one hand under the water, testing and adjusting the temperature. My eyes dragged back to my reflection—to my kiss-swollen lips.

That last round had turned into an hour-long, achingly slow fuck that ended with me spilling over his hand again. Instead of letting me drift off afterward, he'd kissed me deeply, his hands roaming until he pulled me up and into the bathroom.

My thighs were still trembling.

I should've felt exhausted. My body certainly was. But my mind was lit up—completely consumed by him, by this fire burning between us. An insatiable need to have, to taste, to claim. Whatever doubts I'd been carrying hadn't disappeared— they'd become something else entirely. And as I cataloged the bruises marking my skin, the only thought left was how badly I needed to make him mine—to hold on before anything could take him away again.

Bare feet padded across the tile behind me. I felt his presence before I saw him, his gaze roaming over me as well, a low hum of approval leaving him. Goosebumps erupted across my skin.

Because he'd wanted the same thing.

And he'd gotten it.

Sebastian braced his hands on the counter, caging me in, a smile tugging at his mouth as he looked at our reflection.

I leaned my head back against his shoulder. "I'm looking a little rough."

Shaking his head, his eyes swept over me once more. "Masterpiece." That was all he said.

He pressed a kiss to my cheek before moving away toward the shower, and I turned to watch him go—watch the muscles in his legs tense and flex with each step. His ass tightened as he walked, and the low bathroom light caught every line of him, highlighting each perfectly carved groove. He was so tall. So thick. Dark hair dusted over his calves, his thighs, his groin— Sebastian turned onto his side, and my gaze followed that perfect trail up his chest. His hair was a little longer, now mussed from my hands.

I loved him like this—wilder.

He stepped into the shower, the waterfall head soaking him in seconds. Closing his eyes, he ran a hand through his hair, and I swear the moment slowed as I licked my lips.

"What are you waiting for?" His voice carried through the fogged glass, his grin unmistakable even through the steam.

I pushed off the counter, my mouth curling into a smirk.

My turn.

CHAPTER TWENTY

ASH

Every nerve in my body was awake, coiled too tight beneath my skin.

I couldn't remember the last time I'd felt like this—though it was probably with him.

But not like *this*.

There were no walls this time. No pressure. No lies. Nothing holding us back.

Would people be upset about it? Sure. I was guessing his parents would drag my name through the dirt again. But who the fuck cared?

The exhaustion in my limbs—in my mind—felt good. Not the bone-deep strain of holding everything up—just the clean release of finally letting go. It held me there, awake inside the moment instead of letting it slip through my fingers.

I'd probably let him sleep after the shower. But we could indulge in this a little longer. Maybe another round before we had to leave for the hospital again. And who could blame me for wanting him this much? For needing him?

Four fucking years of dreaming about him. Not just being with him like this—fucking him—but actually *having* him. I knew there were still conversations to be had, decisions to be made. But I'd told him I loved him, and he'd come to me so willingly. That had to mean something. Right?

The water washed away the sweat and the grime—and some of my doubt, especially when he stepped in and molded his perfect body to mine. I hummed softly as his arms wrapped around my waist, holding me there with him under the spray. His lips slid across my back, his tongue a warm caress as he caught the rivulets trailing down my skin.

I reached for the body wash, squirting some into my hands before turning in his grasp and taking a step back. Our eyes met as I worked up a lather, my palms sliding over his shoulder, his chest. Warm water traced the lines of his body, carrying the soap downward in lazy streams.

When I finished rinsing him, I tipped my head toward the shelf and reached for the shampoo. Ethan's hair had gotten so long—longer than before, falling into loose, golden curls that clung to his neck. I fucking loved it. And he knew that.

"Come here," I murmured.

He stepped closer without question, turning so his back was to me. I poured a small amount of shampoo into my palm and worked it gently into his scalp, massaging with my fingertips. The curls loosened beneath my hands, slipping between my fingers as I washed him. I combed through them slowly, more reverent than necessary, savoring every second of it. I could've stayed there forever just doing this. Just knowing I was allowed to touch him again—without fear, without distance, without losing him afterward. Listening to those little hums of approval through the rush of the water.

He tilted his head slightly, giving me better access, and I smiled despite myself. "Almost done," I said, my hands stilling for a moment before I rinsed the soap away, careful not to tug, letting the water run clear. I smoothed his hair back from his face when I was finished, my thumbs brushing his temples.

When he turned again, I expected to see fatigue. Some hint that the night had caught up with him. Instead, Ethan was watching me intently—eyes clear, focused, intense. Something warm and steady settled in me at the sight of it.

"My turn," he whispered.

Ethan picked up the body wash, his fingers brushing mine as he poured some into his hands. My gaze caught on the gold bands circling his fingers, the way they flashed softly under the light, right where they belonged. They always had. Ethan was made to wear things like that—meant to be looked at, worshipped when he did.

He stepped in closer, close enough that the warmth of him pressed into me, and then his hands settled on my shoulders, washing me with the same care I'd given him. Slow passes over my chest, my arms. His touch wasn't tentative, but it was thoughtful, like he was checking in with my body as he went.

I closed my eyes, water pounding against my back, his thumbs dragging unhurried circles that made me breathe a little deeper. When I opened them again, he was still watching me, a small curve at the edge of his lips. Then, without a word, he dropped to his knees. He didn't take his eyes off me as his hands came down with him, washing the backs of my thighs, my calves. He leaned forward, placing a kiss on my hip before his attention returned to the task.

I braced one hand against the glass in front of me, Ethan trapped between it and my body. My cock—which should have been more than satisfied for the night—started filling slowly at his attention. At his position.

His hands slid along the inside of my thighs, over the swell of my ass, fingertips just barely dipping into the crease. Then, bold and assured, he wrapped his fist around my cock and stroked.

I moaned softly, drawing his gaze back to mine.

He grinned, nudging me under the stream of water to rinse away the soap before guiding me forward again with a hand hooked under my thigh. As soon as I was close enough, he stuck out his tongue and let the head of my cock brush over it—softly at first, then with more pressure.

One of my hands slid into his hair, cupping his nape, holding him there as he looked up at me with that almost wicked glint, letting me sink deeper into his mouth.

Then he closed his lips around me and sucked, and my eyes practically rolled. He was careful—probably mindful that we were both oversensitized—but still took me deep and eased off again, his mouth working over my cock. Fuck—that felt incredible.

My mouth fell open as I watched him, felt the scorching heat of him, the pull of his lips. My legs threatened to give out every time the head of my cock brushed his throat. He kept at it for a couple of minutes, each second making it harder and harder for me to think, to stop myself from thrusting into that beautifully tempting mouth.

Until he moved back and looked up at me, licking his reddened lips and giving me a slow grin. His hand slid up my thigh, his head tilting. "Did you like that?"

I nodded, fingers twisting in his hair.

He bit down on his lip. "Why don't you turn around for me?"

My stomach flipped.

For half a heartbeat, something in me stalled—not because I was surprised; some part of me had always known we would end up here. The way he carried himself now, the way he touched me, thrummed with that need to claim. It wasn't bravado or recklessness. He wanted this. Needed it.

Ethan must have seen the apprehension on my face, because his grin only widened. He let go of my cock, his nails scraping lightly over my thighs. "Let me eat you out, Daddy."

"Fuck—" My whole body tensed at the request. And that fucking pet name. "Please don't start with that again."

Ethan chuckled roughly. "I'll stop." His face softened as his eyes dragged over me. "I'll make you feel good," he said, voice still thick and sinful.

I hesitated, my breath catching, turning shallow and fast before I could slow it.

He kissed my hip again. "Trust me?"

My chest rose with a longer inhale as I ran my thumb along his jaw, following the line of it, focusing on the feel against my skin. This wasn't surrender. It was choosing to feel safe with him. "You know I do."

"Then turn around."

Something in his tone made heat spark low. I started to move, my shoulders tightening before I allowed the tension to slip away.

"No—right here." He took hold of my hips and turned me toward the glass, positioning himself behind me. My hands came up without thought, palms meeting the surface, fingers spreading as my elbows locked. I leaned forward just enough to hold myself there, breathing through the strange mix of tension and exposure settling along my spine.

His lips touched the small of my back, and instinct made me want to pull away. Instead, I closed my eyes and let a breath leave me slowly, feeling the tightness ease as his mouth stayed there. Ethan's hands gripped me roughly—first my thighs, then my ass—keeping me steady while he kissed me again and again, his tongue warm as it moved over my skin.

Each pass of his mouth drew a deeper breath from me, my stance shifting wider instinctively as he spread me apart and let his kisses drift lower.

I couldn't remember the last time I'd done this, but my body didn't wait for me to catch up. It responded anyway, loosening in small, uneven increments as his tongue slid lower, a hot, wet stroke over the furrowed skin that broke my breathing completely. I gasped when he did it again, my forehead tipping closer to the glass as he stopped teasing and pressed his mouth in fully, licking me over and over.

His fingers brushed my elbow, and I let him guide my hand back into his hair, my grip tightening as I felt the steady motion of his head. My feet slid farther apart, my forearm coming up against the glass as my weight tipped forward, no longer braced so much as held there. Ethan's hand slipped between my legs, rolling my balls, and the sound that left me was loud and unguarded. When his hand closed around my cock and began to stroke, my knees threatened to give out.

I was panting over my arm, every sensation landing harder as his mouth worked against me, firm and unrelenting.

"Ash," he said between licks.

"Yes?" My voice came out rough, scraped raw by my breathing.

Another suck made my breath hitch.

"Look up for me."

I lifted my head on a shaky inhale, my eyes catching my reflection in the steamed mirror ahead. The sight of myself there —flushed, open, barely holding upright—pulled a breathless laugh from my chest. "You did that on purpose."

Ethan hummed behind me, mouth still moving, hand steady on my cock. I watched my own breathing. Watched how my body rocked back into him without thought. How I wasn't even pretending to resist anymore.

He was getting me closer than I had any right to be after already fucking him twice, my breathing breaking down further as I leaned into him, chasing his mouth—

Then he was gone.

My body surged back before I could stop it, a sharp inhale tearing from me as I reached for what he'd taken away. Ethan laughed softly, slapped my ass, and rose to his feet, wrapping his arms around my waist and pulling me back against him until my breathing began to even out.

"Let's go back to bed."

I turned the water off and let him pull me with him. We dried off quickly, moving around each other in the small space without speaking. I stepped into the bedroom ahead of him, wrapping the towel around my waist before sitting on the edge of the bed, the mattress dipping under my weight.

Ethan stayed in the doorway for a moment, a towel slung low on his hips, arms crossed loosely over his chest, head tilted as he watched me. The look in his eyes made my pulse kick harder.

"What are you thinking?"

A slow smile curved his mouth. "That we need to have a conversation about consent."

I lifted a brow.

He pushed off the doorframe and took a few slow steps into the room. "I need to know where you draw the line."

My chest tightened as I drew in a breath. "There are no lines with you."

He stopped a few feet away, gaze steady. "We need to be clear."

"I am being clear," I said, reaching for his hips when he moved within reach, my hands settling on his skin. "We can do whatever you want."

Ethan looked down at me, something measured passing through his expression before he leaned closer, voice low near my ear. "What if what I want is to fuck you?"

The reaction in my body was immediate, a collision of resistance and surrender that left my breath stalling.

"Not just that," he continued, "I want you to let me do whatever I want to you." His voice dropped, softer now, more controlled. "Let me take the reins." His gaze flicked to my mouth. "Let me take care of you."

The words landed deep, settling somewhere beneath thought. My body reacted before I could shape a careful answer, heat spreading as my shoulders loosened despite myself. I stayed right there with him. "You can do whatever you want."

Ethan didn't move. "Is that what you want?" he asked quietly, studying my face. "For me to take what's mine?"

Fuck.

I nodded. A sharp thrill raced through me at the thought of letting go. Of finally being allowed to stop.

"I know you're not used to it, Ash," he said. "I know you like being in control."

A small smile tugged at my mouth. "Can't it be both?"

Ethan's lips curved once more, recognizing the words he'd once said to me. "If I do anything that feels wrong, you tell me to stop."

"You won't—"

"Promise me." His tone sharpened just enough to cut through me. "If you don't, I won't know if you like it. And I need to know."

My chest eased at that, and I let out a slow breath. "I promise."

He held my gaze another beat, making sure. Then he straightened, the decision settling into his posture. His hands dropped away from me, the sudden absence loud in the quiet room.

"Okay." He nodded toward the bed. "Move back."

I did, sitting against the headboard, my pulse thudding in my ears. I focused on that rhythm, on him, on keeping the doubt from pressing in as I let myself give over to what he was asking for.

He walked around the bed until he stood directly in front of me. "Lower. Lie down."

I obeyed, sliding down until my back met the pillows. Ethan's eyes never left me. He let the seconds stretch—

One.

Two.

Three.

—before finally reaching for his towel and pulling it free.

He climbed onto the bed and stood there for a moment, looking down at me like he was taking stock. When his feet settled on either side of my waist, he crouched, forearms braced on his thighs, filling my field of vision. My chest rose and fell too fast for someone just lying there, doing nothing at all.

Then he reached out.

One hand slid over my chest, slow and possessive. The other curled into my hair at the back of my head and tugged, just enough to hold me in place. "Who do you belong to?"

Heat flared under my skin. "You."

He shook his head once, unhurried, his palm resting over my throat. Not squeezing—just there. "My name. Who do you belong to?"

"To you," I said. "Ethan Bennett. Just you."

He tilted his head, watching me like he was listening for something beneath the words. My body buzzed under his touch, the warmth of his hand seeping into my skin.

His thumb brushed my jaw. "Open."

The command went straight to my groin, my cock throbbing with anticipation. I let my mouth fall open, breath shallow and waiting.

"Tongue out."

I followed the order, eyes locked on his as he leaned in, working his tongue in his mouth before letting his spit fall on my own, heat flooding my mouth.

Fuck. Me.

"Swallow."

I did. Eagerly.

His mouth curved slightly as he watched me, satisfaction flickering there before he leaned close, voice rough against my ear. "Good boy."

My breath caught in my chest, but a second later he was kissing me—hot and claiming—his hand still firm at my throat as he pushed his tongue into my mouth, tasting himself, holding me exactly where he wanted me. His fingers hooked into the towel at my waist and gave a sharp tug, the fabric coming off in one impatient pull.

Ethan's body settled back over mine, and my hands lifted

instinctively, reaching for him anywhere I could just to feel him closer.

He broke away, keeping me pinned with his grip on my neck. "Hands up. On the headboard."

My hands flew up, palms flattening against the wood, and he dove back in, kissing me hungrily. Then he started his descent—rough, not slow in the slightest—and the heat of each kiss felt like magma, like he was igniting something inside me that wanted to claw its way out, ravaging everything in its path.

His mouth closed over my cock, taking it deep without warning, and my neck arched back as a loud moan ripped out of me. He held one hand out, and without a word, I reached for the lube and slapped it into his palm.

He never eased, working between my cock and my balls with unbroken focus—tongue, lips, pressure—drawing me tighter with every pass. My hands stayed locked against the headboard as I forced myself to keep them there. The act of not holding him —of surrendering my pleasure to him—had me coiled to the point of breaking.

I felt his slick fingers slide over my balls, then lower, circling me the same way I'd done to him earlier, as if he'd been taking fucking notes and giving them back to me. His mouth returned to my cock, pulling me deep enough that my hips jerked against the bed, my brain barely registering the moment my body loosened and the tip of his finger pressed inside me.

Then the sensation sparked hot, a clean, electric jolt that made my breath stutter. As he pushed deeper, my muscles gave way in small, unguarded increments, the intensity cresting in a way that felt overwhelming and right all at once.

He pulled his mouth free with a soft pop, eyes flicking from my cock to where his finger was inside me. "You're so fucking tight."

"Fuck—" The word left me ragged as heat raced up my chest and into my throat, but he didn't pause long enough for me to catch a breath or process what he'd said. Before his mouth returned, he withdrew just enough to add another finger.

The stretch, the steady push and pull, was unlike anything I'd felt before. My eyes kept slipping closed as my hips moved without permission. When he added a third, whatever tension I'd been holding on to finally broke, my body responding as a whole, nerves lighting up until everything else fell away, with just one thought looping over and over.

Don't move your hands.

Don't move your hands.

Don't move your hands.

Ethan moved away from my cock, flushed and breathing hard, and reached for the nightstand. He tore open a foil packet and rolled the condom on, then he reached for the lube. His hand slid between his legs, his eyes closing briefly, breath catching as he stroked himself before leaning forward again. One hand pressed into the back of my thigh, guiding it higher as he moved in, his cock settling against me, firm and waiting.

I closed my eyes and nodded.

Ethan wrapped his hand around my cock, still slick with lube, stroking once as pressure built, before I bore down and my body yielded, letting him slide inside. He didn't stop. Didn't need to. Whether it was because he'd fingered me into oblivion or we'd just been at this for too long, my body gave in easily, and he kept going until he was fully sheathed inside me.

Ethan was panting, his free hand rubbing the back of my thigh in a soothing motion while the other kept stroking lazily. His lips were parted and glistening, his eyes burning into mine. "Okay?"

Somewhere in the haze it registered—this felt *good. So fucking good.* "Yes."

He sucked in a deep breath, pulled his hips back, dragging his cock out, then thrust in hard.

"Fuck!" My back arched as he kept the pace, working my cock in the same rhythm, my body lighting up every time he pushed deeper. The burn and stretch—the thought of him stroking himself inside me—sent me spiraling, my body begging for more.

Ethan stopped, adjusted his weight on his knees, and started again. The angle changed—it hit deeper—and my hand flew up without thinking.

"Don't," he rasped. "I'll get you there. Don't fucking move."

My palm pressed back against the headboard, my shoulder already feeling the strain of holding the position—and that burn only wound me tighter, my body finally understanding that staying still for him was its own kind of pleasure.

His hips thrust hard into me, the slap of his skin against mine overwhelming my senses.

"You feel so fucking good." His voice was huskier than I'd ever heard it, and it pushed me toward the edge fast.

I squeezed my eyes shut. "Keep talking," I begged.

"I'm about to c-come—fuck." He was breathing hard, the tremor in his voice confirming his words. "I want to see you come all over yourself. Feel you clench around me and suck my cum out."

Jesus—

My legs trembled as I forced myself to stay still, and almost as if he could read my mind, he curled his hand under my thigh and pulled it up over his hips, lifting onto his knees and fucking even harder into me. The change stole the breath from my lungs, the pressure building until it felt like I was being pulled apart from the inside.

His skin was fever-hot against mine—the weight of him pressing me into the mattress had my balls drawing up tight, the edge crashing closer with every thrust.

Our eyes locked.

"Come for me," he said.

There was no willpower left in me to resist. No reason to try.

I groaned loudly as he dragged my orgasm out of me, the release crashing through my body in ragged waves, spilling over my stomach as his hand slowed but didn't stop, stroking me through it. I couldn't look away from him. His mouth was open, breath coming hard as his gaze tracked the mess I was making, the way my body shook beneath him. He thrust a few more times, deep, and moaned my name as he came inside me, his head tipping back, eyes rolling shut.

The aftershocks hit hard. My whole body shuddered, over-sensitive and loose all at once, his cock still pressed deep inside me, stretching the pleasure out longer than it should have. I couldn't move. I didn't want to. Everything felt big and loud, like my nerves hadn't caught up with what had just happened.

He finally let go of my cock and braced his hands on the bed, hovering for a second before lowering himself to press slow kisses over my chest.

I let my arms fall, easing the burn in my shoulders as I did. I reached for him, brushing his still-damp hair back, needing to touch him, to make sure he was still right there. Ethan smirked, breathless, leaning into my hand as he steadied himself. He pulled out carefully and dropped beside me, close enough that I could still feel the heat of him along my side.

I stared at the ceiling, my thoughts slow and scattered as my brain tried to reboot after being knocked sideways. My eyes a little too wide, my mouth still open as I dragged a hand through my hair. "That was… that was…"

Ethan laughed softly beside me, still catching his breath as he tied the condom off. "You liked that."

I turned my head toward him, taking in the smug curve of his mouth, the satisfaction he wasn't even trying to hide.

"A lot," he added.

A laugh slipped out of me too, shaky and overwhelmed in the best way. "I did."

He rolled onto his side, and I followed immediately, drawn to him.

Up close, he looked unreal—half-lidded blue eyes, flushed cheeks, lips still red. Beautiful in a way that hurt a little to look at. His tongue swept over his lower lip as he studied me, that familiar intensity still there. When he looked at me like that, it felt like the world tipped, like everything else slid out of focus.

One hand came up to cup my face, holding me there, close enough that I could feel his breath against my skin. "You're mine, Sebastian."

Warmth spread through my chest, my lips curving into a slow smile.

He pulled me closer, pressing our foreheads together, his grip firm—almost desperate. "I'm not doing this halfway," he said. "Not again."

I kissed him without hesitation, relief rushing through me at his words. He really hadn't let go. He wasn't walking away. "I'm yours."

His arms locked around me at that, like he'd been waiting to hear it just to breathe again, and our bodies fit together as if they'd never been apart.

My lips brushed his temple as I closed my eyes.

"I'm yours."

CHAPTER TWENTY-ONE

ASH

The slope of his neck—that curve into his shoulder I'd memorized years ago—was so tempting I couldn't stop myself. I pressed my lips to his warm skin, inhaling him, eyes fluttering shut as something inside me clicked into place. Finally, I could do this again.

Ethan grumbled in his sleep, and I pulled him closer, wrapping an arm around his chest and fitting myself against his back.

"I can't have sex again," he muttered suddenly, voice hoarse. "Let me sleep, Sebastian."

I chuckled against him, kissing his neck again.

"I'm serious."

"You can sleep all you want, pet," I said. "I just wanted to let you know I'm leaving in a little bit."

Ethan tensed and rolled to face me, giving me the cutest, sleep-rumpled expression I'd ever seen.

"What?" His gaze dragged over me—my hair, my face, my chest—and confusion crept in. "Why do you look so clean?"

I kissed his forehead. "Took a shower. Henny's picking me up in ten."

He scooted closer and nuzzled into my shirt. "What time is it?"

"Seven ten."

He let out a low, tired sound. "We didn't sleep at all last night. Why are you up so early?"

I closed my eyes and buried my face in his hair. "Combination of jet lag, anxiety, and jitters, I'm guessing."

Ethan went quiet for a beat, just breathing close while I dragged my fingers through his curls.

"Anxiety about…?" he asked, more awake now.

"My father. Work."

"Oh…" he exhaled. A small sound, but weighted.

I smiled to myself. "The jitters are about us. About everything that happened last night."

He tipped his head up enough to look at me. "Like… in a happy way?"

"A very happy way." I leaned in and kissed him—softly at first, a few lingering presses that, the moment I remembered I could, started to turn heated again.

"I thought this wasn't about sex," he teased.

I chuckled into his mouth, sliding over him and deepening the kiss. My hand traced up his ribs, savoring the fact that he was still naked in my bed.

"I'm going to get you dirty. I'm covered in cum."

I moved my mouth to his beautifully marked neck. "No, you're not. I cleaned you up after you fell asleep."

Ethan snorted. "I'm sure that sounded romantic in your head, but it came out really fucking creepy."

I poked at his ribs as he laughed. His hands went straight into my hair, and I caught his wrists, pinning them above his head as I settled my weight over him.

Ethan had that shy-turned-smug smile, still looking like he'd been freshly fucked. Perfect.

"I changed my mind," he purred. "Let's fuck again. You can keep holding me down like this—like the good old days."

It was my turn to groan and bury my face in his neck. "Henry's going to be here soon," I said, shaking my head, even as temptation curled low in my gut.

"You're hard."

"Yes." I lifted myself slightly. "I am."

"So, are we just going to waste that?"

"Seems like it."

Ethan writhed beneath me, grinding his hips up. "What's one more round? Blowies for breakfast."

My head fell back with a laugh. "You're fucking perfect, did you know that?" I let go of his wrists and sat back on the bed, slipping off him reluctantly.

"I'm aware." Ethan sat up too, stretching his arms overhead, the movement showing off the lines of his abdomen beautifully. His gaze dropped to my groin, and he flashed me a cheeky smile. Then he moved, crawling across the bed toward me.

I jumped off the mattress the second my brain caught up with what he was aiming for. "We're never going to leave this bed if you keep that up."

He settled back on his heels, his body fully exposed again, his cock hard and heavy between his legs. "Sounds like a plan."

I was one breath away from saying *fuck it,* when my phone chimed. I dragged it out of my pocket, already knowing. Henry. Five minutes.

Fuck.

"They're moving our dad to a room soon," I said, glancing back at him. "I have to go."

Ethan's expression sobered. "Let me jump in the shower real quick. I'll go with you."

"You don't—"

He stood and pressed a palm to my chest, stopping me. "I know I don't have to. I *want* to."

As he turned to leave, I caught him by the waist and hauled him back. "My bathroom."

That same shy smile curved his mouth. "All my stuff's in the other room."

"I'll bring it over. Get in."

His lips twitched before he turned and disappeared into my bathroom.

We moved fast after that—his shower, his clothes, everything falling into place with practiced ease. Minutes later, we were heading toward the black SUV parked out front. I handed him my sunglasses, and he slipped them on like they belonged to him, looking unfairly good doing it.

I opened the back door for him, hesitated for half a second, then shut it and climbed in beside Henry.

"Well, hey," Henry said, already looking between us with suspicion. "Didn't know you were tagging along."

Ethan patted his shoulder easily. "Of course. How are you doing?"

Henry shrugged. "Better. Actually managed to sleep last night." He glanced at me out of the corner of his eye. "How about you two? Get any shut-eye?"

I looked at him evenly. "Not much, no." I had no intention of elaborating.

From the back seat, Ethan let out a small sound—like he'd stretched wrong and paid for it.

Henry twisted in his seat. "You okay?"

Ethan nodded, sunglasses still hiding his eyes. "Yeah. Just kind of sore."

Henry's eyebrows shot up.

"Would you just drive," I said lightly, "and mind your fucking business?"

His mouth pressed into a thin, amused line as he nodded quickly. "I am. I'm minding it. I'm not even going to comment on the size of the hickey E's got on his neck. Not. At. All." He mimed zipping his lips.

Ethan snorted softly and turned to stare out of the window.

"Is Oli there?" I asked, steering the conversation away.

"Yeah. You know he's refusing to leave for more than an hour." Henry shook his head. "Parental overprotectiveness is cranked to a hundred." His hands tightened on the steering wheel, knuckles whitening.

Something was off.

His posture was too rigid, his leg bouncing where it rested against the door. It didn't track. If anything, this should've been the least stressful day we'd had in a while.

"Did something happen with Dad last night?"

Henry glanced at me, lips parting like he hadn't expected the question. "No. Oli didn't say anything." He lifted one hand and bit at the side of his thumb.

A tell.

"Are you okay?"

He nodded too fast. "I'm fine. Just… stressed. Club stuff…" The words trailed off, unfinished.

And then he shut down, clean and sudden, the way I knew too well. A door slammed quietly behind his eyes, nothing getting in, nothing getting out.

Maybe later, when things settled, we could talk about it.

Or maybe Ethan could.

The rest of the drive passed in a quieter stretch of road and silence. Henry's grip on the wheel eventually loosened, the tension in his shoulders easing just enough that I let it go—for now.

My thoughts drifted anyway. To my dad. To the steady rise and fall of his chest the last time I'd seen him. To the word stable—fragile and hopeful all at once.

And then, inevitably, to work.

My phone rested heavily in my palm. No response from Elena. I frowned at the screen, rereading the last message I'd sent before we left the apartment.

ME

Can you brief me on the alternative plans?

Ready to pivot

Loop me in

Nothing.

A week ago, I would've already been on three calls, forcing decisions into place. Now I just… waited. Ready to let it be a shared solution instead of something I had to wrestle into submission alone.

The silence shouldn't have unsettled me. It did anyway.

And then my thoughts drifted right back to Ethan. Like something in me was wired to find him when the ground gave away. He was still leaning back, head against the window, sunglasses on, jaw relaxed but not asleep. A bruise bloomed dark on his throat, impossible to miss.

Mine.

Ours.

We pulled into the hospital parking lot, concrete and glass rising to greet us.

Oliver was the first to spot us, leaning on the nurses' station with his phone in hand. His face relaxed the moment he saw us. Charlotte stood beside him, arms crossed over her chest, hair in a high, messy bun, her lip caught anxiously between her teeth.

"Hey, why the stressed faces?" Henry asked as soon as we reached them.

"Dad's okay," Oliver said quickly.

We all let out a collective breath.

Oliver's eyes flicked to mine, then to Charlotte, and back again. "They're getting him ready for the transfer. It'll be an hour at most." His gaze slid briefly to Ethan. "Ash, let's just—" He waved a hand, motioning for me to follow.

"What's all that about?" I asked once we were out of earshot.

"Our father-in-law is in town," Oliver said.

Anger surged through me—sharp and protective—as my attention snapped back to Ethan. He was still chatting with Charlotte and Henry, face relaxed, unaware.

"Why? How do you even know?"

"Margaret. This thing with Dad is all over the news right now. He must've heard and thought it was perfect timing to show up." Oliver scrubbed a hand over his face. "Char's a mess. She wanted to tell Ethan herself, but she's stressed about him dealing with it." He hesitated, then added, more matter-of-factly, "There are photos everywhere, too. Of all of us coming and going. A couple of you and Ethan together."

I exhaled slowly. Of course. Fucking vultures.

"Nothing scandalous," Oliver went on. "But you know how people are. They like to talk."

My shoulders tightened anyway—the familiar prickle of exposure crawling up my spine—before I forced the tension back down. That wasn't what mattered right now. "I don't want him anywhere near Ethan."

Oliver nodded. "Trust me, I get it. I gave hospital security his information—asked them not to let him up if he shows. I just wanted to give you the heads-up." The casual edge in his voice had vanished; he'd clearly already processed this in his head.

"I haven't talked to Charlotte about it," he added, turning to me fully, his expression serious. "You know… everything you told me yesterday. I thought it would be better coming from you." He paused. "We should rip the bandage off and do it now. Tell them both."

My stomach twisted at the thought. But he was right. Ethan would want to know, and he'd be pissed if he found out I'd known and kept it from him.

Just then, a nurse stepped through the doors and headed toward us. Alarm shot through me, but her posture was relaxed.

"That must be about the move," Oliver said.

"Mr. Langley?" she said once she reached us. "They've already started transferring your father out of the ICU. He'll be settled in his new room shortly. You can head up to the third floor now, and once he's stable, someone will come get you."

"Thank you," Oliver said, relief softening his whole face. As she walked away, he caught my gaze once more.

"Yeah," I said. "Might as well, right?"

Oliver gave me a solemn nod, and we went to them. Our Bennetts.

Henry came with us. There was no reason for him not to, and while we waited for news about the transfer, we settled into a small waiting area, close enough to hear if we were called.

Ethan sat beside me, Charlotte on his left and the rest close.

"There's something I need to tell you," I said, looking at both of them.

Charlotte was worrying her lip, but she nodded right away. Ethan's brows furrowed.

I kept my eyes on him. "About your dad."

He stilled. Charlotte's fingers went around his hand immediately.

"What about him?" Ethan asked.

"Do you remember when I asked if I could look into him?"

Worry crept into the edges of his expression.

"Well… I did."

The muscle in his jaw ticked, his posture going very still. Charlotte had already told him his dad was in the city. At least I didn't have to be the one to drop that part on him.

"I wasn't sure if I should bring it up, especially with everything going on," I continued. "But with him in town… you need to know."

Oliver nodded once in agreement.

"Go on," Ethan said quietly.

"He's not just bad with money." I held his gaze. "He's been running investment scams—taking people's savings, promising big returns, shuffling funds around to make it look legitimate. And he hasn't exactly been honest with the IRS, either. They're starting to take notice."

Charlotte's breath left her in a soft, broken sound.

Ethan didn't react right away. "He's being investigated?" His voice was nearly emotionless.

"Yes," I said. "And it's serious. Financial penalties and possible criminal charges. Maybe not prison, but it won't just disappear this time."

"And my trust?" He swallowed. "Was that—?"

"It was part of it. He probably used it to cover losses. Hid it. Claimed things he shouldn't have. Because it was a joint account, it wasn't technically theft. But it still became part of the mess."

Ethan let out a quiet breath. "So I was useful." A hollow edge crept in. "Convenient."

"Hey," Charlotte whispered, squeezing his hand. "No."

He stared straight ahead, like he was watching the truth assemble itself piece by piece.

"Darling, none of this is on you." I leaned in slightly. "He took advantage of you. That doesn't make you culpable. It makes you exploited."

His jaw clenched hard.

"And now you have a choice," I said carefully. "If you want, you can come forward. Talk to investigators. Your timeline, emails, bank records—it would help establish a pattern. It won't give you your money back. But it could hold him accountable. Legally." My gaze went to all of them. "Publicly."

The room went quiet. Very quiet.

Then the reactions started to unfold. Charlotte's eyes filled. Henry looked furious—his fist pressed to his lips, eyes blazing.

"And if I don't?" Ethan asked.

"Then you don't," I said. "This is your call. Not mine. Not anyone else's. There will be fallout if they can prove it—press, questions, public attention. And both of our families will get called out because of who we are to each other." My gaze flicked to Charlotte and Oliver. "So it's something to weigh. But no one here is going to pressure you. Or blame you."

Charlotte exhaled and nodded. "He's right. E… it's your call."

Ethan finally looked at her. "Did you know about this?"

"Not this," she said. "Not the details. But… about a year after the wedding, he came to Oli and me. He was all charm and family, and *I missed you both*—until he asked for money. Wanted Oli to 'invest' in something vague. Wouldn't show paperwork. He just kept insisting we should trust him."

Oliver drew her closer, his palm steady at her back.

"And when I told him no," Charlotte continued, "he turned cold. Said if I wasn't on his side, I wasn't worth staying in his life. Then he cut me off." She let out a small, disbelieving breath. "I thought I'd pushed him away. But now…"

Ethan stared at her, something clicking into place. Doubt giving way to understanding.

"He left because I wasn't profitable," she said softly. "That's on him. Not us."

Ethan's face didn't crumple. Didn't shatter. But something behind his eyes gave. He dragged a hand over his mouth, exhaling a shaky breath. "So that's it, then. The money's gone." His eyes finally found mine. "Right?"

I reached out, brushing my thumb over the back of his hand. "It is. But he doesn't have to get away with it. You don't owe him silence."

He nodded once. "I need a little time," he said, voice steady despite everything crashing inside him. "To process." His fingers tightened around mine. "But thank you. For not letting him blindside me. Again."

Always, I wanted to say. Instead, I just bowed my head.

Oliver squeezed his shoulder. Charlotte leaned into him. Henry didn't speak but moved in closer.

Our little world closed ranks around him.

Because whatever he chose—

We were already on his side.

Time passed without any of us moving, just breathing

together and letting the weight of it settle. Eventually, people began to peel away—Charlotte following a nurse for paperwork, Oliver stepping aside to talk to a doctor, Henry disappearing with Vivian to check on my father's new room.

And then it was just us, standing side by side.

"Does my mom know?" Ethan asked after a while.

I shook my head. "Oli was the only one who knew. And I only found out a couple of weeks ago. I didn't tell you because… well." I huffed softly. "You know why."

His arms were crossed, but he wasn't closed off. His body angled toward me, leaning in without actually touching.

Then his hands dragged over his face. "Fuck—it's been a week, hasn't it?"

"It has." I watched him carefully. "Do you want to go back to the apartment?"

He rubbed a hand over the back of his neck, staring past me for a moment. "No, but…" His eyes finally met mine. "I think I should go, Ash. Back to Madrid."

My chest deflated a little, but he was right. Our father was stable, and Ethan didn't have to stand here avoiding *his* father if he didn't want to.

"End of semester's coming up," he went on. "Exams. I've already missed enough. And I need to get back to work." A breath slipped out of him. "I can't afford to fall behind right now."

"I'll get the plane ready," I said automatically. "Drive you to the airport."

That earned me a look. "No private jet rescue mission, Mr. Langley." The corner of his mouth lifted. "I'll fly commercial tomorrow night."

I caught his hand before he could drop it. "Can I at least book that?"

He squeezed my fingers once, shaking his head, his lips pressed together with an amused tilt. "And just so you know, I also have to go to the bank and figure out a loan for next semester… and I don't want your input on that either."

I forced myself not to slip back into the role I knew too well. "That's… fine by me." I exhaled through my nose, swallowing the instinct to argue. "I love watching you voluntarily sign up for unnecessary interest rates."

That pulled a real laugh out of him. Then his gaze dropped to our hands, and something softer moved through his expression. "You're staying, right?"

"For a little while," I said. "Until he's really out of the woods."

He nodded slowly, absorbing it. "Life just keeps getting in the way…"

I slid my hand to the back of his neck, thumb brushing just under his hairline. "It does." A beat. "But we're good."

He searched my face.

"You and me." My grip tightened slightly. "We're good, right?"

He hesitated, and I saw it—the fragility, the fear, the history. It hurt, but why wouldn't he be careful with me? I'd earned that caution.

"You're coming back?" he asked.

"Of course."

Another beat. Then he nodded. "Then we're good." And with a faint warning in his tone, he added, "Don't disappear on me again, and we're good."

Relief washed through me. I stepped into him instead of answering, pulling him close. He folded into it immediately, arms wrapping around my waist, holding tight for one long second before easing back.

I frowned at his sudden retreat.

"We're in public." He gave a small shrug. "Eyes everywhere, remember?"

I hated that.

I really fucking hated it.

And I hated that he was right. That we still had things to say. Things to repair. Things to build—properly this time—instead of just falling into bed and pretending none of it mattered. We needed that foundation before rumors spun out of control and everyone decided to weigh in on whether we should or shouldn't be together.

It was going to kill me to watch him leave tomorrow, but a couple of weeks was nothing compared to everything we'd already survived.

I kept hold of his hand. "At least I still have you tonight."

He smiled—softer this time.

I lifted our joined hands and pressed my lips to his knuckles, holding them there for a moment longer than necessary.

He didn't pull away.

So I stayed right there—not ready to test how easily this could break.

———

By the time we reached the apartment, the cold had settled deep into my bones.

The day had passed without incident. I was still waiting for Elena to get back to me, but it was already late in Madrid, so I wasn't expecting a reply tonight.

Dad was asleep when we left, but today had been better. He'd been more present, more himself. We talked about nothing and everything—the weather, his company. Like old times. For the first time since the heart attack, I hadn't felt like I was clinging to him with white knuckles. I told him I was staying a little longer, and he'd smiled—a small step that felt gigantic.

He even spoke with Ethan, and watching them interact so casually was… interesting. Ethan stayed beside me the entire time, his hand warm at the small of my back—steady, grounding, never asking anything in return.

Then he insisted we stop for food. More specifically, at a deli fifteen blocks out of the way in the already bitter November night.

I shifted one of the bags into my grip as I reached for my keys. Ethan stood beside me, burdened with the rest—three overstuffed paper bags balanced with our coats and his satchel.

"This is what happens when you can't make up your mind," I said, eyeing the stack. "What the hell are we going to do with this much food?"

"I wanted to try everything." Ethan adjusted the bags higher against his chest, one slipping until he caught it with his elbow.

"It's wasteful. And excessive—and that's coming from someone with a mild shopping addiction."

Ethan chuckled. "You'll eat it."

"I will not eat four sandwiches." I pushed the door open, still shaking my head, and frowned as light spilled across the floor, voices drifting down the hall. "That's odd."

We stepped inside, the warmth of the apartment settling around us. I reached out automatically to relieve some of the weight from Ethan's arms as we moved toward the living room —then halted.

Everyone turned.

Elena was by the coffee table, Raúl beside her. Mateo leaned against the wall, arms crossed. Aria perched on the arm of the sofa like she'd been waiting for us to arrive, and Oliver lingered near the window.

And Henry—

At the front of the room, Henry stood with a marker in hand, a massive whiteboard set up behind him, the furniture rearranged to make space.

"Oh good," he said brightly. "You brought food."

I blinked, my brain still struggling to catch up. "What's this?"

Henry gestured toward the board. "Isn't it obvious?" He spread his arms like an orchestra conductor cueing a performance, a wide grin breaking across his face. "It's a *worktervention*."

I let out a short laugh, caught off guard, the shock still keeping me rooted in place.

Ethan nudged my arm as he passed, drawing my attention to the unmistakable satisfaction on his face. "Told you it wasn't too much," he murmured, winking. Then, louder, "Okay, who's hungry?" He took the bags from my hand and headed toward the group like he'd known exactly what he was walking into.

"So this is why you weren't answering your phone?" I asked Elena.

She grinned. "Your brothers said you were finally ready to listen to the voice of reason. I couldn't stay behind and let them take all the credit." Her expression softened. "And this is ours, Ash. We built it together. We'll save it together."

The words lodged somewhere deep, leaving me momentarily without a response.

"And I'm here because no one knows how to talk Sebastian Langley out of a crisis better than me," Aria announced, crossing her arms. "Or force him out of it."

A quiet laugh slipped out of me.

Raúl stepped closer, looking as unimpressed as ever. "And I have the connections to make sure you can act fast."

Oliver pushed off the wall, already halfway through a thought. "State contracts are what's bleeding you right now," he said, like we were picking up a conversation we'd already been having. "You don't fix that—you sidestep it." His gaze met mine. "There's room in private infrastructure—energy, logistics, smaller-scale developments that don't get tied up in red tape. Mid-size municipal partnerships, too. Less exposure, faster turnaround."

I held his gaze, caught between pride and something harder to swallow. He'd already mapped it out.

"We reallocate resources out of the stalled contracts, prioritize projects with shorter cycles, and bring in private capital where we need liquidity. You tighten the pipeline, keep cash moving, and you're not stuck waiting on approvals to stabilize."

Aria waved a hand toward Oliver. "See?" she said, giving me a pointed look. "Right on cue—the financial genius."

Something in my head kicked into gear, chasing the path Oliver had just laid out. Not fixed, but within reach.

Then our attention went to the last piece of the lineup—Mateo, still leaning against the wall.

His eyebrows lifted. "I've got nothing." He jerked his thumb toward Henry. "I'm here for emotional support of *this* Langley."

A ripple of laughter moved through the room, and I felt some of the weight I'd been carrying finally ease. Enough that I didn't feel like I was bracing anymore.

Elena's hand came to rest on my shoulder. "When we started this," she said, "you told me you wanted the CFO role so you could have more time. So you could build a life outside of work."

Ethan drifted back to my side, close enough that our arms brushed. I slipped mine around his back without thinking.

"You also said you'd need me to remind you of that," Elena continued. "So here I am. Yes, we're in a crisis. We'll solve it. And then you're going to step back and remember what life looks like outside your office. Okay?"

Life outside my office…

The idea of a life with some balance—of having something that wasn't just work—felt… right. And then it was there all at once—the pull to stay in it. To live in the moment. To enjoy it. To stop thinking five steps ahead and just be in what was right in front of me.

My grasp on Ethan tightened as I smiled through the ache. "Okay."

"Good." Henry clapped once and pivoted into motion. "Okay, people, positions. We have a crisis to solve and sandwiches to demolish. Mateo, stop leaning and start contributing. Raúl, drop the attitude." He pointed at Oliver. "You—keep going. Whatever you've got, that's where we start. And Elena—"

he paused, eyeing her. "You're actually terrifying, so I'm just going to hand the proverbial mic back to you."

The room came alive around me—chairs scraping, coats dropping, voices overlapping—everyone falling into place with an ease that made my throat tighten.

I stayed where I was for a moment, taking it all in. Ethan remained tucked against my side, solid and warm beneath my arm, his presence steadying in a way words never could.

"Thank you," I said, leaning in closer, my voice low.

"Wasn't me." His gaze moved across the room—my brothers, my team, my family. "You've got a lot of people in your corner, Ash."

Something in my chest gave, quiet and undeniable.

"Guess I do."

———

The apartment had only just quieted.

The whiteboard stood in the living room, marker caps scattered across the coffee table, the faint smell of deli sandwiches lingering in the air. Chairs sat slightly out of place. Everyone had filtered out one by one. Only Henry—the last to leave—had drifted to the terrace with Ethan while we sat going over numbers.

Their voices carried faintly through the cracked door as I stepped into my bedroom, loosening the buttons of my shirt as I went, the weight of the day settling into my muscles. Not the bone-deep strain I'd been carrying for weeks—just the heavy pull that comes after you finally stop moving.

I was about to knock on the frame when I heard my name.

My hand stilled.

Through the narrow opening, I could see them near the railing, shapes softened by the night beyond. Henry leaned back against the metal, arms folded loosely, Ethan beside him, shoulders slightly hunched against the cold, head tipped down like he was listening and bracing at the same time.

Something about the sight kept me in place.

Ethan around Henry had always been a slightly different version of himself. Softer. Less guarded. And I couldn't make myself interrupt it—that openness, that rare unarmored honesty.

"I'm just saying," Henry murmured, his breath fogging in the cold, "for someone who swears he doesn't want drama, you really like walking straight into it."

Ethan huffed a soft laugh. "Shut up."

"I'm serious." Henry bumped his shoulder. "So? Should I congratulate you? Are we doing champagne? Flowers? Matching sweaters? What's happening?"

"Nothing's happening."

Henry didn't buy it. "Sure. Nothing. That's definitely what it looked like this morning when you both walked out like you'd been fucked six ways to Sunday."

Ethan groaned. "Jesus, Henny."

"Well?" Henry pressed as he laughed. "You're glowing and bruised. I feel like I'm owed at least a little transparency."

Headlights streaked from far below, the space between them holding.

Then Ethan sighed. "Of course we had sex," he said. "It's Sebastian. What else would you expect?"

I didn't know a sentence could hit two places at once. First, the sting of dismissal. Then the weight of guilt. But lie in the bed you made and all that.

Henry's voice softened. "And?"

"And nothing," Ethan said. "We slept together. That's it."

"Ethan—"

"I'm serious," he insisted, though his voice wavered. "I'm not doing this thing where I build castles in my head and then watch him knock them down again. I'm not doing that twice."

Henry stayed quiet, letting him keep going.

"So no," Ethan continued, quieter now. "I don't know where we are right now—*what* we are. We're... whatever. Temporary. Situational." A humorless breath. "Who knows? Maybe in a few weeks there'll be some article or scandal, and suddenly there's a branch to open in India. Or Singapore. Or Jupiter."

"He's trying," Henry said gently. "Look at what happened here tonight."

"Yeah," Ethan replied. "He is, and I'm not saying I don't believe him. I just... can't afford to believe *too* much, you know?"

My chest clenched—not in anger or offense, but with a deep, aching grief for the damage I'd done.

"Things are always complicated with us," Ethan said. "Circumstances haven't changed. I just need to see if he has."

Henry nudged his shoulder lightly. "For what it's worth, I think he knows that."

Ethan didn't respond.

And I didn't move.

Because, yes—it hurt. But I deserved every bit of it.

He didn't doubt me because he was dramatic or suspicious. He doubted me because I'd taught him to. I'd trained him to brace for impact when it came to me. Reinforced the same lessons life—and his fucking father—kept drilling into him. If that didn't make me want to drop to my knees and apologize forever, nothing would.

Their voices softened after that, the conversation drifting into something lighter. A quieter laugh dissolved into the night air, and that finally broke whatever held me there. I stepped back from the door and moved farther into the room, giving them the privacy I should have given from the start.

Leaning my shoulder against the wall, I pulled in a slow, steady breath.

He wasn't wrong to protect himself... But I wasn't walking away. Not this time.

My resolve came quietly but with certainty as I straightened.

I was done reacting—done waiting. From now on, I was choosing.

If he needed proof, I'd fucking give it to him.

For as long as it took.

CHAPTER TWENTY-TWO
ETHAN

This… was not what I was expecting.

On my last night in the city, Sebastian and I had fallen into bed fully clothed, too exhausted for anything but slow, sleepy kisses. He'd kept me tucked against him, and I'd drifted off with his hand warm at my back, neither of us wanting more than the quiet comfort of staying close.

The next day, when he'd pulled up to departures, I'd already been bracing for a quick kiss, a distracted "call me," and a wave through the glass. Instead, he'd cupped my face and kissed me slow and deep, like he hadn't been in a rush for once in his life.

Long enough that a horn had blared behind us, snapping the moment in half.

Sebastian had been there in a way that had felt unfamiliar. Not even like Barcelona. This had been more. Realer. Softer without losing himself.

He had promised he'd stay in touch.

And then he actually did.

Every day for the next two weeks, there was a message waiting for me when I woke up. More throughout the day. Usually a call at night when he knew I'd be home. We didn't talk about us, but everything else in our lives was suddenly fair game.

He told me about his dad—how some days felt a little easier. Some days harder. How sometimes seeing him dragged up memories of his mom and all that pain, and sometimes it made him furious all over again.

We talked about work. I filled him in on what was happening here, and he walked me through some coursework like it was nothing, explaining concepts in that calm, frustratingly brilliant way that made me mad at him and proud of him at the same time. I told him classes were getting harder by the day, the end of the semester creeping closer, and that I was splitting my time between morning lectures and whatever hours I could carve out at VistaReal.

He told me the crisis was stabilizing. That Elena had the team moving faster than he could have alone. That he was delegating more. Listening more. Letting go where he could.

He told me he was taking time off. Making the most of the time he had in New York—spending mornings with his dad and long lunches with Oliver. Picking up Liam and Amelia from daycare and letting them drag him through Central Park to look at the Christmas lights already going up, like he didn't run a company worth more than most small countries.

He told me he was worried about Henry. Said he wished he would open up to him more. Said he knew he'd made that harder by not being someone Henry could lean on before.

I don't think he realized how big that admission was.

It felt like living in some parallel reality, and I still didn't know if I was allowed to trust it.

Falling into a routine with him was dangerously easy. All our conversations eventually slid into flirting, wanting, waiting. Sometimes more. Because how could they not? After that night together—after four years of nothing and now knowing exactly what I was missing, and not being able to touch him again because of the ocean between us—how were we not going to crave each other like this?

He didn't say the words again—those three little words that haunted me. But I felt them. In the way he spoke. In the way he stayed. In the way he tried.

In the little things.

Packages started showing up at my apartment. The first had pastries from a place he'd tracked down because I'd mentioned —once—that I missed them. The next was clothes, not random but very... me. Soft. Warm. The kind I'd always said I'd buy someday. That was so Sebastian. Always had been. Except this time, it didn't feel like performance or distraction. It felt like care.

Two weeks of that. Two weeks of his voice in my ear every night. Two weeks of wanting and waiting and trying so hard not to hope. By the day he was finally supposed to land, I was a mess of nerves and anticipation, pacing like a kid waiting for Santa. Because I didn't know which version of Sebastian I was going to get when that plane touched down. And I didn't know what it would do to me if it wasn't this one.

I was lying on the couch, scrolling through my phone and waiting, when Henry showed up. It was pretty late already, closing in on 10 p.m.

"You're just getting off work?" I asked as soon as he closed the door.

He looked worn thin—bags under his eyes, clothes rumpled. "Yeah," he said with a nod, walking straight to the bar cart and serving himself a drink. "Things are picking up speed. You know how it is once we're closer to the finish line."

"Is Ari gonna come help?" I already knew the answer before he shook his head. He loved piling responsibility on himself. A Langley trait.

He slumped into the armchair with a heavy sigh. "What are you still doing up? Thought you had an early class tomorrow."

Heat crept up my neck. "Ash is getting back today. He landed a little while ago."

I didn't mention he hadn't called yet. We didn't have plans or anything. I just… wanted to wait. Needed to know he was home and safe.

Henry's eyebrows lifted slightly as he took a sip. "He'll probably be tired, you know."

I smiled to myself, knowing full well he was only trying to protect me—keep my expectations in check. It stung a little that he felt he had to.

I parted my lips, ready to tell him I was doing a fine job of that myself, when the lock in the front door turned and both our heads snapped toward it.

The door opened, and I shot upright, hands braced on the back of the couch as Sebastian walked in.

Well… fuck me.

My stomach swooped at the sight of him. "Hey," I said, unable to keep the surprise out of my voice.

He gave me a tired smile, set his suitcase by the door, and crossed straight to me.

"Hey," Henry said. "Did you come from the plane?"

Sebastian nodded, and when he finally stopped in front of me, he wrapped me in a tight hug. "From the plane," he echoed in that deep rumble of his. Then, more quietly—for me—"Hi."

My arms locked around his neck. "Hi."

He leaned back just enough to press a soft kiss to my lips, and I melted. Completely, stupidly melted.

Then he slipped away, scrubbing a hand through his hair as he turned toward his brother. "Can I use your shower?"

Henry's expression mirrored mine—stunned. His brows were still hovering near his hairline, drink paused halfway to his mouth as he nodded. "Go right ahead."

Sebastian disappeared through the bedroom door, closing it softly behind him.

Henry and I just stared at each other.

"You weren't expecting him, were you?"

I shook my head.

The corners of Henry's mouth started lifting.

I pointed a finger at him. "You keep that goofy smile in check. We're not getting our hopes up."

He quickly covered his mouth with the rim of his glass, but he was very obviously trying not to grin.

My heart was beating a mile a minute, but I still managed to drop back from my knees and sprawl across the couch like I wasn't hovering on the edge of my sanity, waiting. Henry was unusually quiet too, listening as the water ran in the next room and then eventually stopped.

When the door opened again, Sebastian emerged in Henry's clothes.

His house clothes.

Which meant sweats.

Sebastian Langley in gray sweatpants and a worn white T-shirt, barefoot, hair damp and pushed back. He had never looked hotter in his life.

"I took some liberties," he said, glancing at his brother.

Henry chuckled. "I can see that."

Sebastian crossed the room, then climbed onto the couch like it was the most natural thing in the world—stretching out along my side, fitting himself against me, and dropping his head onto my shoulder with a tired sigh.

Okay.

This was cute as *fuck*.

"Do you want a drink?" Henry offered.

Sebastian tucked his head close, his damp hair brushing my cheek. "No, thanks. Too tired," he mumbled.

Tentatively, I brushed his hair back with my free hand. When he hummed in approval, I kept going, stroking slowly. Sebastian settled even closer, his arm looping around my waist, his leg hooking comfortably over mine.

My eyes flicked to Henry.

He just smiled and shrugged before standing. "Well, I'm heading to bed." He took a step, then turned back, his gaze staying mostly on me even though he spoke to Sebastian. "See you in the morning?"

Sebastian nodded, and Henry's smile widened. I shot him a look, to which he snickered and disappeared down the hall.

My heart was still thudding as I lay there, still not totally sure what was happening—other than Sebastian turning from an antisocial cat into an aggressively cuddly one wrapped around me.

"Are you falling asleep?" I whispered.

He nodded.

"Do you maybe want to do that in the bedroom?"

"Here's perfect."

Warmth spread through me. I slipped my arm more securely around him, and he melted into me, like he'd been waiting to exhale until he was right here.

A few minutes passed with nothing but the soft sounds of the apartment at night and my fingers lazily moving through his hair. His breathing eventually evened out, slowed…

Then turned into faint little snores.

I smiled to myself and pressed a kiss to his temple.

Really fucking cute.

———

We ended up falling asleep on the couch. I woke up with a tickle on my neck and darkness surrounding us. There was a blanket over us too, which I assumed was Henry's doing, because Sebastian was out cold. I managed to coax him upright and into my bed. He pulled his shirt off before sliding under the covers, and just seeing him like that—the warmth of his skin right there—immediately sparked my interest. I pressed close, kissing along his neck, his hands already roaming lazily over me.

But when my lips finally met his, he kissed me back… not the way I expected him to. It was soft. Lingering. He rolled us onto my side, curling up behind me, and wrapping his arms tight around my waist before pressing a gentle kiss to the back of my neck.

"Let me just hold you tonight," he whispered against my skin.

I blinked, a little thrown, as a familiar doubt stirred before I pushed it down.

He was tired, after all.

Maybe in the morning.

———

Morning wasn't it either.

When I woke up again, ready to jump him, Sebastian had already gotten up, taken a shower, and was back in his fancy office clothes.

And when I shoved the covers off, gave him bedroom eyes, and very clearly displayed the problem I was dealing with, he only leaned in, kissed me, brushed his thumb over my cheek, and promised we'd get to it later.

There was heat in his eyes—real heat. They roamed over me with the same intensity they usually did. But then he did, in fact, leave.

So I was left to handle my *situation* on my own.

———

Three days.

It wasn't a lot.

But it kind of was.

Three days of him being here… but not really *being here*.

He was doing the cute gift-giving thing again. I'd get to my desk, and there'd be something waiting for me with a little note I knew was in his handwriting, not Vanessa's. We'd see each other around the office, and he'd smile. When we had the chance, we'd talk and flirt. We didn't touch—because touching was still out of the question in public—but anyone with half a brain could see something was going on.

On paper, everything looked perfect. Work was running smoothly. I was back in meetings that mattered. Nothing was technically wrong.

But something was off.

If there was one thing that had always defined us, it was the hunger. That relentless pull toward each other. Even back then, when I wasn't sure of anything and didn't know how to ask for more, the second those walls came down, all we did was have sex.

And that night in New York just confirmed it.

So why, pray tell, was he suddenly keeping that from me?

He didn't come back to the apartment. Didn't spend the night.

I tried telling myself it was the end of the month. That he was buried under numbers and decisions and putting out fires I only half understood. That I was drowning in final projects and group presentations and didn't have the bandwidth to spiral either.

Didn't help.

By the fourth day, I'd had enough.

I tried cornering him in his office, but Vanessa informed me he'd already left for a meeting. So, call it was.

I paced the living room, phone pressed to my ear as it rang.

On the second ring, he picked up. "Hello, darling." His smooth voice rolled out warm and easy.

I smiled despite myself. "Hiya, stranger. Missed you tonight." I made sure my tone was nice and raspy—the way I knew he couldn't resist.

He hummed. "I'm sorry. Got pulled into work. Now I'm going over reports."

"You're back at the office?" I frowned, checking my watch. "It's almost nine."

"No, I'm home."

Right.

His apartment.

The one I still hadn't been invited to.

"Do you need any help?" My fingers traced the edge of the couch. "I could look them over with you." A smirk tugged at my lips. "Or get under your desk and keep you company."

Sebastian's groan lit hope in my chest.

"I have a better proposal for you."

I smiled. "I'm all ears."

"Why don't we skip that tonight? I'll get work out of the way, and we can go out somewhere. Just the two of us."

It was ridiculous how I could get butterflies and still have my stomach sink at the same time.

"Outside?"

"Yeah. Next week."

Next week? What in the actual fuck?

"Are you busy *this* week?"

"Well… it's the end of the month. You know I'm delegating, but I have to go over a million things—"

My rational brain stopped listening. He was doing it again—choosing work, choosing distance. Giving just enough and withholding everything else.

Fuck this.

Fuck Sebastian and his stupid games. Why couldn't he ever just be clear with me?

"Okay, then. See you next week, I guess." I tried to keep my voice neutral, even though all I wanted to do was slam the phone down.

"Promise I'll make it up to you, pet. I'm just incredibly behind after two weeks away. I need to catch up."

"Mhm."

Silence stretched between us.

"Are we good?" he asked.

I nodded, even though he couldn't see it, forcing the words out. "We're good."

"See you tomorrow?"

"Sure."

There was movement on the other end. "Darling, are you sure—"

"I'm getting another call. Talk later," I said too brightly and hung up.

I exhaled hard through my nose, then breathed in for calm.

One.

Two.

Three—

Fuck calm.

My phone chimed.

MY CREEP

Can you call me when you're done?

A pang of guilt flared in my chest, because everything could be true—he probably *was* buried in work—but it still fucking stung. Why did it suddenly feel like having sex with me was a chore? This wasn't another item on his schedule. This was supposed to be ease. Relief. Something we both wanted. So why did it feel like rejection?

Maybe he'd changed his mind. Maybe coming home reminded him that I was still a liability.

Poor Ethan—too many feelings. Always the mess. Always the thing Sebastian had to manage.

I paced.

And of course Henry wasn't here. Not that I should be telling him any of this, but he was usually good at talking me off the ledge.

But was it a ledge?

Or was it time to force him into having a conversation with me and drop all the bullshit once and for all? Either he was in, or he was out. End of discussion.

My brain tried to rationalize. Tried to be fair.

Anger won.

I grabbed my keys, shoved on my shoes, and headed for his apartment.

The cool night air hit my face the second I stepped outside, sharp and dry in my lungs. It should have helped—given me space to breathe, something—but neither that nor the ten-minute walk did a damn thing.

So when I stopped in front of the familiar entrance, I was still fuming and confused—which the doorman clearly picked up on. He straightened slightly as he called Sebastian, announcing that I was downstairs demanding to be let up.

I rode the elevator, jabbing the button harder than necessary, and waited for it to drag itself up five floors and spit me out at his doorstep, where he was already standing with that slightly baffled little smile that, under literally any other circumstance, would've been endearing.

Right now it wasn't.

"Darling, what—" he started, hand still on the door.

I walked straight past him and into his apartment. It was neat, like his place in New York—but this one actually looked lived in. By a human.

There was an empty cup on the coffee table, the pillows on the couch looked rumpled, the whole place smelled like him. It was one of those old buildings turned modern; beautifully redone, and I might have taken more time to appreciate it, because it really was lovely—but then the door clicked shut behind me, and the sound snapped me back to why I was here.

I turned on him. "Why are you brushing me off?"

Sebastian blinked. "I'm not—"

"Oh, you're not?" I crossed my arms.

The small curve of his mouth faded. "Are you mad at me?"

"Yes!" My arms dropped, frustration spilling over. "Of course I'm fucking mad at you."

He looked completely crestfallen as he moved closer. "Why?"

I stepped back. "Because you're doing that thing again. You're pushing me back."

"Darling—when? We talk every day. When have I pushed you back?" His gaze roamed my face like he was trying to catch whatever he'd missed. "Is this because of tonight?"

"Tonight and every other day since you've been back."

His eyes widened. "What?"

I exhaled hard.

"What did I do?" he asked, keeping his voice soft. "Just help me understand—"

"You won't have sex with me."

Silence fell heavy between us.

We stared at each other. I could hear my pulse in my ears as I waited for him to deny it. Admit it. *Something.*

Instead, his lips twitched.

"Don't you fucking laugh at me, Sebastian Langley."

He inhaled sharply, pressing his lips together. "I'm not. I promise I'm not—it's just…"

"What?"

His hands went to his hips like he needed something to do with the impulse, mouth fighting another smile. "I've been back for less than a week."

"Yeah, but we hadn't seen each other for two," I said. "And four fucking years before that. You've been sex-starved since I met you, and now suddenly you're the most patient man alive? Out of nowhere?"

He tried to smother it. Failed. A breath of laughter escaped.

"Don't fucking laugh!"

He dragged his hand over his face, covering his mouth. "I'm sorry, darling." He shook his head, but that stupid glint was still in his eyes. "I am turning forty next year. Have you factored that into your equation?"

"Don't be cute with me," I said. "This distance—it's not you. And we haven't even talked about what's going on with us, and now you don't even want me—"

The humor vanished from his face cleanly. "I don't want you?" he repeated, disbelief raw in his voice.

"What the hell am I supposed to think?"

"Not that. Never *that*." His tone softened, urgent now. "Ethan, I love—"

"Yeah, so you've said. But we're still hiding. Everything is behind closed doors. It'd be very easy to pretend it never happened like that, wouldn't it?"

His lips parted like I'd physically winded him.

"So what is this?" I demanded, throwing my hands up. "If you're not pushing me back, then what are we doing? Because you change your mind constantly, you don't talk to me, and I'm tired of guessing—tired of being fed scraps—"

"Scraps?"

"Yes. That's what you do. It's what you've *always* done. You don't take me seriously—"

"I don't take you seriously?" His voice dropped. "Darling, are you kidding me?"

Anger flared again. "What else am I supposed to think? Should I just keep believing your promises—you don't exactly have the best track record."

His shoulders slumped for the briefest second—then straightened. "I take you very seriously, Ethan," he said quietly. "I always have."

"Fucking *words*—"

Sebastian turned and walked away.

"Hey!" I followed, pulse pounding. "We are not done. You don't get to walk away. I want answers."

He crossed the room to the far wall, reached for the bookshelf, fingers finding something I couldn't see. A keypad chirped.

"I'm serious, Sebastian—"

Metal clicked. The safe opened, and he reached inside.

"You can't just—"

He turned back and placed something on the table with a heavy, absolute thud.

I stopped.

"So am I," he said, his voice calm as he lifted his hand. "I've never been more serious."

A small black jewelry box sat there.

The kind that held promises.

Real ones.

Permanent ones.

My breath hitched.

CHAPTER TWENTY-THREE

ETHAN

My heart was lodged somewhere in my throat, pulse roaring in my ears. "What the hell is that?"

Sebastian stayed exactly where he was. "What do you think?"

"It better be a fucking car." My eyes snapped back to his. "Because the alternative is that you've lost your fucking mind."

The corners of his lips curved, eyes softening just a fraction as he tipped his chin toward it. "Open it."

My body refused to cooperate. Muscles locked, feet rooted to the floor. Frozen. Possibly forever.

"No." My voice came out thin. "You open it."

"It's not for me."

I blew out a sharp breath and stepped back, rubbing my knuckles under my nose, eyes glued to the small black box like it might detonate. "When did you get that?"

"Four years ago."

Something in my stomach dropped hard, violent enough to make me dizzy. He was going to fucking kill me tonight.

My jaw went slack as I looked up at him again, searching his face for any hint that he was messing with me. Nothing. Just that same openness that had been there ever since he got the call about his dad. Hell—since I came to Madrid.

"Oh," I breathed. "So you did lose your mind."

Sebastian let out a light chuckle. But there was a slight tremble to it. Because of how fucking huge this was. This admission.

"Didn't lose it," he said. "The opposite, if we're being honest."

I looked around the room, pulling air into my lungs and trying to understand what any of this meant. "Explain," was what I landed on, taking a few steps away from him. Away from him and that box.

Sebastian's eyes went unbearably soft, and I didn't know how I was supposed to listen to him through the frantic beating of my heart.

"When I left," he said, "it fucking hurt like hell. Being without you."

Heat gathered behind my eyes. I blinked hard.

"But we were still talking. Even if we weren't together, you weren't completely gone from my life. Until…"

"You stopped," I finished for him.

He nodded. "Henny told me it was hurting you. That you never left your apartment. That you were glued to your phone, waiting." He gave a humorless laugh. "He said I looked miserable too. I probably did."

The space between us went quiet.

"When things were really done," he went on, "it got worse. And I just… knew."

"Knew what?"

He gave me a sad smile. "I already knew you meant the world to me, my darling. I loved you back then, even if I was too much of a coward to say it out loud. I felt it."

Every muscle in my body tightened once more. Bracing.

"But when I felt your loss," he continued, "I knew there was no one else. It was you, irrevocably, for the rest of my life." He nodded at the box. "That's when I got it—made a plan."

The burn in my eyes intensified. "You were with someone else." My voice came out small. I couldn't make it anything else. "You've been with other people. You told me that."

"I was," he said. "But they knew too. Luca knew."

"What?"

"I told him we could have exclusivity, but it was never going to be long-term. That I couldn't give him my heart, because it already belonged to someone else."

My chest twisted painfully. "Why didn't you break up with him then?"

"Because I'm an idiot," he said, shifting his weight on his feet. "I convinced myself that if we were going to happen, it had to be done properly. Because things with you were… bigger than anything else." He paused. "You were never temporary to me. I just kept waiting for the right moment. For my life—for yours— to be arranged in a way that made sense. It took realizing how quickly everything can change to understand that I might lose you. I wasn't willing to keep waiting."

I shook my head. "It doesn't make sense."

Sebastian stepped closer, closing the distance like he couldn't help himself. "Darling, our relationship is complicated. It was even more so back then. But the things that kept us apart are still an issue now."

I frowned, brain scrambling to keep up. "Are you talking about my age?"

"Yes."

My mouth pulled downward.

"And before you tear me apart for it, remember—you were *nineteen*, Ethan. You were just starting your life. You still are."

The realization stung more than I expected, knowing he was still holding back over something that felt so fucking trivial to me. I thought we were past this.

"So what?" I asked. "You figured you'd just… keep me away until I was old enough for this to be real?"

"Yes."

I closed my eyes and dragged my hands through my hair. "You and your *fucking* plans."

He reached for my wrists, fingertips brushing my skin, but I shook him off, stepping back. He was closer now. Too close and not close enough.

"I don't believe that anymore," he said. "I want us *now*."

"Because of your dad—"

"Partly. But mostly because of you. Because of what it meant to have you there. Because of how much I needed you. And because of the man you've become."

I stared up at him, every part of me held in place.

"Not that you weren't always… *everything* to me. You were— *you are*," he went on. "But now you know who you are. You stand in it. And I want to be there for all of it. I don't want to keep missing you as you grow into yourself." His throat worked. "But it's so fucking complicated."

"Why?"

"Because I don't want you to give up this part of your life," he said, his voice breaking softly around the edges. "I don't want to steal it from you. I don't want you to wake up one day when I'm gone and realize you still have years left—and you spent them on someone who'd already lived his."

My brows furrowed. "I'm sorry—did you turn thirty-nine last month, or eighty?"

He huffed. "You know what I mean—"

"No. I really fucking don't." Heat flared back into my chest. "Why are you making decisions about *my* life without even talking to me? Why do you get to decide what I want—or what my future should look like?"

His face tightened—not in anger, but in pain.

"I know how old you are, Sebastian. I've always known. And I don't give a fuck." My voice softened, but it didn't lose its edge. "I want you. I don't want to lose out on anything either. Why can't I grow up and live my life *with you*? Why does the only version of my future you'll accept have to be one without you? With both of us miserable?"

"I don't," he said. "Not anymore. I want everything with you, and I don't want to wait anymore to have it. If you'll have me again—if you can forgive me for being an absolute ass—then we'll figure everything else out."

We stayed there for a beat, just looking at each other, letting it sink in.

Some of my anger started to fade, and as it did, this ache— this fucking Sebastian Langley–shaped ache—came rushing back. Because even though I hated what he'd done, part of me was swooning at the thought that he'd been waiting this whole time. That I'd been the only one to ever bring down the fortress he kept around himself. That he was mine. That he had always been mine.

I swallowed thickly. My hands weren't steady when I spoke. "Why were you staying away now?"

Sebastian stilled. A hesitation. Small, but unmistakable.

"Don't," I said, my voice tightening. "Don't decide this without me. I know you. I can tell when you're doing something that involves both of us without actually talking to me about it."

His gaze dropped, a slow breath leaving him. "I heard you."

"Heard me...?"

"You and Henry. On the terrace." He pressed his lips together, offering a small, helpless shrug. "You said you weren't going to build castles in your head again. That you couldn't afford to believe too much."

Heat rushed up my neck. "You were eavesdropping?"

"I wasn't trying to," he said. "But once I realized what you were saying... I couldn't walk away."

Silence pressed in around us.

"I know how much I hurt you," he continued. "When I said we were never going to be love. That what we had was only sex."

His eyes lifted to mine. "I saw what that did to you. I see what it still does. And I realized that if I touched you again without proving this was more—without showing you that I want all of you, not just your body—you might never believe me."

Something inside my chest cracked open.

"So I wanted to show you," he said. "That we could have everything else. That being with you isn't just hunger." His voice softened. "It's home."

The room blurred. That old wound in my chest throbbed—but it wasn't pain this time. It was something loosening. Healing. He wasn't pulling away. He was trying to make *us* safe.

I drew in a shaky breath, my fingers loosening as the truth of that settled under my ribs. All this time, I'd been bracing for the impact. For the moment he'd disappear again.

But he was right here.

"If you ever want to show me what's inside that box," I said, steady despite the way my chest hurt, "you're never going to do that again."

His dark eyes stayed locked on mine. Hopeful.

"You don't get to plan our lives in your head and make choices for both of us. If we're doing this, we're doing it together."

A small smile curved his lips as he nodded.

"I probably lost my mind too, considering…" My lip trembled, the burn behind my eyes flooding back. "But I love you, Ash," I said, my voice breaking on his name.

His expression shattered.

"And I want everything with you too. I always have. So don't fucking hurt me again."

He didn't waste a second. His arms wrapped around me, holding me so tight it bordered on painful. "Never again, pet," he whispered into my hair. "Never."

I clung to him, burying my face in his chest, breathing him in. "If you try to push me away again," I said, voice muffled but deadly serious, "I'll tie you down on the bed and never let you out. You don't get to leave me again."

Sebastian leaned back just enough to look at me, a slow smile pulling at his lips. "Thought I was the one who was supposed to lock you up in my room."

I fisted his shirt and dragged him back against me, heart hammering. "Then show me you mean it, Ash," I said, breathless, aching. "Show me you're going to keep your promises… and fucking *take* me."

Something unrestrained flared behind his eyes. I barely caught it before his mouth crashed into mine. Relief broke through me in a rush, my hands sliding into his hair as the kiss turned wild—not for possession, but for closeness, for proof, for the simple, overwhelming reality of us. Because this was choosing each other again without hesitation, without distance, the way we always should have.

His hands slid down my sides to my thighs, grip firm, and in one swift movement he lifted me, carrying us to the couch and settling me into his lap with practiced ease.

"What happened to the bedroom?" I grinned down at him, cupping his face.

"Too far."

The kiss that followed wasn't slow. If anything, it splintered —teeth, breath, the sharp edge of need scraping against everything we'd been holding back. My hands slid under his shirt, pushing it up, needing skin instead of fabric. Sebastian groaned into my mouth and yanked it off in one impatient motion, tossing it somewhere behind us.

When my own followed, his eyes caught on my chest. He stilled, lips parting, his whole expression softening.

I smiled to myself. "If you'd tried to ravage me at any point this week, you would've seen it."

His dark eyes lifted to mine, brows drawing together in something that looked almost like pain. The necklace he'd given me was back around my neck, where it belonged. Where he belonged.

His fingertip traced the C engraved into the medallion, adoring. "When did you get it?"

"I went to Maya's after I saw you wearing yours."

The look on his face—it was beautiful. The only word I could think of to describe it was yearning. I knew it too well. That feeling had lived locked inside me for so long. For him. For us.

Sebastian leaned in to kiss me again, the urgency returning bit by bit as his hands cupped my neck, one thumb brushing over the chain. Clothes followed in clumsy, desperate pieces. Buttons abandoned. Waistbands shoved down. We kept colliding back into each other between it all, separating only when we had to.

I was dizzy with it. With him.

Sebastian rested his forehead against mine, breath uneven, hands firm on my hips. "Darling," he murmured—a quiet check-in.

"I'm here," I said immediately. "I want this."

He reached for his wallet in the pile of discarded clothes beside us and pulled out a small packet of lube, holding it up instead of assuming. "We're both good?" he asked softly.

I nodded. "Negative. On PrEP."

Relief crossed his face before desire took over again. "Me too. I want you bare."

I nodded again, the decision settling between us, and something about choosing each other so openly made my chest hurt in the best way.

Sebastian leaned back against the couch, eyes dark and intent on me, hands steady as he guided me up. The world narrowed to the way his gaze never left mine, as if this mattered as much as everything else between us.

With his fingers slick and his mouth back on mine, he worked me open, ready for him. The heat eased into something heavier, deeper. I rocked against his hand, and he groaned into my mouth, biting my lip. After long, breathless minutes, he withdrew his fingers.

He moved lower, giving me room, and I braced my knees by his hips as he held himself upright. With our eyes locked, I bore down, taking him inch by inch—hot and perfect, stretching me effortlessly. I didn't stop until I was fully seated, my body settled against his.

His eyes were molten, tracking every inch of me, more than once stopping at my chest and the glint of gold resting there. One hand left my hip, gliding over my stomach before steadying at my neck. "You look like an angel up there," he said, voice rough, chest rising and falling hard.

I grinned, fingers sliding into his hair, twisting and pulling, just how he liked. The first roll of my hips dragged a low, primal sound from him.

My lips parted as his cock slid inside me again—out, then back in. "Do I fuck like an angel too?" I didn't relent, smirk still in place, eyes locked on his half-lidded ones.

A raw chuckle escaped him as his hands returned to my hips, urging me on. "No," he moaned, the corner of his mouth lifting.

I rose and dropped harder on his lap, the impact sharp enough to knock the breath from him, making his lashes flutter.

"You fuck like a *god*," he rasped.

Sebastian spread his legs wider beneath me, hands locking on my hips as he drove up to meet me, forcing my body to take his thrust.

Fuck.

Yes—

My mouth fell open, a broken sound tearing out of me as we snapped into rhythm. All gentleness slipped away as our hands turned rough—his fingertips denting on my skin while my grip tightened in his hair, tipping his head back and dragging a hiss from him that was equal parts pain and pleasure. The smirk never left his lips as we matched each other, bodies pounding together like a challenge, a game of who could undo the other first.

I fucking loved it.

His hard, punishing thrusts, the fire behind his eyes, the sound of skin slapping skin—everything about this, this feral sex with him, made it ten times hotter.

He bit down on his lip, groaning, and for a moment I was sure I had him—until his hand closed around my cock and everything shattered.

My hands pulled free from his hair, bracing on the couch, on his shoulder, nails digging in as heat ripped through me and made my thighs quake. His grip was slick and unyielding, the pressure perfect.

The rocking of our bodies turned frantic, chasing our climax. I needed him with me—I needed to drag him over the edge with me—but then he tightened his hold on my hip and slammed up harder, the angle exact, the constant thrust inside me blowing my vision white.

"Fuck—gonna come," I gasped, barely forcing the words out before my body seized. My thighs locked, release crashing through me. I shook violently, spurts spilling across his chest, a long, deep moan breaking from my throat.

"So fucking hot," Sebastian growled. "Want to come inside you."

I nodded, wrecked, still shaking too hard to speak.

Then I was on my back, the couch warm beneath me as he took over completely.

"God," I groaned as he drove into me, hard and deep, our matching medallions clinking softly together. His hands hooked under my knees, forcing me open, holding me there as he slammed into me again and again, until his moans turned ragged.

His hips stuttered, then snapped forward one last time, his cock kicking inside me as I watched his face above mine, plea-sure stripped bare. He came with my name on his lips, body sagging forward as he filled me, small, involuntary jerks carrying him through the last waves of it.

When he stilled, I clenched around him, smiling when it dragged a hoarse groan from his throat. The aftershocks were still humming through me, made even sweeter by the way his mouth lingered—brushing mine once more before drifting down my jaw, over my collarbone. Slow. Unhurried.

He pulled out carefully, the warmth of him withdrawing inch by inch, then sat back on the couch, one hand still hooked under my thigh, gaze fixed between my legs, lips parted.

Heat spread up my already flushed neck, and I nudged him lightly with my knee, smirking. "Pervert."

Sebastian grinned, still catching his breath. "I'm getting something to clean you up."

"We've talked about this."

"I know," he said easily, already moving to stand. "But I want you in my bed. Clean first." He gave my thigh a light slap on his way past.

I winced. "Neat freak."

"You'll appreciate that when we're living together."

He walked away, leaving me staring after him. Someone had abducted the real Sebastian Langley. That—or I'd definitively broken the commitment-phobe.

"Why the smug smile?" he asked as he came back, a damp cloth in hand.

"Oh, nothing," I said. "Just thinking about you."

He arched a brow, unconvinced, as he sat beside me and dragged the warm cloth over my stomach. I watched him as he cleaned me—over my cock, between my cheeks—careful even when his touch was firm. The low light caught the glint of the necklace at his throat.

"Come on," he said when he was done. "Up."

I followed him into his room on shaky legs, taking in the unfamiliar space. The bed was big, softer-looking than the one in New York, piled with inviting covers and pillows. Everything was done in deep, earthy tones, the walls finished with the same elegant trim framing the living room. Double-paneled doors stood shut against the cold, glass panes reflecting the city lights beyond the small iron-fenced balcony.

My attention snagged on the bookshelves. Fantasy. Rows of it. Well-worn spines, familiar titles I recognized because he'd mentioned them before—books he loved, worlds he disappeared into. It made me smile to myself. This place looked like him.

I sat on the bed facing the view outside while Sebastian stood in front of me, still beautifully bare as I held his gaze.

"What?" he asked, thumb grazing my cheek.

I pressed my lips together, failing to hide my smile. "Would you bring the box in?"

He didn't try to hide his own as he nodded.

I dropped back onto the bed—it was as comfortable as it looked—and pulled the covers up.

When Sebastian returned, he opened the box and set it on the nightstand before climbing in behind me. I turned onto my side, facing it as he curled close, an arm settling around my waist.

There it was—a simple gold band carrying so much weight.

"You're not allowed to ask, by the way," I said. "We haven't even been in a real relationship yet. You might hate the way I don't organize my socks by color."

His arm tightened around me as his quiet laugh warmed the back of my neck. "I can wait." A quick kiss landed on my nape. "But you should consider moving in. I'll brief you on closet protocol."

I nudged him with my elbow. "Don't joke about that."

"I'm not." He played with the medallion hanging over my chest, twirling it in his fingers. "It's not a joke. I meant what I said. I want everything, and I don't want to wait."

My eyes stayed fixed on the reflection of lamplight over the gold, letting that sink in. "Maybe." It wasn't exactly a small step, and you were supposed to think these things through. No matter how loudly my heart was screaming *yes*. "Depends on the amenities."

Sebastian hummed behind me. His warmth surrounded me, the steady rise and fall of his chest at my back making everything feel… right.

"So what was the plan?" I adjusted myself, settling more comfortably against him. "When was all this supposed to happen?"

"When you were twenty-five."

"Of course," I said dryly. "Because I'd be infinitely more mature in a year."

"A year and a month." The rumble of his voice vibrated between us. "And it wouldn't all happen at once. We'd just… start talking. Then a relationship. Moving in together. It was supposed to take years."

I caught his hand and laced our fingers together, drawing it against my chest. "What if I was in a relationship?"

"What?" he scoffed softly. "Like you cared when I was in one?"

I let out a short laugh. "That's not fucking funny."

"It's really not." His chin settled over my shoulder.

I hesitated, then, "I tried to talk to Luca. Apologized for being a dick to him. He told me to fuck off." My gaze dropped. "Which… fair."

"You did?"

I nodded. "Charlotte made me realize that, even if you were mine first, it wasn't called for. Plus, it brought up all the mess with my parents, and I just… I didn't want to be that guy." I shook my head slightly. "But I was."

Sebastian stayed quiet, probably processing what I'd just said.

"I reached out too," he finally said. "Tried to apologize again, but he wouldn't listen. Not that I blame him."

The weight of it settled between us.

"I fucked that up," he added after a second, his voice low. "And I get that it'll make it harder for you to trust me too."

My fingers tightened around his.

Sebastian's ability to stay—to actually commit—had always been a concern to me. But what we'd done to Luca, as fucked up as it was, had been collateral damage from us finding our way back to each other.

If everything Sebastian had said tonight was true—if that ring meant what he said it did—then he'd always chosen me. Above anyone else. And that changed something big, pulling my doubts away from him leaving me for someone else and toward whether he could truly let me in.

"I do trust you, Ash," I said, quieter now. "I get why this spiraled out of control—for both of us. Just promise you won't keep things from me, and we can make it out of this mess."

His hand tightened in mine, holding a little firmer. "I won't."

The moment lingered, heavier than before. I kept staring at the gold band—at the promise of what that future could be.

"And then what?" I asked, trying to push past it. "We'd ride off into the sunset?"

Sebastian sighed, like he was attempting to do the same. "We'd move here if you wanted to. Travel together. Find our rhythm."

"Did you picture kids in this fantasy?"

Sebastian went still. "Is that… something you'd want?"

"It's something you probably should've asked before planning entire lives for us."

He stayed quiet.

"But no," I said. "I don't think I do. It'd be a conversation if you wanted them, but I'm fine being the cool uncle. I figure Henny's going to have five kids. That's enough for all of us."

Sebastian chuckled, tension easing as he relaxed back into the sheets. "That works for me too."

"Anything else?"

He kissed along my jaw. "Spend the rest of our lives like this

—doing whatever we want. Only I'd get to spoil you, like I've always wanted to."

My mouth curved as I tipped my head, his beard brushing my neck.

Then it was there again—the question that had lived in my head ever since that first article came out. "Do we have to hide this time too?"

"No," he said, voice firm. "No more hiding."

I turned in his hold, needing to see his face. "Really?"

"Elena knows, and I updated the report with HR a couple of days ago."

I blinked.

"As for the rest of the world…" He sighed, deeper this time. "Pictures have been circulating for a while now. There are even a couple from the hospital—"

Outrage surged through me. "Are you fucking kidding me?"

Sebastian lifted a shoulder, frustration and resignation mixing in his expression. "People are always going to speculate until we say something. All I want to do is tell them to fuck off, shout it from the rooftops… but I don't want this to hurt you again."

Hurt me? I held his gaze for a second before it clicked. "Who told you about that?"

"Henny. Oli." He brushed a strand of hair behind my ear, his eyes lingering on the movement. "I'm sorry, pet. For leaving you to deal with everything. Alone."

That familiar hollow feeling opened up again. "People are assholes," I said quietly. "Fuck them."

Sebastian smiled and leaned in to kiss me. "You deserve sunlight, my darling. That's what I want to give you. I'll crush anyone who dares say a word to you." His hand slid back into my hair, this time holding. "I mean it, Ethan. I want you on a throne—my fucking *king*. Untouchable. I'll protect you from everything. Stand by your side."

That fire in his eyes, those words, warmed me to my core. I

brushed my thumb over his lower lip. "I don't need protecting," I said. "That's not your job. But I'll take the standing beside me. And the throne."

Sebastian's intensity softened into a quiet huff as he nudged his nose against mine. "I love you."

"And I love you." I pressed a kiss to his lips. "Let's conquer the world together."

The words lingered between us, followed by countless softer kisses, until the edges of the night blurred and we drifted off wrapped in each other.

It felt like the quiet after a fire—smoke still in the air, embers still glowing, but something new already beginning to breathe between us.

We weren't whole yet.

But we were rising.

CHAPTER TWENTY-FOUR

ASH

"You have a meeting with Carlos Rincón at five..." Vanessa scrolled through her tablet, eyes never leaving the screen.

"Call him back and move it to next week. It's not a priority, and I have a dinner to get to."

She nodded. "Consider it done. Do you want me to move the call with Costas at four?"

"No. That one will be quick. Please make sure Oscar is included."

Another nod, fingers already flying. "Do you still want me to go shopping for Ethan?"

I smiled to myself. "No. I'll take care of that later." Two months deserved my own brand of spoiling. I wouldn't miss it for the world.

Vanessa stood from the chair opposite me, her outfit immaculate as she flipped her slick black hair back. "Alright. That's everything. I'll forward your dad's call as soon as it comes in."

"Thank you, Nessa."

She waved me off and strode out like she was walking a runway. I chuckled. Her easy closeness with Ethan made perfect sense.

My phone started buzzing.

I leaned back in my chair, clearing my throat as I answered. "Father dearest," I said lightly, "how are you feeling today?"

"Tired. Which, according to my doctors, is now a sign of progress."

"That's the spirit."

"Still walking every morning," he added. "Slowly. They don't let me forget it." A pause. "And you?"

"Everything's running smoothly. For now. You know how these things are."

"That I do. And… Ethan? Is he well?" he asked, not hesitant, exactly—just careful.

"He is," I said. "He's been amazing, actually. Helping me with some of the research for the expansion project."

"That doesn't surprise me. He was rather ambitious in his time here."

"And too stubborn to be left out."

A faint huff of amusement came through the line. "That too. I'm glad you have him," he said after a moment. "Recovery makes you acutely aware of how much you don't like being alone."

Something about that landed deeper than he probably meant it to.

"There's something else I wanted to speak to you about," he went on. "One of the seats on the Langley Enterprises board will be opening at the end of the quarter."

I blinked.

"I'd like to nominate you for it."

Surprise jolted through me, straightening my spine. "The board?"

"Yes, the board," he said. "You know this business inside and out, and you've been effectively running your own for years. This isn't symbolic. It's overdue."

"That's not a small thing."

"No," he agreed. "It isn't. And I wouldn't offer it if I didn't believe you were exactly what the company needs." He paused, then added, quieter, "What you weathered last year would have sunk most. Instead, you stabilized, rebuilt, and came back stronger. That isn't luck. That's leadership."

The words settled deep in my chest. "And the… enthusiastic press coverage?" I asked before I could stop myself.

A soft exhale. "People talk. They always will. What matters is that you held the line, protected your people, and refused to compromise your integrity. That's what endures."

Pride twisted with something older. Something that still wanted his approval more than I cared to admit. "That's—" I exhaled. "I'm not sure what to say. Thank you."

"Not necessary," he said. "Even if you won't be the head of Langley Enterprises, I want your voice at the table. We need someone with a vision for the future we can trust."

"And you trust me?"

"I do."

Coming from him, that was everything.

"We'll go over the details later," he added. "But I wanted you to hear it from me first."

"Thank you," I said, meaning more than just the job.

"And Sebastian?"

"Yes?"

"Give Ethan my regards."

I smiled. "I will."

The call ended, but I didn't move right away.

A seat on the board of Langley Enterprises. Not a return—a foothold. A way in without giving anything up. I'd spent my life being shaped for that world, craving power over it, then years carving out something that was finally mine. This sat somewhere between the two—a place where I could have a voice without surrendering my autonomy.

For the first time since everything imploded, the future didn't feel fragile anymore.

It felt earned. It felt steady. It felt… possible.

A soft knock pulled me out of it.

"Come in."

The door cracked open, and Ethan peeked inside, hair a little rumpled, eyes bright. "Hey," he said. "Am I interrupting something important?"

I smiled automatically. "Never."

His grin in return was pure sunshine. Ethan crossed the room, bypassing the chairs, leaning in for a kiss before perching on my desk, legs spread at my sides, fully aware of what the image did to me.

"So," he said, badly hiding the excitement in his voice, "I had a thought about tonight."

I ran my palms over his firm thighs. "Tell me everything."

"Let's ditch the reservations. I'll make dinner instead."

I raised a brow. In the time we'd been living together, I'd barely seen him pour himself a glass of water. "You're going to cook for me?"

He nodded, but that smile had an edge now. "Promise you'll love it. I'll make your *favorite*."

I chuckled. "Whatever you want, pet."

He bit his lip and pushed forward, leaving the desk to straddle me. My hands went to his waist automatically, holding him there.

"I wish we could fuck in this office."

I dropped my forehead to his collarbone. "I still have two meetings. Please don't get me hard right now."

Ethan laughed softly, rocking closer, settling right over my groin. "Too late."

"You're a menace."

He hummed. "Tell me what you're thinking about right now so we can both be hot and bothered before tonight," he murmured into my ear.

I palmed his back, feeling the muscles move under my hand. "I keep thinking about that costume. You don't happen to still have it, do you?"

His fingers slid into my hair, a chuckle rumbling out of him as he tugged. "Bet you'd love that. What are you picturing?" He leaned back to look at me. "The mighty Sebastian Langley getting to fuck a Greek god?"

"It's not about power. You just look mouthwateringly divine in it." My hands slid to his ass, squeezing. "Also very accessible."

"It really was. From more than one angle." His eyes lit up. "You know what would be hot too?"

"What?"

"You in one of those little gladiator skirts. All oiled up." His voice dipped as he leaned closer. "I could be, like, a senator's son."

I laughed. "Would you?"

"Yeah." He rolled his hips, slow and teasing. "And I could go to the ludus because I want to see the gladiators training. Maybe even pay to fuck one."

"You know that's Romans, right? Not Greeks."

"Shut up, let me keep going." He was fully gone now, eyes bright with it. "I'd act all noble and bored, pretending none of it impressed me. But then you'd be there—sweaty and dangerous and not paying me any attention." His smile turned wicked. "Maybe you'd hate me at first. Think I was just another rich idiot watching from the stands. And I'd keep coming back, every day, just to see if you'd look at me."

"This is getting elaborate," I said, grinning. "How long have you been thinking about this?"

"As if I'm the only one who ever got hot watching Sparta-cus." He writhed in my lap. "Fuck, I'm not going to be able to walk out of here."

My hand slid between us, over the evident bulge at his crotch. "No. Doesn't look like it." I leaned in, kissing his neck, nudging his necklace aside so I could trace my tongue over his skin.

"Fuck, Ash," he breathed. "We need to do that one day. Now I can't stop picturing you bent over for me."

I slid my hand behind Ethan's neck and pulled him down into a deep kiss, fully prepared to ignore Elena's near-constant warnings about this exact scenario—

A knock at the door broke us apart.

If I were a betting man, I'd put my fortune on who it was.

"Are you decent? Nessa told me Ethan was in here," Henry called.

Ethan tipped his head back with a groan. "It's like he has a radar."

"He probably does," I said. "Come in."

Henry pushed the door open and leaned in first, gaze sweeping over us before one brow arched. "Wow. Zero shame. We're not even pretending anymore?"

Ethan pressed his lips together, color rising in his cheeks. "Give us a minute."

Henry grimaced. "Gross." He stepped inside anyway, shutting the door behind him before dropping into a chair, completely unbothered. His eyes moved between us again, slower this time, a knowing grin spread across his face. "This," he said, nodding toward us, "is exactly what I meant."

"What?" Ethan asked.

But I remembered.

I rolled my eyes at my brother, because he wasn't wrong. When he'd walked in on Luca and me, he'd said it looked like a business meeting. This—Ethan flushed and rumpled—this was what Henry had expected chemistry to look like.

"We had lunch plans," Henry added. "Which you can't cancel. I already have abandonment issues since you stole my roommate slash bestie."

I shot Ethan an apologetic look. "We did have plans."

He scrunched his face like he could will the situation away. "Nobody stole me. We still see each other basically every day." It took him a minute—and one careful readjustment—before he finally settled into the chair beside Henry, still a little flustered, playing it off as best he could.

Henry glanced between the two of us, lips twitching. "So," he said, "should I assume I walked in on something deeply traumatizing?"

"Very," Ethan deadpanned. "Hopefully you'll never recover and finally learn your lesson." He shifted in his seat. "I should get going though—work."

I cleared my throat. "Actually, I have something to tell you both."

That got their attention.

"But I want Oli here too."

Henry frowned. "Why does Oli need to be here?"

"Because this is the kind of thing he'll be offended not to be included in."

Ethan smiled, already catching on. "Is it good?"

I didn't answer, just picked up my phone and tapped Oliver's contact.

He answered on the third ring. "Ash, if this is about the spreadsheet, I already—" A child's voice shrieked something unintelligible in the background. "Hold on—no, not the crayons —Amelia, I swear to god—"

Henry snorted. Ethan pressed his lips together, clearly trying not to laugh.

"Hi to you too," I said.

Oliver huffed. "What's going on? I'm currently being held hostage by my own children. Char's busy."

"I need you for two minutes. You're on speaker."

"Fine," he muttered. "What's this about?"

I leaned back in my chair, aware of how quiet the room had gone. Ethan and Henry were both watching me, waiting.

"I just got off the phone with Dad."

Ethan's expression softened instantly. Henry straightened in his chair, eyes warm and attentive. Oliver stayed quiet on the other end of the line, the small sounds of chaos still filtering through.

This was new.

Not the news. The sharing of it. A year ago, I would have processed it alone. Made the decision alone. Carried the weight of it alone. Now three of the most important people in my life were waiting with me.

I looked at them—my brothers, the man I loved—steady, present, here, and I felt it settle in.

Success didn't feel like distance anymore.

It felt like belonging.

Like family.

———

Later that day, I walked into our shared apartment with a smile, dropping the package with yet another gift by the door. Normally, just coming home to him made my heart skip a beat.

Today it was different.

Today marked two months.

Two months since we'd stopped pretending this was temporary. Two months of building a life that, somehow, already felt lived in.

We'd spent most of that time here, learning each other's rhythms in ways that felt both new and inevitable. Christmas had been loud and warm in Long Island—Oliver and Charlotte, the kids, Vivian keeping my father from overexerting himself, and Ethan slipping into the center of it all like he'd always been part of us. We'd kissed our way into the new year, the world outside the windows forgotten as midnight passed. And somewhere between the holiday chaos and the quiet days that followed, we escaped to the coast for Ethan's birthday—cold air, empty shoreline, his laughter carried away by the wind.

And then we came back to real life.

He dove into his classes and work with a focus that made me

proud just to watch. I learned how to leave the office at a reasonable hour, and my company grew without consuming me. I started running again in the mornings, and reading in the afternoons. Not reports, but actual books. Small pieces of a life I'd once enjoyed and forgotten how to be a part of.

Ethan and I weren't hiding, but we weren't loud, either. We had dinners out. Morning runs in the park. His hand brushing mine beneath tables. Quiet appearances at private events where people could draw their own conclusions. I wasn't sure relationships were meant to feel this intense, this fast. A younger version of myself would've been spiraling about it. But this—whatever this was—felt natural. Easy. *Right*.

And something this right deserved daylight. The world was already whispering about us. This time, I wasn't planning on staying silent. Not for long.

I loosened my tie as I stepped inside, taking in the quiet, pristine apartment, and frowned. "Darling?"

The kitchen was spotless. The dining area was exactly how we'd left it this morning. My mouth curved into a knowing smile. "Where are you hiding?"

"In here."

I followed the sound of his voice toward the home office. "I thought you'd be slaving away in the kitchen."

"I lied," he said. "Can't cook for shit."

The door creaked as I pushed it open—

And my brain stalled.

Ethan was perched on my desk, waiting for me.

For a second, all I could do was stare. He was all bare skin and open invitation, palms braced on the surface as he leaned back, feet resting on the arms of my chair, offered up to me. A gold jock hugged his hips, the metallic fabric catching the light with every small movement, framing him shamelessly. Fine chains draped his torso—one banding his waist, another crossing his chest like a delicate harness, glinting against his skin with every breath. A thin gold garter circled one thigh, the smallest detail, impossibly intentional.

My body answered instantly.

Because this was everything.

My fantasy.

My office.

My Ethan.

Heat flared low in my stomach, and I had to force myself to breathe.

He watched me watch him, eyes bright with mischief and something softer underneath, and lifted one shoulder in a small, not-so-innocent shrug.

"But dinner is still served."

CHAPTER TWENTY-FIVE

ETHAN

Sebastian's gaze was darker than I'd ever seen it, roaming over me as he stepped into the room, not bothering to close the door behind him. His hands slid into his pockets as he shook his head. "What did I ever do to deserve you?"

My tongue flicked over my lips, and his attention followed the motion, hungry.

"Doesn't hurt that you love buying me stuff," I teased.

Sebastian chuckled, dragging the chair back so he could stand between the open V of my legs. Starting with the garter at my thigh, he brushed his fingers over the delicate chains decorating my body, transfixed, following their path slowly upward. When he reached my chin, he curled a finger beneath it, tipping my face up. "What's the plan?"

My grin only grew. "I had a little something installed. Anniversary present and all that. Thought we could finally break this desk in. It's long overdue, don't you think?"

"What?"

I glanced over my shoulder toward the edge of his desk, silently directing his gaze. His lips parted when he saw it—a small iron loop, drilled into the sturdy wood.

When he turned back to me, something awed and curious was written all over his face.

I slid open a drawer, reaching inside and dangling them from a crooked finger—a pair of Velcro cuffs.

A low groan slipped from his throat. By the time his gaze lifted to mine again, his pupils were blown wide. "You or me?"

I bit down on my lip, loving that he felt the genuine need to ask now. "Me—tonight. We can switch some other time."

He leaned down and captured my lips in a searing kiss, one that made my body arch into his, my toes curling. The cuffs dropped onto the tabletop with a dull thud.

"You're so fucking perfect."

I smiled. "So how does this fantasy play out in your head?" I scooted a little farther back on the desk, hands on his hips, keeping him close. "Am I your horny assistant? Did I misbehave?"

Sebastian shook his head slowly, lips still parted. "It was never a power play." His presence suddenly felt overwhelming in the room, the air thick with the look he was giving me. I'd tapped into something new—something wild, dangerous, primal, and exhilarating. His hands slid beneath my thighs, lifting them to his sides, silently asking me to wrap them around him. "Do you know why I've wanted you here?"

My breath was already coming in short. "Not really."

Palms slid across my back, holding me exactly where he wanted as he leaned closer.

"The desk isn't for me," he murmured. "It's all you, my darling. *Your* pedestal. *Your* place of worship." His mouth brushed my ear as his voice dropped lower. "Somewhere worthy of you—where you can be bare and open, and I can give you everything your body's been asking for."

Fuck—okay. This was going to be good.

My whole body was already thrumming with anticipation. I could tease him all I wanted, but I fucking loved that mouth of his. The way he spoke to me, how those words slipped from his lips like honey, trapping me. Only now I knew with absolute certainty that they weren't lies. He meant all of it.

"Do you want to use the gift?"

"Yes." No hesitation.

The corners of my mouth lifted. "Is that part of the worship?"

"A proof of trust," he whispered, then grinned. "And to make sure you'll let me take my time. As long as I like."

A shiver raced through me before Sebastian was back at my lips, his kiss deep, drawing me into him. My head went fuzzy as his body pressed against mine, still fully clothed, and the contrast only made it better.

My breath left me when, in one quick motion, I was on my back—his mouth at my neck, nibbling and sucking as his hands guided my wrists above my head. Sebastian's desk was huge, thick wood and solid beneath me, wide enough to hold most of my body with only a little hanging off the edge.

He made quick work of cuffing me, giving them a firm tug to make sure they were secure before his mouth closed around one nipple. I groaned as his hand slid down my torso, fingers brushing the gold at my waist—cool metal against heated skin— before palming my cock and tugging lightly at the elastic of the jock, testing it.

"I did order food for us," I managed, cutting off on a moan as he latched onto the other side. "It'll get here eventually."

"I hope you told them to come in a couple of hours."

I laughed, breathless. "I did, actually—fuck."

Sebastian gave a sharp suck as his hand stroked me once before hooking his fingers into the band and pulling, stripping it from me without ceremony. He leaned back just long enough to take me in—approval dark in his eyes.

Then he turned me onto my front.

Heat crept up my spine as I heard the chair scrape back, my whole body tightening with need. His hands settled on my thighs, pausing to trace the garter there before sliding higher to cup my cheeks, spreading me apart as he took me in with a low groan. "You look incredible like this."

With the balls of my feet planted on the floor, the edge of the desk pressed into my hips, leaving my hard cock angled down toward it. His lips grazed my skin, breath ghosting over me and making my muscles clench. Then the kisses started—soft at first, brushing over me as he slid the chair closer.

Just the idea of how we must look right now—me laid out for him on his desk at his mercy—made my heart thump and my cock throb.

His hands held me open as his mouth moved closer, until he pressed a kiss right where I was already aching for him. He stayed there for a second, warm breath making me squirm, before the slick drag of his tongue made me squeeze my eyes shut and moan.

He didn't stop. Didn't pull away. Firm hands kept me in place as he worked me open with relentless focus, tongue hot and insistent, breaking only to kiss and suck before starting again.

The scratch of his beard as he went deeper made me want to push back into him, to chase the pleasure he kept igniting over and over. He kept going, coaxing and teasing until my body loosened enough for him to slip into me with that talented tongue.

I shuddered when I felt his hand on my cock, but he didn't stroke it—just held the head between his fingers, thumb brushing over the sensitive slit, already slick. The sensation was too much, my gasps slipping into small, helpless whines.

Sebastian pulled back just long enough to murmur, "I fucking love it when you make that sound," before diving right back in.

My shoulders burned as I strained against the cuffs, like it might help me absorb what he was doing to me. Breathing came in the form of fast and heavy pants against his desk.

When my thighs began to tremble, he released me just long

enough to rub them soothingly, his thumb catching on the little golden chain. "Are you getting tired, my darling?"

I shook my head.

He paused, and before I could ask why, he adjusted me on the desk so my cock was pressed flat beneath me and my hips were fully supported. Sebastian pulled his chair in close, guiding my legs over it on his sides, taking the strain off them—and somehow making everything feel even more exposed.

A heartbeat later, his mouth was back, hands gripping my cheeks to keep me from seeking any friction, and another helpless moan left me.

"Just relax, my pet," he said. "I'll take care of you."

I closed my eyes and let myself melt into the desk, knowing full well what his plans were, and surrendering to him completely.

———

I had no way of knowing how much time had passed.

Only that my body wouldn't stop trembling.

Only that sweat clung to my skin, leaving me slick against the desk.

Only that he'd brought me to the brink so many times now that if he so much as breathed on my cock, I was going to come.

He had worked me with his tongue for a while. Then his fingers—taking his time with each one before moving on to the next, dragging them in slow, torturous strokes against my prostate.

Then his mouth had moved—sucking on my balls, my taint, lapping at my cock just enough to tease, never enough to give me release.

Then back to his tongue.

I couldn't fucking take it anymore.

"Ash," I whined.

He stilled, and I dragged in a deep breath.

"Yes?"

"Would you get your cock in me already? I'm fucking dying here."

He chuckled roughly behind me. Two fingers pressed inside me and curved.

"F-fuck," I breathed, hands curling into fists around the restraints. My feet were back on the floor now, on purpose. The only thing touching my cock was the air around it. Until his fingertips brushed against it, barely there, just enough to make me squirm and groan.

"Maybe we should have used a cock ring," he said in the most infuriatingly casual tone.

"Sebastian, for fuck's sake…" I groaned as he slipped his fingers out and back in again. "Aren't you dying too?"

"I am." And to prove it, he stood and pressed the slick head of his cock against my cheek.

I made a helpless sound. "Fuck. Get that in me right now."

He pulled his fingers free, one hand still holding me open as he slid the head of his cock over my hole. It quivered in response.

"Right here?" His voice was husky with want.

"Yes."

There was pressure. Not enough to push in, just enough to make me rock back, urging him to do it.

He pulled away.

"Oh, come on," I muttered, voice strained as I pushed back, begging without saying it outright.

Another amused sound. "If you stay perfectly still and let me give you what you want, I will. If you move, I start all over."

I nodded against my forearm. "Please."

He came close again, palm pressing to my tailbone as that maddening rub of his cock returned. "On your forearms, pet. Arch for me."

I did, rising onto my toes to follow his order.

Slowly, the pressure built. More and more, until his crown slipped inside, and I let out a broken sound—

Only for him to pull back.

"Oh my fucking god—I'm going to murder you if you do that again."

He chuckled darkly. "Love the sweet talk." A kiss brushed my shoulder as he pushed in again.

I did my best to stay still as he did it a few more times, each one pressing a little deeper before retreating completely.

"You feel so good in here," he rasped, thumb brushing my rim. "Do you want me to tell you?"

My body tensed at the words. Another shiver rolled through me as he pressed in deeper.

I nodded.

"You're hot and slick and so relaxed, practically sucking me in." A deeper push, this one with more force. "Favorite place on earth, right here." His thumb grazed again, then a harder thrust.

I bit my lip, trying not to make a sound.

He stilled. "You know the deal, darling. You start holding those moans in, and I won't give you what you want."

My mouth fell open. "Please."

His hands slid to my waist, fingers stroking once, the chains biting into my skin… and then he yanked me back, driving his cock fully inside.

"Ah, fuck!"

"Yes, my darling." Another thrust. "Like that." His fingertips dug into my flesh, forcing me back again, drawing his name from my throat. "Louder."

I didn't need the order. I wouldn't have been able to quiet the sounds tearing out of me even if I tried. Each hard thrust lit me up, every muscle tensing with the need for release. The desk scraped across the floor, chains clinking as the force of his movement shoved my body over it.

"Push back, pet," he urged. "Show me how you love it."

I did immediately, shoulders burning with the strain as I

used my forearms for leverage, meeting him instinctively, feeling his control slip as his thrusts picked up speed. His hands clamped around my waist like a vise, hauling me onto his cock again and again, filling me, setting me alight from the inside out. My cock bounced beneath us, throbbing with need.

Then he hit exactly right—the pressure perfect on that sweet spot—and I moaned his name loudly.

"Right there?"

"Yes!"

He set his stance, grip firm, and started driving into me hard enough to make my eyes roll back.

"Fuck, yes!" My toes curled into the carpet as I met every thrust I could manage, desperate for more.

Sebastian's hand slid into my hair, fisting it—not enough to tip into pain, but the sure grip sent a shockwave of pleasure straight down my spine.

"Gonna come," I groaned, pulling against the cuffs, my whole body drawn tight as he dragged me closer and closer with every thrust until, with another scream of his name, the heat coiled low in my gut, balls pulling tight, and finally—*fucking finally*—my cock kicked and spilled. Untouched.

"That's it, darling," Sebastian said, voice wrecked. "That's it. Fucking come on my cock."

And I did—for so long and so hard my vision whited out, ears ringing as my body jolted over the desk, pleasure still singing through my nerves while he kept fucking me, each thrust growing more erratic until he finally slowed, and, with an almighty groan, his heat began to fill me.

Time stretched, suspended in that hazy nirvana of pleasure, our harsh breaths loud in the otherwise silent room, until little by little we pieced ourselves back together and drifted down to reality.

He lowered himself over me, forearms braced on either side of my body, panting over my shoulder, still buried deep. Slowly, Sebastian pulled out, pressing soft kisses along my neck as he loosened the restraints, rubbing careful fingers over my wrists to coax the feeling back into my hands.

"There's a cloth in that drawer," I said. "And water."

He hummed. "Thought of everything, did you?"

Sebastian helped ease me onto my back, settling in the chair, and lifting my feet to the armrests again. I watched, entranced, as he pulled what he needed from the drawer, dampened the cloth, and started to clean me, first wiping away the sweat and then the mess between my legs, his focus entirely on what he was doing.

I let my gaze drift over him, taking in his flushed face, the way his chest rose and fell, the strength in his shoulders, and his messy hair, something warm and stupidly fond tightening in my chest.

He noticed and arched a brow in question.

"You're so fucking handsome," I said. "Did you know that?"

His smile was equal parts smug and self-conscious. Cute.

So I kept going. "I could spend all day just looking at you."

Sebastian chuckled, finishing with me before turning the cloth on himself.

I closed my eyes and rubbed at my shoulder, wincing at the dull burn.

"I'll work it out for you later," he said. "In bed."

"It's okay."

"I'm still going to."

My eyes opened when his hands settled on my waist, the cold press of metal against my overheated skin drawing a sharp breath from me.

His eyes were gorgeously dark as he looked down at me. "Come here. I want you close."

I smiled and let him pull me down with him, straddling his lap on shaky legs. Sebastian wrapped his arms around my waist and found my mouth, kissing me the way he always did—slow, deep, and full of heat.

Threading my fingers through his hair, I held on to him as I met every one of his kisses. "I love you."

"I love you," he said back, without a moment's hesitation.

My heart felt too full to contain it. After everything—the distance, the fear, the years we lost, and the work it took to find our way back—we were here. No hiding. No pretending. Just us, still laughing, still trusting, still choosing each other.

Being with him felt like finally exhaling after holding my breath for years.

His eyes were on my face, that soft smile lingering. "What are you thinking?" he asked, because he always knew when something was stirring in me.

"I'm so happy, Ash," I said. "I'm so fucking happy. With you. With this."

"Me too." His fingers brushed slowly along my spine. "I've never felt more… complete."

My hands twisted in his hair, keeping him close. "Let's not ever let this go, okay? You and me, right now. Let's keep this forever. Let's love the fuck out of each other."

He nodded, eyes steady. "I want that."

Emotion swelled in my chest, urgent and overwhelming— and I loved that he met me there, that he never flinched from my intensity. He loved all of me. "Promise me."

His expression changed—set with intent. "I can do more than that," he said, quietly searching my face. "If you let me."

"What do you mean?"

His arms tightened around my waist, drawing me in. "I want you to be wearing that ring right now."

The words were barely a whisper, but they hit me like a blow, my eyes widening—heart stuttering.

"I want to keep this forever too," he said. "I don't want to imagine a future without you in it. And I want everyone to know how fucking lucky I am."

My body felt light, unsteady, like I might drift right out of myself.

"I want you to know that I'm yours," he went on. "That this is ours, and nothing and nobody is ever going to take it away from us." His tongue swept over his lips, his gaze dark and unwavering. "Marry me, Ethan."

My eyes burned. My hands trembled where they held him. "It's crazy," I whispered. "Isn't it? It's too soon—"

"Maybe," he cut in gently. "Maybe for anyone else. But you and me, pet? When have we ever given a fuck about what makes sense? When have rules ever meant anything to us?"

My grip tightened on his hair, my heart racing like it already knew what it wanted.

"What do you say?" His eyes were bright and earnest as they looked up at me. "Let's love the fuck out of each other."

A wet laugh escaped me as I nodded. "Yes," I breathed. "I'll marry you, Sebastian."

His grin was the most beautiful thing I'd ever seen.

And I met it with one of my own. "Let's show them how it's done."

CHAPTER TWENTY-SIX

ETHAN

"I know it's here somewhere," I muttered, digging through the pile of clothes on my side of the closet floor.

"It's fucking hilarious, looking at this," Henry said from the doorway of the walk-in, arms crossed as he surveyed the chaos.

I pulled out a couple of shirts, huffed, then yanked open a drawer. A flash of green caught my eye, and I snatched it up triumphantly. "Aha. Knew it was in here."

"I cannot believe Ash is okay with this." Henry let out a short laugh. "I wasn't allowed anywhere near his closet when we were kids."

"You never borrowed his clothes?" I draped the scarf over my shoulders and reached for a coat on the rack. "That's such a waste. I would've stolen half of it."

"No, he let me wear anything I wanted. He just never let me inside." Henry pushed off the doorframe and stepped in, still looking around. "He'd handpick outfits for me because if I moved one shirt an inch out of formation, life as we knew it would end." He paused, taking in the current state of affairs. "Clearly, you have a special permit."

I rolled my eyes. "First of all, I am trying to be more organized. And second, every few days he dives in here for an hour and re-sorts all of it. He loves it. Color-codes and everything." I slid open the sock drawer and gestured inside. "See?"

Henry snorted and shook his head, already turning away.

I followed him, looping the scarf more securely around my neck as we headed for the door. "He hasn't complained once." A small pinch of insecurity slipped in. "Do you think it really bothers him?"

Living together so far had been… perfect. Sebastian had kept his promise about spoiling me—and not just in bed. He was present. Attentive.

I loved our routine. Breakfast together every day. Him helping me with coursework at night. Talking in bed about work because we both *got it*—because we both craved the high of problem-solving and basked in the admiration that followed when we nailed it.

I fucking loved it.

And I loved that it was forever too.

My thumb brushed over the band on my finger, and a smile tugged at my lips. It had only been two days, but my stomach flipped every time I remembered we were engaged now.

Only the people closest to us knew—Oliver, Henry, and Charlotte, obviously. But then also Aria, Elena, Vanessa, and Maya. Every couple of hours, Sebastian would casually mention someone else who knew, and my heart would stutter all over again. I knew we had to be careful, but, fuck, I wanted to shout it from the rooftops.

I was going to *marry* Sebastian Langley.

Sebastian Langley was going to be *my husband*. Permanently, irrevocably, and one hundred percent mine.

"I don't think there's anything you do that actually bothers Ash," Henry said, grabbing his coat from the couch. "Even when you're being a complete pain in the ass, he still finds it endearing. It's honestly disturbing."

"That's because I give incredible h—"

"Stop." He held up a hand. "We've never tried this before, but I think we need boundaries. Can we do boundaries?"

"Henry—Mr. *I-love-to-toe-on-the-line-of-impropriety* Langley—wants to have a chat about boundaries?"

He shrugged. "It feels icky when you do it."

"I'll agree to boundaries if you actually stick to them too," I said. "Fair is fair."

Henry scoffed, but it was affectionate and completely transparent. "Fine. You'll be begging for my stories. I bet they already fuel your sex life at this point."

"My sex life needs no fueling. I still have the indents from the desk—"

"Stop," he said loudly, hand raised again. "I swear to fucking god, this is the beginning of a truly horrific drinking game."

A laugh escaped me as I pulled my phone out of my pocket. It was buzzing, and I would've bet anything it was Sebastian asking when we were getting to the restaurant for lunch.

But when I saw the name on the screen, my stomach dropped.

Fuck.

"What is it?" Henry asked, his face turning serious.

I turned the phone so he could see my dad's name.

"Oh, fuck." His hands went to his hips, lips pulling down in disapproval. "What are you going to do?"

I stared at the screen, indecision churning—until impulse won. My thumb hit accept, and I lifted the phone to my ear.

"Hello, son. Thought I'd miss you."

My chest tightened immediately. "Hey."

"How've you been? Missed you in the city. Your mother told me you'd left when we spoke."

I hummed, my heart beating too fast. That was over two months ago. Apparently time moved differently for him.

"She told me it looked like you and Sebastian were back together. Good for you."

This… *fucking asshole.*

"Why are you calling, Dad?" I asked, my voice flat.

A pause.

"We haven't talked in a while. I thought—"

"We haven't talked in a while because the last time we did, you admitted to draining my trust fund. So yeah. That tracks."

Silence.

"Ethan, that was a joint investment—"

"A joint investment in which one of the parties—the one who had all the fucking capital—was kept completely in the dark?"

"Don't talk to me like—"

"I'm going to talk however the fuck I want," I cut in. Not loud, but firm. Because he didn't get to hear me fall apart. "I know you're not going to give it back. And the only reason I'm even answering is to tell you not to call me again. And if you thought me and Sebastian getting back together was another money ticket for you after you pressed charges against him for something that he didn't do and that was none of your fucking business, then you are very, very mistaken. Do yourself a favor and delete my number. You no longer have a son."

I ended the call and let the phone fall onto the couch before I could throw it.

That was that.

He didn't get the last word.

"That," Henry said, pulling my attention back to him, "was fucking badass." He grinned and gave me a double thumbs-up, that almost made me smile.

"Fuck," I breathed, the word trembling out of me. My eyes burned, and I scrubbed my hands over my face.

Henry's hand landed on my shoulder. "You okay?"

I shook my head. Then nodded. "Yeah. I will be—I am." Anger still coiled in my chest, hot and sharp, along with indignation and helplessness—the same things he always dragged back into my life without fail. I took another breath.

No more.

I didn't need him.

I didn't need someone who didn't know how to be—or didn't even seem to want to be—a parent. I had more than enough people in my life. A family. Whole and perfect without him.

"I am," I said again, this time with more conviction. "And I'm done." My shoulders finally relaxed as I met Henry's gaze. "I sent the information over for the investigation last week. Talked it through with Ash."

Henry's eyes widened slightly. "Holy fuck, E. Are you sure you're okay?" His hand tightened on my shoulder.

"Yeah. I mean, is it ideal? No. I don't want my father to be part of a legal battle, but if they fine him, that's fair, right? At least he'll think twice before screwing someone over again."

Henry's expression softened. "It's more than fair."

I stepped out of his grasp and shrugged, my head still a mess —but a more resolute one. "We should get going."

Henry nodded, though his dark eyes stayed on me. "Let's. But before we do…" He took a second, like he was deciding how to say it. "You should know that what you just did? It was unbelievably brave. I'm proud of you, E, for a lot of things—but right now, because… you really do know how to stand up for yourself, don't you?"

There was something unspoken in that. Part of it was about me, yeah—but another part of it was about him too. And somehow, that made me settle even deeper into the decision. Knowing it helped him in some way.

"I'll stick up for you too," I said. "Aggressively. If you ever need me to." My lips curved into a smile.

He matched it, and together, we left the apartment.

Closing the door behind me felt like closing one chapter and stepping into another. And as I breathed in the cold February air, I realized how much I fucking loved this—walking into my life instead of being trapped by my past.

And doing so in perfect company.

The city hummed around us, bright beneath a pale winter sun, the cold sharp but alive with movement. Only a few blocks later, we spotted Sebastian and Vanessa lingering outside the restaurant—a tapería—both absorbed in Sebastian's phone.

The sight of my new fiancé sent heat rushing up my neck, and I had to fight the grin threatening to take over my face. All thoughts of my father vanished instantly, and my thumb rubbed absently over the band on my finger once more.

A cold hand reached out and pinched my cheek.

"Look at you," Henry said. "All cute and smitten."

I swatted him away. "Get off me."

That little scuffle caught their attention. Sebastian glanced up and smiled when his gaze landed on me…

…and Vanessa looked downright feral with barely contained excitement.

Huh.

Sebastian met me halfway, and the moment his lips touched mine, I was right back in honeymoon heaven.

"Hello, darling."

"Again." I smiled and leaned in for another kiss. "You're all warm."

A soft huff brushed my mouth as he deepened it.

"You taste so fucking good," I whispered—or tried to.

"Gross," came from our right. Henry was attempting a disapproving face while still somehow looking ridiculously pleased for us.

Sebastian slipped an arm around my shoulders. "We'll talk in a bit," he told Vanessa. "Thank you for everything."

"Good luck," she called, already walking away with a wave. She shot me one last strange look before disappearing down the street.

My hand rested on Sebastian's hip. "What were you two up to?"

"You know… work." His attention—and his other hand—was already back on his phone.

"So?" Henry said, nodding toward the doors. "Food?"

I stepped out of Sebastian's hold, but he tugged me back when I tried to follow his brother. "What?"

He lifted his phone, camera pointed at me. "Just a second."

I pressed my lips together, trying not to smile as he raised our joined hands into the frame. The shutter clicked.

"Did you just take my picture?"

He grinned up at me. "Am I not allowed to?"

"You're allowed," I said. "That was just kind of—"

"Hey," Henry called, holding the door open. "In or out?"

Sebastian's eyes were glued to his screen once more, so I tugged his hand and pulled him inside with me.

The restaurant was nice—a regular spot for us, where they always tucked us into a table in the back so we could have a little privacy. Soft light spilled from hanging lamps, warming the stone around us, and the low hum of conversation made it feel like the rest of the world had been gently turned down. The air smelled faintly of smoked wood and grilled meat as we slid into our seats, coats draped over chair backs, the cold still clinging to us. We settled in with drinks Henry had already ordered for all of us, because of course he had.

"So," I said, glancing across the table at him, "finally got the permits?"

"Fucking finally. Just the finishing touches left, and we're done. Opening date is February fourteenth." He gave me a sly smile. "So you can push the Valentine's plans back a day and be all lovey-dovey over there."

"That's fine by me." I peeked at Sebastian, but he was still zoned out. "And Mateo?" I asked, pretending not to watch Henry's face too closely.

His mouth twitched. Just a little. "Out of town."

"Uh-huh."

"Raúl has Loki," he added. "I'm supposed to pick him up later today."

"Wow. You're being incredibly forthcoming."

"Don't push it."

Next to me, Sebastian was still staring at his phone, his thumb moving in slow, careful taps across the screen. He had that focused look he got when he was doing something he absolutely did not want to be interrupted during.

"Are you going to join us any time soon?" I muttered.

He didn't look up.

"So." Henry smirked. "Oli and I were thinking about a quick States run, around March. Check on Dad. You two should come —and then we disappear somewhere warm afterward. I'm done with winter."

"Do you have your phone with you?" Sebastian asked suddenly.

We both turned to him.

"Yeah."

His gaze dropped back to his screen. "Good."

I was about to ask what that was about when my phone chimed. Frowning, I reached into my pocket, while Sebastian smiled like the cat who caught the canary.

Sebastian Langley started following you.

"That's what you've been doing?" I held up my phone with a light laugh. "Finally crawling out of the Ice Age and joining the rest of the world on social media?"

He nodded.

"What did he do?" Henry asked, leaning closer to look. "Wow. How the hell do you have so many followers already?"

His eyes went wide, and I was pretty sure mine did too. Hundreds of thousands of them.

What the hell?

"All Vanessa's doing." Sebastian's gaze dropped back to his

phone, thumb tapping just before another notification chimed. Then he looked up at me, barely contained excitement written all over his face.

My heartbeat stuttered, sensing something before my mind caught up. I looked down at the screen.

I'd been tagged.

With a tap on the notification, there I was—just minutes ago —smiling in the background, lips pressed together. But what filled the frame wasn't my face, even though it was unmistakably me.

It was the ring.

Gold. Bold. Impossible to miss.

The restaurant noise dissolved into nothing.

"Holy shit," Henry breathed beside me.

I looked up at Sebastian, stunned, then back at my phone.

And then I saw the caption.

My one. My love. My darling.

Holy.

Fucking.

Hell.

I could only stare at it, my hand already beginning to tremble. "What—"

"Did you just—" Henry's gaze jumped from my screen to me, then to Sebastian. "Fuck. Did you just announce your engagement like that?"

Sebastian's grin faltered just a little before his eyes lifted to mine, bright and intense. "Shouting from the rooftops, darling," he said. "The way it was always supposed to be."

Phones began chiming around us—one after another. Mine. His. Even Henry's. But all I could do was look at Sebastian, my heart pounding, because this—this ridiculous, perfect thing he'd just done—was the most incredible thing anyone had ever done for me.

It was the biggest thing *he* could have done.

My eyes burned as he wrapped his arms around me, letting me bury my face in his chest and shut out the noise of the world. After a lifetime of doubt, of questions, of not knowing if I would ever be enough for anyone—enough for him—here we were.

And it wasn't just that he was choosing me so openly—it wasn't about anyone else believing it. It was how we had chosen each other. Now, instead of hiding our love from the world, we got to shove it down everybody's throats. Together.

This was ours.

"Only sunlight from now on," he whispered into my temple.

I closed my eyes, pressed closer to him, and let myself feel it. *Only sunlight.*

———

After all the chaos finally quieted—after the messages, the calls, the congratulations from the people we loved—it was just the two of us again, back in our apartment.

Sebastian sat beside me on the couch, our hands laced together, his thumb tracing slow circles over my skin. He looked at me with that soft, perfectly fond smile that still made my chest ache.

So I took a picture of him.

And tagged him, just like he had done to me. Right below it, I laid down the words I'd been fighting a lifetime to set free. I didn't have to pretend anymore. This was it.

Mine. For-fucking-ever.

EPILOGUE

ASH

One year later…

"Are you about done?" Henry poked his head through the door.

Oliver stood in front of me, hands on the knot of my tie, making sure it was just right. "Just about." His dark brown eyes checked his work for a second before he smiled up at me.

"I'll be right back," Henry said, closing the door again. He'd been running around all morning, bouncing between me and Ethan and everything else he was supposed to be in charge of. His real job today was to relax and be with us, but Henry wasn't built for giving up control when it came to big events.

And this was about as big as it got.

There were over three hundred people attending. I still wasn't sure how he'd pulled that off, considering I wasn't exactly known for having close friends. But between Langley family obligations, our shared social circle, and business connections, we'd actually had to cut the list down.

We'd asked for this, though. We wanted today to be something people talked about. Something they looked forward to. Hell, Henry had even arranged for press coverage, because we'd wanted that too. Public, but on our terms. Exactly how we liked it.

"I can't believe this is actually happening," Oliver muttered as I slipped on my jacket.

"So little faith," I said, running my fingers through my hair, careful not to mess anything up as the sound of liquid being poured into a glass filled the room.

"No, I mean—I knew it would happen. It's just... strange to match the you standing here now with the you from five years ago."

"With Sebastian Langley, the CEO?"

He smirked as he handed me the glass. "With Sebastian Langley, the chain-smoking playboy who swore he was never going to settle down."

I chuckled. "If you remember correctly, I said I would. Just not necessarily with the person of your choosing."

Oliver smiled at me, soft and fond. "I couldn't be happier about the person you chose."

That warmed something in me, but I couldn't resist the jibe. "Five years ago, you had a different opinion."

"Absolutely no one could have predicted this." He raised his drink. "But we can toast to a reckless plan working out in your favor."

I clinked his glass.

The door burst open again, and Henry frowned at the sight of us. "Hey. No celebrating without me. New rule—all toasts include the three of us."

"Everything okay?" I asked.

"Yeah," he said, looking a little frazzled but grinning. "Double best-man duty is getting interesting, but everything's perfect. Let's drink and make an honest man out of you."

Oliver's lips parted.

"It's too easy," I said dryly.

Henry laughed. "Way too easy."

After we drank, Henry ushered us out of the room.

My heart picked up its pace—fast and unprovoked.

It made no sense. There was nothing fragile about us anymore—no hiding, no glances over shoulders, no calculations before touching him in public. Just life, unfolding at our pace.

Mornings that started together and didn't feel borrowed. Calendars that overlapped because we wanted them to. Flights booked without secrecy. Dinners that turned into plans, plans that quietly turned into habits.

We argued about groceries. About whose turn it was to order out or attempt cooking. About whether fantasy novels counted as "serious literature." They absolutely did. We worked too late and still went to bed tangled together, bodies familiar enough to sleep through.

It was ordinary. And today was just a formality—because this was already our life.

But my heart didn't seem to care.

This wasn't something I was chasing anymore.

And that realization hit harder than all the risks ever had.

Henry walked ahead of us, talking quickly into his phone as we moved through the back of the venue. Kitchens. Offices. Then finally, a wall of soft white curtains.

"Ready," he said into the phone. "Two minutes. Start it up."

The music dipped, then swelled again.

"You have the song I asked for, right?" I murmured.

Henry scoffed. "The one thing you asked for? Please."

"Just checking. In case you haven't noticed, I'm a little nervous."

Oliver's hand settled on my shoulder, and Henry's joined it on the other side.

"We've got you," Henry said gently.

And then he pulled the curtain back.

Hundreds of people stood, all eyes turning toward the Langley brothers as we stepped into the room.

Into the event of the year.

The second Langley-Bennett wedding.

For a moment, I just stood there, taking it all in.

The space had been transformed into something stately and almost unreal. Rows of sleek dark chairs filled the room, every seat occupied, every guest dressed in black, creating a sea of shadow and silk that made the aisle glow in contrast. Tall arrangements of white flowers and soft gold accents lined the walkway, candlelight flickering between them like a path of fire leading straight to the raised stage at the far end.

Behind everything rose the grand staircase, wide and sweeping. The aisle stretched from those steps all the way to where we now stood, waiting.

Waiting for him.

Henry and Oliver took their places beside me, both in dark blue at my sides. My own suit matched Ethan's, cut from the same white cloth, tailored carefully.

I let my gaze drift, just for a second, over the front row.

My father stood there beside Vivian, his posture straight, his expression soft in a way I wasn't used to seeing. He was smiling —really smiling—and there was pride in his eyes that made something in me ache.

A few seats over, Charlotte was practically glowing, Liam and Amelia beside her barely containing themselves, their excitement bubbling over in quiet giggles, trying very hard—and failing—to look subtle as they edged closer to the aisle, craning their necks for a better view.

All of them here.

All of them watching.

The music changed once more, and the first notes of the song I'd chosen poured into the room. When Henry had played it for me earlier, I hadn't even tried to hide my smile. In a funny way, it had been ours from the start.

I leaned slightly toward my brothers, eyes already locked on the staircase. "Watch his face."

At the top of the stairs, Ethan appeared, and the world narrowed to just him.

He stood there for a breath, framed by light, golden curls a little wild, his suit fitting him like it had been designed by someone who knew exactly how to love every inch of him. His eyes lifted, searching—and they found me. That shy smile settled on his mouth, soft and devastating all at once.

Then the song hit him. His shoulders loosened, emotion slipping through, and he shook his head with a quiet laugh before mouthing *fuck you* in my direction.

Henry and Oliver both chuckled beside me, and my face hurt with how wide my grin was as laughter rolled through me.

Ethan's lips curved into something wicked as he started down the stairs, his gaze never leaving mine. He mouthed the lyrics as he descended, picking up speed with every step, energy practically sizzling around him.

He held his arms slightly open at his sides, eyes blazing, fixed on me as he mouthed the words straight to me.

But you dragged me through the fire…

I had.

And I would again.

For us.

His pace quickened, and I couldn't stop myself from moving too, meeting him halfway with my arms already open. One hand flew to my neck to pull me in as I caught his waist. Foreheads touched, eyes closing as the weight of everything around us pressed in, charged and electric.

We were getting married.

He and I.

Who would have thought?

"You just had to use that fucking song," he muttered, lips a breath from mine.

"I *am* feeling particularly *lucky* right now," I said, biting down on my lip as he pulled back just enough to glare at me, a smile he wasn't even trying to hide tugging at his mouth.

Our eyes were locked together, the music still swelling around us, the room full of people and light and expectation.

"You ready?" he said, his tone changing to match this moment.

I smiled. "For a while now."

His thumb brushed under my jaw, that small, gentle touch igniting something in me—something that had only ever been his.

Ethan's grin was bright as he tilted his head. "Then let's go get married."

And together, we turned toward the stage.

———

The reception had already slipped into motion around us.

Music hummed through the room, warm and low, laughter rising and falling in soft waves as people moved between tables, glasses catching the light. Candle flames flickered against crystal and gold, turning everything hazy and unreal, like the whole night was wrapped in a gentle glow.

And in the middle of it all, Ethan and I were sitting shoulder to shoulder, still not quite believing this was real. There was a strange, floating feeling under my skin, like the ground hadn't caught up with us yet.

Married. Officially and irrevocably.

We didn't need to cling to each other to feel it, but somehow we kept finding small ways to stay connected anyway. Our knees brushing when one of us shifted. Hands resting on thighs. Fingers reaching without really thinking about it.

Every now and then, he glanced at me, eyes soft and a little dazed, like he was still trying to process what had just happened. I felt the same. A year of waiting, wanting, building toward this moment—and now here we were, sitting in a room full of people who knew. Who could see us. Who were celebrating us.

It was overwhelming in the best way.

"You know," Ethan said, pulling my attention back to him. "I know we agreed on this, but isn't it weird seeing just us two in white?"

I pressed my lips together to keep from smiling as I leaned in closer. "Why would it be weird?"

Ethan gave me a look, humor dancing behind his eyes. "Come on, Ash. You and I aren't exactly the paragons of purity, are we?"

A laugh broke out of me before I could stop it, and Ethan followed, folding into me for a second, his forehead brushing my shoulder.

I slid a hand along his jaw, tipping his face back toward mine. "We're not in a religious ceremony, but no, I wouldn't say we embody restraint."

That shy smile spread across his face, lighting him up in a way that hit somewhere deep in my chest.

"The choice wasn't ever meant to show that," I said, my thumb gliding just under his cheekbone. "It was meant to make us stand out, because that, my darling, is what we have always done."

His fingers curled tight in my jacket, pulling me in just enough to close the space between us. "We're *married*, Ash."

Something in me gave at that—quiet, but final. I leaned into him, resting my forehead against his. "We are."

"You and me," he said, his voice edged with wonder.

"You and me, pet."

He pulled me down to his lips, and the kiss felt bigger than any we'd shared before, like we were trying to ground ourselves in it, to hold on to something that was already ours.

There was the bright, familiar sound of a spoon tapping against a glass.

Once.

Twice.

I lingered there, close enough to feel his breath for a second longer before we turned to the front together, the room slowly quieting around us.

Henry was already standing, a drink in his hand, wearing a grin that meant he was very aware all eyes were on him, and he was enjoying it entirely too much. Oliver was beside him, amused, while Charlotte perched at the edge of her seat, eager, the kids clustered near her—all of them waiting.

Henry cleared his throat, lifting his glass. "Okay, okay," he said, looking around the room. "If I could have everyone's attention for just a minute…"

Ethan pressed a little closer to me, anticipation buzzing between us.

"Oh no," he muttered. "Here we go."

Everyone sat a little straighter. People angled in their seats to get a better view, and my heart started picking up the pace once more.

"As you all know, this is a very important night," Henry said. "One most of us thought might never come. Not because these two don't love each other—but because one of them has a tendency to run, and the other has a dangerous habit of blowing things wildly out of proportion."

A ripple of laughter rolled through the room.

Ethan groaned beside me, shaking his head. I rested my palm on his neck, chuckling under my breath.

"I knew it was going to happen," Henry added smugly. "And I'll let you all in on a little secret. Even you two." He lifted his hand, drink still in it, pointing at us. "I knew this was going to be big from the moment they met."

His gaze softened as it landed on me. "And I would know. You see, Ash isn't just my big brother." He swallowed hard, clearly trying to hold it together. "He was a parent when I needed one. My protector. My comfort. My teacher. He's been a lot of things that are making me dangerously emotional right now—but the biggest one is friend."

My heart clenched tightly as my eyes prickled.

"I've got a couple of those." His eyes flicked briefly to Oliver. Then to Ethan. "But Ash was the first person who really wanted that role. He taught me how to be myself, how to be proud of it, and he's been beside me every step of the way, making sure I got everything I wanted out of life."

The room was silent, hushed around his words.

"You might see him as this important man. Charming when he wants to be. Serious when the moment demands it. But I see the real him—even when he's fighting tooth and nail not to show it. There's a softness under all those layers of armor. And that softness came to life the day he saw Ethan for the first time.

"He tried to deny it. Tried to fight it." Henry paused, smirking. "Tried to pretend it was something else, even though it was painfully fucking obvious to the rest of us."

More laughter.

"But what he didn't realize yet was that Ethan wasn't just another conquest. He was his match."

Ethan's hand found mine and held it tight.

Henry lifted his glass slightly, eyes bright. "I'm here on double best-man duty tonight because it wasn't just my brother who got married today. I know Ethan well enough to tell you this with complete certainty." He looked straight at my husband. "Ash never stood a chance. Because once E decided this was it… it was it. And today is proof."

The room went quiet.

"The thing about Ethan is that he loves like that in everything. Fully. Without bargaining. Without an exit plan." Henry smiled. "He walks into a room and makes it feel like home. He shows up when it matters. He stays when things get hard. And he has this stubborn way of believing in you until you start believing in yourself." He glanced at me. "That's why my brother loves him." Then back to Ethan. "And that's why I do too. Not just as Ash's husband, but as my best friend."

Ethan sniffled beside me, his free hand coming up to his face. His shoulders shook once, like he tried to stop it and couldn't. I tightened my grip on his hand, threading our fingers more securely together, my thumb pressing slow circles into his skin. He leaned into the touch without looking at me.

"Watching this love story unfold has been absolute fucking chaos," Henry said with a soft laugh. "It's been anxiety-inducing, hilarious, and heartbreaking. But it's also been beautiful. Because from the very first day, you could see them changing. Like something deep inside each of them was calling to the other. They fought. They broke. They rebuilt. They became the best versions of themselves so they could fit together. So they could stand together at the top."

His words landed deep, and I felt every part of them.

I looked at Ethan beside me—really looked at him—at the way his fingers clung to mine, like he was holding himself together inside this moment the same way I was. His eyes shone, glassy with everything Henry's words had stirred loose: relief, disbelief, and the quiet astonishment of being seen and loved so openly.

I thought about every version of us that hadn't worked. Every fight. Every mistake. Every time we'd hurt each other because we hadn't known yet how to love without fear.

And somehow—against all the odds, against our own worst instincts—we'd made it here anyway.

To this.

To each other.

I brushed my lips softly against his temple, and he squeezed my hand tighter.

Henry exhaled, shaking his head in disbelief. He glanced around the room, like he needed witnesses for what he was about to say. "I don't know if this is how love is supposed to work—but it's how *they* work. And the only thing I can think of when I see them together is fireworks. Fire. Explosions. And somehow… perfect control."

A few people laughed softly. Others wiped at their eyes.

"This day is very special to me. But it should be special to everyone in this room. Because this isn't just my brother and my best friend getting married."

His eyes went back to us. "This is power colliding with power. Fantasy blending into reality. Resistance pushing back against rules and time. And I honestly can't wait to see what you two unleash on the world."

He lifted his glass high.

"Because it never saw you coming—and it better be fucking ready. Let's make some noise for the newlyweds."

The room erupted into applause—cheers, whistles, the pop of bottles, and the clink of glasses crashing together. But I barely registered any of it. All I could feel was Ethan's hand in mine as I pulled him with me toward Henry.

I let go of Ethan just long enough to wrap my arms around my brother. He folded me into him without hesitation.

"Thank you," I managed, my voice thick.

Henry gave a slightly shaky laugh. "I did good?"

I pulled back just enough to look at him. "Always, Henny."

His lips pressed together, his eyes shining, before he reached for Ethan and wrapped him into a hug too.

For a second, I just watched them—my brother and my husband, laughing quietly, foreheads close, sharing inside jokes that kept them smiling.

I let my gaze drift.

The room was alive—cameras flashing, glasses raised, music swelling into the air. People were smiling at us. Not whispering. Not staring. *Smiling*. My father stood near the front of the room, his hand resting at Vivian's back, pride unmistakable in his eyes as he watched me. Oliver and Charlotte shared a kiss, Amelia and Liam bouncing at their sides, too excited to stay still.

All of them here.

All of them with us.

I looked back at Ethan. At the way he was glowing, still a little stunned. Our hands found each other again, fingers sliding together automatically. The rings caught the light when we moved—two matching bands, simple and perfect.

Inside them, where only we could see, were the words we'd chosen:

From our ashes.

Because we hadn't been made from something soft.

We'd been burned down.

And somehow, we'd built everything from what was left—stronger.

Truer.

Ours.

We rose from our ashes together, ready to set the whole damn world on fire.

ACKNOWLEDGMENTS

This book... man, writing this book was *really* fucking hard. It took me over a year to finally give these two their HEA, and it was a very hard-fought one. Not because I don't think Ash and Ethan were meant to be, but because they really loved fighting me on how they would get there.

Anyway, I wanted to say thank you to the people who helped them (and me) finally get this story out.

First and foremost, my wonderful husband, for supporting my daydreams and watching me turn them into books with pride behind his eyes. And my kids, for always showing me the beauty in chaos, even in the middle of the mess.

Next, my editor, Jess, who is so much more to me than just what her title entails. But right now, I really want to highlight her abilities as both an editor and a writer. The way you break things down, challenge my choices, and help me dig deeper into these characters has shaped this story in ways I couldn't have done on my own. And the way you understand voice, pacing, and emotion, not just technically but as a writer yourself, is something I lean on more than you know. Without your constant encouragement and our talks about these two, I don't think I would have ever had the courage to publish this book. You don't just make these books shine; you make me a better writer with each one, and I will never have enough words to thank you.

To my beta readers, I want you all to know that this book exists because of you. I cannot stress enough how important you were to this process. I think you can tell, from the first version you read to the one in your hands now, just how much you've shaped this story.

Lore, your understanding of these characters' emotions and your belief in their arc gave this book its well-rounded narrative and helped the found family aspect shine. I'm so grateful for how thoughtful and kind you always are with your feedback.

Abbey, you pushed me to sit with the messy parts and be brave enough to tell this story exactly as it was always meant to be: unapologetic and chaotic.

Laura, my absolute chaos gremlin, you somehow managed to make me laugh out loud while still calling me out in all the right ways. Your feedback helped these two finally get their act together, and we have you to thank for our beloved desk scene.

Brandy, you've been hyping up our boys from the very, very start. Your support has always been unconditional and so full of love, and I felt safe handing them to you. You also helped me crack the biggest plot hole and turn this story into something so much stronger.

Jeannine and Bryoni, your honesty pushed me to clarify everything and dig deeper, making the most difficult emotional moments land with greater impact. Your belief in this story gave me the courage to turn the mess-o-meter up to a thousand.

And finally, Taylor, my sensitivity reader, thank you for helping me tell this story with care and for making sure the queer love in these pages was always represented thoughtfully and with intention. It meant a lot to me to know this story landed the way it needed to with you.

A big shout-out as well to my cover artist, Lina Ganef, for bringing these two to life with such a stunning, fiery cover and giving them the comeback they deserved.

And to my amazing readers... thank you for suffering through that first cliffhanger, for trusting me to bring you this second part, and for staying with these characters through all their chaos. I hope you're walking away from this with a full heart and a hundred memories of them that will live on. Thank you for being here.

ABOUT THE AUTHOR

Alex Cross is a professional daydreamer with a knack for overanalyzing and creating drama out of thin air. She's a chef, a mother of two, and the organization fairy of her household.

When she's not chauffeuring her kids around or making her hundredth attempt at baking the perfect brownie, she's listening to music and drawing inspiration for her next or current story.

If you want to know all about new releases or are just in the mood for some awesome book recs, follow her on Tiktok as @alexcrossauthor.

ALSO BY ALEX CROSS

Echoes of Us

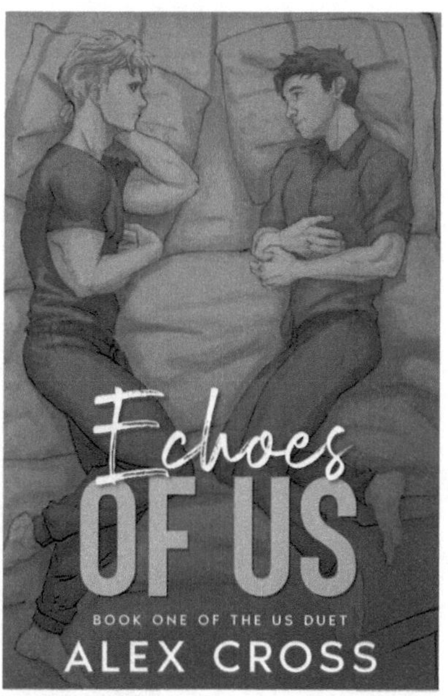

Atticus King had his life mapped out—train hard, play volleyball, keep to himself. That is, until Noah Rossi burst onto the scene: charismatic, impulsive, a storm that tore through Atticus's carefully built walls and set his world on fire. They didn't fit—Noah was everything Atticus wasn't—but somehow, they found a rhythm in their shared love for the game and an undeniable pull toward each other. It was everything Atticus never knew he wanted.

But just as quickly as Noah entered his life, he disappeared. No explanation. No goodbye. Only silence that left Atticus drowning in confusion and pain.

Two years later, Noah walks back into Atticus's world as if nothing ever happened, stirring up old feelings Atticus has tried to bury. The bond they shared is undeniable, but so is the hurt that lingers beneath the surface. Why did Noah leave? And can they rebuild something from the shattered pieces of their past?

Love isn't easy. But for Atticus and Noah, it might be the only thing worth fighting for.

An MM story about real love—messy, complicated, and raw. About addiction, toxic relationships, and the struggle to claw your way out of the trenches. About facing the truth, even when it's ugly. About second chances that may or may not come with new heartbreak.

Becoming Us

Noah Rossi met Atticus King in the worst year of his life.

While everything around him was falling apart, Atticus stood out like a lifeline. They were nothing alike, but Noah was drawn to him, to the quiet warmth he never believed he deserved.

Now, two years later, they're finally finding their way back to each other. Picking up the pieces of a love that never really ended, Noah and Atticus are trying to move forward. But rebuilding trust doesn't erase the wreckage left behind, and Noah's past still lingers in the shadows of everything they're trying to become.

As their relationship deepens, the story shifts between present day and the past, revealing the grief, trauma, addiction, and emotional scars Noah has spent years trying to outrun. Slowly, piece by piece, he begins to heal, not just for Atticus, but for himself.

A companion novel to Echoes of Us, Becoming Us is an MM story about recovery and redemption. About choosing love in the aftermath of destruction. About learning that you can be broken and still be worthy.

And that sometimes, the hardest person to forgive is yourself.